More praise for
The Bad Luck Bride

"Readers, rejoice! We have a new writer to celebrate. Janna MacGregor writes with intelligence and heart. *The Bad Luck Bride* is a full-bodied romance about what it truly means to love, to forgive, and to heal. Plus, it introduces us to characters we will enjoy as they grow and develop. Smart, smart romance."
                    —*New York Times* bestselling author Cathy Maxwell

"Delightful! Janna MacGregor bewitched me with her captivating characters and a romance that sizzles off the page. I'm already a huge fan!"
                    —*New York Times* bestselling author Eloisa James

"*The Bad Luck Bride* is a stroke of good luck for readers—the intricate plot, arresting characters, and rich emotional resonance will leave you swooning."
                    —*New York Times* bestselling author Sabrina Jeffries

"Janna MacGregor's *The Bad Luck Bride* is a seductive tale filled with suspense and unforgettable characters. A must-buy for historical romance readers."
                    —*USA Today* bestselling author Alexandra Hawkins

"A diamond-bright debut, with a passionate heroine and worthy hero to root for."
                    —Maggie Robinson, author of *The Unsuitable Secretary*

The BAD LUCK BRIDE

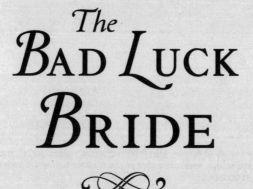

JANNA MacGREGOR

St. Martin's Paperbacks

THE BAD LUCK BRIDE

Copyright © 2017 by JLWR, LLC.

All rights reserved.

For information address St. Martin's Press, 175 Fifth Avenue, New York, NY 10010.

ISBN: 978-1-250-11612-3

Our books may be purchased in bulk for promotional, educational, or business use. Please contact your local bookseller or the Macmillan Corporate and Premium Sales Department at 1-800-221-7945, ext. 5442, or by e-mail at MacmillanSpecialMarkets@macmillan.com.

Printed in the United States of America

St. Martin's Paperbacks edition / May 2017

St. Martin's Paperbacks are published by St. Martin's Press, 175 Fifth Avenue, New York, NY 10010.

10 9 8 7 6 5 4 3 2 1

To Greg,
the author of my romantic life

Acknowledgments

To my wonderful agent Pam Ahearn, who read the story of Claire and Alex and made my dreams come true. To my fabulous editor Holly Ingraham, who helped me turn Alex into someone special. Without your vision and brilliance, the poor guy might still be sitting in the study and waiting for the next bottle of whisky. Jennie Conway and the rest of the superb team at St. Martin's Press, you are the fairy dust that makes everything sparkle.

Many compare the publication of their first book to giving birth, sending the first-born to school, having a root canal, or "it takes a village." All true. Nevertheless, for me, it opened a wonderful new world of friendships for which I am forever grateful.

Thank you, Eloisa James. Your time and company at the wonderful Tuscany workshop taught me so much and in so many lasting ways. Cathy Maxwell, thank you for making me believe in my storytelling. Sabrina Jeffries, Maggie Robinson, and Alexandra Hawkins, you have my eternal gratitude.

The final thank-you goes to Wilma, aka Willie, my

loving mother and the woman who first introduced me to the swirl and twirl of Regency romance. During high school, I know you saw those hidden romance novels under my bed. Truly, I was studying. I love you.

The
BAD LUCK
BRIDE

Chapter One

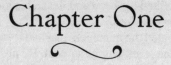

The raw wind pounded every inch of Alexander's body and lashed at what little remained of his compassion. As Marquess of Pembrooke, Alex had fought for years to cultivate the fine art of patience. Today proved that to have been a waste of time.

He should have ignored the lessons of forbearance and studied the intricacies of inflicting vengeance. Never again would he take for granted the epithet of "friend"—not when friend meant betrayer. The barren, snow-packed field was a perfect stage for a duel. Mere feet separated him from Lord Paul Barstowe, the man who had destroyed his family.

Alex's bay stallion edged closer to Lord Paul's white gelding. From this distance, the weather-roughened face of Lord Paul, the second son of the Duke of Southart, failed to mar Alex's childhood memories. In their youth they'd been inseparable. They'd witnessed each other's milestones. They'd celebrated each other's successes and suffered through the failures. Their friendship should have lasted until their deaths. Instead, it died instantly when Alex found his sister's letter explaining her suicide.

"Alice is dead." The bay stomped and blew out a breath of steam. By rote, Alex stilled the beast with a soft pat. Nothing good would come from delay. His eyes burned. The north wind's fury strengthened, but he refused to turn away. "I buried her two days ago."

Lord Paul tilted his head and flexed his gloved fingers. "I'm sorry for your loss."

Alex attributed the numbness that had invaded his body to grief and the weeklong bitter cold. He pushed the misery aside and subdued the anger that nipped at his sanity. Even if his pursuit of justice caused his own blood to stain the snow, the sacrifice would bring some peace. Bile took refuge in his throat. He dismissed it with a hard swallow.

Alice Aubrey Hallworth, his youngest sister, lay in the Pembrooke family crypt. A week ago, she'd laughed and charmed the entire family at dinner. When they'd finished the evening meal, she had excused herself, then taken a tonic before bed.

She never woke.

Now, there was nothing left but Lord Paul. How one so dissolute could ruin one so young was a question Alex would never understand. He drew a gulp of air in a desperate attempt to keep his pain buried deep inside.

Alex tightened the reins. "She was carrying your child."

In the distance, a disturbance arose, upsetting the desolate, snow-encrusted field. From the west, a man upon a black horse raced across the icy stretch of open land. Time was of the essence. Lord Paul had to agree to the duel before Nicholas St. Mauer, the Earl of Somerton, arrived. It had been a mistake to tell Somerton his plan.

"How do you know the child was mine?" Lord Paul's voice rose in defiance.

"She left a note and told me not to blame you. But now, all those times I encountered you both together during the fall hunting party and the holidays—" The words and memories made Alex physically sick; the nausea churned in his belly. "She was happy. I thought it all above suspicion."

Alex waited for Lord Paul to show some remorse, even if only to ask if Alice had suffered. As the silence lengthened, the weight of the two flintlock pistols in his pockets offered the only comfort he'd accept this day.

By this time, Somerton had closed the distance by half. Clouds of snow rose from the ground, the peace disrupted by the horse's churning hooves.

"How unfortunate for all." Lord Paul squinted toward the rider.

"Indeed." Alex leaned forward as his entire body tensed. He fought the desire to reach inside his jacket for one of the pistols. Instead, he coaxed his horse to stand within inches of Lord Paul's white gelding. "Do me the simple courtesy of looking at me."

Lord Paul made no move in his direction.

The unrelenting need to hear the man's betrayal and remorse firsthand spurred Alex to continue. "How could you seduce Alice, then abandon her like a piece of refuse on the street? How could you leave her with child?"

"I don't suppose telling you I had nothing to do with it will change our situation." Lord Paul finally looked at Alex. "She pursued me—"

"Damn you." Alex's voice rang out like a shot across the empty field. "Why didn't you stay with her? You should have done the honorable thing and married her."

As the last words faded, Lord Paul's face paled. "Careful, Pembrooke. Don't rush to a judgment you'll regret."

"We'll settle it, here and now." Before Alex uttered the rest of the challenge, the Earl of Somerton arrived on horseback and came to an abrupt stop.

Lord Paul held his hand away from his face to block the swirl of snow that engulfed him at the arrival of the earl.

Somerton brought his mount forward to separate the two men and their horses. The earl's jaw clenched, and his eyes narrowed. "Pembrooke, enough!"

"Dashing entrance, Somerton." Lord Paul's smile was pure provocation. "Come to save him? Too late. Your friend is well on his way to hell in a handcart."

"You'd best leave." Somerton's voice thickened with emotion. *"Now."*

Alex refused to acknowledge the interruption. Lord Paul was his sole concern. "You will pay for your treachery tonight." He cared nothing about facing a trial in the House of Lords for killing the man in a duel of honor.

Somerton blocked Alex's view and reached for the horse's bridle. "Pembrooke." The timbre of his friend's voice turned mellow and even, as if trying to tame a wild animal. "Alex, come on, old man."

Whatever he had done in the past to deserve Somerton's loyalty was a curse today. In one tug of the reins, Alex coaxed the horse away from the earl's grasp. "No. I will finish this one way or the other." Resolved to deliver a day of reckoning for Lord Paul's deception, he turned to face him. "We don't need the luxury of surgeons or seconds."

Somerton moved his horse forward and demanded, "Lord Paul, leave." The snowfall stopped as if on command as the earl raised his hand to slap the hindquarters of the white gelding.

"Somerton, stay out of this!" Alex's outcry caused a flutter of movement in the nearby trees as several birds fled.

Before the earl dropped his hand, the horse bolted. Lord Paul fled into the nearby woods and the oncoming night.

Alex reached with his right hand and grasped the handle of a pistol. As he pulled the heavy weight from his pocket, his conscience made a spontaneous and regrettable appearance. He bit off an oath, then slowly released his hold.

The fallen snow had deadened every sound except the subtle creaking of Somerton's leather saddle as he shifted his weight. Alex's grief, still raw, scored his every breath, his every thought, his every hope of future happiness.

He would not live this way. He'd find another way to force Lord Paul to atone for his sins. Memories of Alice, once bright and clear, were now stained a dirty umber.

Sleet replaced the snow. Raising his face to the gray sky, Alex embraced the razor-sharp pelt of ice against his skin. When he became accustomed to the stinging pain, he broke the silence in a steady voice. "I will take everything from him. I do not care the cost or sacrifice. Everything he holds dear will be mine."

Chapter Two

April 1812
London—The Reynolds Gambling Establishment

Lord Paul repeatedly slapped his gloves in the palm of his hand. Again. And again. The movement reminded Alex of an angry cat twitching its tail when treed by a persistent hound.

"*You* bought my vowels?" Lord Paul's face darkened with disbelief.

Alex raised an eyebrow and lifted the corners of his mouth, though there was no humor in the moment. "No need to thank me."

Lord Paul narrowed his ice-blue eyes. "When hell freezes or there are thirty Thursdays in February. Whichever occurs first."

Alex ignored the sarcasm and withdrew a piece of paper from his coat pocket. "I agree to pay all your gambling debts, including the ones from today. In exchange, you give me the deed to your Dorchester property, Willow House." He lowered his voice and handed the single sheet of paper to his nemesis. "Also, you will sign this."

Lord Paul snatched the paper from his hand. He didn't spare a glance at the entrance of Alex's two solicitors.

The suffocating weight lifted from Alex's chest. Tonight,

after months of devising the proper punishment, he could breathe freely again. His honor had dictated such satisfaction. Alice and her baby were dead, and nothing would bring them back, but the retribution he delivered would alleviate Lord Paul's betrayal.

Alex forced himself to appear calm, but his fist itched to take a swing at the swine in front of him. "Sign the note, and we're through. You're safe from your creditors, and this outrageous circus you created."

Lord Paul finished reading and looked up with a start. "You bloody bastard! If I give up Lady Claire, I won't be able to pay my debts. I'm as much as ruined."

"She's not your responsibility anymore." If he had it within his power, no woman would be Lord Paul's concern ever again.

Lord Paul's angry demeanor slipped when a brief hint of panic widened his eyes. With a blink it was gone, but Alex knew he'd scored a deep blow. "You ruin me, you'll destroy Lady Claire, too. She can't afford the scandal of another broken engagement. Besides, she's a lovelorn calf. Can't keep away from me. Of course, I oblige her."

"What are you suggesting?" Alex leaned across the green felt gaming table. It took every ounce of self-control not to kill the miscreant before him. The thought that Lord Paul had ruined another innocent made his gut turn. "Careful of your answer. If the Duke of Langham heard—"

"Don't be tedious. Of course I've had her." Lord Paul's face twisted into a smirk. "You can force me to sign it, but what good will it do? If need be, I'll marry her by special license tomorrow. The chit would be ecstatic and think it romantic."

"If you make the attempt, I'll know. Any foolish move on your part, I'll sell you back to your creditors. A rather nasty lot prone to violence, I hear." Alex mimicked Lord Paul's tic by popping his own gloves into his palm. The sound echoed through the room like a whip against bare skin.

With a hatred unmasked for all to witness, Lord Paul glared at Alex. Both knew there was no other recourse. With minimum movement, he dipped the quill into the inkwell and signed the note.

As casually as possible, Alex took possession of the paper and sprinkled sand over the signature.

Lord Paul leaned close. "I didn't realize I was worth this much to you."

"You aren't, but Alice was." Alex drew a breath for patience and summoned every speck of poise he'd collected over his lifetime. "You should have played deeper. I'd have paid much more."

He threw the black greatcoat over his shoulders and walked to the door with the paper in hand. With each step, part of the burden fell further away. Yet his own remorse lingered and weighed heavy on his conscience. He should have taken greater care with Alice. Too engaged in the daily management of his estate, he had missed numerous opportunities to spend time with her. What had she hoped for her future? Had she looked forward to her debut in society? Now, he'd never know. He should have seen Alice's humor and good cheer were nothing more than masks to hide her pain.

He took one last look at Lord Paul. The bastard would soon realize the extent to which he was ruined. "It was fortuitous I didn't kill you, as that would have been too easy. I'd much rather see you suffer as Alice did." He breathed in the stale remnants of cheroots, cheap spirits, and Lord Paul's desperation. The combination was a heady scent, one he'd remember until his dying day. For the first time since he'd discovered Alice dead, he felt alive.

His solicitors would expound every excruciating clause in detail, but Alex could explain it in far easier terms. He had crushed Lord Paul. To put the final nail in the coffin, he would attend this evening's ball, where he would ask for Lady Claire's hand.

She would need him when her engagement to Lord Paul ended.

With little success, Alex tried to quash the truth that forced its way into his thoughts. He needed her as much as, if not more than, she needed him.

There was only one problem. He needed to persuade her to ruin herself and jilt her fourth fiancé.

Alex was actually looking forward to Lady Anthony's ball. Normally these functions were a bore, akin to a fatal, gut-churning plague, but not tonight's event. He was eager to dance and converse with Lady Claire, the woman he would convince to marry him. He studied the perimeter of the dance floor from the second-floor balcony. The dance crowd slowed to a stop. The graceful sway of the ladies' dresses didn't hold his interest. Only one woman commanded his attention tonight.

He would recognize that radiant crown of dark red anywhere. Lady Claire's hair was a beacon, guiding his gaze. The last time they had met, she had been a tall, gawky girl who had reminded him of a skittish filly. A rare frisson of excitement caught him by surprise. She was no longer such a creature burgeoning into adulthood, but a lovely woman.

Lady Claire Cavensham, the only child of the late Duke of Langham, laughed with a group of young women. From the corner of the ballroom, a liveried footman walked in her direction with a note, the claret color of the Barstowe family stationery recognizable even from the second floor.

The horror of the moment pummeled him as hard as a direct punch. "The bastard," Alex said under his breath. The insipid arse hadn't possessed the decency to see her in person.

The footman moved closer to Lady Claire, and time slowed to a crawl. The scene below unfolded like the few seconds before a carriage accident. A person saw the wreck coming but lacked the ability to stop the damage.

Regret bled into his musings. She was hardly at fault. With haste, he made his way downstairs in an attempt to lessen the damage. With a bit of luck, he could intercept the footman before he delivered the note.

Alex dodged several guests as he made his way to Lady Claire. It would be inexcusable to run through the throng of attendees, but that didn't stop him from ignoring several greetings from friends as he passed. Only twenty feet separated him from saving her.

"Pembrooke! What the hell are you doing here?" A euphoric Lord Fredrick Honeycutt blocked Alex's path. "I haven't seen you in ages. Are you headed to the card room?"

"Not now, Honeycutt. I'll find you later." With a brief nod, Alex sidestepped the man and continued toward Lady Claire.

The footman extended the silver salver containing the missive. She pursed her brow before her eyes grew wide. She must have recognized the color of the stationery. In a barely perceivable instant, she masked her concern. With a slight smile, she nodded and took the note.

Alex's gut slammed to the floor as she stepped away from her friends and with a flick of her finger broke the seal.

Bloody hell. Claire wanted to scream the words aloud as she crushed the note in her hand. The thick paper's sharp edges, a painful reminder of its contents, gouged her palms through her cream-colored satin gloves.

She held the note from her fourth fiancé. Short, terse, and in an annoyingly elegant hand, Lord Paul informed her that he would not be attending their engagement announcement. The words were nothing more than a release from another promise of everlasting matrimony.

True, she did not love Lord Paul, but she had thought of him as a friend. Perhaps, over time, a friend she could have learned to love. There was no denying what had happened tonight.

The hateful curse had struck again.

One more sorry rejection she could add to her collection. Dazed, Claire bowed her head in shame, her glance skimming the beautiful engagement dress, a confection designed and carefully crafted to celebrate tonight's betrothal announcement. Within the hour, she had planned to dance with Lord Paul in front of the guests, her gown sweeping the curse out of the ballroom and out of her life. Now, all she had in her future was the humiliation that waited for her once the *ton* heard she had suffered yet another broken betrothal. Only this time, the *ton* would have a front-row seat.

All she'd ever wanted was a family of her own. To have a family, she had to marry. Truthfully, she wasn't particular whom she married—just determined.

She blinked to make certain she wasn't dreaming. "Ruined" did not express the calamity of the evening. The term might have explained her situation two fiancés ago, but "destroyed" was a more apt description of the night. She dreaded the inevitable snorts and snickers from onlookers when they pounced upon the discovery that her fourth fiancé had taken the much heeded advice and jilted her a mere hour before the announcement.

Long live the Lady Claire Curse.

She was not one of those women who lost the resolve to fight. With every breath and every muscle in her body, she vowed to make her escape. She pasted a serene smile on her lips. Head held high like a proper duke's daughter, she backed away from her cousin Emma and her friends. A second step increased her momentum. One more, and she would be out of sight of the guests gathered near their group, then she could hasten her departure.

As she made the step to pivot, the hard edge of a serving tray slammed into her back. Glass shattered around her. The tinkling of the shards echoed throughout the large room as the orchestra's last strains faded to silence. Claire pressed her eyes shut, then opened them to see the damage. Dancers, dowagers, and debutantes turned in unison at the catastrophe. The all-too-familiar heat bludgeoned her cheeks.

She faced the unfortunate footman who held the upended tray. "Pardon me. That was my fault. Are you hurt?"

The footman shook his head. "I beg *your* pardon, my lady." He bent down to pick up the fragments of broken glass.

Stomach sucked in and shoulders squared, she returned her attention to the dance floor. The other guests had resumed their festivities, except for the onlookers closest to her. Several smirks alighted across the sea of faces at her embarrassing attempt to escape.

"Claire, is everything all right? You look a little . . . unsettled?" Her cousin Emma stood by her side with a brilliant smile that brightened the entire room.

If Claire hinted what had transpired within the last few moments, she doubted her cousin would be able to keep the worry from her beautiful face. "I'm fine. I just need some air."

Emma's nod made her honey-colored curls shine in the candlelight. "Your anxiety is perfectly understandable. Personally, I cannot wait for the announcement. Finally, I'll get a full glass of champagne, maybe two." Apparently satisfied all was well, she patted Claire's arm, then returned to her friends.

Tonight, Claire's aunt and uncle had planned to raise a toast to her future happiness. They'd already asked Lady Anthony if they could make an announcement. Thank heavens they hadn't specified what it was.

The liveried footman who had delivered the note stood by her side, ready to assist. With his black-and-gold attire matching the ballroom decor, the man looked like a worker bee in an active hive. Footmen in similar costumes moved in precision throughout the room to attend the other guests. The first strains of a quadrille floated into the air.

The servant bowed slightly. "My lady, will there be a response?"

Where was it? In her shock, she must have dropped the missive. A quick survey of the floor revealed the note a mere foot away.

She knelt to pick it up. At the same time, a large male hand reached for the paper.

A burst of pain exploded at Claire's right temple as she bumped heads with the man. Horrified at her clumsiness, she jerked backward. What more could go wrong this evening? Miraculously, she didn't fall into a heap. "I'm sorry. . . ."

The rest of the apology melted when Claire found the most arresting pair of gray eyes studying her. Without a thought to the consequence, she snatched the note directly out of his gloved fingers to stop him from reading it. "Excuse me, but that's mine."

Alexander Hallworth, Marquess of Pembrooke, crouched before her. "Lady Claire, allow me to assist you." The half smile he offered appeared almost compassionate.

His whisky-dark voice caused a warm tingle to spread from the top of her head to her toes. His black evening coat accentuated the breadth of his shoulders. Even resting on his haunches, he towered over her. Mortified at her earlier incivility with the note, she averted her eyes, and her serene smile collapsed. "Thank you."

He lightly clasped her elbow and helped her stand.

With a dismissive turn, Claire faced the footman. "I need to send a message to my uncle, the Duke of Langham. Is there someplace private, away from the noise?"

Claire ignored the urge to steal another peek at Pembrooke for fear he would discover her secret. Where had he come from? He never attended these events.

She followed her bumblebee escort into a dimly lit salon decorated in colors of the footman's livery. The plush gold carpet muffled her steps, and she wished it could perform the same magic on her pounding heartbeat. The footman produced a sheet of paper with a sharpened quill and a fresh pot of ink.

The effort to pen a quick note was more difficult than expected. Her hand shook to such a degree that a large smear of iron gall ink stained her pristine glove, one more blemish on the evening. Somehow, she composed her thoughts, a simple request that her aunt and uncle meet her in the vestibule so she could leave without notice. The ink had barely dried when she sealed the missive. "Please deliver this immediately. I'll not wait for his reply."

"Yes, my lady."

The footman opened the door, and the noise from the ballroom festivities barged into the room like an uninvited guest. After he left, she welcomed the sweet comfort of silence. Another broken betrothal. Her chest tightened with the familiar pain. The hurt was not from the string of unsuccessful engagements, but more, the undeniable truth she would never have a family to replace the one she'd lost.

With a glance around the salon, she let out a tiny sigh of relief. Fortune bestowed a brief grin on her dire circumstances. The room overlooked Lady Anthony's formal gardens. Any other night she would have been content admiring the promised tranquility from afar. Tonight, it conspired to act as her accomplice.

Through the ornate floor-to-ceiling French doors, she made her escape onto the terrace and down the steps. She couldn't chance another walk through the ballroom and face a plethora of curious stares from the vultures who masqueraded as guests.

Small lanterns swayed in the gentle breeze. Light danced upon the pathway. A chill ran across her arm, and her skin prickled. There was no cause to worry about discovery since the gardens would most likely be empty. The midnight supper guaranteed to keep the party inside.

Within fifteen minutes, she would find some peace of mind safely cocooned with her aunt and uncle in the family's coach. The late evening dew soaked her silk dance slippers and, undoubtedly, the hem of her beautiful dress. It was a small price to pay for freedom.

A brief flash of lightning appeared in the west. Claire stopped dead in her tracks, then straightened her spine. She quelled the new worry that joined her current discomfort and continued on her way. A few gentle drops of rain fell on her shoulders. *Dear God, not this. Not now.* She hummed the lullaby her mother had taught her to keep her fears at bay.

Completely unprepared to face a storm, she took several deep breaths to bolster her courage. Thunder rolled from behind and grew closer in a strange rhythmic pattern. Her chest muscles seized and held her breath prisoner. With no warning, her heartbeat revolted and exploded in her chest.

The garden around her disappeared, and once again she was ten years old. The crack of splitting wood accompanied by the boom of thunder spilled into the carriage as they crossed the bridge to Wrenwood. The vehicle lurched to the right. The din of the storm swallowed the horses' screams and the outriders' frantic shouts. End over end, the carriage tumbled. The coach groaned as the paneled wood splintered. Suddenly, she was plunged into the frigid water that stole her breath. Her skirts tangled around her legs. Alone, wild with fear, and unable to kick free, she fought the surrounding blackness.

"My lady?" The deep voice brought her back to the present. Her racing pulse slowed. The footman must have seen her exit. She turned to assure him all was well, but her short-lived reprieve transformed into a full sense of dread.

"Lord Pembrooke," she whispered. Now she faced a delay in reaching her aunt and uncle besides the risk of discovery.

At least she had company. . . .

Enough! She had to control her panic. All she needed was another two minutes to reach the vestibule.

He surprised her with a sudden enchanting smile. "You must be enjoying the ball about as much as I am. It was quite a feat to catch you."

Claire managed a small, tentative smile in answer. What could he possibly want with her this evening? The distant notes of the supper waltz faded to nothing. "You wanted to catch me?"

Pembrooke took a step closer. She muffled the whimper that threatened at his sudden nearness. A brilliant flicker of lightning caused his eyes to flash like a blaze of fire. His black hair made it nigh impossible to see where his head ended and the night began.

"In the ballroom you appeared distraught. I'm here to offer assistance."

His words set alarm bells clanging. If he had seen her agitation, who else had?

"Assistance?" Claire winced as soon as the word escaped. She was not a blasted parrot. She swallowed the lump in her throat before casting a glance over his shoulder. No one else accompanied him.

Another charge of light rent the sky, causing an uncontrollable shiver to skate down her back.

Pembrooke leaned into the pathway light. The lantern's flame cast his strong chin and chiseled cheekbones into prominence. His eyes scrutinized her with the intensity of a scientist cataloging an insect's features under a magnifying glass.

Her parched throat prevented another swallow. If he continued to examine her in such detail, he might discover the true magnitude of her distress.

"Lady Claire . . ." His whisper surrounded her. "Let's discuss Lord Paul."

A fiery flash lit the sky. At Claire's sharp inhalation, Alex extended his hand in invitation. "Shall we escape the rain?" A small alcove attached to the house and located to the right of the pathway would provide a safe cover.

"I'm expected in the ballroom." The feigned strength in her voice reminded Alex of a wounded animal desperate to defend itself. The tremble of her hands corroborated the true extent of her turmoil.

The warm glow from the garden lanterns caused the droplets on her shoulders and hair to glimmer like tiny diamonds. She made Botticelli's *The Birth of Venus* look plain. With a chuckle designed to alleviate some of her anxiety, he closed the distance between them and confided their shared secret. "You do realize you're headed in the wrong direction?"

Her eyes shimmered with a sheen of moisture.

The urge to brush away any wayward tears on her cheeks came from nowhere. "That was artless." He lowered his voice to a whisper. "I apologize. It was not my intent to make light of your situation." Tonight was difficult enough for both of them. He wanted her to accept his offer, not be frightened of him. "Please. This is important. On my honor, you have nothing to fear."

Claire took a tentative step toward the alcove.

Alex followed with his hand at the small of her back, ready to stop her if she tried to run.

She paused before crossing under the arched doorway, and the lantern's light bathed her in a golden hue that enhanced the creamy complexion of her skin. A slight breeze delivered a hint of her fragrance, a spicy citrus. The aromatic blend was pleasant but rather unique for a woman.

"Shall we sit?" He pointed to a granite bench.

"No, that won't be necessary. What do you want?" Curtness tinted with something heavier dripped from her voice. Perhaps despair, since she looked as if she had seen a ghost and had barely lived to tell the tale.

He stepped closer. Lady Claire stood stock-still. She looked like a very brave, very small soldier. Or perhaps a very cold soldier.

He slipped off his tight-fitting evening coat. Instead of handing her the garment, he placed it around her shoulders.

Her body tensed as he leaned in. "Th-thank you," she said softly.

Even with a minimum amount of light, her hair held the color of rich auburn. From nowhere, the urge to run his hands over the curves that defined her hips and rounded chest caused his body to tighten. The only explanation for such a visceral reaction had to be tonight's events. She was beautiful, but he'd been in the company of beautiful women before. No, it was her poise under the most difficult of circumstances, the humiliation of another broken engagement, that caused his pulse to drum a pounding rhythm.

Alex swept the errant thoughts away. He had a tricky proposition in front of him: marriage. "Lady Claire—"

"Why are you following me?" She eyed the archway and pulled his coat tighter to her body. "I'll be missed if I don't return to my family promptly."

He wasn't certain whether she was afraid or annoyed. Her behavior was unusual.

"How are you planning to manage the rumors of Lord Paul's absence tonight?" Alex gentled his voice to soften the impending blow. "I say this not to be cruel, but by morning the entire *ton* shall share the news of another lost fiancé unless you act tonight. I might add they will revel once again in your latest mishap."

"You mock me?" Her eyes pierced his gaze like an arrow.

"Not at all. I want to help." He needed to tread carefully. He had enough experience with the women in his life to know he was in danger of receiving a cordial but thorough tongue-lashing. "I'd like to discuss your unfortunate circumstances in an honest and forthright manner."

Her stoic face reminded him of Italian Renaissance paintings, the subjects' serenity marred by a subtle hint of discontent. "The Lady Claire Curse has taken on a life of its own," he said finally.

She flinched so slightly that he almost missed it.

Her discomfort caused a surge of protectiveness to blast through him like a thunderbolt. "The *ton* feeds on such scandal regardless of the truth." He locked his hands behind his back. "To shield yourself from the gossip that will erupt once it's discovered, you should announce you broke the engagement with Lord Paul tonight. If you don't act first, you'll be laughed out of town once and for all. London will not discern if you are a duke's daughter, niece, or laundry maid."

"One can only have so many proposed trips down the

matrimonial aisle before all the potential groom candidates empty the nave for good." Her face was devoid of emotion. "I'll convince him to change his mind before anyone knows."

"Lady Claire . . ." This was more difficult than he thought. The poor woman obviously felt trapped, and Lord Paul was her unlikely savior. "Do you know where he is right now?"

"No."

"He's at the Reynolds, deeply in debt." He lowered his voice. "Are you hesitant because of the witch's curse . . . ?"

She glanced at the sky, then scoffed, "Please. You think too narrowly. Some attribute my misfortune to blood curses, curse tablets, and even Roman book curses. I have quite a collection to choose from, with the added talent of losing fiancés to death, disease, and dismemberment. Shall I list them all?"

He smiled at the challenge in her voice. "If you want to share."

A small defiant smile broke across her lips, and her eyes flared. She was even lovelier than he'd first thought.

"Well, Lord Thant lost a leg after a nasty accident not more than an hour after proposing. Lord Riverton left the country because of a duel. The day he proposed to me, he chose to celebrate in a peeress's bed. He was found by her husband." Her voice softened when she added, "Lord Archard died of a fever." Finally, her eyes betrayed the hurt he expected she must feel over tonight's events. "Now you understand why I need him." With a silent dignity, she turned away.

Alex lifted his hand to take hers but thought better of it. Without much talent to deliver comfort, he would rely on nonchalance to hide his unease. His goal had never been to ruin Lord Paul at the expense of another. As long as she didn't cry, he could finish this.

With a clench of his fist, his resolve returned. He could not afford to lose focus. His actions tonight defined this woman's future and his. "Tell me exactly, counting Lord Paul, how many fiancés have you had? Four? You'll find another to marry, I guarantee it."

With a swift turn, Claire faced him, and her narrowed eyes shot daggers before she inched her chin upward. She grabbed her skirts in her one hand and brushed past. The sheer volume of silk and satin rubbed against his legs and made a heavy *swoosh* sound. With a flick of her wrist, she dropped the skirts and spun around.

"How did you discover Lord Paul broke the betrothal?" She asked the question with a strength in her voice that spoke volumes about her character and intelligence. "I just received word myself. Last I knew the two of you weren't friends."

A twinge of pity smoldered deep inside. The sentiment was something of a novelty since Lord Paul had taught him to doubt his own kindness. With perseverance, he worked through the brief moment of conscience, and certainty came to the rescue. He had worked months for this night and refused to succumb to the tortured look in her eyes.

She had become part of his plan when she took up with Lord Paul. Her part required she marry and become his marchioness, and his part required he keep Claire and her wealth from Lord Paul. Alex knew the man well enough not to trust him. If desperate enough, Lord Paul would likely convince her to escape to Gretna Green.

In theory, the plan had seemed perfect, but it was harder to execute with a real lady, and one he was drawn to, at that.

"News spreads fast. I don't want to see an innocent ruined by his actions." Alex lifted his shoulders in a shrug. "How are we going to get you through this scandal un-scathed? I saw how upset you were in the ballroom."

She shivered as if still cold.

"Let me help. We may be able to agree upon a mutually satisfactory solution."

Claire tilted her head to the side and delivered a mulish look. This woman had a backbone and had recovered from the earlier torment. She wasn't going to take his proposal lying down like some simpering miss. An immense sense of pleasure rushed through him at the sight of her newfound confidence. He vowed not to allow her to fall prey to Lord Paul.

"Lord Pembrooke, what precisely do you want? If you seek something degenerate, you are mistaken if you think I'd agree."

"I have no more depraved designs on you than I have on any other young lady in the ballroom." His body was telling him differently, but he was a gentleman and would never act on it. "My motives are honorable."

"Why?" She crinkled her brow. "Why help me?"

"Simple. You're a lovely woman who deserves a better life than what Lord Paul can offer." He summoned a smile designed to convince her of his sincerity. "You should go back into the ballroom and announce you're jilting him for another. I'll stand by your side."

"I see. Your suggestion is that in front of Lady Anthony's guests, I personally ruin myself by announcing I'm throwing Lord Paul aside. What will that accomplish but feed the curse?" Claire's voice held an edge of cynicism. "Did someone put you up to this?" She didn't wait for an answer. "With my luck I should have expected this type of play. See how many men she can lose. Which club holds the bet? White's? Brooks's? What's the payout?"

"Stop, my lady. Any man would be honored to call you his wife."

Her lips parted on a sigh as if she didn't believe him.

Something much like chivalry rose within him. How

had a dissipated rake such as Lord Paul sunk his claws into such a wonderful creature? "The truth is I'm trying to save you from another humiliation. Break with him. Now. Tonight. Before anyone knows what he's done."

Faint thunder rumbled, and a flash of lightning followed far off in the west. The ornate lanterns bobbed up and down from the sudden gust of wind. Claire's head jerked in the direction of the coming storm, and her face blanched.

He was losing her interest. "Lady Claire, my reputation suggests I'm honest and above suspicion. Just ask my friends."

There were only a few he considered to be worth his time. Since Lord Paul's betrayal, his only close friend was Somerton.

Alex smiled in earnest. "I would never allow you to be humiliated in front of society. I'm trying to help you." Somehow, he had to convince her of that fact, then the idea of marrying him would be much easier to accept.

She blinked rapidly, then turned back to him and, for an instant, appeared startled to see him there. "That's very gallant, my lord. Truly, thank you for the effort. But I must leave."

This night could not end with her escaping, so he tried another tactic. "You need to protect your Wrenwood estate and your wealth from lechers who would feed upon your vulnerability. Not to mention stop that ridiculous curse."

"I have two." She held up two gloved fingers.

"Two? Two what? Curses?" No one at his club had uttered a peep about another curse.

"Estates. I have two estates, Wrenwood and Lockhart." She returned his stare.

Her answer was unexpected, but his business experience had taught him to show nothing. The report from his private investigator had not mentioned additional properties.

Thoughts were percolating if she chose to disclose this information.

A razor of lightning split the sky. She flinched and took a step closer to him, but her reaction had nothing to do with him. *It was the storm.*

Her gaze darted to the exit of the alcove, then she returned her attention to him. With a slight shrug of her shoulders, his evening coat fell into her hands. She offered it to him. "My lord, good night." Outside their hideaway, the voices of a man and a woman floated in the air.

Alex put his hand on her shoulder to prevent her escape. "Will you give me some assistance? I seem to have lost my valet." He quirked an eyebrow. "Besides, if you leave now, whoever is out there will see us."

She ventured a halfhearted grin and held his garment in two hands. With a little persistence, he wrestled his way into the evening coat. Her hands smoothed the material across his shoulders and back, causing a pleasant sensation to cascade through him at the slight touch.

Claire took several steps toward the pathway. In a flash, he moved beside her and grasped her elbow. When he brought her close, something flared between them as he gazed into her haunted eyes. Whether the desire to keep her next to him was passion or the need to protect a vulnerable woman made little difference. He pulled her into the shadows and brought his mouth to her ear. "Wait until they pass." The warmth from her skin beckoned.

A flash of lightning lit the gardens and the alcove.

With a gentle hand, he pushed her against the wall and stood to the side so he blocked her body from view.

A clap of thunder cracked as if the sky were breaking. It rolled into a loud rumble that refused to die.

"Please." Her whisper grew ragged as she struggled for breath. In one fluid motion, she pulled the lapels of his evening coat toward her. She buried her face against his chest and pressed the rest of her body to his, almost as if she sought sanctuary inside. "Don't leave me." Her voice had weakened, the sound fragile, as if she'd break into a million pieces.

"I won't. I promise." Alex pulled her tight. One hand sank into the soft satin of her skirts while the other slid around the nape of her neck to hold her close to his chest. It was the most natural thing in the world to hold her. Her body fit perfectly against his.

With the slightest movement, she pulled away. Her eyes wildly searched his. For what, he couldn't fathom.

He lowered his mouth until his lips were mere inches from tasting her. Madness had consumed him. All he wanted was to kiss her thoroughly until she forgot her fear—until she forgot everything but him.

Her breath mingled with his, and the slight moan that escaped her was intoxicating. Nothing in his entire life felt as right as this moment. He bent to brush his lips against hers.

"Pembrooke? Have you seen Lady—"

Claire leaned back and released his lapels. Without her warmth, he experienced a sudden loss of equilibrium. He turned with a snarl to greet the intruders.

Immediately, Lord Fredrick Honeycutt and his sister, Lady Sophia, took a step back as their eyes grew round as dinner plates.

The first to recover, Honeycutt announced, "I see you found Lady Claire." He bowed his head slightly, then lowered his voice. "The Duke of Langham is looking for his niece and is directly behind us."

A sense of wariness flooded Alex's mind when Claire's uncle strolled forward and came into sharp focus. As he stood, his feet spread shoulder width apart, the duke's presence commanded everyone's attention. His visage held the hint of a smile, but the two large fists resting by his sides were the real barometer of his mood. "Claire, are you all right?" The affection in his voice was at odds with the fury flashing in his eyes.

"I'm fine." She stepped out of Alex's shadow but stayed close to his side.

Surprised by her decision not to run to her uncle, Alex placed his hand on the small of her back to give her courage.

Claire's cousin Michael Cavensham, Marquess of McCalpin, stopped abruptly at his father's side, followed by his younger brother, Lord William. Both men stood approximately the same height as the duke.

With grim amusement, Alex considered how he might scale such a wall of Cavensham men and come out alive.

A faint rumble of thunder faded. Even the elements of nature were leery of a confrontation with the duke and his sons.

"What are you doing with my cousin?" McCalpin made a move to charge Alex, but the duke held his arm out to warn his heir away.

Lord William stood on the other side of his father. The duke's youngest child, Lady Emma, joined their group. She called out, "Claire? Do you need my help?"

Alex fully expected Claire to launch into some type of explanation as to why they were alone. Instead, with a slight tilt of her head, she turned so her back faced the gathering gawkers. If it was a move designed to safeguard him, she needn't have bothered. He'd shield her from the growing crowd.

"I'm sorry." Her warm breath caressed his cheek much like a kiss.

"Don't be," he whispered. With a slide of his hand, he took hers. With their fingers intertwined, he gently coaxed her to stand by his side. He raised her hand to his lips in a slow motion so the crowd had an unfettered view.

Her eyes widened.

"Everyone, please give us your attention." His deep voice carried through the garden so even the stragglers heard. He held her gaze and smiled.

The crowd quieted.

"It gives me great pleasure to announce Lady Claire's engagement to Lord Paul officially ended tonight."

"Have you lost your mind?" she whispered.

Murmurs broke through the gathered assembly.

Claire tried to break free of his grasp, but he refused to let go and gently squeezed her fingers. "Trust me." The soft words held a tenderness only for her. To the throng, he continued in a voice that resonated. "Because Lady Claire has agreed to become my wife."

Honeycutt's eyebrows hit the top of his forehead, while his sister seemed ready to twirl into a faint.

Emma darted forward into the alcove. "Claire!"

McCalpin followed Emma. "Pembrooke, so help me God, if this is your idea of a joke . . ."

Langham pushed his way into the arched doorway, and the breadth of his shoulders hid the view from the onlookers. "Sweetheart, what is this?"

Alex answered before she could respond. "I'm protecting her from being dishonored by a morally bankrupt rake."

The duke raised an eyebrow. His skepticism melted into a mask of ducal haughtiness. "Lord Pembrooke, I shall see you at Langham Hall tomorrow to discuss your obligations to my niece."

"It will be my pleasure, Your Grace." He turned and, without a care who witnessed his next move, brought his mouth to Claire's ear. With the slightest touch, he caressed her lobe with his lips. "You will not regret tonight. I swear it."

"You're wasting your time." She walked toward her uncle and never looked back.

Relief coursed through Alex's blood. He had accomplished tonight's goal with the unsuspecting help of Honeycutt. Marriage to Lady Claire might have been by a circuitous route, but forcing her to marry him saved him the time of a long courtship and enduring ridiculous talk of the curse from the *ton*.

With an abundant sense of satisfaction, he left the alcove. When he passed a sculpture of Eros, the distinctive curl of its marble lips drew his attention.

The damn thing grinned at him.

The carriage rocked gently as the team of four brought Claire closer to Langham Hall. Once she reached the solitude of her bedchamber, she'd concentrate on tonight's events. When she'd left her home earlier this evening, her future husband was Lord Paul. Now Lord Pembrooke had declared to the world, or at least to the majority of Lady Anthony's guests, that she would marry him. She struggled to understand this topsy-turvy upheaval in her life. Thank heavens a canopy of starlight had replaced the earlier storm.

She sat beside Uncle Sebastian, her father's brother and the current Duke of Langham. His arm around her gave her the courage to face her distraught aunt.

"Tell me what happened." Aunt Ginny sat on the edge of her seat, waiting for every word. The worry in her voice cautioned Claire to proceed gingerly with her explanation.

"There's not much to share. Lord Paul broke the engagement."

"I'll skewer him like a piece of meat," Uncle Sebastian announced.

Aunt Ginny inhaled sharply.

"I couldn't face another joke over the Lady Claire Curse," she murmured, her voice raw. She forced the unruly mass of humiliation marching through her stomach into submission. "Lord Pembrooke escorted me outside, then Lord Honeycutt, his sister, Uncle Sebastian, and the others found us."

"My dear girl . . ." Aunt Ginny squeezed her eyes shut and grabbed Claire's hand. "Did you kiss him?"

"It might have appeared so, but I assure you he was helping me. He acted honorably this evening. He was the one—" Claire swallowed hard. "He knew about Lord Paul before I did. He wanted me to announce I broke the engagement before people learned Lord Paul would not appear this evening."

Aunt Ginny patted her hand between her own. "Why were you in the garden alone?"

"I couldn't risk returning to the ballroom. It was the shortest way to the entry vestibule."

"Sebastian, we can't let Claire marry under these circumstances. What would her mother and father say if they were here?" She stretched to touch her husband's knee. "Margaret would never have let this stand. I can't, in good conscience, allow this to go forward without knowing more." Her voice softened. "You know what your brother Michael would have wanted."

Her uncle scooped up Aunt Ginny's hand and brought it to his lips. "Sweetheart, she has no other choice. Pembrooke made the announcement they would marry."

Her aunt shook her head and exhaled a sigh.

"We won't let you face tonight's gossip alone. Not after everything you've gone through." The warmth in her uncle's voice encouraged Claire to lean against his protective embrace.

Aunt Ginny turned to Claire. "What are your thoughts?" Clearly, she sought another ally in her crusade against Lord Pembrooke.

"At this point, what does it matter? I have to marry." Her words were sharper than she would have liked. "I'm sorry, Aunt Ginny. It's just—" She took a deep breath. As long as there was a chance for happiness, she could face another day, even with the gossips.

Her sweet aunt's intentions were heartfelt but would only make things worse. She had to marry if she wanted her own children. With marriage came respectability, which she needed desperately if she wanted to increase her role within her mother's charity. Lord Pembrooke might be her last chance. She couldn't afford to lose him. She let out a sigh of exasperation. Claire examined every event of the evening and tried to make sense of the chaos. Pembrooke had just finished mourning his sister. Now, he was here in London warning her of some dire gambling debt that would ruin her life. The effort made little difference since Lord Paul had already broken with her.

None of it made sense. Not unless it was the curse or some twisted game between Pembrooke and Lord Paul. Somehow, she'd find a way to discover the truth.

If it was painful going from betrothal to betrothal, she could only imagine her stature in society if she was forced to become a renowned spinster. At the ripe age of twenty-four, Claire was too old to be on the matrimonial market. Marriage to Lord Pembrooke had to take.

Claire hesitated, but her curiosity got the better of her. "I know Wrenwood borders the marquess's ancestral seat. What else do you know about him?"

"He's well regarded by his peers." Uncle Sebastian thought for a moment. "He and I don't agree on many things when the House of Lords is in session. Nevertheless, he is passionate about issues of agriculture and the rights of tenants. He's quite wealthy."

Aunt Ginny humphed. "A ringing endorsement for any man."

"At least he's committed to something." Uncle Sebastian laughed, then grew serious as he faced Claire. "No one, including Lord Paul or Pembrooke, will take advantage of you."

Chapter Three

❧

A housemaid stoked the fire into a welcoming blaze of heat. "Will there be anything else, my lady?"

"No, thank you."

When the maid opened the door to leave, her cousin Emma bounded into Claire's sitting room like one of her father's retrievers, always willing to swim the deepest waters to capture the fallen prize. She collapsed on the sofa next to Claire. "You and Pembrooke in the garden alone? How did you accomplish such a feat in a single hour? I've been out for years and still can't get LaTourell to sneak away for a kiss."

"Em, it's not what you think," Claire said gently.

Her other cousins, McCalpin and William, arrived at a more leisurely pace and took the seats directly opposite.

"Kiss?" McCalpin's jaw tensed. "Did Pembrooke touch you?"

William leaned toward McCalpin. "The marquess wants to test the bounds of propriety with our cousin? I say we take the blackguard—"

"No. Of course he didn't," Claire said. William and McCalpin always cared for her welfare, but sometimes their zealousness to protect both their sister and her spiraled outside the limits of acceptable behavior.

"Brute force is hardly the answer," Emma continued. "Goodness, not long ago we were at the modiste's for the final fitting of your first wedding dress. The *ton* called your wedding to the Earl of Archard the romance of the Season." With a dramatic sigh she continued, "Last month, I was there for the fitting of Lord Paul's gown."

"Lord Paul's gown?" She laughed as she threw a pillow at Emma's head. "It's my gown."

With a coquettish smile, Emma cooed, "Another gown is in your future."

Claire grabbed another pillow to toss, then hugged it to her chest as the levity of the moment evaporated into thin air. Most women practically caught kissing another man besides their intended would die from mortification. After the years of whispers and insinuations from "polite" society, she was immune to such shame. Instead, her overriding concern was doubt about his motives. There was no logical reason Pembrooke would offer for her unless it was a hoax.

With her cursed luck, she half expected him not to show in the morning.

McCalpin reached behind his back and pulled out a small rectangular pillow. Without dropping his gaze from Claire, he lobbed the pillow and hit Emma square in the face. "Quit teasing her, Em."

Emma tossed her head. "That wasn't very nice."

"I'll take you to any bookshop you want tomorrow without time restraints to make up for it," McCalpin said.

"Prepare to be gone all day on a grand adventure, dear brother. I'm hunting for Jeremy Bentham's first book of essays."

"The philosopher?" William scratched his head. "McCalpin, why do you do this to yourself? God knows, once she sets her mind to acquiring a book, she's like a terrier and won't let go."

McCalpin's full attention settled on Claire. "Are you acquainted with Pembrooke?"

"Not really."

"Why did he announce this supposed engagement?" McCalpin pressed.

"I have no answer. We're just acquaintances. He must want something, but your father says he's wealthy and well respected." Claire's hold on the pillow in her lap tightened. "What do you know about him?"

McCalpin leaned against the chair and relaxed, but the intensity in his blue eyes never wavered. "We belong to the same clubs. For years, at White's he had a table reserved every day at three o'clock. Most days, Lord Paul joined him for a drink. If he didn't attend, Somerton joined him. Never all three together."

"There's bad blood between Somerton and Lord Paul," said William. "After Lady Alice's death, Pembrooke let the table go. Now, he only socializes with Somerton. What caused the break with Lord Paul has never been discovered."

"Let's finish this tomorrow when we're rested." Claire caught a glimpse of the sky from the window where the moon reigned over the night. A hefty dose of contentment swept through her at the sight. Tonight, she could concentrate on Pembrooke.

Emma leapt from the sofa and settled into one of the chairs in front of the fireplace. "Oh, we don't mean to keep you, but I must share something." She curled her long legs under and continued as if she hadn't heard Claire's request. "Tonight, Lady Lena told me Pembrooke has an arrangement with Monique LaFontaine."

McCalpin heaved a heavy sigh. "Em, for heaven's sake,

that's not an appropriate subject to discuss in mixed company."

"I'm sure William's tender ears have heard worse," Emma countered.

Will shot a devilish grin to his sister. Emma straightened in her chair. The two siblings baited each other relentlessly. Even though they argued with an annoying vigor, they were close.

Emma focused once again on Claire. "How will you manage a mistress?"

"Don't be naïve. There's nothing to manage. Whether he keeps a mistress is simply a tale batted about by people who have nothing better to occupy their minds." She, above all people, knew how gossip was woven into a false truth.

When she had sought refuge in Pembrooke's arms to escape the storm, he had accepted her without question and had stayed by her side. Even when her deepest fears were exposed, he hadn't questioned why—he had protected her.

How he had handled the gaping bystanders in the garden when he defused her broken engagement and claimed her for his own was unforgettable. The man had been magnificent in his command. She would be forever grateful he had shielded her from the scandal as best he could. The least she could do was to return the favor and safeguard his reputation.

"Claire, I'll discover if he has an arrangement." McCalpin reached over and grasped her hand. "If it's any comfort, I haven't heard such rumors."

Emma cocked her head and knit her eyebrows together. "What if it's not a rumor? Now who's being naïve?"

Claire bit her tongue hard to stop the doubt that skipped across her thoughts. Pembrooke had never explained his reasons for the proposal. What right did she have to question his motives, as long as he came to her tomorrow? It shouldn't matter if he kept a mistress. With a resigned sigh, she knew it made a world of difference. Granted, her overriding goal was a marriage that would provide her with her own family and respectability. Nevertheless, she'd not marry if Pembrooke carried on with a member of the notorious demimonde behind her back. No matter how desperate, she'd not marry under such circumstances. What remained of her reputation, she'd protect fiercely.

Since Archard, she had never expected to have a husband in love with her. Pembrooke's arms around her had been an unexpected comfort, one she would not share with another.

Claire yawned. "Let's talk tomorrow. Shall we?" She had dropped her tone and was hopeful the hint would do its magic. She would never rest if Emma continued to dredge up old tales.

Emma stood and stomped her foot. "What if he makes you a laughingstock?"

Claire groaned. "Many consider me such already."

Emma bristled with outrage but continued, "How can you dismiss this so easily? What if he's nothing more than a contemptible rogue?" Emma stood at attention much like a field marshal rallying the troops for a take-no-prisoners battle. "He frequents gambling hells and never attends society functions. What suitable husband does that?"

"Contemptible rogue or not, perhaps we should hold our judgment. He sounds like a jolly entertaining fellow to spend time with," William added.

Emma didn't bother to hide her attack. She hurled McCalpin's pillow at William, where it landed at his feet. "We're talking about Claire's future. Be serious, for once."

"I'm not privy to his exploits in gambling hells. Besides, your father thinks he has admirable qualities." Claire knew there was no use arguing the point, but she had to explain.

"He just came out of mourning for his sister. I have no other options."

"Claire, you have choices. You always have. We'll not let Pembrooke or that ridiculous curse force you into marriage." McCalpin stood. "He all but disappeared from town after his sister's death. I didn't hear one mention of him or the rest of his family while they were in mourning."

"Nor I." William joined his brother. "We'll see what we can discover."

With an exaggerated puff, Emma blew a stray piece of hair out of her eyes. "Dreadful business about Lady Alice. His other sister, Lady Daphne, just arrived into town, too. I'm anxious to see her."

"I appreciate your concern, but I believe Lord Pembrooke is honorable. He knew about Lord Paul and offered to help me before anyone saw us." Claire softened her voice. "He could have made an excuse and walked away when we were discovered." An honorable man would protect his wife from ridicule. She had to believe Pembrooke would give up his mistress, if she existed.

"I hope for your sake he is, Claire. You deserve only the best." McCalpin turned to leave, with Will following suit. "We'll bid you good night."

Emma narrowed her eyes, as if debating whether to accept Claire's argument. A simple shrug of one shoulder signaled her surrender to the challenge. With a quick spin, she made her way to leave. "When you marry, I'll miss"—she turned from the door—"these talks." Her voice wobbled. "I don't want you hurt anymore."

Claire jumped up from the sofa and gathered her cousin in her arms. "Sweetheart, don't worry. With my history, you might have me until *you* marry." She had made her voice light, but the familiar dread emerged from its dark cave inside her chest to keep her company. She pushed it aside. She had more important things to consider.

After the door closed, Claire made short work of preparing for bed, then drew the draperies around her bedframe. Settled under the covers, she caressed her lips with her fingers. Might a kiss from the "contemptible rogue" be so different from that given by any other man?

She had come close to discovering the answer tonight. He would have kissed her if they hadn't been interrupted by Lord Honeycutt. Surrounded in the safety of his embrace, with all her attention narrowed on him, she had forgotten the storm completely. When had that ever happened?

Pembrooke's offer of marriage might change in the light of day. No doubt his friends and others would encourage him to avoid her and the curse. Proof once again that romance and love were fairy tales. She didn't believe in them, at least not for herself. The only reasonable expectation was respect and honor from her husband.

If Pembrooke's mettle had him somewhere other than her doorstep tomorrow, she hated to think of the ramifications.

She dared hope he was the answer to her prayers. Otherwise, she'd be crushed by the curse and completely ruined.

Alex descended the main staircase of his town house. He had important matters to iron out at Langham Hall, namely negotiating his marriage to the lovely Lady Claire Cavensham. His butler, Simms, stood at attention beside Somerton.

"Ready?" Somerton checked his pocket watch, not hiding his irritation. The earl had been Alex's friend since their early years at Eton and knew him better than anyone.

"In a moment." Alex was not worried. He had fifteen minutes to walk the two blocks to Langham Hall.

Somerton delivered a long-suffering sigh. "I have to be at Goodwin's by nine."

"What in the devil for this early in the morning? No. Do not answer. I have an excuse. You don't." Alex smoothed his waistcoat as Simms held out a beaver hat. Without a look in a mirror, Alex donned the hat and walked out the front door. The earl was right beside him.

"I heard you managed to become betrothed last night. How will the Duke of Langham receive you today?"

"I'm not certain. He was not pleased last night. I'll show him my sincerity and hope that's enough." It made no difference to Alex. He had to marry Claire. Sunshine broke through the gray clouds and chased away the gloom of the London morning. The sun's effects matched Alex's mood. "I'll not allow her reputation to suffer at my hand." He quickened his pace.

"It's a little late for that. This morning every gentleman at White's had you, Lady Claire, and her curse as the topic of discussion." Somerton pulled his hat at an angle to lessen the sun's effect. "Do you realize what you're undertaking this morning?"

"I assume you're referring to Lady Claire. Rest assured, I know what I am doing. It's the final piece. We'll marry Friday morning and arrive at Pemhill by nightfall."

"Marriage is a lifetime commitment." Somerton's voice lowered. "Seriously, perhaps you need to think this through. There's something not quite right about her. Why has she been engaged so many times?"

"Please, Somerton, I never took you as one to believe in curses."

"Sometimes you can be so obtuse." The earl shook his head. "She has the worst luck of anyone I've seen."

"Her luck's about to change."

"Don't be an arrogant arse. It would be tragic if she were hurt again because you rushed this engagement. Just take your time and become better acquainted before marriage."

"Don't be an old hen. Save the speeches for when you're in the House of Lords. She's perfect." Alex grinned. "I was pleasantly surprised by her person. There's a quiet elegance about her."

"Do you think you can come to care for her?" In typical fashion, his friend had found his jugular.

Alex released an inward groan and gritted his teeth. With a sudden stop, he faced Somerton. The sun reflected off the earl's light hair, nearly blinding him. "It's none of your bloody business."

"She'll be your wife and the mother of your children. She'll be by your side, God willing, when you grow old." Somerton stared with narrowed eyes, as if calculating the return on one of his complicated investments. "Neither of us witnessed sterling examples of happy marriages growing up. Your parents were indifferent to each other. My father was miserable after my birth when my mother died, and he never remarried." Somerton hesitated. "Based upon the law of averages, don't you think this deserves more consideration? What if she's in love with him?"

Unease inched its way into Alex's thoughts. He tried to tamp down the concerns Somerton had unearthed. He'd never intended to hurt Lady Claire, just safeguard her future. "Do you think there's reason to believe she is?"

"How would I have knowledge? Lord Paul isn't my friend either." Somerton continued his trek. "All I'm saying is you need to come to terms with this betrayal, or your grief will never heal. You'll continue to live in isolation. That doesn't bode well for a happy life or a contented wife."

"Have you looked in the mirror lately? Your social calendar is nonexistent."

"Pembrooke, that's a poor analogy. I choose not to attend events because I don't enjoy them and have no responsibility to attend. You do. You sit in the House of Lords, and you have a sister in her first Season. You need to make appearances."

Alex refused to admit Somerton had a valid point. "Weeks ago, I shared my plan to marry her as the final punishment for Lord Paul. You made no objection."

"I didn't endorse it either. I never thought you would go through with it." Somerton slowed his pace as he continued to offer his opinion. "Some of your most admirable traits are the deep love and sense of responsibility you bear for your family. Don't confuse that with Lady Claire. She isn't your obligation." Somerton offered a grim smile. "Marriage, much less love, has never been something I understood. Nonetheless, it seems to me you should have some reason to marry her other than revenge."

The short answer was "yes," he had a reason. He already cared for her. Whether the feelings came from chivalry or his desire for revenge wasn't easy to determine. He'd protect her from Lord Paul. He had failed to do it for his own sister, but Claire would not suffer the same fate. A shadow of annoyance darkened Alex's earlier mood. "This conversation is getting monotonous."

Somerton ignored the comment, which was typical. "Lady Claire is a lovely woman. Some fellow will be lucky to have her—under the right circumstances. I'm not convinced it's you."

"Last night was the right circumstance. I could not have planned it better." Alex slowed his stride. Before him was Langham Hall, where Claire resided with her aunt and uncle.

Located in fashionable Mayfair, the mansion was one of the newer residences, specifically designed and built for the crème de la crème of the aristocracy. The large structure was a perfect example of Georgian architecture. With red brick and a wrought-iron railing around the perimeter, the home loomed like a veritable fortress.

"After last night, Langham will press for a quick ceremony, which works to my favor. I don't trust Lord Paul. Unless he marries another heiress quickly, he's ruined. The faster our marriage vows are said, the better."

Somerton's face turned to stone. He tugged the sleeves of his dark gray morning coat. "Make the attempt to woo her. The effort will provide you both an opportunity to become better acquainted."

"When did you become an expert on courtship?"

Somerton's lean body tightened as if he were ready for a fight. With a quick glance skyward, he appeared to reclaim his patience. "Lady Claire deserves better than what you're offering, and so do you." He continued to push his point. "For all that's holy, make certain you're on the right path."

Alex lifted an eyebrow to halt the lecture. His friend's worries would not squander what promised to be a spectacular day. "This is my life. I expect your good wishes at the opera this evening."

He turned from Somerton and entered the gate to Langham Hall.

Claire stood ramrod straight and waited for Pembrooke to enter the blue drawing room. Small compared with the others, this room had been her mother's favorite. Ivory silk covered the walls, while Oriental rugs the color of a kingfisher's blue feathers carpeted the floor—an appropriate place for her first visit from Pembrooke. Never before had she met any of her fiancés in this room. A change of scenery when discussing marriage might change her chance of success. For luck, she wore her favorite morning gown in a shade of emerald green, trimmed with black rosettes around the hem and sleeves. It was striking, and she wanted to look her best. More important, it gave her confidence.

Good Lord, how pathetic. Now, she was allowing the curse to dictate her choice of dresses in her everyday life.

Before breakfast, she'd contemplated how to explain tactfully, of course, that she wasn't interested in his offer of marriage. He had no valid reason to marry her. If she rushed this engagement and it didn't work, the curse would hang over her head for the rest of her life. But after the morning's visit with Uncle Sebastian, she didn't have another choice.

Last night after they arrived home, her uncle had read Lord Paul's note. He'd immediately sent out investigators to find the man's whereabouts. Sure enough, as Pembrooke had stated, Lord Paul sat at the Reynolds's gaming tables. She'd come in second to a roulette wheel.

Perhaps Pembrooke offered sage advice. Her life might be hell with Lord Paul.

Aunt Ginny broke the silence for the fifth time in five minutes. "Are you sure you don't want me or your uncle present? I still think this is highly improper. What if you are forced into something not in your best interests?"

"I haven't changed my mind." Claire grasped her aunt's small hand, its warmth reassuring. "Thank you, but I need to talk to Pembrooke. Four previous engagements do provide one with some benefit. If we come to an understanding, I'll be living with him for the rest of my life." She smiled in hopes of relaying a good spirit. In reality, she was desperate for this to work.

Concern lined the corners of Aunt Ginny's eyes.

Claire gently squeezed her aunt's fingers. "I'm wise enough to know I'm not marrying for love. Don't worry. I'm not afraid to tell him no if I grow uncomfortable with his demands." She released her aunt's hand and wiped her damp palms on her dress.

Her poise cast aside, Aunt Ginny grabbed Claire in a tight embrace. "I *wanted* you to fall in love."

Claire's eyes stung at the words. "What you and Uncle

Sebastian have is rare. I'll be content if Pembrooke and I are comfortable."

She drew a deep breath for fortitude and stepped away from her aunt when Pitts, the family butler, announced Lord Pembrooke. A quick sigh of relief escaped her. His appearance this morning proved he was a man who kept his promises.

The room magically narrowed when the marquess entered. His gaze captured hers with a gleam of interest. Keenly aware of his scrutiny, she curled her toes in her slippers and forced herself not to bolt from the room.

After the appropriate greetings, Aunt Ginny announced, "Lord Pembrooke, you and Lady Claire may talk in private. No one will disturb you."

A slight smile hinted at the corners of his mouth. "Your Grace, if you and the duke would have a moment after Lady Claire and I finish, I'd be grateful."

Her aunt tilted her head and nodded her assent. "Claire dear, if you need anything, Pitts will find me." Without waiting for a reply, she glided out of the drawing room.

He continued to stare at her long after her aunt left. Claire's face grew hot. To show vulnerability before a word was spoken spelled doom. Claire met his gaze even though last night's wanton memories of their shared imaginary kisses left her on edge. "Won't you sit down, my lord?"

"Thank you." The velvet richness of his voice soothed some of her nerves. He waited for her to sit before he took the chair directly across from her. "You look lovely."

Like a girl in her first Season, her breath quickened at the kind words. Though he appeared to relax in the chair, his eyes were sharp.

Alex lowered his gaze and came right to the point of the day's visit. "Have you given any more consideration to our circumstances?"

"Some." Claire swallowed to stop the flutters in her

chest. He leaned close. The clean smell of citrus soap and his unique masculine scent encircled her, much like last night when he'd held her in his arms.

"The same for me." His tone held an unexpected degree of warmth and, with it, concern.

"I am truly sorry about last evening." Her voice turned wooden, and her throat closed around the forced words. The bevy of earlier flutters had roosted in her stomach. "My actions alone caused you to be in this situation. I appreciate your help, but I—"

"I am not sorry," he interrupted. His gray eyes held hers with an intensity that reminded her of the sea bashing against a rocky shore on a stormy day. "What happened in the alcove?" His voice turned gentle. "Why were you so frightened?"

She had dreaded this moment. He was the only person outside the family to glimpse her naked fear of storms. If she confided the real reason, he'd think her a loon and leave Langham Hall at a full run, an outcome that might be best for both of them. "I was out of sorts from the whole evening. Please, it was nothing."

He narrowed his eyes, his doubts clear.

After an eternity, he reached across the space that separated them and took her hand in his long fingers. The warmth of his palm offered comfort, and she desperately needed it. She should pull her hand away, but her arm refused to move.

"Lady Claire, it would be the greatest honor if you became my wife." His sinfully smooth voice coaxed her to move closer. "Will you marry me?"

Completely captivated, she stared at him. Then reality intruded. As the result of last night, she had to answer another proposal. She should be thankful he'd made the effort to appear this morning instead of wary.

After she croaked out, "Yes," a balm of relief coursed

a path through her until it settled in the center of her chest. There, she had said it. Another added to her collection. Maybe five was her magic number.

His eyes flashed with humor. "That wasn't so hard, was it?"

If he only knew.

"I've already discussed the major issues with my uncle. If we come to an agreement, his acceptance will be a certainty."

"We'll reach an accord." His mouth eased into a smile that curved like a sinuous cat. "Thank you for accepting my offer. After we parted last night, I wasn't certain how you would answer."

She couldn't stop staring, and he wouldn't look away. Everything he said was so—so perfect. Didn't he realize she had no other option?

Taking a deep breath, Claire took the plunge into the unknown. "My dowry is fifty thousand pounds. I haven't visited Wrenwood in fourteen years and have no objection to giving the land to you. Three families have farms on the land. Their shares are small, but I ask that you allow them to remain."

He nodded. "They'll be a great help to my steward as he inspects the property. It's all very generous."

"I want the house and all other estates and holdings to remain mine."

Pembrooke continued to smile but added a single nod of his head, his movement slow and measured.

"I have three hundred thousand pounds. I want the money, without question, for my use at my discretion. At the end of my life, any remainder placed in trust." She waited, certain a rejection was forthcoming.

Alex gazed at her through half-lidded eyes. "Done."

Claire found it difficult to determine if he was bored or

ready to strike. Nothing seemed to alter his controlled demeanor.

Maybe luck was with her today, as he was so agreeable. "I'm dedicated to my mother's and the current duchess's charitable works and will continue to be so. It requires I attend several fund-raising events throughout the year. I'd like to host one after we marry. I'll expect you to attend and help me at these events."

"I'd be happy to."

"There's something else you must know. I've always loved children." She studied her clasped hands. "Every year I host a yuletide holiday party for orphans associated with those charities. It's always been at Langham Hall, but I want to host it in my own home."

"Are you asking for my permission?" He furrowed his brow.

"Not really, my lord. It's a commitment I keep every year, and I don't want to continue to rely on Langham Hall's staff and the duke's generosity after I'm married." With a calculated insouciance, she adjusted her smile. "The expression on your face tells me you'd be appalled if there were children running amok at your house."

"Ah . . . no. I wasn't aware of your interests. Of course you can host it at our home. It'll be yours as much as mine."

Claire tilted her head at his perfect answer. Interestingly, he didn't seem the least perturbed with her wishes. Thankfully, he didn't ask for her reasons. She'd started the tradition when she was eighteen to privately remember she had suffered the same loss as the children she'd entertained. Such a small effort on her part brought immeasurable joy to the children. Equally important, it helped soothe her guilt over surviving the carriage accident that caused her parents' death.

"Believe it or not, I like children also. How many shall

we have? I'll go first. I'd like at least a boy and a girl." Humor inched its way into his response.

This was an unexpected topic, but if he wanted to discuss children, that was fine with her. "I want as many as we can have. It makes no difference to me."

"I want to know which I prefer. That's why I want a girl and a boy to start." His gaze appeared thoughtful as he studied her. "I've heard if seasoned properly, they're quite tasty."

Shocked, she raised her hand to her heart, the pounding beat indicative of her unease at their whole conversation. The smile that tugged at his lips softened his face, and he laughed, the rich sound filling the room. She could easily grow accustomed to such banter, particularly with him. She bowed her head to hide the effect he had on her. "You're incorrigible."

"You're beautiful," he countered.

"No. I'm adequate."

He drew closer. "Little liar. The truth is when you smile or laugh, you take my breath away."

Aware of his gaze, she tingled all over. His words gave her hope their future marriage might work splendidly.

She started to relax and allowed herself a study of his face—the sharp angles of his cheekbones, his square chin, and the slight indentation at the center. The curve of his lips was nearly perfect. The only flaw, if one could call it that, was the fullness of the lower lip. He was the one who was beautiful.

This was no time to moon over her future husband. She scrambled to break the silence that rose between them. "I want a trust created to hold the rest of my wealth for our children. My father kept my estates separate from the duchy. It was his wish I have something from my mother's side of the family."

"Done." He leaned back in the chair and contemplated her with a lazy grin. "Are you nervous?"

"No." She tilted her chin and narrowed her eyes. "Why do you ask?"

"Sitting on the edge of the seat, you appear ready to bolt from the chair. Let's discuss something else besides settlements and trusts, shall we? I'll tell you something about myself that no one else knows, and you do the same with me."

"Is this a game?" She bit her lower lip to keep from scowling. His gaze flew to her mouth and lingered. What was he about?

"No. I thought it would help us get to know one another better."

"Oh," she whispered. There was no need, as she'd just agreed to marry him, but inside a little of her melted. He'd completely captivated her with the simple gesture.

"I'll go first." He tilted up one corner of his mouth. "Now, do I have your solemn promise not to disclose anything we discuss?"

"Absolutely." She put her fingers to her lips and twisted as if locking away the secret.

His eyes darkened for a moment, turning a steel gray. "I shall test the lock later for safekeeping, you understand."

A deep heat fell across her cheeks.

He seemed pleased with her response, and his smile returned. "When I was a boy, I wanted a pet, but my mother had a strict rule, no animals in the house. So, I snuck one of the tame barn cats into my room. For two months, I kept Athena hidden."

"Athena?"

He raised an eyebrow. "Appropriate for a mouser."

"What happened?" She breathed deeply to keep from laughing.

"My sisters let it slip one evening I had a cat sleeping on my bed. My mother marched into my room and demanded I hand over Athena."

"Poor kitty and poor you."

"No need for sympathy. This story has a happy ending. I simply informed my mother that after seeing a mouse, I took matters into my own hands. Athena deserved to stay inside. Shocked at the news of a mouse infestation, my mother readily agreed. From that day forward Athena had free rein at Pemhill."

"Did she do her job?"

"I have no idea." He leaned back in his chair, completely at ease. "The mouse I saw was in the lower pasture. Athena never ventured beyond the courtyard."

She put a hand over her mouth and shook her head to hide her mirth. "You didn't tell anyone?"

"Never," he whispered. "Only you."

She shivered, then pulled away to study him. Was he teasing her? Or was the low thrum of his voice something else?

"Your turn."

She swallowed. With so many secrets, it was hard to settle on just one. "Several years ago, I stole away from Langham Hall without anyone knowing."

"Scandalous," he murmured, but his eyes were bright with merriment.

"There was a gypsy camp about an hour away. I visited and bought a witching ball." The confession proved she believed in the curse. How could she explain her desperation to protect her family after her first fiancé, Archard, had died?

The room grew quiet. Without breaking his gaze, he took her hands in his. "What's a witching ball?"

"A glass sphere that traps curses and keeps them from harming loved ones." This was beyond foolish to have disclosed. She stilled but forced herself to push through the answer. "The old gypsy promised it would keep evil spells from a house. It's in my bedroom to stop the curse—"

Suddenly, he tilted her head with his fingers. His lips gently brushed hers. He drew back and studied her, his eyes liquid pools of silver. "If you like, bring it with you when we marry."

"Are you scared of my curse?" The words slipped free, as if his kiss had released all her doubts and fears.

"No." His lips brushed hers again. "My kiss simply locked your secret in me."

She blinked slowly. What if she was scared of the curse? Scared of getting close to another person again and losing him? She shook her head to clear the momentary weakness. They were discussing marriage settlements, not baring all their secrets.

The next term held little, if any, financial worth but was as important as any dealing with her fortune. Fidelity within marriage fostered respect for the union and each other. She had seen the effect it had on her aunt and uncle.

If Pembrooke acknowledged he kept a mistress and refused to give her up, she could not marry him. Otherwise, his affair would give the *ton* another excuse to make her life miserable. She brought enough of that to their marriage and didn't need any additional fodder from him and his mistress.

"I want us to commit to one another completely." With a complete lack of grace, she blurted, "You must give up your mistress immediately."

His mercurial gray eyes sharpened, and his show of lighthearted humor lifted instantly. He leaned closer and brought his face level with hers. "How do you know whether I have a mistress or not?"

"People believe you keep Monique LaFontaine." Claire stayed glued to the chair. If she moved an inch, he would perceive her as weak. "If you have an arrangement, you must break with her. My cousin McCalpin will verify it before we marry."

He was so close, but she refused to blink. Without moving a muscle, she waited as if she had all the time in the world. Truthfully, her insides jiggled like a blancmange. She might have pushed him too far, far enough for him to walk out the door never to return. Even so, she must present a face that was unwavering in her resolve.

"My God. You're serious," he said.

"Yes." Claire raised her eyebrows and set her jaw. A hint of unbridled panic started to buck within her chest. What if she had made a mistake? She had just insulted him. She couldn't lose this last chance at marriage. Could this be any more of a bloody blunder on her part?

Pembrooke broke the silence in a tone that, though quiet, held an ominous quality. "I have no such arrangement. I've been in mourning for the past year and didn't leave Pemhill. I'll not comment any further about my past. It has no impact on our union."

A modicum of dread tightened in her chest. What about her past? If he had any inkling of the truth, he'd recoil in horror. Every thought and concern she wanted to pursue congealed into a huge pool of muddle in her mind. With a slight shake of her head, she attempted to gather her wits.

How could she have been so cruel, bringing up the subject of mistresses while the man had been at his ancestral seat caring for his family? "I'm sorry. Losing a family member is one of the hardest things I've ever had to face. I'm sure you still grieve."

He stared out the window, completely distracted and unaware of her inner turmoil. Finally, his gaze returned to hers, and his face softened. "Thank you. We all miss Alice very much." He took a deep breath and released it, his pain evident. "Let's continue. What else would you like to discuss about the settlements? Or is there anything else you'd like to share?"

Taken aback by his question, she relied on her greatest nemesis to save her from floundering anymore. "No, I think we're done. Might I suggest you call upon the *ton*'s gossips if you want to know about me? They know more about the past and the curse than I do." If he pursued this line of questioning, she was going to lose him, too. Only this time she would be the reason for the loss.

His eyes crinkled, betraying the humor he found in her comment. "Indeed. Probably the same applies to me."

Claire remained still. If she shared any of her secrets, the remains of her reputation would be in tatters, but more important, her dreams for her own family and the children's home she was building in her parents' memory would be shattered. Who would trust innocents to her?

A muscle flickered in his jaw. "This is an extremely delicate subject, one I'm afraid will cause you embarrassment but needs to be discussed." He spoke softly, his voice deep with a mellifluous timbre. "You may think this is a tit for tat, but I assure you it is not. Nasty rumors have surfaced that you . . . have a lover. Rest assured, I'll do whatever is necessary to silence such talk and protect you."

She studied his face for a sign, any hint he knew the truth about her. Without warning, shame slammed into her chest. She choked with memories of Lord Archard. To show the depth of their commitment, they had made love and given their virtue to each other all those years ago. "Thank you for your concern. I've not heard those rumors."

"I apologize if I've caused you distress." He plowed his hands through his black hair. The long length brought to mind a pirate. For a moment, he appeared to be as lost in the past as she was.

"Who's spreading that tale?" She struggled to sound nonchalant.

"It's hard to identify. It's innuendos and rattles from people who have no—" The pain on his face turned into a rueful smile. "Don't worry. I'll put a stop to it."

"There's no need. No one can stop the rumors about me." Desperate to escape the torture, Claire bit her lip to gain control as her pulse raced. Her heart whispered it was time to tell the truth and bare her guilt. For years, she had carefully protected the secret deep inside. But this man and his vow to protect her made her want to confess all.

Oh God, she couldn't. He'd walk away, and society would waste little time in labeling her a pariah.

He rose from the chair and stood before her. "I should take my leave and see your aunt and uncle."

She took a deep breath to settle the rampage of emotions coursing through her. "They'll want to go over our agreement again. Be patient with my uncle. He has a reputation for being quite tenacious."

"I don't think your uncle cares one whit for my patience. He's concerned for your welfare, as he should be."

Claire felt her cheeks heat once again.

"That pink is enchanting on you. I must make you blush at every opportunity if that is my reward." He clasped her hand and brought it slowly to his lips. The warmth sent shivers through her. "I'm very pleased with our union. I'll call again soon." His retreating steps grew silent.

Deep inside, she knew the only true course of action before her. She had no other choice or option in life. The costs of not moving forward with the marriage outweighed any temporary relief of escaping his disapproval once he discovered the truth.

She was Pembrooke's. God save them both from the curse.

Chapter Four

❧

Nothing inside Claire stirred. The hot, sticky air in the attic had more movement. Her stupor made her doubt she had a heartbeat.

After Pembrooke left, her world tilted on its side and circled much like a top coming to the end of a spin. His graciousness and honesty were a true testament to the type of man he was. A man who would care for his wife. A man who deserved love. A man who deserved the truth.

None of her other fiancés had ever stirred her feelings of want and guilt and shame into such a frenzy. There was no denying she was cursed. The glimpse she'd caught of her future life with such a man offered the promise of everything she wanted, but deep in her heart the reality of her situation refused to grow quiet.

She flipped open the chest before her, a massive cedar piece that held each of her wedding dresses. Kneeling, she searched until she found the silk bag that held the pink gown she had planned to wear when she wed Henry, the Earl of Archard. She gently lifted the dress from the chest and searched the hidden pocket in the bodice.

She pulled out the locket he had given her the day they

had made love. It was no more than an inch and a half tall, surrounded by diamonds. The real beauty of the piece was the likeness of her betrothed. The artist had captured him with a hint of mischief etched around the eyes. Henry had asked she pin the piece inside her wedding gown as a remembrance of his love.

Her finger caressed his face. The sound of her heartbeat and the accompanying pulse returned along with her confidence. Within a span of five minutes, she'd come to a conclusion—she had not made a mistake giving her virtue to this man. She had loved him, and he had loved her. Any repercussions from her actions were minuscule in comparison with what she had shared with Henry. She would confess to Pembrooke and deal with the results.

Her lady's maid, Aileen, stepped into the attic. "My lady? Pitts told me you were here. They're waiting for you in His Grace's study." She tilted her head and narrowed her eyes at the open trunk. "You're not considering wearing one of those gowns when you marry Lord Pembrooke? You don't want to wed with a dose of bad luck."

"No. I was feeling a little nostalgic." Claire returned the locket to its resting place and took her leave of the attic. She'd had enough bad luck to last a lifetime. She let her newfound inner calm blossom into the strength necessary to face her future.

Once Pembrooke discovered her secret, he'd have every right not to go through with marriage, nor could she blame him. However, if her aunt and uncle discovered the reason they wouldn't marry, they'd be devastated. The disappointment on their faces would crush her. They'd provided a home when she had none and had given her their support over the years. She couldn't repay their kindness with the humiliation they would suffer at the knowledge that their niece had lost her virtue years ago.

She could break the engagement with Pembrooke. But

she'd be forced to leave London for her Lockhart estate in southern Scotland. This morning, the gossip had exploded about her break with Lord Paul and her new attachment with Pembrooke. If she didn't marry him, it would take little to run her out of town by Friday. As certain as the sunrise each morning, the curse would follow.

Claire stood outside the study and bowed her head. She squeezed her eyes closed until the emptiness in her chest subsided. Somehow, she had to find a way to tell Pembrooke before they married.

When she advanced into the room, her aunt and uncle were poring over a monstrous pile of papers on the desk. Alex was nowhere in sight.

"There you are." Aunt Ginny pushed a wisp of silvery-blond hair out of her face. "I told Aileen to prepare your blue satin gown for the evening's engagement." Her aunt smiled, but her voice betrayed her unease. "Sebastian and Pembrooke decided you will appear together before the announcement of your wedding later this week."

"Why ever should we appear in society?" It was impossible to think they'd go out in public as a betrothed couple. After Lady Anthony's ball, the curse had stirred anew. The morning paper, *Midnight Cryer*, had featured her broken betrothal and new engagement on the front page. The headline simply stated, LADY CALAMITY'S ALLURE IN FULL FORCE LAST NIGHT.

Her uncle's face softened. "Pembrooke and I thought an evening out together will keep the rumors to a minimum. You're going to the opera this evening."

Aileen curtsied in front of her. "Shall I lay out your mother's sapphires?" she asked in a soft lilt.

"Yes, that would be lovely." Some of her uneasiness dissipated as she focused on the twinkle in her maid's eyes. Aileen was seven years older than Claire and had been with her since she was thirteen. Her aunt proclaimed every young woman required her own personal maid to present one's self in the best possible light. More important, Aileen willingly stayed by her side when the nightmares threatened.

The room grew quiet, in contrast to Claire's emotions. Excitement that she would finally marry clashed with the fear of what her marriage to Pembrooke would entail. This moment was unique from the other four times she had sat down to discuss marriage settlements. Alex wanted her and not her dowry. None of the other fiancés could make such a claim. Not even Archard, who had needed her dowry for his estate. She chose the seat next to Aunt Ginny, as she would provide unwavering support.

With an air of finality, her uncle finally turned. "Claire, the terms with Pembrooke have my blessing."

She swallowed hard and squeezed her eyes closed to regain her composure. He'd agreed. She embraced the immediate sense of hope and allowed it to unfurl deep inside her chest. Their marriage meant her reputation could be repaired. Whatever her future held, if Pembrooke still wanted her after she confessed, she would find a way to make her marriage a success. "Please continue."

Aunt Ginny held a piece of paper in her hand and extended it to Claire. "You need to be prepared in case anyone asks you about the curse and Lord Paul. His gambling is worse than we thought. He lost his fortune last night at a gambling hell and had no recourse but to sell his late mother's estate. This morning, he sent Sebastian a note with an explanation for last night."

"No, thank you. I'd rather not." Now the *ton* would add debt to the list of curses to accompany death, disease, and dismemberment. Claire paused to consider the letter with Lord Paul's broken seal on the outside. Last night, a similar piece of foolscap had held such great power over her life. Now, it was nothing more than a piece of rubbish.

Her aunt's eyes were sympathetic. "Sweetheart, this is cruel, but you need to hear the latest. Rumors abound that Lord Paul's misfortune is a lie." She moved close and clasped Claire's hands. She squeezed as if trying to give Claire some of her strength. "Some say he personally spread the tale so he could cry off without penalty. No one knows who owns the property now. We cannot afford for any more scandal or suspicion to come your way. Thank goodness Pembrooke was here. He's given you great consideration."

"What do you mean?" Wariness swept from Claire's toes to her head.

"Lord Pembrooke believes Lord Paul is trying to secure private funding to recoup his losses. If he is successful, his reputation will survive, while yours . . ." Aunt Ginny paused. "Let's just say the curse will remain alive and well. He'll not suffer if he doesn't marry you. There are always other heiresses."

"What does Pembrooke suggest?" Claire had to ask but dreaded the answer.

Finally, Uncle Sebastian found his voice. "You and Pembrooke will venture into society the next couple of days and present a happy couple smitten with each other, laying any hint of Lord Paul or a forced marriage to rest. At week's end, you'll marry by special license. To the *ton,* you'll appear wise to be free of Lord Paul's debts." He surveyed her face with raised brows. "Your thoughts?"

She wrestled her disquiet into a somewhat tenuous submission and turned to her aunt. "Do you have an opinion?"

"If you aren't sure or are uncertain about marriage to Pembrooke"—Aunt Ginny patted her hand in comfort—"we'll find another way."

Claire took a deep breath and stood. "I want to marry him."

Uncle Sebastian let out a breath of relief. "I approve. He

gave us his assurance he'll protect your holdings and reserves."

"We'll make plans regarding the rest of the week later today." Aunt Ginny's eyes brightened. "You'll be married Friday."

Claire squared her shoulders. "Thank you. With all the turmoil, I forgot to ask what's playing at the Royal Opera House?"

Uncle Sebastian had already walked back to his desk and laughed over his shoulder. "Who cares? You and Pembrooke will be going to the theater *to be seen playing,* not to see what's playing. Enjoy tonight."

Claire fidgeted as fourteen thousand imaginary ants marched across her back while Aileen adjusted a wayward lock of hair.

"My lady, you look magnificent, if I do say so myself. No man will be able to resist you, particularly Lord Pembrooke."

If her maid had an inkling of the truth about Claire's virginity, she'd see how easy Pembrooke's regard could be lost.

Claire held still as Aileen closed the clasp of her favorite necklace, a massive piece of jewelry that her mother had said matched her father's eyes. Tiny diamonds surrounded a large royal-blue sapphire stone. The rest of the necklace consisted of perfectly matched diamonds separated by smaller sapphires and set in a gold collar that encircled her neck.

Her gown was a perfect accompaniment to the necklace. The décolleté scooped low but was still modest enough that Claire didn't feel overexposed. An overlay of matching tulle with tiny sapphires sewn in a pattern on the dress's hem gave the appearance of stars twinkling from a heavenly blue sky.

Claire reached for her gloves as a brisk knock sounded on the bedroom door.

Aileen returned with Lord Paul's calling card. "Serves him right to see you as beautiful as you are this evening," she groused.

Within minutes, Claire entered the yellow drawing room. She took a steadying breath and waited beside the sofa for Lord Paul to notice her arrival. The room was silent except for the occasional crack of wood splitting in the fireplace. Tonight, the salon's warm gold colors made his complexion look sallow.

He stood before the fire, looking down at the floor. After a few moments, he lifted his head. Claire's heart pressed against her chest when she saw the extent of his dishevelment. His torn superfine coat and mussed hair were evidence of what the last couple of days had cost him personally. Likely he had not been home, or his valet had given notice based upon the turn of events.

"Claire, how beautiful you look." Lord Paul's eyes were kind as he glanced over her dress. A ghost of a smile eased across his lips.

"Thank you. I—I don't have much time. I have plans for the evening." She clenched her teeth to keep from inviting him to sit. It was odd not to ask him to stay. During their engagement they'd enjoyed each other's company, a sign they might have developed a true affection for each other in their marriage.

"I had to see you." He looked away for a moment before walking to her.

If anyone saw him enter Langham Hall, the winds of rumor would blow across town within an hour. She had to think of a way to get him to leave immediately.

"You've undoubtedly heard I'm financially destitute." His voice softened, but the words were abrasive. "I'll not associate your good name with mine."

His eyes narrowed in pain. She lifted her hand to give comfort, then let it gently drop. She could not offer any succor until he explained why he had left her to fend for herself last night at Lady Anthony's ball.

"That's the reason I broke the engagement. Some say I was convinced of the curse or I had deliberately misled you. Rest assured, it's not true."

His light blue eyes were normally luminous with humor, but tonight they appeared dull with defeat. The tragedy of his incessant gambling had cost him everything. He appeared lost, almost forlorn, as if he'd lost his last friend.

"Thank you for the consideration. I'm not certain I can offer you much else except I hope you find happiness in your life. A footman will show you out." The evenness in her voice surprised her.

Desolation spread slowly over his face. She prayed he wouldn't plead for forgiveness.

"Claire, I deeply regret that I've placed you in this position. If there is anything"—he cleared his throat—"anything that will salvage our friendship . . ."

Her heart pounded heavily in her chest, as if announcing *I told you so.* She ignored the litany. He had offered for her without any qualm about her curse. She owed him her friendship. "You'll need to give me some time. Your actions have put my family in a difficult position. The social calls today have been nothing but a false veneer of concern. Every single person wants to know if the rumors are true. You understand?"

"If it offers any comfort, tomorrow's fodder will be about me. I don't want to lose your friendship, too."

The sound of the hall clock signaling the hour sounded like a death knell. Pembrooke was due any minute.

Alex's decision to make the evening as pleasant as possible for Claire fell into a trough of disbelief. A small opening through the drawing room door allowed him to watch and listen to the conversation as it unfolded between his fiancée and Lord Paul. Claire's soft words made it difficult to hear everything she said. His mind raced in an attempt to come up with a rational answer. Surely she wasn't involved with him.

"Why put me through such a public humiliation? I thought you wanted this marriage." Claire's voice was barely above a whisper, the desperation clear. For a moment, he believed she was in pain.

"If you only knew the full anguish I feel. My apology isn't enough, but it's all I can offer you now." Lord Paul hesitated. "I'm responsible for my actions, but you should know there are other forces at work I can't control. If I had known the true costs, I would have never put either of us in this situation."

Across the room, Claire had crossed her arms at the waist. "I wish you had told me in person. Why didn't you give me the courtesy of breaking with you? At least I'd be called a jilt instead of being the butt of a cruel joke."

The hairs on his neck stood on end as Lord Paul seemed ready to disclose Alex's part in his ruin. Claire either didn't understand the hint or didn't care at this point.

Lord Paul slowly came forward and took her hand in his. "I wanted a life with you." His other hand brought her chin up, forcing her to look into his eyes. "I thought we'd suit in every way. Give me another chance, and you'll not be sorry. Give me until Friday. Say yes, Claire."

Alex's body tensed as he closed his eyes to block the vision of Lord Paul's hands on her. It would ruin everything if he interrupted their interlude. It was pure torture to wait, but her answer would define his next action. He held his breath and waited.

"The damage is done." Claire's voice never wavered, with words clear and precise in her enunciation. "Your absence at our engagement announcement broke the betrothal. It's best this way."

"What if I told you I loved you?"

Claire fell back as if Lord Paul had struck her. She broke the silence with a firm voice. "Please, don't." She shook her head. "We both need to move forward with our lives."

Alex slowly let out the breath. His self-control hung by a thread. It had taken every bit of discipline he possessed not to barge into the room and drag her away when Lord Paul begged her to take him back.

"I disagree, my lady. I'll not give up that easily. Enjoy your evening." With a quick nod, Lord Paul turned toward the door.

Alex moved himself into the shadows, waiting for him to exit. When Lord Paul closed the door, Alex approached from behind without a sound. He took advantage of his superior height and grabbed the dejected man by the scruff of the neck. "A word, if you please."

Lord Paul looked more like a desperate vagrant than the son of a duke. Before he could spit out a reply, Alex shoved him into the music room across the hallway.

"Bloody hell, Pembrooke." Lord Paul tried to straighten his rumpled jacket. "You've caused enough trouble this week."

Alex clenched his fist. "Apparently not. I heard enough of your conversation to conclude you bear a striking resemblance to a stuck pig. You almost squealed the terms of your rescue."

"Why should I hide the fact you made me break with Lady Claire? The entire town talks of nothing but my demise and the curse." Lord Paul retreated to a pianoforte and softly played a minor chord. "My life is over. I'm broke, destitute because of you. I've nothing to lose." When he lifted his head, all emotion was gone, as if a curtain had fallen, signaling the end of a tragic play.

"Then the rumors at the club are true. Your father cut you off completely." A hint of guilt sprang into Alex's thoughts, but he slammed the emotion behind the door of his hardened resolve. "Do as agreed or I'll pull the guarantees. Otherwise your pick, Australia or America."

Lord Paul closed the distance between them. "Go to the devil."

"Stay away from Claire." Alex's voice turned callous. "If you hound her, I *will* call you out. I beg of you, give me a reason—any reason."

Lord Paul's eyes suddenly cleared. "You're after her for revenge. Goddamn me, why didn't I see it earlier?" His voice deepened. "You set me up with unlimited credit at Reynolds. Anything I wanted to play with no limits. How long did it take you?"

Alex delivered a bored inspection of Lord Paul's mussed clothes. "Not long with your taste for debauchery."

"You don't give a damn about anything except settling the score. You were the one who destroyed Alice. Not I."

Alex reined in the overwhelming urge to attack. If he hit the man, he wouldn't stop until Lord Paul's lifeless body littered the floor. "We both know why she died. How do you live with yourself?"

"My conscience is as pure as a choir of angels." Lord Paul delivered an appraising glance. "Let me share a secret. Lady Claire is an incomparable. A jewel of the finest quality. There is no comparison to any of the other women I've had. Trust me."

Alex's breath hitched. That was the crux of the problem. He had trusted Paul. When Alex had prepared his first speech for the House of Lords, Paul had spent the afternoon with him. Politically astute, Paul had rewritten entire sections. He'd listened to Alex give the speech, then advised which points to emphasize. The next day, Alex had received a standing ovation.

They had shared the same life experiences—attended the same schools, belonged to the same clubs. There were once friends. He knew where Paul came from and how he thought. But could he believe Paul's claim that he'd slept with her? He'd lied about Alice, and he had to be lying now. There couldn't be another explanation.

Lord Paul lifted a corner of his mouth in an arrogant smirk. "Claire has the most delightful set of—" He brought his hand up to his heart and sighed. "You'll discover the treasure trove on your own."

The vision of Lord Paul's hands on Claire tainted his final act of revenge. He forced himself to focus on Lord Paul and closed the distance between them. "You are foul"—he gritted his teeth and narrowed his eyes—"but I've never thought of you as a liar."

"You always were a judgmental prig. Maybe that's why Alice always sought my company instead of yours when she was troubled." Lord Paul cocked an eyebrow.

Lord Paul spoke the truth. Alice had always sought Paul's counsel. But he'd be damned before he showed any reaction to the pain inflicted.

"For what it's worth, the next time I finish with a lover, I'll send a note. If Lady Claire is any indication, you obviously enjoy following me in bed," Lord Paul said.

Alex grabbed him by the neckcloth and twisted. Only the toes of Lord Paul's shoes touched the thick carpet. "If you as much as hint any of these tales to others, I'll kill you without thought or ceremony. Now leave before my good humor escapes me." He gave a forceful push, sending Lord Paul crashing into the closed door.

Lord Paul flashed a rancorous grin as he brushed his

coat. "You will pay for what you've done. I promise. I will not let you ruin Claire the way you did me. Or Alice."

Before Alex entered the drawing room, he took a moment to smooth his coat and cravat as he composed his anger and pain. He refused to give countenance to the claim Lord Paul had Claire in his bed. She was a lovely, well-bred woman. Such lies would not follow her once they were married. No one would sully her. He'd risk duels and curses before he'd let her suffer.

The taunt that he had ruined Alice was close to the truth, as he had failed to protect her from such evil. It mattered little at this point. Everything he'd done in the past year was for Alice. That was the only thing that mattered. If he sheltered Claire, it might provide a semblance of salvation and some relief from his ever-present guilt.

Claire faced the fire with her back to him. She either had not heard him approach or didn't care.

His gaze slowly followed the sweep of her dress before coming to rest on her shoulders. The image of the dark blue silk against her ivory skin presented a charming tableau, one that any master would be delighted to paint. The fire caught the shimmer of her hair, reflecting flames of dark red. She was beautiful.

With a whirl of her dress, she greeted him with a genuine grin before it faded into a practiced smile. She drew a deep breath, then waited for him to approach. Authentic smile or not, he was drawn to her almost as if he were caught in a magical web, the pull too great to resist. Silently, he acknowledged the inevitable truth. He didn't want to resist her—no matter how inconvenient for him.

Whatever this was between them, he couldn't lose perspective. He had to remember Alice. His hoarse whisper broke the silence. "Lady Claire."

She regarded him with clear, observant eyes. "Lord Pembrooke."

"Please, it's Alex. That's what my family calls me." He smiled slightly to put her at ease, but remnants of hurt still shone in her eyes. Was she mourning the loss of Lord Paul? He resolved to make her forget everything except for him.

Neither of them had their gloves on for the evening. He took her hand, the warmth and softness of her skin threatening to whip his amorous thoughts into a full frenzy. With deliberate ease, he bowed and turned her wrist to meet his lips. Her spicy scent, a bergamot orange with sandalwood, brought back the memory of her clinging to him at Lady Anthony's ball. He allowed his lips to linger before tasting her skin with his tongue.

Her quick intake of breath at his forwardness encouraged him to continue. His thumb lightly toyed back and forth across her palm. He needed to touch her for his own reassurance. She bewitched him like a temptress.

Her lips parted as if she would welcome his kiss. Her green eyes darkened when he lifted his gaze to hers.

"I saw Lord Paul as I arrived. Is everything all right?"

Claire stilled, then responded in the gentle tone he was coming to recognize. "I told him it was finished between the two of us." Her expression held little emotion. "It's hard to explain. Yesterday, I expected to marry him. Today, I'll be with you."

Inside, Alex relished his triumph. In that moment, she had agreed to relinquish her fate into his hands. Her acceptance was a heady start to the evening.

"Shall we leave . . . Alex?"

The slight hesitation before she spoke was a lightning rod. Desire shot through him again as his name fell from her lips.

Claire tugged her hand free and donned her evening gloves. "Let us continue the conversation in the carriage."

He mimicked her movements with his own gloves. The absence of her warm touch was a loss, but her acknowledgment that she was his lightened his mood considerably.

Claire considered the Marquess of Pembrooke's black carriage. It rivaled any of the Duke of Langham's vehicles. The coach looked like Alex—big, dark, handsome—and the devil to drive. Six restless horses, anxious to start the journey to the opera house, snorted and stomped in unison.

Alex reached out to help her into the carriage. His gloves accentuated the elegance of his large hands and the power that resided there. After she entered, he squeezed her fingers and lingered before releasing them. His touch caused her heartbeat to perform the same erratic dance she'd experienced in the drawing room when he had kissed her wrist.

After she settled in the front-facing seat, Alex quickly entered and sat opposite her. Although cloaked in shadow, his presence filled the carriage. It pushed at her from every angle, almost as if he touched her. She looked out the window for some diversion, trying to keep her thoughts from wandering back to him. After an eternity, the carriage lurched into motion and the clip-clop of the perfectly matched team set off.

"Do you love him?" His low voice hummed.

The unexpected question caused Claire to choke with a cough. She covered her mouth with her hand in an effort to hide her distress. Alex came out of the darkness and handed her his handkerchief. She shook her free hand in an attempt to stop his gesture.

He took her upheld hand and pressed the cloth into her palm before he closed his fingers around hers. Alarm crossed his face. "Claire?"

She regained the ability to speak, but her throat protested

the effort. "No. I have no . . . I meant what I said earlier. I never want to be reminded again."

"Good." His unfathomable, slate-colored eyes darkened to a lustrous obsidian hue.

She became increasingly uneasy under his scrutiny. It was as if he enjoyed watching her discomfort. His silence made it difficult to find anything to converse about. Nevertheless, she was not a coward and forced herself to watch him in return. His evening attire enhanced his masculinity and did nothing to hide his strength. All of it—his body, his smell, and his allure—overpowered her. He reminded her of some wild animal and, caught in his lair, she was unsure what he would do. None of her other fiancés had affected her this way. She closed her eyes in an effort to collect her composure.

Finally, he broke the silence. "I consider myself most fortunate to have such a beautiful and fascinating bride."

"Alex, please. There's no need." She shifted in her seat and took a deep breath to ease her discomfort. "I'm not the type of woman who has admirers outside the suitors who find my investments my most attractive feature."

She waited for a response, but none was forthcoming. The lull in conversation turned into a noose around her neck, one she had to escape.

"In truth, I lead a boring life. I work at a charity and take social calls. I rarely attend entertainments or *ton* events." Even to her own ears, she sounded dull.

Still, he said nothing.

"It's true my fortune is legendary in more ways than one." She couldn't stop the ramble of her words. "We both know it isn't large enough to overcome most men's fear of the curse."

"Do you believe you're cursed?"

"Sometimes." Why else would she have traveled to a gypsy camp on her own, desperate to find some relief from her bad luck? She'd even thought of going to Scotland and finding a white witch who could reverse the curse.

"There is no curse." His deep baritone resonated throughout the carriage. "Do you know why I want you?"

His voice was a potent elixir that had her relaxing . . . until she understood the question. Her chest ached from a ragged intake of breath. She couldn't form a response. The air pulsed with the tension of his statement. At this moment, she would give every pound she possessed to escape her past. She would like to be Claire and not a bank account or a piece of property or a cursed joke. And he was giving her that chance.

His silence settled around her, causing her stomach to tangle into knots. She waited for ages, the rattle of the carriage wheels and the rhythmic clop of the horses the metronome of time passing.

In a deep, gentle cadence, he broke the silence. "Claire . . ." His voice caressed her as he leaned toward her and emerged from the shadows as if he were a hero in a gothic novel. A grimace crossed his face before he continued, "When I announced our engagement at Lady Anthony's ball, I thought we'd have a typical marriage between a peer and his wife. A comfortable friendship. But . . ." He stopped and let his gaze follow the length of her body before coming to rest on her face. "I didn't expect to find you so desirable that I no longer trust myself with you. If I had my way, I'd topple you in that seat this very instant." He moved closer without touching her, but the heat of his body enveloped her.

She stiffened in shock, not knowing how to stop the building thrum of desire between them, or if she even wanted to. His scent, spicy and all male, so different from hers, wrapped around her willpower, and she shamelessly drew forward. She waited for his touch.

Alex's voice dropped to a low, sensual pulse, stirring

the warmth low in her belly. "I'd kiss and suck until your lips were red and swollen." He sighed before he brought his mouth to her ear to whisper, "Then I'd nip at your earlobes while telling you every wicked thing I'd do to you. I'd undress you ever so slowly, every inch of your satin skin unveiled for my enjoyment. I'd bite with my teeth, then soothe with my mouth until I laid your breasts bare. I'd worship your nipples until they hardened and you begged for relief. While I pleasured you, my hand would wind its way under your dress. I'd caress a path on your skin until I found your most secret place."

Her body vibrated. My God, his words raged a storm inside her body.

In slow motion, he braced his hands on the leather seat framing her hips and leaned forward until their bodies were a scant inch apart. "I'd put my fingers inside you and give you the sweetest torment with each caress, over and over until you screamed my name as you surrendered to the rapture. Then, Claire, I'd mount you until we both cried out our pleasure . . . together."

She couldn't move. White-hot heat swept through her body with the force of a tidal wave and hampered her simple ability to breathe. His scent covered her, marking her as his.

The carriage came to a halt. The sounds of various voices drifted into the vehicle. Alex reached toward her, and with the barest of caresses, the gloved knuckles of his hand slowly rubbed her cheek. Her body screamed for more while her mind cried, *Stop!*

"Take a minute. My driver and groomsmen have instructions not to intrude unless I signal." He took charge with quiet assurance. "If I've shocked you, forgive me. I look forward to the day I can have you. Until then, know the depths of my desire for you." Alex exhaled his frustration. "There is nothing I want more than to have you in my bed."

She closed her eyes and placed her hand over his while he gently caressed the apple of her cheek. Her emotions were so convoluted, she doubted she'd ever regain control. "Alex—"

He moved as if to embrace her in a kiss.

Every muscle in her body tensed into tight little knots she doubted could ever be untangled. To her utter despair, he drew away.

"The next time you believe you're cursed, come to me. I'll show you that you aren't." Power radiated from his body as he relaxed. "Give me a few moments. Then, shall we go inside? I want the entire audience to see you're mine, my future wife."

Chapter Five

Claire didn't wear provocative gowns to the opera, or anywhere else, for that matter, but the dress she wore tonight was vibrant in color and movement. It was the perfect choice after Alex's declaration in the carriage that he wanted people to notice they were together.

His private box fell conspicuously direct center above the stage and set back a sufficient distance from the other boxes. Any sense of privacy vanished when several audience members ogled them with their opera glasses. Holding the single-lens contraptions to their eyes, they gave the appearance of formally dressed pirates ready to claim the spoils of the fight—namely, the first to spread the gossip that Lady Claire Cavensham had attended this evening's performance with the Marquess of Pembrooke.

As Alex escorted her to a seat in the back, his hand, possessive in touch, rested on the curve of her lower back. After they settled, he leaned intimately toward her. "My mother and sister shall be joining us. I want to share our announcement."

Claire's earlier prurient tension had melted, only to be replaced by another desire. She would meet his family. "I look forward to seeing Lady Daphne again. However, I haven't had the pleasure of meeting Lady Pembrooke."

"My mother doesn't go out much in society since my sister's death. This year is different now that Daphne's out." A hint of a smile crossed his face as his eyes lit from within. With a slight shift in his seat, he claimed the edge of her chair as if sharing his innermost secrets. His leg pressed against hers, and the heat of his touch transfixed her. "Daphne is confident and poised in social settings, yet her warmth and humor readily shine. I'm really quite proud of her. She's grown into an accomplished young woman."

Claire's heart did a somersault when she gazed upon his face. He was charming in his attitude toward his sister. His love of family was readily evident. She experienced a jolt of immediate joie de vivre. Within a week, she would become part of their family. She wanted the current marchioness to become a fast friend and hoped their relationship would blossom into one as close as mother and daughter. The joy was short-lived when she remembered that any such future happiness would be tied to Alex and his reaction to her secret.

"I only wish Alice were here to see Daphne's Season." He leaned forward and placed his elbows on his knees. His gaze settled on the other side of the theater. "She'd be euphoric at her sister's success." He was lost in thought for a moment, his face expressionless except for the fine lines at the corners of his eyes that made his pain obvious.

Claire didn't want to intrude upon his grief, but she had to offer some comfort. "I was acquainted with your sister, but I wish . . . I wish I'd known her better."

He straightened and wordlessly placed his hand over hers and gently squeezed. The movement was so subtle that no one in the theater would have noticed the gesture. However, it told her volumes. Her sentiment had brought him a respite from the sorrow.

His lips tugged upward as he leaned close. "You and she would have become fast friends. I'm sure of it." With a shift of his body, he increased the space between them.

His movement signaled that the topic was closed for discussion. He'd share a part of himself, then pull away. He'd demonstrated that skill in the carriage this evening and now with Alice. It made the truth hard to deny. He might have said he didn't believe in the curse, but perhaps he'd pushed her away so as not to risk it. A wise decision, as the curse couldn't affect him if he kept his distance from her. Still, tonight left her wanting more. She wanted to know everything about him.

The private door opened, and an elegant lady in her mid-fifties entered with Lady Daphne. Both were dressed at the height of fashion. The woman had to be Alex's mother, as his gray eyes were the mirror image of hers.

Alex rose to greet them, and Claire stood at the same time to observe the exchange. He met his mother with a grin and brought her gloved hand to his mouth for a quick kiss. "Good evening, madam."

The Marchioness of Pembrooke nodded with a smile. "Alex, you look well."

"Indeed. May I introduce Lady Claire Cavensham?"

The marchioness turned her attention to Claire. In a melodic voice she said, "It's a pleasure to make your acquaintance." With a wave of her hand, she proclaimed, "I'm happy you could join us this evening."

Lady Daphne jumped into the conversation. "This is marvelous. I'll not have to suffer the same old boring crowd at intermission. Pembrooke's friends are wonderful, but dreary. We'll have to rely on each other for amusement." The young woman offered Claire a sudden, winsome smile.

The marchioness studied Claire. "Are you here by yourself?"

Inwardly, she cringed at the marchioness's question but

squeaked out a lame "Yes, my lady." This was not the way she wanted to start their relationship. The curse was enough to scare away any person, but a fast reputation was unspeakable.

Alex came to her rescue, smoothing any rough waters. "Mother, I want to share our news. Claire has consented to be my wife. She and I are to be married by special license at the end of the week." His lips twitched into a smile worthy of a rogue. "You and Daph must retire early on Thursday. I want you at Langham Hall eight o'clock sharp this Friday."

Daphne grabbed Claire's hands in hers and delight lit her face. "Married! This is marvelous news."

Claire looked at both women, and happiness rose like cream in a cup of milk. If she didn't control her rambunctious emotions, she'd never make it through the night. "Thank you for such kind words."

The marchioness smiled with warm affection. A few telltale tears sprang to her eyes when she turned to Alex. "Well, you have taken me by surprise. I was not expecting this announcement." She laughed through her tears. "How wonderful! Lady Claire, welcome to the family. Congratulations to you both. I shall invite your family over for dinner to celebrate."

Alex's mother didn't mention or acknowledge the curse. She didn't question Alex about his decision at all. No matter what happened from this day forward, the marchioness had already become one of Claire's favorite women in the entire universe. She had accepted Claire and their marriage without objection.

As the orchestra finished their warm-ups, it was time to take their seats. Alex motioned toward the front. "We'll continue our conversation at the intermission."

Alex seated his mother and sister in the second row. Then he brought her front and center. The cat was out of the bag if anyone wondered whom the Marquess of Pembrooke had escorted to the theater. Everyone could see her seated close to him. Rumors of Lord Paul would fall silent by morning.

When the first act ended, footmen entered the box with bottles of champagne and glasses. As soon as everyone had a glass in hand, the marchioness raised her glass. "May you have a long and happy marriage," she said with a bright smile. "I know I'm presumptuous, but let me add, may you bring me lots and lots of grandchildren to spoil. And soon."

At the marchioness's kind words, Claire almost deferred to the overwhelming urge to fall on her knees and thank the merciful heavens.

Daphne joined in with a resounding "Huzzah!"

Before either Alex or Claire could answer, the box door swept open. One of the *ton*'s most handsome and eligible men, the Earl of Somerton, strolled into the box like a sun god. His golden hair and tanned skin magnified his stunning looks. His turquoise-colored eyes added an exotic feature to his tall and lean physique.

"Well, well. Pembrooke decided to grace us with his presence tonight. There are no words to describe the honor." Somerton greeted the marchioness and Daphne before his gaze fell to Claire.

At his sly smile, Claire felt unease start to crowd out her earlier happiness. She didn't know Somerton well, and if he teased about the curse, her entire night would be destroyed.

"Lady Claire, a pleasure." He bowed over her hand and then slowly rose. His startling gaze held hers as if trying to ascertain a secret.

Claire darted a glance at Alex and relaxed. His eyes twinkled, and an affectionate smile—the same one she'd seen when he had talked about Daphne—transformed him into the most dazzling man she'd ever seen. With ardent envy, she wanted that smile for herself.

"Somerton, thank you for appreciating my good taste. You are greeting the future Marchioness of Pembrooke, so I suggest you release her hand. Otherwise, I'll have no other recourse except a sound thrashing at Gentleman Jackson's."

The earl let his hand linger longer than was socially acceptable. "No, thank you." He gently squeezed, then finally released her fingers. "The last time we raised fists, I couldn't move for a week. Getting on a horse was pure torture." He faced Claire. "My lady, I apologize for monopolizing your attention. I offer my congratulations to you both." He bent his head in a mocking bow and whispered loudly, "Alas, I fear Pembrooke is getting the better part of the bargain."

With a devil-may-care smile, Alex clasped his friend's outstretched hand in a firm handshake. "You're trying to goad me into the ring. Still, I thank you."

The two men's antics reminded her of her cousins McCalpin and William when they teased and prodded each other. Soon, others entered the box while the two men continued their conversation. Claire excused herself and made her way to Daphne and her friends and found Emma among the women. They chatted about upcoming events, and the conversation turned into a rousing discussion about which balls would host the most eligible men.

Claire listened with amusement before she returned her attention to Alex. When their eyes met, she was caught and unable to turn away. There was a spark of something indefinable in his eyes that demanded she hold his gaze.

She met his demand and raised it with a small smile.

"Lady Claire, I didn't expect to see you today."

Claire found the Hailey's Hope solicitor before her.

Completely immersed in her task, she hadn't heard him approach. Wallace Perkins had been with the charity ever since her mother had started it more than twenty-five years ago. His usual good cheer was replaced by the slight line of a frown.

"Good morning, Mr. Perkins." Claire placed the quill carefully in its stand. "I wanted to start on the solicitation letters to the potential donors for the children's home. The duchess will write her share later on this week."

He nodded his head. "Excellent thought."

"If we receive another twenty thousand in donations before we hire the architects, we'll be able to add another floor to the building." Since arriving in the cozy office, she had allowed the work to consume her. It was her passion and her refuge.

The solicitor closed the door behind him. "I wondered if I might have a moment of your time."

"You may have as many moments as you need."

"I understand congratulations are in order." His cheeks colored into a ruddy apple red.

Her happiness faded a little. He must have seen yesterday's "Lady Calamity" article in the *Midnight Cryer* that informed all of London she was engaged to Lord Pembrooke. The gossip rag was the bane of her existence, always taunting her with pithy comments about her curse. "Thank you."

"Perhaps we should discuss your wedding plans." He cleared his throat. "What I mean is . . ."

"Mr. Perkins, there's no need for embarrassment. I saw the article too."

"Will it have an impact on the children's home?" Mr. Perkins asked.

"I'm not certain. The curse talk is usually bandied about as a joke. If patrons actually believe—"

"Lady Claire, that's not at all what I meant." His gentle

gaze finally met hers. "I'm talking about after your marriage."

Claire shook her head. "Lord Pembrooke and I will travel to his estate for a month. He understands the charity means a great deal to me."

"Will the marquess support your work?"

"Completely." When she'd informed her future husband that her work was non-negotiable, it hadn't caused him the least concern.

Mr. Perkins leaned closer. "Someone came around several days ago asking about you."

"Oh really?" She scooted to the edge of her chair.

Mr. Perkins nodded. "He interviewed several of the men and staff, but didn't ask to see me. It was quite odd. According to the staff, the questions asked pertained to your acquaintances, work schedule, and how you spent your time."

Claire let out a silent breath. None of this boded well for either her or Hailey's Hope.

"The man identified himself as a Mr. Thornley. He said he was gathering information for a thorough exposé on the real Lady Claire. I assumed he was from the *Midnight Cryer.*"

Who was the real Lady Claire? At Hailey's Hope, she was someone who knew her course in life, simply a woman fortunate enough to have the opportunity to help others. Outside these walls, she was someone ridiculed. She straightened in her chair. "Was the curse discussed?"

The solicitor pushed his wire-framed spectacles higher on his face and swallowed. "Yes, my lady."

Her mother's presence was everywhere within Hailey's Hope. Once Claire walked through the door, she left the curse behind. It held no power over her. Now, it threatened to taint everything important to her.

She'd rather be hunted by jackals than face another

article mocking her. "I don't want our good work or the orphanage jeopardized because some scandal sheet wants to sell papers."

His brow folded into soft lines. "Every single man declared the curse was utter nonsense. They told Mr. Thornley all about your good work. Mr. Napier was quite vocal in your defense. He threatened to throw the man out on his ear."

Claire clenched her fists under the desk and smiled. "That's very kind of him, but I don't want anything disparaging said about Hailey's Hope or any of its residents. It's imperative nothing impacts our fund-raising for the expansion. I'll inform His Grace and ask for his assistance. We'll find out exactly what Mr. Thornley is writing."

"My lady, I was hoping you would say exactly that."

She nodded. Nothing would harm the haven she'd created for others. Or the peaceful sanctum she found every time she stepped foot in this place.

Simms waited at the foot of the stairs. Alex descended and pulled his snow-white linen cravat away from his itching neck. His valet, Jean-Claude, was a grand master in the art of starching shirts and neckcloth until the offending pieces could stand on their own.

"My lord, this arrived by special courier." Simms held a note with Macalester's seal.

"Thank you." His private investigator, Macalester, had finally sent word. Alex didn't think anything damaging would be unearthed. Still, he needed to discover any surprises before his marriage. He wanted all information gleaned kept under wraps, since Claire and her small staff would join his household within the week.

Alex rode his horse, Ares, to Macalester's office, letting the horse set the pace. For a split second, guilt clouded his thoughts for investigating Claire. Last night in the carriage, he had wanted nothing more than to take her in his arms and push away the unhappiness on her face when she'd described her life of isolation and rejection. Besides the Cavensham family, she seemed to be a loner with no real confidantes.

He had intended last night's actions to convince her how much he wanted her. As God was his witness, it was the truth. No matter how inconvenient it was for him. It had taken him hours to finally sleep. All he could think about was Claire in his bed, by his side. It was pure torture.

He had to find a way to keep her from encroaching any further into his thoughts. Not only was it driving him insane, but she distracted him from work. For the first time in over a year, Alice wasn't the first thing he considered when he woke.

It was Claire.

She was a duke's daughter and would make a perfect marchioness. However, for his sake and their future, he had to find answers. Alex wouldn't allow anyone through his defenses. He'd learned from his mistakes not to overlook any trifling matter that involved Lord Paul.

Claire's integrity had never appeared as fodder for gossip. If there was something in her past, he would have caught wind of it. He had never heard one word against her until that foolish curse had taken root. Like tinder, her misfortune fueled a hungry fire of gossips until she became the *ton*'s favorite amusement. Alex had never paid much attention until the opportunity to ruin Lord Paul had come to light. Only then did he concentrate on protecting her from that rake.

Alex wasn't certain when she'd been introduced into society. That was not surprising since he could hardly remember Daphne's entrance in society this Season. Claire had never held the title of a declared incomparable, a woman crowned a diamond of the first water. Gentlemen never sang her praises. She merely existed along the fringes of society.

Last night at the opera, she'd mesmerized him. Her beauty had easily surpassed that of every other woman in attendance. Her poise and charm shimmered. The fact she had remained unattached for years astounded him.

A simple redbrick building housed Macalester's offices. With a young man acting as escort, Alex found his way upstairs to the investigator's office. The room exuded comfort, with supple leather chairs that surrounded a heavy wooden desk. Nothing appeared on the desktop except an inkwell and a quill. He anticipated Macalester's report would be the same, brief and to the point. With firm proof nothing sordid existed in Claire's past, he'd attend to his other matters.

Macalester entered and greeted Alex with a slight bow and a reserved deportment.

"Tell me what you have." Alex wanted the information as quickly as Macalester could deliver it.

"Certainly." Macalester shook his head. "You'll be relieved to hear nothing exists of real consequence. For the most part, the ducal staff is extremely loyal to the family. However, some were freer in conversation. All told me not to approach her lady's maid, Aileen Findley. She is fiercely protective of Lady Claire."

"As expected," Alex agreed.

"Lady Claire has never been linked with anyone suspect, either man or woman. Not a sniff of a scandal. She keeps to herself except for the companionship of her family and a few close friends, even at social events."

Alex allowed himself to accept the first tinges of relief. "Her other engagements?"

"Ah, yes, the Lady Claire Curse is in full regalia for the *ton*'s entertainment." The investigator continued, "The first engagement was to the Earl of Archard, who died a month before their wedding. According to one of the duke's staff, strong affection existed between the two."

Alex took care not to show any reaction. It was best not to dwell on Archard for both their sakes. He'd help Claire forget the heartache.

The investigator rattled off the second name. "Her second engagement ended shortly after the proposal. As soon as the Earl of Thant asked for her hand, he suffered a tragic accident. His horse collapsed and died while he was riding. Within hours he went under the knife and the crushed leg was amputated. I could not discover who broke the betrothal."

Macalester stopped abruptly. Apparently, he sought permission to continue. Alex nodded and waited for the end of the litany.

"That accident was the source for the curse."

"Thant claimed she was cursed?" He'd always been rather remote—not one to spend much time in London.

The investigator shook his head. "A gossip rag published the story after the break. Proclaiming her cursed, it detailed her parents' deaths, Archard's, and Thant's unfortunate accident. At the end of the article, it warned the *ton*'s eligible men to be wary of seeking Lady Claire's hand even with her great wealth."

"How long ago was the article published?" He closed his eyes. Claire's first taste of the curse probably caught her unawares at some ball or soiree. If he'd known her then, he'd have rallied every acquaintance to dance with her to dispel the rumors.

"Archard died three years ago. Thant's accident was two years ago."

God, the strength it had taken to act as if none of this nonsense bothered her. The curse had dogged her for years. "I never realized how long she's suffered through the innuendos."

"I'm not finished, my lord. The third was a vicious case, really. Lord Berkeley caught Lord Riverton in flagrante delicto with Lady Berkeley within an hour of asking for Lady Claire's hand. After the duel and the subsequent death of Lord Berkeley, Riverton fled to the continent."

"Did you uncover how Lady Claire became involved with Lord Paul?" It had to be desperation to escape the rumors.

"He took an interest in her after his taste for gaming increased to the point of addiction. The Duke of Southart is a friend of the Duke of Langham, and both approved the match. Southart's heir is a sickly sort and rumored likely not to inherit. Thus, Lord Paul would be the next in line. Both men thought such a union advantageous, a way to unite the two houses."

In silence, Alex contemplated the information. Southart's heir had completely disappeared from society. Still, how could Langham have allowed Claire to become involved with Lord Paul?

The investigator cleared his throat. "I do want to mention a couple of peculiar business transactions."

"Transactions she handles through her solicitors or independently?" With her fortune, it was probably nothing more than investment dealings. He'd be interested in understanding the extent of her business acumen and how she managed her fortune.

"Both. Lady Claire has personal accounts with the boot maker Hoby and a small but fashionable men's clothier named Grigby near her favorite modiste's shop on Bond Street."

Alex sat stone-faced. He didn't expect a review of her purchasing habits to be included in the report.

"Lady Claire has in the past two years purchased four pairs of boots, all from the same form and in the same style—standard men's riding boots." The investigator continued without regard for Alex. "Within the last week, she ordered two additional pairs. From Grigby, she recently ordered two pairs of buckskins and two shirts, all for immediate delivery."

Alex's grip on the chair tightened, and sweat broke across his brow. Macalester's recitation had lasted forever. A simple reason for the purchases was bound to exist. He would have surmised they were a wedding gift for him, except she'd been buying these items for years. No denying the items were ordinary. He must have twenty of each in his possession. "Do you know what she plans to do with her purchases?"

"Grigby refused to share any information. I stole a peek at the books for what little information existed. The items are sized for a man half our size. Does Lady Claire have a younger male relative she's responsible for?"

"I'm not familiar with her mother's side of the family."

"Scottish, I believe. Her mother was an heiress in her own right." Macalester's brow creased into neat lines. "Lady Claire is involved in Hailey's Hope. Perhaps there's a young man at that charity she's taken under her wing?"

"I don't know much about the charity except Lady Claire is quite dedicated to it."

"Her mother founded it when His Majesty's soldiers, specifically the Black Watch, arrived home from war with no employment prospects." Macalester's voice held an unmistakable pride. "The current Duchess of Langham continues the work in remembrance of the prior duchess. Lady Claire volunteers several days a week and is spearheading a children's orphanage that will be located next to Hailey's Hope. She's well regarded by the soldiers. Fiercely."

"Meaning?"

"I made the mistake of mentioning the curse to one of the residents. He actually was prepared to charge me in her defense."

"I see." Macalester's details didn't impart anything to disparage Claire, though the clothing purchases were confounding. He let out a breath. "Is that all?"

"One final item. Lady Claire recently sent a sum of one hundred and fifty pounds to a solicitor located in Leyton near the south part of Essex. I've not been able to ascertain what the solicitor did with the money. It's minuscule in comparison with the total amount of her fortune. Rest assured, I'll track the funds."

Alex responded with deceptive calm. "How will you discover the information? I don't want a nasty public suit coming back on me."

"Not to worry. No one will know," Macalester replied. "I'm continuing my inquiry as we speak. As soon as I uncover the purpose of the money and the recipient, I'll send word. Anything else, my lord?"

"No. Thank you. You've done enough. I'd appreciate your continued discretion. Everything, even a minute detail, known to me alone." Alex stood and approached the door he had entered.

"My lord, I have my own private entrance in the next room. Perhaps you'd like to leave from there? Your privacy is assured that way." Macalester walked Alex to the next room.

"Thank you for the consideration."

"Don't let the information cause distress. There's a reasonable explanation. I've done hundreds of these investigations. Lady Claire's secrets appear to be quite harmless."

Alex looked the investigator in the eye. "Good day."

A tight knot of dismay snapped loose in his gut, much like a flag caught in high winds. He never looked back and continued down the private passageway to the street.

He couldn't remember exactly the streets Ares traveled, but the horse had taken him home. Every scrap of information Macalester had divulged today led to another secret, another facet of Claire he didn't understand. The investigator hadn't discovered any direct evidence of an affair, but just when he thought he'd solved one mystery, another presented itself.

Upon reflection, Alex breathed with some relief. The size of the clothing and boots certainly wouldn't fit Lord Paul, who was slightly smaller than Alex. Why was she buying men's clothing? For a man or a boy? Was this the same person she sent money?

Within minutes, Alex was inside his Mayfair address with an unmitigated resolve to become better acquainted with his future wife.

The only way he knew to put the pieces together was to make Claire fall in love with some of his renowned Pembrooke charm.

Chapter Six

With a heaviness of heart that weighed upon tonight's celebration, Claire arrived at Lady Hampton's dinner party. Within hours, her engagement to Alex would become official. After the evening at the opera, she was determined to tell him about Archard tonight. She couldn't live with the secret anymore. Not after he'd treated her so warmly, always putting her interests ahead of his. Plus, he didn't seem the least concerned with her curse.

Throughout the day she'd had to pinch herself to believe it was real—she was so close to marrying. She followed her aunt and uncle through the door, where she came under Lady Hampton's scrutiny.

"My dear girl, I'm delighted you were able to attend tonight. I promise it will be an evening to remember." Lady Hampton beamed as she pushed her way between Aunt Ginny and Uncle Sebastian. Ignoring the others, the grande dame grasped Claire's arm and led her away into the drawing room. She lowered her voice and confided, "I received word earlier you *must* sit next to Lord Pembrooke."

Like a schoolgirl with the latest secret, Lady Hampton continued in a singsong voice. "I hear he's set his cap for you." She looked both right and left to see if others could overhear before she continued, "I've known Pembrooke since he was in the nursery. Such a smart girl to grab him. I never believed in that silly old curse, anyway. I don't know why I didn't think of introducing you two before."

Dazed by the whirlwind in front of her, Claire stayed silent.

Stepping back and leveling her gaze, Lady Hampton cooed with delight. "My goodness, dear, you're striking. I'd venture to say radiant. Did Alex do that to you? He's brilliant to snatch you up."

"I agree, Lady Hampton." Alex came from nowhere and settled Claire's hand into the crook of his arm. He lowered his voice in a conspiratorial tone. "Is there a private room where Lady Claire and I might have a word?"

"About the wedding, heh, boy? All right, I'll let you sneak off for three minutes. Not one moment more." Lady Hampton matched Alex's sotto voce intonation. "Go to the study, third door on the right down the hall." She chuckled and winked as if she shared their secret. With a quick bob of her head that sent the plumes of her headpiece waving, she left to greet the other guests.

Alex's smile of amusement remained when he placed his hand over Claire's. Although she was caught off guard at the impact of his gentle grip, her apprehension faded when his impish grin captivated her attention. In two days, she would be married to him. His merriment was a good omen. "You're close to Lady Hampton?"

"Is my mother here yet?" Alex's tone warmed with laughter as he looked about the room. "She tells Lady Hampton everything. They were best friends growing up and have continued to be thick as thieves into adulthood. Some things cannot be kept secret in my household."

"Pembrooke, I heard that," Alex's mother called out as she entered the drawing room to greet them.

She gave Claire a hug, then kissed Alex on both cheeks. "Hello, darling."

Alex smiled and returned a kiss to his mother's cheek. "Madam, you look beautiful as always."

The marchioness batted his arm at the compliment. "Thank you."

His affection for his mother was endearing and completely uninhibited. Claire wanted to beg for entrance into his secret world. What would it take for her to earn his regard? Would she ever have it? She pushed the nagging doubts aside and forced herself to enjoy the moment.

"I know you want privacy to talk," the marchioness continued. "Do not tarry. I want you both at the table before Lady Hampton sits down." Without waiting for a reply, she left them on their own.

"Come with me," Alex murmured. He let her walk ahead through the hallway and gently guided her with a touch of his hand. When they arrived at the study, Alex reached around her to open the door. A whisper of his warm breath brushed her neck.

She didn't have the foggiest clue what was so urgent. Every inch of her skin tingled as thoughts of last night's carriage ride leapt to mind. She tried to tamp her excitement into submission, but it was nearly impossible since Alex made the evening brighter.

With a devilish gleam in his eyes, Alex ushered her through the doorway and closed the door. "How are you handling all of this attention?"

"Well enough. You?" She kept her voice light, but secretly her insides stiffened, waiting for any sign the attention from the papers and society was making him wary.

"Perfect now that you're here with me." He closed the distance between them. "All I've thought about since the opera is how much I want to kiss you." The low thrum of his voice made her body ache, and a flush swept through her. "May I?"

"Yes," she said, surprised he had asked her. When he took her in his arms, she focused where their bodies touched—chest against chest, leg against leg. If she had her preference, they'd stay here for the rest of the night. This was much more comforting than having Lady Hampton's other guests observe them like a pair of caged lovebirds.

The familiar smell of citrus and spice drew her closer. "We're long overdue for this." His hand brushed her check.

She couldn't form the words, so she nodded her head. The moment stretched, and her whole body ached for his mouth to cover hers. It had been such a long time since anyone had wanted to kiss her.

Claire should have known what to expect. She saw him coming closer, but still, she stiffened. His lips were surprisingly soft and gentle when they settled over hers.

For a second kiss, it was somewhat chaste. Eyes closed, she concentrated on his touch. Before she drew back, he deepened the kiss by slanting his mouth over hers. With relentless patience, he coached her lips to match his movements. She parted her lips on a soft sigh. This was the kiss she had imagined all along. When she acquiesced, Alex moved his tongue over hers, caressing in a slow, exaggerated dance.

Claire became lost in his protective embrace until she heard moaning and, through the sensual fog, recognized her own voice. She drew away, shocked by her reaction. Starved for affection, she had completely forgotten herself.

In a slow, languid motion, Alex leaned back and looked deep into her eyes but held her close. "I've missed you."

Gentle and with the ease of an engaged lover, he placed a tender kiss on the corner of Claire's lips with a matching one on the opposite side. Encouraged by his overtures, Claire met his lips with a tentative kiss of her own. A deep groan vibrated in his chest in response. He tightened his embrace.

With a slow, deliberate movement, he kissed her jaw before trailing his lips upward until he reached her earlobe. "Claire, what you do to me," he whispered. He eased back to study her face, then drew her close and placed his forehead against hers.

Claire's lips throbbed as if demanding she return to kissing Alex. She closed her eyes and focused on his touch. "We should get back before our three minutes are up," she whispered.

"What if I don't want to?" He grimaced, then unveiled the most seductive smile. He raised his hands as if weighing something on a balancing scale. "Kissing you or dinner? Selfishly, I'd much rather stay here, but I want to make our announcement as quickly as we can."

They were becoming better acquainted. That's all the kiss represented. If only her brain would share the information with the organ in her chest, the one that pounded in a rush beat and demanded she give him everything. There was only one wise course of action—tell him everything tonight no matter the consequence. He deserved that much.

"My lady, shall we return to the others?"

Alex's forearm was not a safe place for Claire to rest her hand as he escorted her into the dining room. She didn't want to let go. Within minutes, most of the ladies had taken their seats. Alex waited until the stragglers sat down, then sat on Claire's right. Lady Hampton sat at the head of the table with Alex by her side. To Claire's left sat the elderly but lively Earl of Linscott.

Rumor had him enjoying a sordid affair with the lady on his left, the widowed Lady Tottin. The earl hadn't bothered to glance in Claire's direction once. He seemed more than happy to divide his attention between his glass of wine and Lady Tottin. That suited Claire perfectly. Lady Hampton had relaxed the formal etiquette rules for their small group, and Claire needn't worry about entertaining him with conversation.

As the liveried footmen served the first course of turtle soup, Somerton addressed her from across the table. "Lady Claire, I understand discussions are under way for expanding Hailey's Hope. Has an architect been chosen?"

"The choice of the architect will be made by Her Grace and the others who serve on the expansion committee." Claire's confidence rose with the familiar subject. "With luck, the final plans and a groundbreaking before autumn would be a cause for celebration."

Aunt Ginny nodded her approval. "Lady Claire gave a substantial contribution for the expansion. The men require a larger dormitory, but a greater need is to establish a home and school for the widows and children. With proper education, a hope for securing good-paying jobs can become a reality." Her aunt's loving gaze caught hers. "She also created a trust for a new orphanage."

Somerton inclined his head in agreement. "If I may lend assistance? I recently finished a renovation on my London residence. Many of the architects considered were top-notch."

"Would you have the time to come to Langham Hall next week?" Aunt Ginny asked. Soon, the two were entrenched in the most myopic discussion regarding wall reinforcements.

"Claire."

She jumped at Alex's whisper.

"The charity is lucky to have such a generous benefactress. I'd contribute substantially to your cause and entice Somerton to give also." The warmth in his voice was almost a caress. "The duchess is fortunate to have you working with her at Hailey's Hope. Your own passion and commitment shows."

"Thank you." Custom dictated her formulaic answer. When she turned to acknowledge his compliment, the intensity of his gaze made her gawk as if she were a love-struck girl of seventeen.

He lifted his glass in a silent toast. "I look forward to discussing it in greater detail with you . . . in private."

As the others continued their conversations, Alex's eyes never left hers. The world fell away, and it became the two of them. When he delivered a wolfish grin before taking a sip of wine, Claire couldn't hide her enchantment as heat swept up her neck and settled in her cheeks.

What would her marriage be like if Alex truly came to care for her? To have a husband who valued your efforts to help others would be the start of a strong foundation for their union. Even more, to have a husband who valued you as a person would make all the heartache she'd experienced in life a trifle.

Claire forced herself out of the self-induced fog of euphoria. The temptation to believe he was developing a genuine fondness for her drifted away, to be replaced by a familiar feeling of foreboding—something would go horribly wrong tonight.

She concentrated on keeping her breath even when the end of the meal brought forth a delicious assortment of jellied oranges, apricot tarts, sliced fruits, and her uncle's announcement of her upcoming nuptials. Before the ladies left the gentlemen for their ritual of port, her aunt and uncle stood next to Lady Hampton and Alex's mother.

The act signaled that Claire and Alex were to join them at the head of the table. She tried to push away the fear the curse would make an appearance. Her mind filled with grim images of Alex walking out of the room never to return while Lady Hampton's guests fell to the floor in a chorus of boisterous guffaws. Her legs turned into lead. She stared at her untouched plate.

"Lady Claire." Alex placed his hand under her elbow to help her stand.

Like an automaton, she let him lead her to stand with their families at the head of the table. His hand never left the small of her back as he stood beside her.

Uncle Sebastian raised his glass. "Will you all join my duchess, the marchioness, and me as we share our joyous and heartfelt wishes for the upcoming marriage of our niece, Lady Claire, to Alexander, Marquess of Pembrooke?"

A thunderous round of "Hear, hear!" and claps exploded in the room.

Alex leaned in and whispered, "It's over." His hand moved to the side of her waist, and he gave a gentle squeeze in reassurance.

She struggled to maintain her taut hold of control. The black cloud of the curse tightened its stranglehold on her happiness. She turned to Alex. His eyes never left hers as he raised her hand for a kiss.

When she let out the breath she'd been holding, everything tumbled out.

Tears, laughter, and an audible sigh of heartache.

Selfishly, how could she chance his rejection? Whatever could she tell him that wouldn't leave him disappointed?

Gentle rain transformed into a foggy mist as the carriage made its way through Mayfair to Langham Hall. Claire found it harder and harder to maintain the façade of calm.

"The evening was a complete success based upon the way the guests rushed to congratulate us." Alex captivated her with an irresistible, devastating grin. "I didn't hear Lord Paul mentioned once."

"Not a single peep. I can't thank you enough for everything you've done tonight." The entire magical week was a memory she would keep forever—whatever happened tonight. Something she would find comfort in as she grew old, and Alex was the reason.

Nothing about the evening had been real, and if she allowed herself to think otherwise or permitted her foolish heart to hope for a happy outcome after she told him about Archard, it was a recipe for disaster.

The horses pulled in front of the mansion, and Alex helped her down. Not letting go of her hand, he kept her close to his side as he escorted her to the door.

She made her way into the front hall, where Pitts stood at attention. "Thank you for the wonderful—"

"Let me help you with your cloak," Alex interrupted. "Let's talk for a few minutes."

With a step back, she squared her shoulders. She had to put some distance between them if she wanted to survive tonight. "Yes, we have much to discuss."

Side by side on the sofa, Alex reached for Claire's hand and laced his fingers with hers. For some reason, he could not keep his hands off her. He took his thumb and rubbed her wrist while he wrestled with how to end the evening.

Tomorrow his agenda was full. First thing, he needed to sign the final settlement agreements. The solicitors would deliver the documents early. Then, he had to finish preparations for travel to Pemhill. Within two days, he would escort Claire to his ancestral home. Proud of what he'd accomplished, he wanted to share its history and his efforts toward the betterment of the property. He wanted her to fall in love with it.

"I secured the special license today. I likely won't see you tomorrow." Alex took a deep breath. "You won't come down with a case of cold feet, will you?"

Claire inhaled sharply before turning from his side. The quick glimpse he caught of her face reminded him of a kicked puppy unsure where to turn.

Alex closed the distance between them. "My God, I apologize. My lame humor went awry." Stupid. No other word could describe his actions. After he'd charmed her tonight, he had ruined everything with a careless quip. "I'm not really certain how to part this evening. I thought if I was humorous, it might settle the discomfort we're experiencing."

When she faced him, she'd managed to veil any expression of pain, but her pallid face told him another story—the damage was done.

He brought her into his embrace and kissed the top of her head. "You have no cause to worry. Tomorrow, if you need me, send your maid to my valet. He'll know where to find me."

Claire softened in his arms. When she placed her head against his chest, he allowed himself to relax. She snuggled closer and her scent rose to greet him. The curve of her figure exquisitely matched his.

"I suppose it's natural to make light of my situation." Her chest rose against his as a quiet sigh escaped. He caught her gaze for an instant, then she faced the fire. The quick glance was enough to see her sorrow. "There's something I must tell you. Whether you still want to marry or not will be your decision alone."

With a gentle pull of his hand under her chin, he forced her to face him. "Please don't tell me you're nervous over Friday." She didn't return his slight smile.

Claire didn't disagree. His body tensed at her silence, the familiar bitterness burning his gut. He adjusted his position to watch the emotions wash across her face and tried to relax. The constant reminders that Lord Paul was once part of her life must be making his mind weary.

"There is nothing you could say that would convince me not to marry you." He attempted to pull her close, but she stiffened in his arms.

"Claire?" Alex released his hold but caught her hands in his. Under his astute gaze, she could hide nothing. His thumbs gently stroked her wrists. "What's wrong? I'll help you."

The lightness and fledgling happiness that followed her this week grew dark faster than a candle flame snuffed out. Would she ever accept the curse was real? It would make the disappointments in her life so much easier.

She withdrew her hands from his and clasped them together to still the uncontrollable shaking. She fought to appear calm. "When you asked me to marry you, I wasn't truthful about my past," she whispered. "I . . . I gave my virtue to—"

His large hand covered hers and squeezed. "You don't have to say any more."

If she risked a glance and saw disgust on his face, she'd never get the words past her lips. "You see, I loved him so very much and . . . we were to be married within a month. I never thought I'd lose him."

Claire studied the blue rug on the floor for fear the condemnation in his eyes would crush her. The day of reckoning had come, and the shame scorched every inch of her soul. Every young woman knew from day one never to give the prize of her virginity to someone other than her husband. She had rationalized her actions because their wedding had been only weeks away. Then Archard was gone, along with her hopes and dreams.

"It was wrong of me not to share this with you before the announcement this evening. Before you offered for me, I should have told you of my past." She stood, determined not to cry. "I'm so sorry."

He had every right to expect a pure and virtuous bride.

The room grew quiet except for the rhythmic rustle of her dress as she clenched and unclenched her fist in the fabric. She turned slightly and shifted her gaze to receive whatever censure he delivered.

Alex rose from the sofa and stood beside her. More surprised than frightened, she looked into his eyes and found nothing but her own reflection. "He intimated as much, but later he taunted me with the fact. Don't worry, we'll still marry. Far be it from me to judge, Claire. My life has been anything but perfect."

Everything within her stilled, as if her heartbeat slowed to a gentle stop. "Who could have told you? I've never uttered a word of this to anyone. Nobody knows except for me . . . and now you."

"Obviously, he knows and is not above spilling your secrets. I'll do everything in my power to protect you—"

"Archard has been dead for over three years," she interrupted. He wasn't leaving, at least not yet, but she willed herself to stay strong and face whatever the outcome was this evening.

"Archard?" Alex asked. The long black lashes that shadowed his eyes flew open in astonishment.

Reason pushed the shame and grief aside. "Yes, Archard. I gave my virtue to him." Disbelief at the current situation sped through her. "There is no possibility someone could have told you. Henry fell ill the next day and never recovered. Who are you talking about?"

Alex took her hands in his, and the warmth, normally a comfort, overpowered her. A sudden acceleration of the flames in the fireplace snapped and caught her attention.

"Some things are best left alone." By the tone of his voice, he intended his words to soothe, but it was pity she heard.

"Tell me who?" The fire's blast cast a suffocating heat into the room. She stood there amazed and waited.

Alex left her side to pace before the fire. The fast rhythm of his steps propelled her dismay to a new level.

Before he could say another word, Claire joined him in front of the fireplace and forced him to stop. "Tell me," she demanded.

He stared at her.

"I don't understand. Why won't you tell me?" She paused and straightened her body as if ready for war. Everything clicked into place as if unlocking a great riddle. "There's only one person in London who could have told you that lie. Lord Paul."

He blinked, but it didn't hide the truth in his eyes.

"You believe Lord Paul's word over mine?" The disbelief in her words ricocheted around the room. A new wave of white-hot anger extinguished her earlier guilt. "I've only had the one experience with someone I loved. I'm telling you the truth."

"Let's focus on our future," he said.

With all the grace she could summon, she walked to the window and gazed into the inky-black night. Several lanterns lit the pathway of Langham Hall's park, the light muted because of a misty drizzle. The foggy night was as murky as her future. However, she still had control over her current life.

"Someone is investigating me for an article. He's visited Hailey's Hope and asked about the curse. I expect a scathing exposé tomorrow just in time to cause all of London to explode in another round of rumors before our marriage." She continued, although each word sliced through her tenuous composure. "With all that's been said this evening and with what's going to happen tomorrow, we should postpone the wedding. Let's determine the damage caused to both of us before we rush to any decisions."

"No, Claire. I'm not giving you up that easily. I don't care about Archard or Lord Paul. I don't care about some damn newspaper article." He stood beside her, and there was fire in his eyes. "I care about you. I'll be here a quarter of eight as planned."

"With all your doubts and all the rumors, you still want to marry me? You don't want my money. You're not in love with me. You don't need the political connections of the Langham family. None of this makes any sense."

"The simple truth? I want you. I want you as my wife." He took her hand and pressed his lips against her skin. He bowed slightly and made his way toward the door. His gaze caught hers one last time. "I've made my choice. Nothing will change it. Please, I beg of you, don't make a decision you'll regret."

Curled into her favorite chair, Claire stared out the window at nothing as she weighed her options. After Alex left her this evening, she had a decision to make. Marry a man who doubted her word or risk going through life always subjected to the hellish curse. She'd not risk another engagement, at least not for several years to come.

Most of the decisions she'd made in the past had brought little happiness to her life. Havoc was her usual reward, and she began to doubt her ability to make the wisest choices. This time, for her own preservation, she had to make the right choice.

It would be so easy to marry Alex and put the rumors and jokes behind her. She could concentrate on what truly mattered—building a family and leaving a legacy that would honor her parents. She could accomplish all of that with her marriage to Alex and the creation of the orphanage. Every day he'd be by her side, and he'd lend his considerable wealth and prestige to her causes. Alongside her aunt and uncle, they'd finish the vision her mother had created for Hailey's Hope.

It would allow her to leave the guilt and curse behind.

More important, she'd be married to a man she found quite charming and considerate.

At what cost? She couldn't bear to live with his doubts—particularly when they shared a bed.

Pain swelled inside her chest. She'd forever lose the remarkable man who had laughed and flirted with her, the man who gazed upon her as if she were special and someone he wanted. Tonight, it was all a figment of her imagination.

With her mind in an upheaval, Claire made the hardest choice of her life. She would not marry him. He believed Lord Paul's lies over her. She'd not go through life after shedding the curse only to find herself in a marriage that was built upon disbelief.

She wrote a terse letter at three o'clock in the morning. Composed on her personal stationery and sealed with a wax imprint of the Scottish thistle, a signature her mother had always used in her correspondence, the note held few words.

> *My lord,*
> *With the deepest of regrets and apologies, I release you from our betrothal. I wish you happiness in your future endeavors.*
>
> *Lady Claire*

When Aileen came into the bedchamber, Claire greeted her dressed in her riding habit, ready for the day.

"My lady, why are you up so early?" Aileen inspected Claire's attire with raised eyebrows. "Are you going riding? Has something happened to your wardrobe? Most of your things are packed already, but I made certain you had a couple of day dresses to wear."

Claire's old riding habit was a convenient design she could don without calling for assistance. But her auburn locks were another matter. She had sent Aileen to bed when she retired and had forgotten to braid her own hair, which was now a knotted mess around her head. Not that it would have made any difference. She had little time to waste on such details.

Before she could ask Aileen to deliver the message, a brisk knock sounded at the door. Whoever it was at this time of the morning, Claire wanted them gone.

Aunt Ginny barged in before Aileen could answer. "Good morning, Cla—" With a flick of her hand, she directed Aileen to give them privacy.

Claire hid the note in her pocket while her aunt locked eyes with her. "Are you sick? What's wrong? Is it Lord Pembrooke?"

Whether it was the lack of sleep or her aunt's tone, Claire couldn't hold off the tension or the tears anymore. First one glistening tear escaped, then two. She tried to speak the words and announce her intentions. But when everything became a watershed, she couldn't catch her breath.

Aunt Ginny gently escorted Claire to the bed and sat her down. "Sweetheart, I know what you're feeling. So many emotions swirled inside me before I married Sebastian." Her aunt soothed her by running a hand up and down her back. "I didn't think we'd suit. Scared and knowing nothing about running a household, I cried for two days before the wedding."

Aunt Ginny studied the floor, then bowed her head and closed her eyes as if in prayer. With a deep breath, she turned to Claire. "My mother mumbled her way through a stumbling diatribe of what to expect from the marital bed. She painted such a grim picture, my legs barely kept me standing on my wedding day. The suspense of waiting for the night didn't make it any easier." She brushed Claire's hair away from her face. "I promise I won't let you be so fearful it ruins your special day. The wedding night is a celebration for both of you. I only hope Pembrooke is—"

The bedroom door opened wide. Emma stood at the entrance. A pasty white pallor had replaced her normal rosy glow. "Mother, something dreadful has happened." Her voice rang with a faint thread of hysteria before she closed the door. "My friend Lady Lena sent a note." Without a clue of what she had walked into, Emma breathlessly launched into the most bizarre story about her brother William, Lord Paul, and betting books. "Lord Paul placed a wager at White's that Claire won't marry Pembrooke tomorrow." Vivid fear glittered in her eyes.

"What?" Aunt Ginny gasped.

"Apparently, no one cared if Lord Paul could cover the bet or not because it's the most popular wager today." Emma's soft voice halted. She looked at Claire, then focused on her mother. "William was there and placed a—"

"What did he do?" Before Emma uttered another word, her aunt stood. "Please don't tell me he challenged him to a duel. Dear God, please no."

Emma swallowed and replied in a low, tormented voice. "He bet one thousand pounds Claire would marry Pembrooke. No one has seen McCalpin or Lord Paul." She collapsed in her favorite chair in front of the fireplace.

Claire stilled, her mouth suddenly dry.

Aunt Ginny clasped both hands together, her knuckles white. "If William made a wager, then McCalpin will double the amount or worse. What have they done?"

Tears had gathered in Emma's eyes. "Lena's brother arrived home an hour ago with the tale. William is still at the club, ready to fight."

"Sebastian must know immediately. Our only hope is that McCalpin has yet to discover the wager. He's looked for any excuse to call Lord Paul out since Lady Anthony's ball. I pray it's not too late." Aunt Ginny choked on her last words.

Claire stood and reached for her aunt's hand.

"Darling, excuse us." Aunt Ginny bowed her head briefly before she broke the silence with a quiet but determined softness. "Will you lie down and get some rest? Aileen and I will have you ready for tomorrow. I promise."

"Shall I stay with Claire?" Worry lined Emma's face.

"No, dear, come with me. I want to see Lena's note." Emma and her mother rushed out the door.

In a miraculous moment of clarity, Claire's thoughts calmed with the knowledge that her world had changed yet again. She took the letter out of her pocket and traced its edges.

Five short minutes could change the course of one's life. She threw the letter into the fire and watched it burn to black ash.

Faintly, above the crackle of the wood, the wax sputtered in protest.

* * *

Dear Claire,
   My grandmother wore these on her wedding day. They're my gift to celebrate the first day of our new life together.

Yours,
A

Somerton strolled into Alex's dining room without an announcement from Simms. With a fierce scowl, he leaned against the chair closest to Alex. "Why did you do it?"

Alex stretched his legs and laid the note to Claire next to the perfectly matched string of pearls. Dressed and ready for the day, he extended his buckskin-clad leg in such a lazy manner, his boot heel rested on Somerton's chair. The man possessed enough intelligence to take the hint and leave or, at least, sit at the other end of the table.

"Can't a bridegroom, the day before his wedding, have a private, peaceful breakfast without any unnecessary cater-wauling from the hoi polloi?"

Somerton ignored the insult and kicked Alex's leg out of the chair. He sat down and grabbed the last piece of bacon off Alex's plate. In one move, he popped the morsel into his mouth. After two chews and a swallow, he said, "You know damn well what I'm talking about. It's all over London."

Alex went back to the morning post. "What exactly is all over London?"

Somerton reached for the last slice of toast on Alex's plate. "The bet at White's under the initials *L. P.* Supposedly, Lord Paul placed a wager your lovely bride would not be married to you tomorrow. Exact words 'not be married to you,' not 'marry you.'"

Alex shrugged. "What's the difference?"

The earl answered, "A world of difference, and you know it. Conjecture is that Lord Paul phrased the bet as an insult to Lady Claire. Makes it appear you'll leave her at the altar. Not the other way around. The curse feeds upon itself. The book is accepting the wager as either she will or she won't be married tomorrow, unqualified either way."

Alex lifted his gaze. "The curse again?"

"If I had to lay odds on the matter"—Somerton narrowed his eyes—"I'd say it was you that placed the wager. To let you know the havoc you've created, Lord William Cavensham placed a thousand pounds against Lord Paul. McCalpin wagered two thousand. Rumor has it McCalpin is looking for Lord Paul as we speak. He wants to challenge him the day after your wedding."

At the last bit of information, Alex looked up from his

paper. "Now, that's something of interest. When will the books close, today or tomorrow?"

Somerton leaned back in the chair and shot him a withering glance. His gaze slowly settled on the opened velvet box that sat on the table. "You're sending her jewelry to ease your guilt?"

"My grandmother wore it on her wedding day. Lady Claire will look lovely in these." He inspected the necklace. Such a shame he couldn't strangle his friend with the strand. "Now you're an expert on gifts for the bride?"

The earl's silence caused every other sound to become louder, more amplified—the maids' steps in the entry hall, the fire crackling in the fireplace, and the clock ticking every second.

At last, Alex's patience broke. "Why are you here?"

"I want you to cease manipulating others' lives to get what you want." Somerton's voice was stern, with no vestige of sympathy. "For your own sake, you have more important things to do than act as if everyone around you is part of a game for your amusement. You have a chance for a wonderful life with a spectacular woman. Don't let life's disappointments give you reason to spoil your current good fortune."

"Exactly what are you accusing me of?" Alex lowered his voice. "Be careful. Even though you're my closest friend, I will not allow you to disparage me, Alice, or my intended. I assure you that my actions for Alice are not a game or an amusement."

Somerton shook his head and chuckled in a manner that lacked any real humor. He rose from the table and walked toward the door. "Don't be absurd. I predict a bad ending. For your sake, I hope you don't bring everyone else down with you when you fall."

"For someone who doesn't plan to marry, you're quite sure of yourself regarding matrimony."

Somerton didn't acknowledge the comment. "Don't fool yourself. You will fall."

How well he knew the truth of that statement. Last night he'd been in awe of Claire's quick strong-mindedness, just as he had been in Lady Anthony's garden. When he'd reached his residence last night, the truth had hit him square between the eyes. Any postponement was a risk. If he didn't come up with a solution to stop her from breaking the engagement, Lord Paul's threat that he'd win her back would come to fruition. The man would pounce upon her break with Alex and try to woo her back.

Besides, his feelings for Claire were more than just about avenging the wrong done to Alice. He hadn't expected to care for her so quickly. To put it bluntly, all of this—last night and this morning—was a damned nuisance.

Alex had left Claire on terms that racked him with shame. He had stained every happy moment they shared because of doubts instilled by Lord Paul's crude insinuations. He had counted on the Lady Claire Curse and the bet to guarantee Claire's presence at their wedding. Otherwise, Lord Pembrooke's Plague might become the newest fodder for the *ton*.

Inside, a bitter misery darkened his soul. God, what had he done?

With his hand on the door, Somerton said, "Pembrooke, take my advice. Consider it an early wedding present."

For hours, Claire paced while she waited for news of her cousin McCalpin. Uncle Sebastian had dashed to White's, hoping to discover when Lord Paul had initiated the awful wager.

The sound of her uncle slamming the carriage door echoed through the entry hall when he returned home. He entered, erupting into curses as colorful as a sailor's. Maids and underfootmen scattered downstairs to avoid his wrath. Aunt Ginny's attempts to calm him failed as he declared heads would roll. Claire had never witnessed him angrier or more distraught.

No one had seen or heard from McCalpin. He had disappeared without leaving word of his whereabouts.

That night, her aunt confided that Uncle Sebastian had paid an afternoon call on Lord Paul's father, the Duke of Southart, for any news. Southart had given assurance he'd support Uncle Sebastian in any reprobation necessary. Her uncle had personally searched the gambling hells Lord Paul frequented in hopes the effort would lead him to his son.

Claire could not give two farthings if McCalpin thrashed Lord Paul. Her cousin outweighed the man by at least two stone. The real danger was a duel.

There was little else to do but go forward with the wedding as planned. She prayed she was in time to stop McCalpin.

It was far easier to live with Alex than bear the guilt if her cousin died over her cursed reputation.

With only a few hours of rest, Alex sprang from his large bed and ordered a bath and shave. Jean-Claude had anticipated his request. Everything was ready.

Whether relieved or nervous, Alex found it difficult to define his mood. He hadn't received word that Claire had backed out of the wedding. The magnitude of his actions did not escape him. To put it mildly, he was more than hesitant to see how she would greet him on their wedding day. He wouldn't be shocked if she didn't make an appearance, after the way they had parted. A sudden stab of emptiness created a hole inside that grew with each second.

Within the hour, Alex had his entire retinue, formally dressed in full livery, outside Langham Hall, waiting to take him and his new marchioness to Pemhill. He entered the grand house, and the ubiquitous Pitts escorted him into the drawing room. Alex had welcomed the fact that Claire's family had wanted to make all of the wedding arrangements. The whole affair was neither extravagant nor commonplace, but it had its own charm.

Arrangements of roses, the color of the rarest Oriental rubies, and white tulips adorned every available surface within the large room. With such a collection, the duchess must have purchased every flower within the city of London yesterday.

Earlier in the week, Alex had given Jean-Claude and Aileen free rein to plan the wedding apparel for the day. Jean-Claude insisted that a rush order be placed for a formal morning suit of blue silk with navy silk trousers. Alex smoothed his hand down the red waistcoat embroidered with silver thread. His black boots shone with a gloss achieved only by using the very best champagne.

He turned and glanced at the people in attendance behind him. All were immediate family members or special guests. His mother and Daphne sat in the front row. The delight on their faces welcomed him and sent another stab to his heart. His behavior over the last several days would shame them both if they knew what he had done to secure his bride in marriage.

Claire's cousins Lord William and Lady Emma stood next to his family and conversed with Daphne. Alex noted McCalpin's absence with unease. No doubt the man was still searching for Lord Paul. With any luck, his search would lead him to a dead end. Somehow, his plan had spiraled into a spider's web, a sticky mess that unintentionally trapped others. If McCalpin was successful in his hunt for Lord Paul and blood was drawn, it would forever haunt Alex.

Langham appeared by his side with a scowl. "A word before we start."

"Your Grace?" Perhaps the duke had discovered the truth about the wager and wanted a quart of blood before the ceremony.

The duke cleared his throat. "My niece has not had the easiest time of things, the loss of her parents and others." His mouth turned grim as his brow furrowed. He stood with his back to the crowd to block their view of the conversation. "Someone questioned the residents of Hailey's Hope about Claire for an article. I've hired an investigator to discover who he is and what he plans to print."

Alex tried to swallow the lump that had charged up his throat at the duke's words. "Any luck?"

"None. It's like the fellow disappeared into thin air. Your idea to leave for Pemhill is sound. It'll keep her away from the predators for a while."

"She's strong in the face of adversity, Your Grace."

"She has an undeniable fortitude, and she has her weaknesses too. Just like we all do." The duke clenched his hand in a fist. "She's carrying her mother's Bible, and her dress is decorated with her mother's plaid. It's exactly what her mother wore when she married my brother. It's Claire's way of remembering." The duke's gaze narrowed. "Do you understand?"

Alex regarded the duke as he contemplated his answer. He had no earthly idea what the duke was trying to relay.

"She hasn't visited Wrenwood since her parents died. Take that into consideration when you arrive at Pemhill." Langham looked toward his duchess and nodded before he turned back to Alex. "Privilege is one thing, but happiness is another. Claire's precious to us. Take care of her."

"I promise I'll see to her every need." Alex forced himself to hold the duke's gaze. "She's under my protection now."

The sliver of concern in the duke's glare turned serious. "These last two days with that damnable curse and the bet at White's . . . she's exhausted. If anything arises, send word."

Alex steeled himself against any show of emotion as guilt colored his enjoyment of the day. His actions to force Claire into this marriage had had the unintended consequence of harming her.

Somerton decided to stand beside him at that moment. With a nod to the duke, he said, "Your Grace."

His friend's anger was still apparent, but the commitment to stand by his side meant more than words could express.

Langham straightened his jacket, then tugged his lace cuffs. "Gentlemen, I must see to the bride." He turned and left the room.

"I need your assistance." Alex kept his voice low.

Somerton bowed his head as if trying to hear the words. "I've been trying to help, but you're too damned pigheaded to realize that."

Alex ignored the slur. "After the register is signed, go to White's and announce the marriage. See if there's any word on McCalpin's whereabouts. Send word to Simms. He's on his way to Pemhill and will know what to do."

"On one condition." Somerton leveled a glare designed to peel Alex alive. "You tell her everything when you reach Pemhill."

Alex nodded once. With his friend's help, there was a chance word would reach McCalpin and disaster circumvented. It was almost over, and relief started to swell inside his chest. In moments, Claire would be his wife.

Alex had not attended many weddings and couldn't recall the details of those he had graced with his presence. The majority were nothing more than trumped-up excuses to get foxed and stupid. However, he'd never forget this day.

For a moment he forgot to breathe when he caught the first glimpse of Claire, her alabaster skin glowing. Langham escorted her. She wore a silver-and-ivory gown adorned with real red roses on the hem and neckline. She was a vision, the most beautiful woman he'd ever laid eyes on.

Reverence swiftly replaced his earlier unease and threatened to burst through as his eyes watered. He bent his head to gain control. When he looked up, he concentrated on Claire's dress. She wore her mother's plaid tied around her waist, the navy and red colors bold against the ivory and silver. She carried no bouquet but held a Bible in her hands.

On her neck, she wore his gift of pearls, which heightened the delicate creamy color of her skin. He had counted on the gesture to soften her feelings for the day, but more important, to soften her feelings for him.

As Claire came nearer, Alex studied her carefully. She kept her head bowed until her uncle gave her hand to him. Only then did Claire raise her eyes and kiss her uncle. She murmured, "I love you. I'm the person I am today because of you."

When she turned to him, he knew, down to the marrow of every last bone, an undeniable sense of happiness. With the first glimpse of her face, remorse banished his sense of awe. The full effect of the last two days had taken its toll. Fatigue had settled into blue circles under the hollows of her eyes. Her body swayed slightly, as if exhaustion and weariness would soon overtake her. Reserved, she placed her gloved hand in his and faced the Bishop of Elan, a distant cousin of her aunt who had agreed to perform the ceremony.

Alex squeezed her hand as the Lord Bishop began. He waited for Claire to return the gesture, with little success. The chill from her demeanor could frost the entire kingdom.

When it came time to say his vows, he recited his with a strong, deep timbre and watched her profile. She tensed, and her cheeks flushed. Claire didn't bestow a single glance in his direction through the entire ceremony. When she said her vows, the whispered words flowed in a rigid cadence, as if she were trying to hold in her outrage.

When directed, he slipped a plain gold band on her finger. The end of the ceremony came with the announcement they were man and wife. Alex turned and waited for their first kiss as a married couple.

"Claire, we need to kiss." With his whisper, Claire turned and allowed his lips to touch hers. Only he knew her response was, at best, tepid.

As the cheers rang out, Claire addressed him without a hint of a smile. "I want to be gone within the hour."

Alex congratulated himself. They had married. He and his bride greeted their well-wishers, and with remarkable little effort, he shoved Lord Paul and revenge out of his thoughts. He focused on Claire and their trip to Pemhill.

After they signed the marriage register, Claire darted upstairs to change. Within ten minutes, she appeared in a riding habit. The jacket was a coarse ivory material in the military style currently at the height of fashion. Frog tabs from the same tartan plaid she had worn at the wedding lined the jacket front, while the dress flowed with an endless drape of cloth to allow for modesty when riding. Unless she was preparing for a hunt with obstacles and jumps, it was a peculiar choice to wear on one's wedding day. Alex had never considered his knowledge of fashion reliable, as he left that chore to his valet, but even he knew she would have been more comfortable in a traveling gown and coat.

He made his way outside of Langham Hall. When he breathed in the cool morning air, exuberance replaced his misgivings. It was time to take Claire home. He'd already sent the majority of his baggage and extras to Pemhill with Simms, who had traveled ahead with a couple of others from his London staff. Only Jean-Claude remained behind to assist him. Thinking Claire would have only Aileen, he was not prepared for the spectacle before him.

Claire had her own carriage, which contained her maid, as well as a curricle and two vocal, massive horses restless to start the journey. The groomsmen assigned to tend the beasts had a hard time controlling the animals.

After saying his farewells to both families, Alex waited for Claire at the Pembrooke carriage. She kissed Daphne and took his mother in her embrace. Pure pleasure illuminated his mother's face as Claire addressed her. She then moved to her own family. First, she hugged and kissed her aunt. Then Langham clasped both of her cheeks in his hands and kissed her forehead. Claire said something that made him laugh. On tiptoes, she kissed his cheek. Finally, she reached Alex's side.

"Are you ready, Lady Pembrooke?" He smiled to relieve the tension between them.

Claire walked past his outstretched hand and climbed into the carriage without a glance, her back straight. Alex lifted his eyebrows. He felt his lips twitch, but he suppressed the grin. Whether she liked it or not, he'd have her undivided attention for the next nine hours as they made their way home.

As the coach and horses ambled through town, Claire would periodically lean to the side before she'd jerk awake. She appeared to startle herself each time. With a straight posture, she'd swallow, then rearrange her riding habit. Her eyes would drift closed again, and the pattern would repeat itself.

Alex sat across from her until he could take no more. He'd not see her suffer. With one quick move, he sat beside her. She never uttered a word. He doubted she had the capacity for speech at this point. She leaned against him, and he cradled her in his arms. As her lean immediately turned into a slump, Alex rested one leg parallel against the seat and used the other as an anchor on the floor. With a gentle nudge, he moved into a position where her bottom was nestled between his legs and her back rested against his chest.

"That's better now, don't you think?" He sat braced against the side of the carriage and held his new wife in his arms. "Claire?"

She mumbled something and succumbed to the gentle swaying of the carriage.

Every couple of miles, Alex looked to see how she fared. She was perfectly still in his lap, warm and soft. He continued to hold her as the carriage rumbled toward his countryseat. He corrected himself—*their* countryseat. When he pressed his lips to the top of her head, her bergamot scent rose to meet him.

She didn't move for several hours. Looking out the carriage window, he took note that they made excellent time, considering the entourage that followed.

With Claire in his arms, contentment set up residence in his thoughts. She'd make an excellent marchioness with her decorum and lineage. Outside of her opposition to him and his worries about her past, he had made a good match. Others, namely Somerton, might think the success of his marriage highly doubtful, but the closer they traveled to Pemhill, the stronger his confidence grew. Whatever misgivings Claire brought with her, his efforts over the next several days would wrest away her concerns. He owed it to her to make up for his abysmal behavior. He relaxed and closed his eyes for the last leg of the journey.

The coachman's call to slow the team of six woke Alex. Claire continued her deep slumber but had shifted position. Her hand rested against his heart. They'd arrived at the last coaching inn to change horses.

The cramp in his leg demanded a stretch, but he ignored it. He would not disturb his wife just to take a short walk around the inn's courtyard. Within an hour or little more, they'd be home.

A brisk knock sounded on the carriage door.

"Enter," he said. A quick glance reassured him that the noise had not disturbed Claire.

Aileen opened the door. "My lord, Lady Pembrooke asked I attend her when we arrived at the final stop." She looked at her mistress, and an affectionate smile tugged at the corners of her mouth. "Has she slept the entire way?"

"She didn't make it too far outside London." His left arm rested on Claire's hip, keeping her secure. "We'll be at Pemhill shortly. You can see to her then."

"With all due respect, my lord, I received specific instructions from Lady Pembrooke. I must attend her." Aileen's voice was calm, but a shadow crossed her face.

"Why?"

The maid's expression melted into nothing, reminding him of a Venetian mask. "My place is not to ask questions. I follow the instructions of Lady Pembrooke." She turned to look at something over her right shoulder.

With an air of casualness Alex said, "Leave her. I'll attend to her needs if she wakes."

The maid opened her mouth to answer, but Alex cut her off. "You're part of my household now. Don't worry. I'll take care of her."

"Yes, my lord." Aileen took another look at her mistress and then closed the door.

An ear-rending neigh broke the peace of the early evening. Alex pushed the carriage curtain aside. One of Claire's horses stood beside his coach with full tack, ready to ride. The black beast stomped in agitation, as if preparing to bolt. Aileen shook her head at the groomsman. The man fought for control as the horse reared up on its hind legs and blew air from its flared nostrils. With one last bellow, it submitted to the lead.

Alex creased his brow over the events outside. The maid must have directed the horse be readied for Claire's use. A ride would explain his wife's choice of attire for the trip. She had planned on leaving the carriage this leg of the journey. A simple answer for her actions escaped him.

Within minutes, the sky had darkened, along with his mood.

Chapter Seven

The carriage hit a bump, and Claire jumped from the jolt. She doubled her fist and hit the roof of the coach to give the signal to stop. As she flew from Alex's embrace to the other side of the bench seat, the carriage slowed. Her hands brushed her face to wipe the sleep away. She had to escape before they crossed the river.

Alex leaned out the window and ordered, "Drive on." The carriage picked up speed. He turned and softened his voice. "We're at Pemhill."

Claire struggled for her bearings and pushed the curtains away from the window. Lush, rolling meadows emerged from their winter sleep. In the far distance, plowed fields and new spring crops popped up from the rich black soil. On the opposite side, pastures with elaborate stone fences and wooden stiles separated the cattle from the sheep.

"The staff will be outside to greet you. We'll allow Simms and the housekeeper, Mrs. Malone, to make the introductions." Alex held the curtains aside as he took in the view. "Since it's late, I thought to order a light repast and retire. It's been a long day for everyone. I'll make certain your maid knows which room is yours. I'll come up after attending to a few matters. I promise not to be long."

Claire struggled to make sense of what had happened since they departed London. A wave of unease rolled upward to catch in her throat. "Did we cross the river?"

"Several minutes ago. Did you want to see it? I'll take you there tomorrow if you'd like. It will be our first stop when I show you Pemhill."

She fought the urge to crawl under the seat and hide. The river was the last place she ever wanted to see.

"Are you all right?" Alex waited a moment for an answer before he turned his attention elsewhere. His eagerness for home was apparent in his stance. He sat on the edge of the seat with feet apart, ready to jump out as the carriage pulled to a stop.

If only her own eagerness at reaching Pemhill matched her husband's.

Pinching her cheeks and straightening her attire, Claire prepared for her introduction as the new Marchioness of Pembrooke. She reached to touch Alex's arm, and his muscles tightened. "I'm ready."

"Welcome home, Lady Pembrooke," Alex said. The vehicle slowed to a stop in the center of a large circular drive. He opened the door and held out his hand to assist her.

Not yet ready to surrender to the night, the sky still held a hint of pink and red from the sunset. Claire stepped down into the cool evening, where the smells of recently cut winter barley, sweet hay, and clean country air welcomed her. Alex's warm hand held hers as she stood in front of a magnificent building. Pemhill's staff stood en masse to greet and give welcome.

The house was impressive, built in the style of an Elizabethan manor. The main section spanned the width of the drive, with two identical additions, best described as classical, at each end. Light stone and brick comprised the house's three symmetrical levels.

Claire walked forward with Alex. Simms and Mrs. Malone, the housekeeper, were the first to approach and offer greetings. "Welcome, my lord and my lady." Simms gave Claire a slight smile and a bow.

"Thank you, Simms. It's good to be home," Alex responded. "I'd like you to meet my wife, the Marchioness of Pembrooke." The staff gave a hearty cheer of welcome. Alex lifted her hand in his and gave it a kiss for the benefit of the crowd.

The next few minutes were a flurry of faces and names as Claire met everyone. When Alex escorted her into the house, the soft glow of candlelight greeted her with its warmth. The interior was light and airy, with two white marble staircases framing both sides of the massive table in the middle of the entry. Beautiful was too tame a word.

The housekeeper approached Claire. "Lady Pembrooke, I've made up the marchioness's suites. If you're ready, I'll escort you to your rooms. I'm sure you're exhausted."

The hint of shyness Claire had experienced upon entering the house evaporated with Mrs. Malone's warm gaze. She was small in height, but all the staff had looked to her for direction when introduced. Even Simms stood in her shadow.

"Thank you, Mrs. Malone." Claire followed the housekeeper and Aileen up the right staircase.

Once she entered her new apartments, Aileen commenced unpacking clothing and personal items needed in the morning. Since Alex promised to visit, Claire fought her exhaustion and the urge to climb into bed and sleep for a week. She tried to lift a bag packed with her dressing robe and slippers but managed only to trip on the rug.

"My lady." Aileen rushed to Claire's side. "I'll not see

you hurt the first night here." She helped Claire into bed as if tending to a small child.

Claire didn't resist the care. She watched her maid's efforts in silence and tried to ask why Aileen didn't come for her at the posting inn. She couldn't form the words as she drifted to sleep.

Alex opened the connecting door to the marchioness's suites and unintentionally scared Aileen.

Bent over the largest of Claire's trunks, the maid pitched forward and caught her fall by clamping hard on the sides. "Hell's fire!" She pushed back and righted herself, then turned. "Oh, I beg your pardon, my lord." With little embarrassment, she brushed the loose hair from her forehead and continued her work. Something silver flashed in her hand before she placed it on the dressing table.

Holding a bottle of champagne and two glasses, he examined Claire's prone body. From her even breathing, Alex quickly deduced the evening with his new wife was over. "My marchioness had other ideas for how to spend her wedding night?"

Aileen's good humor laced the lilt in her voice. "Indeed, my lord. Lady Pembrooke has been awake for the past forty-eight hours. Serving her over the years, I'm confident she'd have preferred nothing better than to spend her wedding night with you. Unfortunately, her body wouldn't cooperate."

"Go ahead and retire, Aileen. You must be as exhausted as the marchioness. I'll make certain someone is here if the need arises."

"Thank you, my lord." Aileen curtsied before leaving the room.

Alex walked to Claire's bed. As he gently stroked her hair, warmth welled from someplace deep inside that he attributed to a sense of accomplishment and real affection.

Marrying Claire protected her from Lord Paul. What he failed to do for Alice, he had done for Claire. Alex let the moment wash over him. It was over.

Claire opened her eyes and sat up.

"Come to me if you have need of anything." When he kissed the top of her head, a rush of contentment ran through his body. He turned to leave, and a flash of light caught his eye. A man's hip flask sat in the center of her dressing table next to a large golden glass bulb.

Alex picked up the glass sphere. His hand caressed the cool glass. She'd brought her witching ball. Tomorrow, he'd help her find a place to hang it. If it helped her, he'd let her put it anywhere, even in Pemhill's chapel. The village rector might protest, but if it made his wife feel safe, then so be it. He turned his attention to the sterling silver flask, a piece heavy in weight with the initial *M* engraved on the front. Around the neck, rubies had been set to form a collar. When he opened the cap, the distinctive odor of whisky permeated the room.

His first and only thought—she'd kept a memento from one of her fiancés. "Whose flask?"

After hearing a murmured mumble, Alex turned. Claire's head had tumbled back upon the pillow. What was wrong with him? Jealousy was not at all typical for him. He needed to give her the benefit of the doubt and allow her to explain. It had to belong to her cousin McCalpin.

His day could not get any stranger.

He'd never considered he'd spend his wedding night holding another man's flask. He had imagined he would hold his new wife instead.

When Claire opened her eyes, the sun's brightness cast beams of welcome around the brilliant peacock greens and blues of the room.

"Good afternoon, my lady. You slept practically the

whole day away. Ready for some coffee, or would you prefer tea this afternoon?" Aileen's cheerfulness brought additional warmth to the room.

"What time is it?" Claire stretched her legs and arms wide. Soft linen sheets, fluffy feather pillows, and a plush coverlet surrounded her in a cocoon of warmth. If her bed was any indication of the comforts available at Pemhill, she looked forward to being spoiled.

"It's after one." Aileen carefully unwrapped several evening dresses. With quick hands, she forced out the wrinkles.

"Why didn't you wake me? Mrs. Malone will think I'm the lazy laggard lady of the manor."

Aileen put her hands on her hips. "Don't fret. The marquess ordered no one disturb your sleep. I've already informed Mrs. Malone you'll be down when you're able."

"Thank you." Claire quickly scooted to the dressing table. Their privacy allowed her to discover what happened yesterday. "Why didn't you come for me?"

Aileen pulled a silk chemise and stockings from a drawer. "Lord Pembrooke ordered me not to wake you. You slept through the royal fit Hermes threw when not allowed to run. It took two groomsmen to settle the spoiled firebrand."

"Do you think he knew?"

"Hermes or Lord Pembrooke?" Aileen quirked an eyebrow as she took out Claire's braid. "No, my lady. The marquess asked, but I didn't tell. You should." Her maid's voice grew tender. "He will understand your fears about crossing the river."

Claire stared at her reflection in the mirror. "I'm going to Wrenwood tomorrow." Eyes flashing with wariness, Aileen slowed in her task of taking down her mistress's hair.

"I need—no, I have to overcome this fear. What if he

sees how I react during a storm? He'll have me locked up or worse."

Aileen's attention returned to brushing Claire's hair and arranging it for the day. "Shall I go with you?"

"I want to go alone this first time." She took a deep breath. She'd not be persuaded otherwise. "Don't worry."

"You should take your husband." Aileen was fixated on a tangle as she gently combed. "If you had seen the expression on his face last night when he saw you in bed—"

"No, promise me you won't say a word."

The maid's hands stilled.

To expose another weakness to Alex or anyone else at Pemhill would spell a disaster she'd never recover from. She'd seen the effect her fear had on her aunt and uncle. They loved her and had suffered through her parents' deaths. Nevertheless, with all they'd shared over the years, Uncle Sebastian and Aunt Ginny lacked the ability to understand the depths of her despair. She couldn't expect Alex to understand the demons she faced.

Claire softened her tone. Aileen was only trying to help. "I want to face this by myself. Promise me."

"My lady, you ask too much of me." Aileen gave a long sigh. "If you're not back by noon, I'll come get you myself." She continued to work the tangle and gave a hard yank with the comb.

"Ow." Claire bit her cheek to keep from scolding her maid.

"Ah, I believe that bugger's out." Aileen finished combing and leveled an assessing gaze that melted into concern. "For your own sake, please take one of us with you."

Claire ignored the advice. She didn't want to start her new life at Pemhill with more explanations. She wanted to face her grief alone and leach every last piece of guilt from her memory.

After dressing in a green muslin morning gown, she was ready for the day, or what little was left.

She found Mrs. Malone and began her duties as mistress of the house. Together, they planned the meals for the upcoming week, the cleaning schedule, and staffing needs. Afterward, the housekeeper took Claire to tour the kitchen and discussed preferences for the morning breakfast buffet and even the entertainment expected by the local gentry while she and Alex were in residence.

What were Alex's preferences? They'd never had a conversation about what either of them liked to eat or drink or how often they should host their neighbors. Did Alex like to read? What did he consider proper evening amusements? Until she understood his routines, she planned on keeping to herself the majority of the time. Meanwhile, she'd run the household as her aunt had taught her.

After the cook and Mrs. Malone took their leave to attend to the household duties, Claire inspected the marchioness's private rooms. Earlier, when the housekeeper had shown her the salon, Claire's mind leapt with ideas. Her first order of business was to turn it into a cozy nook with several informal sitting areas designed to encourage people to linger. The room would serve as her sitting room and a working study. Claire proceeded down the hallway, where several male voices rang with laughter.

"Thank goodness the marquess brought home a proper lady when he married," a young man said. "Can you imagine? She's a duke's daughter. You can tell by looking at her she's quality. I can't wait to send word home to me mum. I'm serving a duke's daughter. She'll think I'm putting on airs."

Claire rounded the corner where three young men were huddled together. Charles, a groomsman, talked to two under-footmen named Benjamin and John. When she'd met them last night, they were completely tongue-tied but managed a mumbled greeting without looking her in the eye.

They suffered the same affliction today. With red faces, each bowed.

Amused, Claire decided to put them at ease. No one would lose his job over harmless remarks. "Good afternoon. I'm curious. Who was speaking about their mother?"

The groomsman spoke first. "My lady, Benjamin and John were forced to listen. We meant no harm."

Claire smiled brightly. "None taken. You're Charles? I'm flattered for the kind words. If you had known my father, you would know my good fortune. He's the one who was special, not me." She gave her first order as the new marchioness. "I need you to have my horse, Hermes, ready to ride tomorrow morning."

"Thank you, my lady," Charles gushed, exposing a toothy grin.

"Excellent. I plan on leaving first thing in the morning. Please have him ready by seven." Claire smiled and walked away as Charles bragged about his promotion to the position of the Marchioness of Pembrooke's own private groomsman. It said a lot about his character that he wrote to his mother regularly.

After unpacking her belongings and organizing her books on the shelves in the salon, Claire rang for tea. The maid brought the tea tray, a letter from her cousin McCalpin, and a note from Alex. Claire hurried to open McCalpin's letter.

Dear Claire,
    When I returned home after my unsuccessful attempt to locate Lord Paul, a letter from Pembrooke was waiting for me. He wanted to assure me that he had never had an arrangement with Monique LaFontaine. I confirmed the truth of

*it. She's involved in a long-term arrangement with
another.*

*I apologize about Lord Paul's horrible wager. I
never found the devil. I finally located his former
valet, who took a position with Lord Westin. The
whole episode stinks of rotten fish. Lord Paul left
for Scotland the same day he let his valet go with a
letter of reference. Mind you, Westin hired the
valet the day before the bet's placement at White's.*

*Since I missed your wedding, I never wished
you happy in your marriage. Consider it done,
Lady Pembrooke.*

> *Yours,*
> *McCalpin*

The weight she had carried for two days lifted from her
shoulders. McCalpin was safe. She closed her eyes and
said a small prayer before turning her attention to Alex's
note. With no salutation or closing, it demanded, *Dine with
me at eight.*

Claire dressed in a simple gold gown of Italian crepe silk
for the evening. The material draped her body in soft folds
and enhanced her natural curves. The only jewelry she
wore was her mother's emerald earrings and her wedding
ring.

Tonight signaled the real start of their marriage, and she
was nervous if her rapid pulse was any indication. She'd
never considered herself an excitable person when faced
with new circumstances, but she had no clue what to expect tonight. Frankly, she had no idea how to act. To ease
the strain, a pleasant evening with Alex might calm the
waters for both of them. They hadn't discussed the night
after Lady Hampton's dinner party—the night she'd
learned Lord Paul had told her husband she was his lover.

When she made her way toward the dining room, Alex was waiting at the bottom of the steps. He held a rakish smile, one that hinted he knew secrets and would share them. Which begged the question, what kinds of secrets would he keep from her?

"Good evening, Lady Pembrooke." Alex caught her hand before she descended the last step and briefly kissed her cheek. Moving his mouth to the side of her head, he whispered for her ears only, "Beautiful wife."

The smile lit his eyes from within. She immediately responded, desiring more of his touch. Instead of pleasant, dinner might turn into pure torture if her traitorous body wouldn't behave.

Stepping away, Alex placed her hand on his arm to escort her. "I'm delighted you joined me this evening. All day I've looked forward to spending time with you."

"With such a note, I didn't consider it a request but a command performance, my lord." His scent of fresh soap, starch, and male surrounded her. For a moment, she imagined burying her nose in his shirt to get closer, much like the night he'd discovered her in Lady Anthony's garden.

Alex chuckled. "Come." He escorted her into the drawing room, where a bottle of champagne awaited them. Alex twisted the cork until the light pop sounded. He let the wine settle, then poured two glasses.

The sparkle in his eyes matched the wine, as if his pleasure in seeing her were authentic. This was a new game he played, and she didn't know the rules. It was only days ago that he thought she was Lord Paul's lover. Since they were married, it offered him little advantage to be pleasant.

"I wanted to toast our marriage last evening, but I found you asleep." His voice carried a hint of disappointment. Their fingers brushed together when he offered the glass. The casual touch caused a spark of awareness to smolder low inside her body. "To my lovely wife, the siren of my desires."

For a long moment, she stared into his eyes and tried to understand his toast. Unexpectedly, he winked and raised his glass to his lips. Claire relaxed and matched his movement. The wine's bubbles tickled her throat as she swallowed. "What a charming toast, one any wife would appreciate. What's caused this humor?" Claire kept her gaze steady and congratulated herself on her composure.

With a sinewy grace, he took both glasses and carefully placed them on the table. "Darling, the thought of you distracted me all day. Tonight, I want our first dinner as a married couple to be special. I hope we have tens of thousands more."

Claire lowered her gaze. His efforts to win a spot in her good graces were quite entertaining, but she didn't want to surrender that easily.

He leaned near, and his lips brushed hers with the barest touch. With a deliberate motion, Alex drew back and looked into her eyes as if trying to see her innermost thoughts.

"When I saw you yesterday, I knew I was the luckiest man in England. Somehow, you found the resolve to marry me." He cupped her cheeks with his hands, his thumbs brushing slightly up and down. "The way we parted after Lady Hampton's still haunts me. The unhappiness I caused you didn't set right with me. Forgive me." Slowly this time, he lowered his mouth and captured hers.

Claire's determination to remain in control fled when his arms tightened around her. The softness of his full lips against hers fascinated her. Warmth settled into every limb of her body.

His hand skated across the soft silk of her dress as his tongue danced with hers. He clasped her hip with a gentle squeeze and pulled her closer. His fingers traced a path upward until his thumb circled her nipple with the lightest caress. He groaned into her mouth.

Claire lost sense of time and place. The friction against her skin made her want to plead for more. The stroke of his thumb sent pleasure racing through her veins until it settled low in her belly. When she arched into his hand, he kissed her again. Hard. Possessive.

Her thoughts tumbled into a mishmash. Her legs grew weak, as if they couldn't bear her weight. His incendiary kiss brought back memories of their kiss at Lady Hampton's dinner party, where she had practically melted in his arms. She wasn't ready for the same loss of control, not until she understood Alex better. Not until they trusted each other better. She stepped back and gazed into his desire-filled eyes.

"I'm hungry. Are you?" Claire asked, breathing heavily.

Alex drew back, his voice sinfully low. "If only you knew. Come, let's eat."

They made their way to the dining room. Her pulse still raced as he seated her. The evening was fraught with challenges, namely his talent to make her forget everything except for him. Every touch, every word, and every glance he gave her threatened what little ability she possessed to make it through the meal.

Claire took a sip of the dry, fragrant white Bordeaux that the footman served. Her breath caught when Alex extended his thigh and leaned it against her knee. The table covering hid his actions, but the heat of his leg against hers still shocked her.

Grasping her hand, he pushed his thumb back and forth against her fingers with a knowing smile on his lips. "Darling, are you all right?"

She nodded, not trusting herself to speak. He deliberately teased her with his attention. She moved her leg to stanch the blatant hint of intimacy between them but allowed his hand to remain on hers. It was above the table and in view of the servants.

Alex's eyes never left hers as the footmen delivered course after course. If quizzed in the morning on what she had eaten, she'd fail completely. Her nerves were wound up tighter than a ball of twine. When Alex offered a bite of his dessert, custard with a vanilla sauce, he held the spoon while she ate. Unconsciously, she licked her lips and found a smoldering fire light his eyes.

"I'm very happy you're here." With a wave of Alex's hand, the footmen retreated from the room. Even though they were alone, he leaned toward her so no more than a hand's distance separated them. "I dreaded coming home, but with you by my side, things are different. I don't feel the oppressive silence in every room."

"Perhaps it's a new chapter in both our lives."

"I think you're good luck." The upward twitch of his lips was devastatingly handsome, and she faltered in the silence that engulfed them. "Spend the day with me tomorrow."

"I'm not certain of my schedule in the morning." She shook her head, desperate for her mind to tackle her heart and take control of the conversation.

"Of course. You're still getting settled." He brought her hand against his lips. "Will you spend the afternoon with me?"

The whisper of his words washed across her skin like silk. It distracted her. No, he distracted her, but she forced herself to focus.

"You mentioned the river yesterday. Shall we ride to it?"

"No." The sharpness in her voice startled her. "What I mean . . . I—I—"

"Pardon me." His formidable gaze captured hers, and his voice deepened. "Until now, it never occurred to me . . . your memories of the river."

"It's all right."

"We both possess memories from here that aren't pleasant to revisit." He squeezed her hand. "Let me take you on a picnic. How does that sound? We'll read and visit some of my old haunts on the grounds. Whatever you'd like."

He was trying to make her feel welcome with a sincere gesture. Her husband was truly a nice man. "I'd like that very much."

He pushed away from the table—a signal their time was over. Claire rose to leave Alex with his evening port or whatever he liked to do after dinner. Tonight, her single desire was to retire with a good book and settle the riot of sensation he had stirred.

"What are your plans?" he asked.

"I'm retiring to do a little reading."

Alex glanced in the direction of his study. He gave her a winsome half grin. "I've got a few letters I need to answer. Afterward, may I join you?"

Claire nodded. "I'll leave you to your work."

She had no idea what he meant. Was he going to join her in reading or consummate the marriage? As she made her way to her chambers, her mind raced as she recalled the kisses they had shared not an hour ago.

Aileen was waiting for her and made quick work of undressing and preparing her for bed. The maid turned to leave but stopped.

"My lady"—Aileen wrinkled her nose as if smelling something not to her liking—"I had the strangest conversation this evening. His Lordship's valet wants *me* to report to *him* daily."

The request shouldn't have surprised her, but it did. Alex never mentioned how he wanted to incorporate Aileen into the staff. Neither she nor Aileen was accustomed to reporting to anyone. Cavensham through and through, she refused to succumb to any discomfort in front of her maid over the announcement. "How did you respond?"

"I told him he was the worst excuse for a man, particularly a Frenchman, I'd ever seen. When he stood to argue, I leaned over the table and pushed him back into his chair. I informed him I don't take kindly to his orders and made it clear if he needed to know, I'd tell him or he could ask the marquess."

Claire retreated to the turquoise-colored Louis XV writing desk and busied her hands with old correspondence. She loved her maid's strong, lilting voice and imagined how it had sounded in the kitchen. The conversation between the two servants facing off against each other would have been a sight—a Scot against a Frenchman. Aileen would stand her ground in any match that might arise with Alex's valet. However, the relationship was tense between the two servants, and both she and Aileen needed to fit into their new household.

"Thank you for defending my privacy, but share the information." She kept her tone even, as if it didn't bother her.

"My lady"—her maid's voice reverberated with indignation—"he's a valet to a marquess. I'm a lady's maid to *you,* a Duke of Langham's daughter."

"And I am now the Marquess of Pembrooke's wife." Claire released an exasperated sigh. "Just do as I ask for now. I'll discuss the matter with Lord Pembrooke."

Aileen folded her arms across her stomach, and her voice softened. "While the valet was interrogating me, an under-footman mumbled something about the curse. His Lordship's valet stood immediately and ordered him back to work. Apparently, the staff holds the valet in high regard. There wasn't a single peep afterward."

"Bloody hell." Claire held her hand against her forehead. She didn't need the curse to follow her to her new home, or the rumor that she and Aileen were standoffish.

"Wish I could say the same," Aileen sniffed.

"Pardon?"

"Wish I could say I held *Jean-Claude* in high regard." Aileen busied herself at Claire's dressing table.

"Tell him whatever he asks." Claire took a deep breath. "Do it in a manner not to upset the staff."

Her maid straightened to her full height and planted her hands on her hips.

"Good night, Aileen."

Her maid took one last look before she left the room.

The welcome quiet did not stop the burn of Claire's cheeks with humiliation. The room became her private sanctum, one she might never leave.

She tried to lose her thoughts in the novel. When she turned the page, she stared at the first paragraph over and over again. It was no use trying to concentrate on anything but Alex and his staff's penchant for her curse. For once in her life, she had dared to hope the curse was over. Alex had been wonderfully kind this evening, and she'd naïvely assumed his staff would see his attention as acceptance.

Uneasy, she wandered to the window and raised the sash. The light wind delivered the sweet smells of spring, encouraging her to take a deep breath of the fresh night air. When something stirred behind her, she turned and found Alex with a bottle and two glasses.

"I'm not interrupting, am I?"

Her breath caught at the sight of him—perfection personified. He stood relaxed without his evening coat or waistcoat. His white linen shirt opened at the collar, revealing a hint of sun-kissed skin and a slight dusting of black hair. She let her gaze travel down his broad shoulders to his narrow hips.

The earlier pulsing in her belly returned. "Please come in." She walked toward a pair of azure damask chairs that faced the fire and waved her hand for him to join her while her heart skipped with excitement. She felt like a moth flying close to the light. She knew better but couldn't resist the allure.

Alex walked to the chair and shrugged his shoulders. "I thought you might like a drink of your family's whisky before bed."

"Are you trying to see me tipsy?"

"If I did, what would you do?" Alex put the bottle and glasses on the table in front of her as if he were offering her a gift.

Claire ignored the question. She poured a finger of whisky for both of them. They raised their glasses and saluted each other. Alex drained his in one swallow, while she took a small sip to savor the smoky flavor.

Alex poured another. With a relaxed ease, he sat in the chair, and she followed suit. "Did your mother's family distill this whisky?"

She nodded, then closed her eyes as the fragrance of malted barley fermenting stirred her memories. "I only visited the distillery once. My grandfather was so proud whenever a new barrel was ready. He gave a bottle to everyone who visited. Do you like it?"

"It's the best I've ever tasted." Alex leaned back, and a smile broke across his lips. "How are you settling in?"

"Well, thank you. The house is beautiful, and your staff is everything efficient and attentive. I couldn't ask for more."

With Alex in her room, it shrank in size. His attention entranced her, and she didn't trust herself with him. Whether he knew it or not, he held too much power over her desire for his tenderness. With little effort on his part, she would make a fool of herself. Restless, she stood to return to the window and walked by his chair.

With an indulgent grasp of her fingers, he laced them with his own. Claire looked at their intertwined fingers. He had strong hands with long fingers, almost double the size of hers. She let his fingers play with hers while she attempted to relax.

"You're thinking too much."

She raised her gaze to his.

"You're like me. You pace when you're unsettled." The low hum in his voice soothed the tightness building in her chest. "Last night I stopped by to say good night, but I'm not certain you remembered."

"No, I was too tired."

"I hung your witching ball in your window." He pointed to a miniature bowed window above her bed, where the glass sphere rested against the center of the windowpane. He brought her hand to his lips. "I want you to feel comfortable here."

How could he turn something so silly into something so sweet and lovely? "You did that yourself?"

He nodded.

"Alex, the staff—" She cleared the frog bouncing in her throat and slipped her fingers from his.

With a quick tug, Alex pulled her onto his lap and into his arms. He traced his finger along her lips before tilting her chin upward. He leaned down and kissed her slowly.

Claire could taste his whisky, smooth and smoky, with a touch of the forbidden. As she sank into his kiss, all her thoughts focused on his lips on hers. Their kiss along with his heat stripped any hope she had of hiding his effect on her. Good God, she was undisciplined to allow his touch without thought to where the actions would lead. When she'd left London, she'd forgotten to bring any good sense with her.

He lifted his mouth from hers and kissed her cheek before he pulled her close to him. He took a deep breath.

He slowly ran his lips along the outline of her jaw. "Claire, I don't want to talk about the staff at this moment."

Whatever this was between them was happening too quickly. "You don't believe me, but I don't have much experience." She hesitated, her defenses stripped away. "I'm not certain what you want, let alone what I want."

"Maybe together we can find answers." Alex pressed a kiss into her palm. "We won't do anything you don't want." His gray eyes had turned the color of dark smoke. "We'll just get comfortable with one another. Hmm?"

She nodded.

He picked her up in his arms as if she weighed nothing and placed her on her bed.

Claire's heart raced as his knee came to rest beside her hip. He pulled his shirt over his head. Nothing would give her greater pleasure than to be held and comforted in his arms. She wanted to feel his hands touching and caressing every part of her. For years she'd yearned for this night, but not like this—not if he had doubts. She closed her eyes to concentrate on the right words to stop this from continuing.

When she opened her eyes, her breath caught at the sight of his chest, chiseled with muscle, fully defined from his shoulders to his waist. Her gaze traced the subtle patterns until a small line of hair beckoned her to follow its path below the fall of his breeches. The urge to explore took hold. She raised her hand tentatively, then pulled back.

Alex grasped her fingers, then brought them to his lips. "Touch me." His warm breath still carried the scent of whisky as it caressed her fingers. "Touch anywhere you like."

Claire spread her fingers across his chest. His skin was hot, and the sinewy muscles flexed under the light touch of her exploration. He must enjoy physical labor and the outdoors. Something else she had to learn about him. She took her time and clasped his shoulders with both hands.

He encaged her body with his, resting his weight on his forearms. With deliberate ease, he lowered his mouth to hers and lightly brushed his lips against hers.

Desire pooled in her belly as she concentrated on his full lower lip.

He teased her lips by tracing his tongue over the seam of her mouth before he coaxed her to open. With little resistance, she let him take control. His tongue danced with hers, slow and languid.

Claire attempted to return the kiss and twined her fingers into his soft hair. The movement of his mouth against hers was like a waltz. He stopped and looked at her. Unable to read his face, she felt adrift. She had no idea what to do. "What do you want from me?"

His gaze grew tender. "I want you to feel tonight. Just feel me. I want to touch and taste every inch of you." With a natural athletic grace, he shifted to her side. His hand stroked her breast through her silk robe.

The hot caress of his fingers caused her to move closer to his side, her earlier concerns forgotten as she melted under his touch. Her nipples came to hard peaks. Instinctively, she arched up into his hand, desperate to relieve the heaviness in her breasts.

Alex sighed. "You're a perfect dream."

Before she could utter a peep of protest, Alex untied her dressing gown. As he pushed the fabric down the length of her body, his hands stroked her bare skin. Frantically, she tried to hide her body by turning away.

Alex stopped her retreat. He leaned down and brought his cheek to hers as he whispered, "I don't mean to frighten you. I want to see you."

The roughness of his evening beard against her skin reminded her of a cat's tongue. He was the most masculine creature she'd ever seen, and he was in her bed. The idea he wanted to inspect her left her unbalanced and unsure, ready to fall.

Alex lifted his face from hers, his gaze earnest. "I've always thought you were beautiful."

She caught her bottom lip between her teeth. If his expression hinted at any disappointment, the only thing she'd remember about this night was his regret. His weight shifted as he leaned over her. With a gentle touch, he framed her face in his hands and turned her toward him.

He must have caught the doubt in her eyes. "I want you to watch as I look at you. It's important for both of us," he commanded. He drew back. His gaze perused her chest and down her abdomen before following the lines of her legs.

Alex's mouth curved into a smile. "Just as I imagined." He returned his attention to her breasts and took a nipple into his mouth. As he sucked, a twinkle of devilry shimmered in his eyes. With a flick of his tongue on the tip of her breast, he contemplated her. "Hmm. You taste perfect. Much better than the custard." He delivered a smile worthy of a rogue.

Claire wanted to close her eyes to relieve the sudden burst of light-headedness, but she was mesmerized as he continued to lave her nipple. A tingle tantalizing in intensity came straight from her center and exploded through her body. When his engorged cock pushed against her thigh, she couldn't help but moan and rock her breast into his mouth as she angled to feel him between her legs. The touch of his lips was a hot brand against her skin. His tongue circled and teased while his hand cupped and squeezed her other breast.

She had little experience with lovemaking, but he was a master with his gentle touch and caresses. His ravenous feasting was the most erotic sight she could ever have imagined.

"Alex . . ." Her fingers threaded his thick black hair as she tried to sit up. She had to find a way to keep her equilibrium in this tempest he had started. Cautious, she scooted away and sat up. "Alex, please."

He groaned as if he enjoyed hearing his name on her lips. "Please more? Please harder? Tell me what you want. I'll give everything to you."

The look on his face was so sincere, it pierced her heart. There was only one answer she could give him. "More of your touch."

Alex lowered her to the bed before he descended to continue his exploration. She watched his tongue meander its way onto her curved belly and her navel. Suddenly, he was too close to her most intimate parts. To stop his movement, Claire pulled at his shoulders. He looked at her briefly with a boyish smile and continued to her hips. Claire twisted, trying to calm the storm raging within her.

She couldn't believe he wanted to look at her there. No one had examined her that closely before. She inhaled sharply as she watched him kiss her mons. She jerked to scramble away on the bed.

He grasped her hips and anchored her to the bed. "Claire, stop. I'll not hurt you." He looked at her through hooded eyes, then continued his exploration. She froze, unable to turn away.

"I promise you'll enjoy this." Like a feral beast, he pinned her with his gaze, eyes flashing as though aroused by her scent. Within seconds, his expression became languid with a lazy smile. With the slightest touch, he brushed through her curls before he found her center. He groaned and closed his eyes. "Sweeting, you're wet."

With those words, he lowered his head and kissed and licked her most private area. His touch brought her off the bed. She grasped the bedding, trying to find purchase as he fondled and excited her. Unhurried, he placed one finger into the entrance of her sex. In a gentle rhythm, he moved it slowly in and out. He kept using his tongue and lips as he kissed and sucked, totally captivating her. Claire arched her body to shift closer to his mouth. She could feel something building inside, a pressure, a need for more of Alex's touch, for more of him.

Claire doubted she'd survive his sensual attack. "Alex, please . . . ," she whimpered, her breathing fast and shallow. A rush of new sensations raced through her body. All the while, he worshipped her with his tongue.

He pleasured her by replacing his mouth with the pad of his thumb as he continued to stroke her in a movement that was unlike anything she had experienced before.

His eyes flashed. "You're ready, aren't you?" His words were an aphrodisiac, taking control of her body. "I've thought about this moment for days. I want you to fall apart. Do it, Claire. For *me*."

His fingers continued to entice as he tempted her to reach higher. Claire let the pleasure spill into every part of her body. It flowed from the end of her toes through her legs. The sensation rose, and an explosion of light cascaded through her body as it reached its pinnacle. She went over a cliff and kept on flying.

Eventually, her heartbeat slowed, and her body came back under her control.

She didn't move when Alex came to lie next to her. His mouth met hers in a slow pursuit, learning every sensitive area of her lips. She could taste her essence, tart and wildly forbidden, when his tongue penetrated her mouth.

Alex brushed the hair from her face, and his eyes met hers. "That's how you taste. You. And *only* you." He closed his eyes. "Delectable."

Claire turned on her side and faced him. He was slowly

slipping past her reserve. The last time she had allowed that to happen, Archard had died. What if the same thing happened to Alex?

He brushed his lips across her jaw, settling his kiss into the tender skin of her neck. "I want to make love to my wife."

She drew back and her gaze darted to his. "I need more time."

Alex stopped unbuttoning the fall of his breeches. They stared at each other across a sudden ringing silence, the divide deafening. His eyes narrowed. "Why?"

"I can't. This was a mistake. It's too soon." Using the sheet as a robe, she scooted off the bed and faced him. God, how could she deny him? She wanted him more than anything.

He sat on the edge of the bed, his focus never wavering. "What is it?"

She blew out a short breath to gain control. "Your doubts. My curse."

He raked one hand down his face as if he could wipe away her arguments, then exhaled. "You have every right to say no, but hear me out—"

"Alex, please understand. I care a great deal about our marriage." Her cheeks grew hot. Restless, she started to pace. "We need to discuss what happened after our engagement was announced. And . . . and there are other things."

"Such as?"

The last time she let someone close to her, he died. The last time she was near Wrenwood, she lost her parents. How could she make sense of any of this? She stopped by the bed and faced him.

"Claire," he whispered. "Talk to me."

"I'm sorry."

"Don't apologize. I'm the one that ruined this night for

us with my thoughtless words. We should have had a discussion before I took you to bed." He rocked to his feet, and his mouth tightened into a straight line.

"No, please. I'm the one—"

He held up his hand to stop her words. "There's no curse, Claire. You realize this. As to my doubts, I didn't come to you tonight with any reservations." He slowly picked up his shirt. "Perhaps it's best if you tell me when you're ready. When you're settled and comfortable."

He held her gaze for what seemed like eternity, then without another word, he left. The click of the door reverberated through her chamber.

She should never have allowed him into her bed. She was such a neophyte to marriage, beddings, and husbands. Trying to navigate this new life without a compass left her stranded with her only companion, the curse. A curse capable of stealing every bit of her happiness.

The harder she ignored the truth, the more it persisted. She was alone in this room, in this house, and in this marriage. His physical touch was an intimacy she craved, longed for, but not when there was so much to lose. Uncertainty hung over her bed along with that damned witching ball, like black clouds ready to burst.

When he gazed into her eyes and caressed her with his hands and lips, she felt cherished, protected, like someone significant. Someone desired by another human being. In those brief moments, she allowed herself to believe she could attain her dreams.

Could she take the risk? What if the curse struck Pemhill? What if she lost Alex?

Any rational person would think she deserved a room in Bedlam. She even thought so sometimes. Yet she couldn't ignore what she'd lost in her life.

She was intelligent enough to acknowledge there wasn't a curse. She had to remember that this time was different.

He wasn't in love with her, nor she with him. It would have been so easy to let him into her bed, doubts and all. During those sweet moments, she could have pretended he valued her while pretending she'd not lose another person she felt close to.

Deep waves of frustration rolled through her, and hot, stinging tears fell down her cheeks. She turned to the window and tried to focus on the black sky.

Tomorrow would bring a new morning and Wrenwood, where she would face the rest of her demons. If she had any luck on her side, perhaps she'd finally cleanse herself of the curse.

Alex leaned heavily on the connecting door. Still bloody hard from the effect of pleasuring his wife, his cock protested the wisdom of his decision to leave her chambers. His wife—beautiful and responsive with barely any coaxing—was more than he had ever imagined.

She said she was inexperienced, but it was difficult to tell. She was tentative but capable of letting her passion rise between them. When she'd found her release, her body had clamped down hard on his fingers.

Afterward, the expression on her face reminded him of the night at Lady Anthony's. The rapid rise and fall of her chest accompanied by her wide eyes was something he'd never forget. She truly was unsettled, almost frightened.

Plus, he'd added fuel to her distress over his reaction to her confession regarding Archard. Did he have doubts about her truthfulness? Instinctively, he believed her.

Damn Lord Paul to hell. His claim of having had her, the innuendos and sly comments, marched straight into his wife's bed and pushed him out. It had no place between what he and Claire had shared.

Christ, what had they shared together tonight? He closed his eyes and concentrated on her touch. He'd been without a woman in his bed for so long. At first, he'd thought it nothing more than confusing physical release with something else. However, deep inside, there was little doubt what the truth was. He was developing a true regard for his wife.

If possible, his cock throbbed harder as his thoughts returned to Claire's creamy breasts and her sweet, wet center. He reached to take himself in hand.

The sound of low weeping came from Claire's room. He attempted to recapture the pleasure and closed his eyes. He clenched his hand around the swollen cock-stand. Tugging up and down its length, Alex could remember only the stark devastation in her eyes. He tried pumping harder, but his cock revolted and softened in seconds.

He had lost his mind.

Chapter Eight

◡

T he thwacking of the straight edge against the leather strap was the only sound in the room. Alex sat under the customary hot towel that tamed the black stubble of his morning beard. Every morning, and sometimes in the evening, Jean-Claude prepared the straight edge for his shave before his bath. The valet sharpened the blade until it could split a spider's silk in two with little effort.

A sudden eruption from the valet interrupted the normally tranquil ritual. "That infuriating maid asked to see me before retiring last night."

"Aileen?"

Jean-Claude pulled the towel from Alex's face and gave a terse nod. "In her snooty way, she demanded to know if I'd sought information about her mistress without your knowledge. I informed her I am *your* valet. Information I obtain about any subject while on duty is for you and you alone."

Alex quirked his eyebrows. "Did she now?"

"Did I mention her arrogance? Because the woman is Scottish, she puts on airs. Must be why they call her 'Airleen' in the kitchens."

Alex sat speechless. His cautious valet normally kept everything close to his vest. He debated whether to shave himself under the circumstances. Extra starch in his cravats was one thing, but razor cuts were another.

"Last evening, I asked Aileen to keep me informed of the marchioness's schedule. I thought it best under the circumstances." Jean-Claude dropped his hands, the razor a safe distance from Alex. "She turned livid at my request."

"Why do you need the information?"

"I only want staff attending the marchioness who are comfortable with her. I've already discussed it with Simms and Mrs. Malone." His valet took the towel and wiped the razor. "If I know the marchioness's schedule, it'll make it easier to make the assignments."

"For what purpose?" His valet had his full attention.

"Rumors are swirling through the staff about Lady Pembrooke. One of the footmen asked Aileen outright about the curse." Jean-Claude straightened. "Before I could send him away, the damage was done. Aileen appeared ready to tear his head off."

"Of all the bloody times," Alex murmured. Was this part of Claire's unease from last night? He'd made a muck of last night on his own, but if his wife had heard a whiff of the staff's unrest . . . She was facing an uphill battle to win their loyalty. "I'll address it. Bring the footman to me."

"There's more, my lord. The staff thinks Aileen possesses the gift of sight since she's Scottish." His valet's normally staid expression turned sour. "If you ask me, it's more like the gift of a witch."

"Need I remind you to play nice?" The strain between his valet and Claire's maid was like a row between two siblings. "You two will work closely together."

With a stiff nod, Jean-Claude lifted the razor to his neck. Apparently, it was safe to proceed with his shave.

The coming days would be busy in their household. With their respective days integrated, they would have to accomplish what was required of the marquess with a new wife. He was anxious to introduce her to his tenants and the village. It would cement her place within Pemhill.

With a scrape of the razor against his face, Alex released the breath he'd been holding. The image of her face last night haunted him. She was truly terrified of something. He only hoped it wasn't of him. The best outcome for all would be to address Lord Paul's claims as soon as possible. Away from the estate, they could repair what he'd done and never address it again.

With that thought lingering, Alex decided to seek her company earlier than the afternoon. They'd spend the day riding and enjoying each other. Whatever the housekeeper had planned for Claire could wait for another day. Time together was too important. While waiting for Jean-Claude to determine his wife's whereabouts, he instructed Mrs. Malone to personally pack a picnic lunch for the two of them. It contained light and elegant delicacies such as boiled partridge eggs, breasts of chicken, cherry tarts, oranges, and a variety of cheeses. Perfect food he could feed to Claire with his fingers along with a bottle of wine.

The effort might allow him to come under her good graces again when he told her he'd had it specially prepared for her pleasure. It was the least he could do. The manner in which he'd left her to cry her eyes out sullied his best intentions last night, but this morning proved Claire correct. He shouldn't have stayed in her bed, not when she was unsure of him.

Jean-Claude approached with deep lines engraved in his forehead. "My lord, the marchioness is not on the property. One of her horses is missing. Aileen refuses to tell me where she is."

Alex's blood pounded a heavy beat through his veins.

"Get her maid now! Have Ares saddled. Ask if anyone saw her this morning."

"Yes, my lord." Jean-Claude ran up the steps to the family quarters.

Alex twisted his gloves in his hands. He'd wring the maid's neck until she confessed where Claire was. Images crowded his mind of last night, and an ominous foreboding grew inside his gut. She was vulnerable. What if that damn curse caused her to flee, and she hurt herself? He had no idea how accomplished she was on a horse.

When the maid appeared at the top of the steps, Alex barked, "Where is she?"

Aileen's eyes grew wide. She gripped the banister with both hands, as if it would protect her.

"Tell me," Alex demanded.

The maid flinched at his tone. With quick, even steps, she descended into the entry-hall atrium where he waited. "My lord, the marchioness had an appointment this morning."

"Where? With whom?" He fired the questions and took a step closer.

Aileen's chest rose and fell with deep breaths. She held her ground and lifted her chin. "Wrenwood. I'll bring her back."

"Stay here. I'll find her." Alex turned for the stables. Aileen ran ahead and blocked his path. The idiotic woman dared to risk his ire.

"Please, my lord, I beg of you. Be gentle with her." Tears streamed down her face.

He ignored her plea. Disgusted with the maid for not immediately complying with his demand and himself for leaving Claire crying her heart out last night, he mounted Ares and galloped for the neighboring estate. Aileen's attitude ensured that whatever he found at Wrenwood, he would not be pleased. He just prayed to God she was still there.

Within minutes, he reached the main entrance. The young groomsman, Charles, attended his own horse and the stallion Claire had prepared to ride at the posting inn. When Alex reached him, he swung off Ares and handed the reins to the young man.

Charles delivered a short bow.

"Is Lady Pembrooke inside?" Panic wasn't an emotion he had much experience with, but his throat clenched as if stuffed with cotton.

"I believe so, my lord." He looked down and shuffled his feet. "Beggin' your pardon, I don't mean to overstep, but I followed her here. She didn't want any company, but I didn't know how familiar she was with the estate. Yesterday, Lady Pembrooke was pleasant and free with her kind words. Today, she is quiet. I thought you should know."

"How do you mean, quiet?"

Charles's face reflected worry as he rushed the words. "She didn't speak to anyone and never smiled. She gave me instructions last night what horse to saddle and what time she'd leave. This morning, I asked if she wanted me to accompany her. She rode off without a word."

Alex turned and walked straight into the house. Damnation, he had to take his time and make her feel welcome and secure with him. One fact was certain. Once he found her, he'd not let her go.

Alex walked straight through the entry. He made quick work of the massive staircase that led to the family quarters. With a methodical system, he opened each door. Every room and each piece of furniture lay entombed in Holland cloths, as if in mourning.

When he encountered the first bedroom, he scoured every conceivable hiding place. Without a sign of another living soul, he continued his search, thoroughly examining every inch of the upstairs. His mind's paralysis allowed him to survey the surroundings as if disconnected from the moment. One by one, he made an orderly sweep of the second floor.

When he descended the staircase to the main floor, a soft mewling sound broke the eerie silence. With a quick turn, he proceeded past the library and the study. He walked across the grand ballroom.

He exited near the rear and continued into a narrow hall, well lit by floor-to-ceiling windows facing north. Alex stepped briskly into the entrance of the portrait gallery.

Claire lay huddled on the floor in front of a large portrait.

The sobs grew more distinct. He didn't hesitate or announce himself as he ran the length of the long hall. His footsteps echoed through the room as his boot heels hit the wood floor.

She bowed her head while whimpers broke the silence. Curled into a tight ball, she held her knees, taking up as little space as possible. She didn't acknowledge him, nor did she start or protest when he picked her up in his arms.

"Oh, Claire," he murmured. "What has happened to you?" His head fell back, and he closed his eyes. She was safe. He carried her to the nearest sofa and sat down. She fell to his chest in the manner of a small child who needed rescuing from the world.

Powerless and not knowing what to do or how to offer comfort, he held her tight to compensate. She had told him she hadn't been to Wrenwood in fourteen years. He should have known—she was here for her parents. Soon, the need to say something came from a place deep inside him.

"I'm here," he whispered. He cleared his throat. She didn't seem to care. "Sweetheart, I have you." Alex bent and kissed the top of her head and gently held her to his chest. He studied the portrait and rubbed her back for what seemed like hours.

She didn't stop weeping until physically spent. She took

a big breath and shuddered in his arms. Quiet filled the hall. Alex leaned against the sofa. His shirt and waistcoat were soaked and stuck to his chest. The muscles in his arms ached from holding her. Once he had found her, his worry receded. Anyone who rode a large stallion had to be an accomplished rider. Any blistering fool would have figured out she wanted to come here to grieve.

Several moments passed before Claire broke the silence. With her face splotched and her eyes swollen and bloodshot, she looked as if she'd gone thirteen rounds with Lucifer. He pushed the hair that had fallen loose behind her ear and rested his hand on the back of her neck. The gentle slide of his thumb across her cheek wiped away the remnants of her tears. Touching her softness was as essential in that moment as the air he breathed. More important, he wanted to give assurance he would not abandon her as she leaned her face against his hand.

"Alex . . ." She squeezed her eyes shut. Sorrow lined her face as she grimaced in pain.

He tightened his hold on her face. No one in the area knew much about the accident and her parents' passing. The estate had closed immediately after the duke's and duchess's deaths. "Tell me what happened that night."

She trembled in his arms and took a few moments to answer. "I've never spoken of it, not even with Uncle Sebastian."

Alex allowed Claire to lead. She should decide what information to share. He watched her face for any sign she'd crumble again.

Claire was strong, and her determination did not surprise him. She stood and walked to the family portrait. "When I was five, my father wanted our portrait done before any more children were born. My parents didn't conceive easily. It took three years before another child was on the way after my birth, and my mother lost the pregnancy early in her confinement. Uncle Sebastian teased they were trying too hard to produce an heir. My parents' retort was their toil had its own rewards."

"No truer words were ever spoken." His response garnered a faint smile from his wife.

"When I was older, I loved to hear that story over and over." Claire returned her gaze to the portrait. "My father thought the artist captured both my mother and me perfectly. At least that's what my uncle tells me. My father had an exact copy painted, a gift for my mother."

Alex stood and walked to her side. "Where's the original?"

Claire took a deep breath. The strain on her face was agony, but she kept the tears at bay. "The portrait's home is at the Langham family seat, Falmont. It isn't displayed in consideration for me. As a child, I suffered nightmares. My aunt thought it best to keep it in storage. That's part of the reason I'm here. I want my father and mother to take their rightful place in the history of our—." Claire wrapped her arms around herself. "Because of me, there is not a single trace of my parents at any of the Langham residences. It's as if they didn't exist."

Raw emotion broke across her face. She was in such pain. It made him want to punch something, anything, to take away her suffering.

"Wrenwood is where I belong, where I don't forget who I am. It was my mother's and my grandmother's. I want my daughter—" Her breath hitched, and she bit her bottom lip. "But now . . . perhaps it's best to put it to another use."

Alex took her hand in his and concentrated on the portrait. Indeed, the detail and coloring were lifelike. Claire, the little girl in the painting, was holding her mother's hand. With a slight smile, the duke was a handsome fellow with an air of authority. The artist caught the gentleness in his eyes as he looked at the two ladies in his life.

By far, the most captivating person in the portrait was the duchess, who was radiant with warmth. The classic beauty looked directly at the artist. Her happiness was readily apparent in her eyes. It was easy to see the love between the duke and duchess. The emotion between the couple was laid bare for all to see, an intimate moment shared by a loving family.

Claire was the spitting image of her mother, except her hair was darker than her mother's red locks. She had displayed the same contentment as the duchess the night of Lady Hampton's dinner party.

Taken aback by the portrait and its effect on him, Alex turned to Claire. "Will you show me the others?"

Claire walked to the next portrait. "These are from my mother's side. Beside our portrait is my grandfather."

Alex studied the man carefully. A big bruiser of a Scotsman with a twinkle in his eye looked back at him. He was dressed in the traditional plaid and kilt of the Clan MacDonald, mounted on his horse with his gun tucked under his arm. In his hand he held a hip flask similar to the one on Claire's nightstand the night of their arrival at Pemhill. Rubies surrounded the neck, but the engraving was not identifiable in the portrait.

"Who was your grandfather?"

"Farlan MacDonald. His friends called him Mac. He gave the flask in the portrait to my mother when she married. He told her there was no argument a drink of good whisky couldn't set to rights. When I married you"—Claire closed her eyes and swallowed—"I brought it with me, hoping it would help us. I like to think my mother would have shared the same words with me on the eve of our marriage—" When her voice cracked, she faced the window.

Alex stepped back from the portrait and pulled her closer, her hand still clasped in his. He'd not let go anytime soon. "Sweetheart."

"It's the first time I've seen a likeness of my parents since their death. I almost forgot their faces." Her defeat was complete as she let out an unsteady breath. "Can you imagine a child forgetting her parents?"

Alex kept her from leaving by taking her into his arms. He held her close for a moment before he lowered his face to hers. "You haven't forgotten. You're here to remember. Next time, I want to be with you." He put his arm around her waist and escorted her back to their mounts without another word spoken between them. A sense of calm—dared he think it, let alone say it?—a sense of family had settled over them.

Without asking Claire's preference, Alex directed Charles. "Take the marchioness's horse back with you to Pemhill. Inform Mrs. Malone and Aileen we'll be home shortly."

Alex would be damned if he'd let Claire ride home without him. His judgment proved sound. She swayed before him, but he caught her before she fell. In one smooth flow of movement, he swept her into his arms and lifted her onto Ares. He followed, then settled her between his legs.

He reached around and embraced her by placing both hands on the reins. The position of his arms kept her secured and steady. Holding her close calmed the torment that had gripped him this morning. He whispered into her ear, "I've got you."

Claire didn't answer.

He gave a nudge, and the horse took a leisurely pace to Pemhill. Why he felt such strong emotions toward Claire in such a short period of time was beyond explanation. Her dignity and vulnerability led him to reconsider his perceptions. Whatever he thought, there was no denying she felt perfect in his arms.

Mrs. Malone and Aileen met them outside when they arrived at Pemhill.

"Ach, the poor lass." The maid gently petted Claire's hair after Alex helped her dismount.

"Mrs. Malone, will you see to the marchioness's comfort?"

The housekeeper escorted Claire inside while consoling her in a quiet voice.

He turned to Aileen. "I'd like a word with you."

The maid's eyes widened.

"Aileen, earlier, I didn't realize—" Alex looked toward the house as Claire entered. "If I caused you concern, it was unintentional."

Aileen studied him without a hint of embarrassment. "I've served Lady Pembrooke since she was thirteen. I know the difficulty she faced in that trek to Wrenwood. I begged her to allow either you or me to accompany her this morning. She was perturbed at my insistence. It was a blessing you were there."

Alex softened toward the woman. Her concern was heartfelt. "It was fortunate I arrived when I did. The next time she decides to travel these hills and valleys to face her grief, I expect you to inform me. If I had escorted Lady Pembrooke, perhaps her pain might have been lessened."

Aileen bowed her head in acknowledgment. "I will, my lord, only if she does not ask otherwise. I mean no disrespect to you, but I owe my allegiance first to her."

"Do you think my interest in Lady Pembrooke's well-being is in conflict with your *allegiance*?" His body tightened as he waited for the answer.

The maid boldly surveyed him as if she were judging his worth as a husband. "My mathair always told me some things are best not shared unless you're willing to halve them." With that cryptic phrase, the maid left to see to her mistress.

Later, Claire sent word she was not feeling well and would not be joining him for dinner. Every morsel on the light tray he'd requested tasted like burned paper. He pushed it away and tried without much success to finish his work in the library.

He leaned back in his chair as a pang of sympathy hit him square in the chest. Claire's grief was raw and overpowering—too strong for an event that transpired fourteen years ago. His own with Alice had faded somewhat, still present, but not disabling. His plans for how to avenge her death had given him another avenue to focus his attention on instead of his own misery.

Aileen's words about sharing halves took on a new meaning. Under normal circumstances, he would never pry into Claire's daily activities. After today, it had become impossible to ignore them.

Something about Claire left him unsettled. He never expected such affection in his marriage. What he did expect was convenience. Ideally, they would have children until they had the mandatory heir and another. If there were daughters in between, Claire would have something to do when they made their debut in society. Nevertheless, after the male heirs, Alex assumed they'd discreetly go their own ways. After such a short time with her, he would never agree to that arrangement.

What surprised him most was the pleasure of her company. He missed her this evening. A visit to her chambers on the pretense of seeing how she fared was a perfect excuse. Hell, she might lock him out after last night, but he'd take the chance.

Within minutes, Alex tapped on the connecting door to Claire's suite. Holding a book, he thought he might look less presumptuous.

"Come in."

Leaning around the corner, he asked, "Are you feeling better?"

Claire nodded. She sat in one of the two chairs facing

the fire. She had her legs tucked underneath and a novel in her lap.

Her chamber was comfortably quiet, with the exception of the occasional pop from the well-tended fire. It was damned difficult to determine if she welcomed his intrusion. She showed no reaction except for her green eyes, which held a glitter of wariness.

He decided to take the chance. "May I join you for a while?" He held his book in the air, signaling his intent.

Claire nodded again and went back to reading.

Alex found their interlude rather cozy. They sat peaceably for a half hour, with neither saying a word. Resolute not to wear out his welcome, he walked over to her chair and delivered a kiss on the top of the head. "Good night."

"Before you go, I want to apologize."

He knelt at her chair. "Apologize?" He should be the one apologizing, for last night and myriad other indiscretions. The guilt over his actions still burned his insides.

She twisted her wedding ring several times, then put her book aside. "I received a letter from McCalpin yesterday."

Alex took her hands in his and squeezed. He searched her eyes for any indication of what she was about to say. "Is he all right?" The knife slid in deeper. If he had caused McCalpin to suffer because of his bet, he couldn't think of the consequences. The Duke of Langham's wrath would be nothing compared with his wife's pain. He would never survive that.

She nodded and released a deep breath. "He's home."

Alex closed his eyes and said his thanks to the powers above. "I'm relieved he's safe." He took a deep breath. The smell of fire and brimstone flooded his senses. Hell was closing in on him for manipulating her life for his cause.

"He also said you were never involved with Monique LaFontaine." Claire swallowed and looked him square in the eye with a steely determination that he recognized had served her well when she was uncomfortable. "My thoughtless remarks when we discussed the settlements impugned your honor—"

"It's forgotten." He couldn't bear her apology. What she had done was a trifle compared with his actions. If anyone had cause to ask forgiveness, he did for tricking her into this marriage, for doubting her word. He needed to tell her now before they passed a point that could never be repaired. He attempted to form the words to start the confession, but his mouth and mind warred against each other. All he could offer was another squeeze to her hands. He needed her to trust him more before he exposed the truth.

Claire released a deep sigh and closed her eyes. "Thank you. Now, if you don't mind, I think I'll retire."

As Alex walked through the connecting door, his conscience screamed and kicked at him to stop and give her his confession.

Thank God he had enough experience to ignore it.

The early morning sun lit the breakfast room in a golden hue of sparkling rays. Claire entered with a lightness that melted when she found the room silent and completely empty.

One of the under-footmen she'd met the other day came in with a fresh pot of chocolate. "Good morning, my lady." He quickly held out the chair to the right of the head of the table.

Claire sat as he pushed the chair in. "Good morning, Benjamin."

"Would you prefer tea or chocolate this morning?"

Claire smiled. "Neither. I prefer black coffee in the morning unless I ask for something else the night before."

The young man gave a hard swallow. "I will let Cook know. A full buffet is prepared for when you are ready to eat. May I serve you a plate, my lady?"

"No, thank you. Do you know where Lord Pembrooke is this morning?" Claire made her tone nonchalant.

"I'm here. Perfect timing to join you," Alex called as he strolled into the room.

The sight of him took her breath away. Fresh from a morning ride, he was intoxicatingly masculine with his windblown hair and his boots all splattered with mud. He gave her a dazzling smile that highlighted his straight white teeth, and Claire met his grin with one of her own.

As he walked toward her, Claire expected him to take his chair at the head of the table. When he bent and kissed her on the cheek, she held her breath, especially since Benjamin was witness to the show of affection.

"Morning, darling," he whispered. In a louder voice, he directed the under-footman, "I'd like coffee as well." Benjamin gave a nod and left the room.

Alex leaned her way, keeping their conversation intimate. "Where did a gently bred lady like you learn to enjoy a brew as foul as black coffee? The truth now, and no tall tales."

Claire gave him a half smile. "If I told you the reason I like coffee, you'd think I was much too hoydenish for a duke's daughter."

His face broke into a boyishly affectionate grin. "Oh, now I must hear this story."

His smile lifted her mood instantly. She delivered a saucy one in response. "When I was a little girl, my governess would walk me to the stables and return directly to the house. Her daily mission was to flirt with my father's secretary. She wouldn't return for hours."

"What would you do?" His breath and the fresh scent of peppermint kissed her cheeks.

"The stable master took pity. After every riding lesson, he'd escort me into his office, where there was always an abundance of fresh-baked biscuits and cakes. He taught me to dunk my biscuits in coffee." She closed her eyes for a second. "Delicious."

Alex leaned even closer. "Go on."

"Afterward, he taught me how to care and mend the tack. By the time my governess would return, I'd be covered in filth."

A wry but indulgent grin tugged at his lips. "She should have been fired."

Claire shook her head, then widened her eyes for a dramatic effect. "Her face would turn the brightest color of purple while she called me a hoyden the entire way back to the nursery. It stands to reason I prefer coffee in the morning."

Alex raised one eyebrow in an indignant manner. "You are quite right. You are too much of a hoyden for a duke's daughter." They stared at each other and burst out laughing.

Before Claire could say another word, he grabbed her hand and raised it to his warm lips. "But you're perfect as a marquess's wife."

His quick gray eyes flashed with an infectious humor. His words, sweet and endearing, caused unexpected warmth to heat her cheeks.

Benjamin entered with the coffee, and the spell was broken.

"I see you went riding. Is that part of your morning routine?"

"Most days when I'm here. Today, a tenant had trouble with one of the granaries for the barley. I rode over to inspect it and gave him my thoughts. I have to return tomorrow. Would you join me? I'll show you every inch of Pemhill." He leaned closer and took her hand in his. "Years have passed since you've been here. It's still beautiful. I know I'm biased, but I want you to see and experience all that it offers. I want to share everything with you." He squeezed her hand and let it linger.

Delighted, Claire nodded her agreement. "Thank you."

Breakfast started in earnest, and conversation flowed with a natural ease about topics ranging from their respective schedules to their preferences for food. Both despised kippers and kidney pie. Who would have thought kippers would be the perfect segue to the obvious topic no one wanted to address?

"I'd like to talk about yesterday." The unease running through her thoughts was torture. She'd rather face the rack, but now was the time to discuss her reaction to Wrenwood.

Alex swallowed his last bite of food. He stood and turned to Benjamin. "Leave us." He positioned his chair to face hers.

"Yes, my lord."

The sound of the heavy door clicking shut dampened all of Claire's newfound confidence. It became difficult to swallow, let alone speak. She struggled to start the conversation without losing all semblance of control. Truthfully, she didn't know what to share without sounding like a ninny.

Taking a breath, she plowed ahead. "I want to thank you for your kindness yesterday at Wrenwood. I was beside myself with grief and . . . didn't handle it well. I assure you it won't become a regular habit."

There. She'd said what she needed to say. She'd listen to whatever response was forthcoming and turn the topic back to safer waters. After a few moments, she'd leave and start the day with a ride on Hermes.

She waited, expecting a simple one-word answer or acknowledgment from Alex. Instead, he took both of her hands in his and bowed his head. He brushed his thumbs over their grasped hands.

"Claire, I don't have any experience with what you went through when you were a little girl." The gentle caress of his fingers against hers was like a soothing balm, encouraging her to stay and share more. "I'm fortunate my mother is still alive, but I lost my father years ago. Our relationship was close, I'd say, for a nobleman and his heir."

Her throat tightened with Alex's unexpected response. The low cadence of his words thrummed through her.

"When I discovered my father had died, a black hole opened in me that I thought would never heal. I was right. It never closed, but it changed. I've changed along with it and have come to accept it. It's a part of who I am now and will forever be. Alice's death . . . is a wound that still hasn't healed. However, every day the pain lessens. I believe we owe it to our loved ones' memories to live each day to the fullest. Who we are today is because they touched our lives."

Claire didn't try to mask her grief as she squeezed Alex's hands in return. His loss was like hers, a heartache she felt every day without her parents. He understood. Her response to her parents' death was her own, and he accepted her. Always, she had tried to keep her sadness hidden unless it was with her aunt and uncle or the old Langham butler, Mr. Jordon.

His gentleness was soothing, a gift she'd never forget.

"Claire, however you choose to honor your parents' memories is your prerogative." He closed his eyes for a moment and shook his head. "What I saw yesterday broke my heart. I saw a little girl still trying to gather herself and understand. As your husband, it's my duty to comfort and protect you. Don't thank me for that. I want to be more than a husband. Yesterday, I came to you as your friend and more. We still have to define what more means to us. But, as your friend, there was no place else I'd rather have been than with you."

Claire sat dumbfounded. Alex was kinder and gentler than she had expected or wanted to admit. She was lost in how to respond. Her confounded hope raised its head again, begging for recognition. Was it possible something meaningful was within their grasp, waiting to be created between them? She dared not dwell on the thought, since she'd been down this road so many times. The destination was always a disappointment.

Yet here he was, throwing it out as a rope, tempting her to grab it. She wanted to believe it was possible. She wanted to believe he was sincere. "Alex, I don't know what to say except thank you."

His warm gaze held hers before he settled his lips on hers.

He tasted like the coffee they'd shared, strong and alluring. Without touching him anywhere except for his hands, Claire welcomed his kiss with one of her own. She savored his touch, and more important, she savored the moment. In that speck of time, she blindly decided to take the risk.

She knew the pitfalls that lay ahead, but, without much protest from her heart, she'd fall in love with her husband.

Chapter Nine

A fter dinner, Alex and Claire retired to the library. He poured himself a finger of whisky. He'd had several perfect days finding comfort in his routine at Pemhill. Each started with sharing breakfast with Claire, a long ride visiting the estate, and afternoons working on his correspondence and estate books. Her presence brought a fresh vibrancy to the estate that diminished the sorrow and regret of the last year.

The sight of Claire wandering the rows of books pleased him. Every passing hour, she appeared to be more comfortable with him. They'd developed an easy ebb and flow to their routine. He would wait as long as it took to gain her trust. It was the least he could do to ensure she felt at home—to make her feel safe.

"Find anything that catches your interest?"

"No, I'm curious about what you like to read." The brilliance in her eyes made his breath catch. Without even knowing the effect she had on him, she returned to browsing the shelves.

Alex came from behind and bent down low to place his mouth next to her earlobe. With a gentle nudge he whispered, "My lady, I'll let you in on a secret. This room won't tell you what you want to know. You'll have to come to my private place in the study if you want to know the truth. That's where I keep all my favorite tomes, including the naughty ones."

Her scent of bergamot and sandalwood tantalized him. He could stay here for days listening to the rhythm of her words, learning her secrets. Images of them together in bed made his heart pound. He craved her touch, but what they were building between them was too important to risk just for his pleasure.

He gently bit her ear. "We'll be lost for days. I'll show you things you never in your wildest dreams could imagine." He placed both arms on the bookcase to frame her within his embrace. He kissed her neck and followed with a nip of his teeth. "Would you read with me sometime?"

"Yes," she whispered. She turned in his arms and wrapped herself around him.

He wanted to shout in celebration. This was the first time in days she'd wanted to kiss him. He lowered his mouth, desperate to taste her. "We'll lock the world out and concentrate on us."

The thud against the closed doors vibrated with a force equal to a battering ram. Masculine groans accompanied the noise.

"Stay here." He had no idea what was happening, but he didn't want Claire anywhere near the commotion.

He crossed the room and opened the door. The grooms-man, Charles, and a relatively new under-footman named Lloyd rolled on the floor. Blood and sweat dripped across Lloyd's face. Charles pulled his fist back for another swing. The crushing blow landed on the under-footman's left eye.

"You fucking bastard!" Charles grabbed Lloyd by the shirt and started to shake him senseless. "If you ever say she's cursed again, I'll kill—"

"Enough." Alex hauled the groomsman away by his collar and separated the two men.

Mrs. Malone and Simms stood dazed as Jean-Claude and Aileen rushed toward them. Charles stared at Lloyd as he wiped the blood from his cut lip.

"What is the meaning of this?" Alex narrowed his gaze to Charles, who appeared to be the winner of the fight.

"Just a little disagreement, my lord." The grin on Charles's face didn't reach his eyes. "I believe we've come to an understanding, haven't we, Lloyd?"

Lloyd's chest heaved as he tried to capture his breath.

Alex released Charles, as the two men had clearly lost their desire to continue the fight. "I'll see you both in my study."

"Yes, my lord," Charles said.

Lloyd nodded.

The two servants kept their distance from each other as Simms escorted them to Alex's study.

"Was anyone hurt?"

Alex's attention snapped to the library door. Claire stood with her hands clasped, her normally pink cheeks pale. The flash of her green eyes was the only hint of her distress.

Aileen rushed to her side, her shock dissipating. "My lady—"

Claire held her hand up. Aileen stopped immediately.

"My lord?" His wife's voice was calm and cool. "Why were they fighting?"

Alex exhaled. Just as he had settled down to a nice evening with his wife, that damnable curse and all its trappings ravaged her again. "I'm not certain, my lady."

"I believe I'll retire. Aileen, please assist Mrs. Malone with attending to any injuries." Claire nodded briskly and straightened her shoulders. Without another word, she headed toward the stairs to the family quarters as if the recent events were an everyday occurrence.

With a gentle tug on her arm, Alex caught her before she reached the steps. "Sweetheart, it's probably just some rivalry between the two men."

"I'm sure you're correct." She continued up the steps without another word.

He turned on his heels for the study. For upsetting his wife, he would personally thrash them both.

He swept through the door, and Simms immediately closed it. With a deep breath, Alex rested his fists on the blotting pad of his desk. "Charles, tell me your side of the story."

The groomsman swallowed. "I heard him make some nasty comments about . . . about the marchioness. I didn't take too kindly to them, and when I told him to stop, he didn't."

"Lloyd," Alex commanded.

"You should know he's awfully fond of your wife, my lord." The under-footman glared at Charles. "Perhaps too fond. I mentioned the marchioness has a witching ball in her room, and the lout took offense."

Alex lifted an eyebrow. "That's all?"

Lloyd nodded, but Charles didn't move.

"Mrs. Malone and Aileen will see you in the kitchen." Simms escorted the under-footman out of the room. Alex turned to Charles. "You, stay here."

Charles bowed his head. "If you're going to dismiss—"

"I'm not going to dismiss anyone." Alex took the chair behind his desk and nodded for Charles to sit as well. "Are there rumors amongst the staff about the curse?"

Charles's face reddened. "A few. I try to nip any such talk as quickly as possible. Lloyd refuses to leave it be."

Alex held up his hand. "From now on, you're assigned

to help the marchioness. If I'm not available to escort her, then I want you to attend her. Every time she rides, goes to the village, travels to London, or takes a stroll in the garden, you'll be with her. No exceptions. I'll not have that curse nonsense upset her, understand?"

"Yes, my lord."

"Have your face attended to."

The door shut. Alex leaned back and closed his eyes. This evening's drama had unraveled all the progress he'd made with Claire. All he wanted to do was pound his fist through the wall. It could wait until later, as his attention was needed elsewhere.

He needed to convince his wife there was no curse.

Claire pulled her favorite dressing gown, a dark gold brocade with black ruffles framing the neckline, tight about her waist. A sharp rap on the connecting door was the only warning before Alex stood before her with book in hand.

Abruptly, he sat in his usual chair and rubbed the back of his neck. "Claire, we need to discuss . . . some things."

With all her practice of suffering through the *ton*'s taunts, it was relatively simple to master a serene expression. Remarkable, as she wanted to throw the witching ball and all it represented from the highest parapet in England. For good measure, she'd like to stomp her feet and scream at how unfair it was that the damn curse had followed her to Pemhill.

However, she stood and waited with an outward tranquility that defied the turmoil swirling inside of her. She released the breath she'd been holding and blinked her eyes to clear her wayward thoughts.

"The scuffle between the two men broke out because . . ." By the last word, his discomfort with the conversation was apparent to both of them.

"We both know what happened."

He rose from the chair and paced the length of the room. Her husband was as agitated as she was over the fight, perhaps even more so.

"My lord, you can't stop this. I've lived with it for years. Trust me. If there was a solution, I'd have found it by now." Her ability to say "curse" had surrendered without a whimper. Such a hateful-sounding word. With a quick turn, she fell into the chair at her dressing table and opened a jar of lotion. "Did you let them go?"

"Is that your wish?" His voice was deceptively composed. "Claire, whatever you want."

"No. I've not had occasion to converse with the under-footman. However, Charles is very kind to me. He followed me to Wrenwood." She raised one brow. "Just between you and me, he wouldn't make a very good spy."

The faint sound of Alex's chuckle filled the room. "Perhaps not, but he's very loyal to you. All will be well."

"Please, don't make such promises." Her body quaked inside, but remarkably she kept a calm outward appearance.

He strode to the dressing table and took her hand in his. "Come and sit by the fire with me. You're too far away."

Once seated, he brought her hand to his lips for a gentle caress. "It's tradition the Marquess of Pembrooke celebrates his marriage and shares his good fortune by introducing his marchioness to the tenants."

"After this evening, you think that wise?" she quipped. "I'd hate to scare off any of our tenants."

"Be serious, you minx." He still held her hand.

She squeezed his hand in answer. "Go on."

"We'll deliver baskets of food as we introduce ourselves as married." He continued, "Let's spend the day tomorrow in the village and pick up what we need. Mrs. Malone will have the details on the twenty-five families who live on the estate."

"That's a charming tradition. I'd enjoy that very much. When shall we deliver the baskets?"

"Perhaps tomorrow afternoon or the next day." He leaned toward her and kissed her cheek. "I want to show you off to everyone."

The brush of his lips against her skin lit a fire that rushed through her. It was getting harder and harder to ignore this need for him. Perhaps tonight she would ask him to stay.

"I'll leave you for the evening." He stood over her. "Will you be able to sleep?"

"Of course." She hid her disappointment that he wanted to leave.

He searched her face. For a moment, she thought he was going to say something.

"Good night," he whispered.

After the door shut, she collapsed in the chair. Of all the nights, this should have been the one where she asked him to stay. Over and over, he'd demonstrated his kindness. What more was she waiting for? The curse was never going away, as evidenced by tonight's events.

If he had asked if he could sleep with her, she'd have said yes, without hesitation. Why couldn't she summon the words herself?

"Alex, stay," she whispered.

Alex approached the carriage with a light step. Claire was already waiting, early for their ride to the village. He looked his fill at the delightful sight before him. His wife was a beauty. Her skin glowed with a natural vibrant color as she happily conversed with the groomsmen who would accompany them.

The attendants scrambled to make the team of four ready. The corners of Claire's mouth turned up more than they did down, a good sign this morning. If the servants' argument over the curse bothered her this morning, she hid her discomfort with grace.

"Good morning, my lord." Claire glanced his way before she took Charles's hand for assistance into the carriage. The warmth of her smile echoed in her voice.

"Good morning, my lady." Alex closed the door to the carriage and gave the signal to start. "You must have had a good night's sleep to put the bloom in your cheeks."

Claire's eyes twinkled with mischief as she tilted her head to examine him. Her morning gown, a simple design of turquoise muslin with pearls sewn on the bottom of the dress and a matching ivory spencer jacket, set off her figure. "I'm certain sleep is part of it. I got up early and rode Hermes around the estate. Nothing too strenuous, I assure you. Charles accompanied me, if you're concerned I rode alone."

"Darling, that's wonderful you've found the time for a ride." Charles had taken his wishes to heart. This was excellent news, and a brilliant idea on his part if her exuberance was any indication. She'd taken a keen interest in exploring Pemhill. "I will attempt to have you back early enough for a rest before dinner."

Claire answered with a smooth hint of laughter in her voice that reminded him of honey, sweet and rich. "How thoughtful, but I assure you I'm up for anything today. As a way of showing our support to the local village, I thought we'd eat at the tavern."

Alex raised an eyebrow. "I wish I had known earlier. I have some estate matters that need attention today. Would you mind if we postponed that outing for another day?"

"Please go ahead without me and take the carriage. I'll have Charles accompany you to Pemhill, and he can return to escort me home."

With a spirited single-mindedness, Claire had outmaneuvered him. As the only recourse, he delivered his most roguish smile, regrouped, and attacked her flank from another direction. "I was hoping later in the afternoon we could plan the tenants' baskets for the twenty-five families. Maybe go on that picnic I promised you. We could start the deliveries tomorrow."

All he wanted was time with her alone without any interruptions.

Claire cocked her head as if examining a rare animal. A flash of humor fell across her face that caused her eyes to widen. He remembered that look from Lady Anthony's ball. It still had the power to turn his insides out.

He resorted to his last tactic to keep her visit short. "In the village, there's not much to keep a lady entertained. My sister complains repeatedly that the shopping is nonexistent. You'll be bored waiting for the carriage to return for you."

"You're too kind, but I'll have plenty to do. I thought I'd see if the butcher has enough smoked hams available for every tenant. I'd also like to purchase candies, toys, maybe some fresh fruit for the children. Mrs. Malone told me how many families have small children and their ages. Please, I want to meet everyone and see everything the village has to offer."

How could he deny such a simple request? He only hoped their day wouldn't be too tedious for either of them. All he wanted was to spend time with her, preferably alone. If that was how she wanted to spend the day, it would be his pleasure.

Alex found himself smiling like a fool in answer to his own wife's excitement of spending the day in the village. If he could keep that expression on her face, he would deem today a success.

He made a show of helping Claire down from the carriage when it stopped. When she stepped out, her eyes brightened as if the sun had favored her with a kiss. Quite a contrast from her mood when she'd first arrived at Pemhill.

The village was small by most standards, but it had everything the community needed. There was a sundries store, a butcher, a blacksmith, and a small shop that carried fabric, trims, and other sewing items. It even had several ready-made dresses hanging in the window. Other businesses lined the rest of the street. There was a doctor, a solicitor, a church, and the local tavern.

Alex escorted Claire into the sundries store, where the proprietors, Mr. and Mrs. Brown, waited and gave an appropriate bow. "My lord, to what do we owe the pleasure of your visit today?"

Alex returned a nod. "Good morning, Mr. Brown. Lady Pembrooke, I'd like to introduce you to Mr. and Mrs. Brown. My wife, the Marchioness of Pembrooke. We'd like to acquire some necessities for the tenants' baskets."

Claire carried herself confidently as she said, "It's a pleasure to meet you both."

Mrs. Brown curtsied. "Good morning, my lady. What an honor our shop is part of your visit. Please accept our congratulations."

Claire returned her smile. "Thank you, Mrs. Brown. You have a lovely establishment. I'll be picking up quite a few things for our baskets and for Pemhill, too. If you don't mind, I'd like to browse before I start my selection."

Alex watched his wife work her magic on the Browns. She asked Mrs. Brown her opinion on the quality of the sugars and the flours available. Mrs. Brown's face grew animated as she divulged all her knowledge within a one-sided fifteen-minute conversation.

As Claire listened intently, she glanced at Alex and gave a quick wink. The day got a little brighter, and Alex quickly answered with a wink of his own.

Midmorning they stopped at the butcher's shop. Harold Higgenbottom was a beefy man with fists the size of a ham and an apron that readily displayed remnants of his work. Alex wondered how his wife would handle the big fellow, but before he could introduce Claire, she jumped to meet him herself.

"Good morning, is it Mr. Higgenbottom? I'm Lady Pembrooke. I could smell the wonderful smoked meats from a block away," Claire called as she walked right up to the man.

Mr. Higgenbottom didn't bow, no doubt because his large, rounded stomach got in the way. In fairness, he gave his best effort and briefly nodded toward Claire.

Without taking his eyes off her, the butcher acknowledged Alex's presence. "Good morning, Lord Pembrooke. I see the rumors were true. The Browns rushed to tell me I was on the list to meet Lady Pembrooke." The butcher gave one of his rare, toothless smiles and asked Claire, "How may I help one of the prettiest ladies to grace my store outside of my own missus?"

Alex's mouth dropped open, until decorum and the buzz of a wayward fly demanded he close it. Claire had the curmudgeon eating out of her hands.

"Thank you, sir. I am in high company indeed, if you're comparing me to your wife." Claire laughed. "Tell me, how many of those hams are available?"

Claire and the butcher went to the back of the shop to work out the details of her purchase. She complimented his work after sampling, then ordered thirty hams, one for each basket and five for the house. Mr. Higgenbottom promised, as a special favor for the marchioness, to deliver the order tomorrow.

Alex allowed Claire to lead him to the village doctor's office. The young doctor, Wade Camden, met them outside.

"Good morning, Lord Pembrooke," Camden called out in greeting.

Alex's hand rested on Claire's lower back. "Lady Pembrooke, this is Dr. Wade Camden."

Claire stepped forward. "It's lovely to meet you."

"My lady, the pleasure is mine." Camden bowed.

She proceeded to inquire about his practice, her eyes trained on the good doctor. Intermittently, she asked about the scope of his work, if he had any assistants, and the special needs of the community. Her genuine curiosity kept the doctor fully engaged.

Alex gave his undivided attention to the conversation as the doctor explained that he had taken over the practice from the previous physician, who had retired last month. Camden, who had trained at the University of Edinburgh, was tall and about Alex's age.

The good doctor had an easy countenance and tawny-colored hair. His manners were kind, and he focused keenly on Claire. In Alex's opinion, he was a true asset, and they were lucky he had wanted to settle near Pemhill.

"If there is anything the marquess and I can do to help your practice, please don't hesitate to ask. The community is a top priority for Lord Pembrooke." Claire's attention turned to Alex, and he was immediately lost in the serene green of her eyes. "My husband is very generous and committed to bettering the lives of his tenants and the others that are a part of Pemhill."

Their proximity and her praise drew Alex's attention to her lips. The need to interrupt the doctor's conversation and kiss her in front of the entire village became his only interest. She was pure sweetness and light. The faint blush on her cheeks and the slight flutter of her pulse mesmerized him.

They had to return to Pemhill or he'd likely do something he'd regret, like swing her into his arms and find some private place where he could ravish her lips with a proper kiss. Alex shook his head to clear the fantasy. They still hadn't met everyone.

"Dr. Camden, it is a pleasure to see you again. My wife and I don't want to take up any more of your time. Thank you."

Claire looked at Alex and said her farewell. Once out of hearing, she pursed her lips, then relaxed them into a smirk that announced she knew his game. "We weren't finished."

"Darling, I didn't want us to monopolize his time. I'm certain he has calls to make."

Claire grew pensive for a moment. With a quick recovery, she delivered a smile he could get lost in. "I never thought to keep him from his patients. You were right to take us away."

His relief was immediate at her swift acquiescence. With any luck, they could have a short meeting with the rector, then proceed to the tavern for a bite. His goal was to hurry home. He had lost his appetite when Claire announced she'd invited the young doctor to Pemhill so they could continue their discussion. How in bloody hell had he missed that part of their conversation? Proof he was completely disarmed when she appeared confident and happy in her role as his wife.

God in heaven, what was the matter with him?

Finally, after meeting the rest of the village proprietors and the rector, and securing various toys, candies, and ribbons for the tenants' children from the last shop, they sat down at the tavern for a meal and a glass of ale. The increase in business had everything to do with his wife, as the entire village had decided to join them. He heard "the duke's daughter" in several conversations.

His wife was a success.

Claire was in rare form. She welcomed and engaged

every villager who crossed her path. After last night, he wasn't at all certain how she would respond to his interests today. There had been nothing to worry about. Alex was proud to introduce her as his wife and pleased with their reception. They'd accomplished today's agenda, and he was eager to leave. He wanted her attention devoted solely to him.

He'd earned it.

The next two days went by in a blur. Claire and Alex made the rounds to their tenants, presenting the celebratory baskets. Mrs. Malone and Cook had added fruited breads, fresh-baked cakes, and apples from Pemhill's pantry to the supplies purchased in town until each basket overflowed. Every tenant matched the gifts with their expressed joy and warm thanks. To Claire, their congratulations were the best wedding presents of all.

The last stop was the Stoddards' home, where two young children rushed out of the cottage to pet the horses. Claire had made a special addition to their basket—peppermints, gingerbread, ribbons, and knucklebones.

Alex's strong hands circled her waist, and he lifted her down as if she weighed nothing. He clasped her hand with a gentle squeeze.

Mrs. Stoddard greeted them before they reached the door. She held a baby, a girl named Mary. "Welcome, my lord and my lady. Adam will be in shortly. I sent our Robbie to fetch him from the field. Please come in."

When Claire entered the homey cottage, the sweet smell of baking bread made her mouth water. It was a relief to escape the sunshine and the heat from the day. She'd noticed the wind coming from the west and a scattering of clouds during her morning ride with Alex. None of it had provided a respite from the heat.

"How are you and Miss Mary this morning?" Claire

rubbed the back of her finger across the baby's red cheeks, hot with fever.

"She's still not her usual self. I'd like to call on Dr. Camden, but we need to wait until I sell some goods at market this week. She doesn't seem to be getting any worse," Mrs. Stoddard answered with worry in her eyes.

Claire cooed to the baby. "May I hold her?"

Alex came to her side after Mrs. Stoddard went to the other room for tea. "You look quite fetching with the little one in your arms." He brushed his own finger against the baby's hot cheek. "Perhaps we need one of our own?"

Claire's cheeks heated. "Hush." She continued to keep her voice low so the others wouldn't hear. "I met Mrs. Stoddard last week at the house, and the littlest was sick then. She's such a tiny thing. I'd like to ask Dr. Camden to examine her. What if it's worse than a simple fever?"

Alex smiled at the baby in her arms. "Consider it done. I'll send for him as soon as we return to Pemhill."

"This means so much . . . to me." Claire's heart skipped a beat at his tenderness and concern for the tenants and their families. At the idea of having a baby with Alex, the familiar quiver of longing began to take hold. He had no idea how much she wanted their own baby in her arms.

After saying good-bye to the Stoddards, they started for Pemhill. At the end of the day, the sun was barely visible as the clouds had thickened in the sky.

Claire's skin glistened with sweat, while Alex appeared immune to the sweltering heat. Without a hair out of place or a wrinkle in his clothing, he drove the empty wagon looking as if he could step into a drawing room ready for an evening of entertainment with the local gentry. When she attempted to take her spencer off, the sleeves entangled her arms.

Alex laughed at her antics and stopped the team with a one-word command. "Perhaps I could offer some assistance?" He slowly peeled the tight jacket from her, revealing her white gown underneath. He leaned over and kissed her full on the lips. "Your efforts with the farmers and their families made quite an impression."

Claire sighed and placed her neatly folded spencer on her lap. "I enjoyed the last two days more than you can imagine. All of your tenants are hardworking people, and the changes you've implemented have helped them become more productive. It's no wonder your estate is profitable."

The compliment seemed to have pleased him. He leaned close and asked, "What scent are you wearing? What is that, bergamot mixed with something else?"

Claire cheeks grew warmer. "Actually, it's orange and sandalwood. My father's favorite. A perfumer in London makes it exactly as he did for my father. He only makes it for me."

Alex pushed a stray strand of her hair behind her ear and his fingers lingered, stroking her neck.

Claire worried about revealing this tidbit but prattled on. "Hopefully, it doesn't offend your sense of smell. McCalpin and William always accused me of smelling like a man." She offered a thin laugh to hide her embarrassment.

A subtle look of amusement flickered in his eyes. "I find your scent to be a part of you, and you, my sweet wife, are very enticing." Alex lowered his head to hers and kissed her again quickly. "Let's go home."

His smile promised good things to come in her future.

Claire soaked in the warm bath and listened to the wind whistle through the window. She enjoyed everything Pemhill offered. The past couple of days had showcased a variety of colorful people who offered her companionship and a sense of community. From Mrs. Stoddard and little Mary to the gruff Mr. Higgenbottom, the tenants and village represented people linked to her past, to Wrenwood and now Pemhill. Rationally, she needed to guard her heart in case of disappointment, but the words "kinship" and "belonging" pervaded her thoughts.

She dressed for dinner and walked to the window. Clouds gathered in the distance. With the air heavy with moisture, unease made her skin prickle. A heavy cloak of dread held her chained to the window as she waited for the storm. The hairs on her arm lifted, and every one of her senses went on alert. She vowed not to succumb to the fear as she made her way downstairs.

Alex had asked her to join him in his study before dinner. Handsome dark wood paneling surrounded the walls. Where the paneling ended, a navy silk wall covering extended to the ceiling. The entire room was a reflection of Alex's taste, and Claire couldn't help admiring it every time she entered.

At the other end of the room, books lined several shelves. She pulled out one of the leather-bound tomes and began to examine the selection, a book of poems by Robert Burns.

The door opened, and Claire looked up. The last remnants of Alex's conversation with the steward entered before he did.

Straightaway, he went to his desk. "If you're looking for something naughty, you won't find it there." Without looking at her, he opened a drawer. "I keep mostly books on soil cultivation, livestock husbandry, and other titillating subjects on that shelf."

"Really? I found this book of poems here. Was it not shelved correctly, or are you not familiar with your own study?" she teased.

"Madam, I know where everything is within my domain. Always." He nodded his head at the book in her hands. "It belongs on that shelf because the majority of his poems reflect the nobility of agriculture."

His impish tone announced a cheerful mood. She almost shared that she was ready to consummate their marriage but dismissed the thought. With the promise of tonight's storm, she'd better not take the risk. After dinner, she'd venture out for a short walk to see the movement of the clouds.

"Would you like a glass of sherry?" he asked.

"No, thank you. Not tonight."

Alex approached and gave her forehead a quick kiss. "Why is that?"

Claire stumbled for a response. He wouldn't understand her need to be alert if a storm hit while she slept.

Without waiting for an answer, Alex took her hands in his. "I know we've had a less than auspicious start to our marriage. I'd like to start anew and hope you're in agreement." He handed Claire a large jewelry box. "This is a promise to our future."

Inside was a large opal pendant the color and size of a robin's egg. Diamonds surrounded the stone and sparkled like stars. The rest of the necklace was made of graduated diamonds that ended in a clasp made of sapphires.

Claire was at a loss for words as she stared at the exquisite necklace. "Why—why are you giving this to me?"

"I've seen how hard you've worked. You've given tirelessly to the tenants with little thought to yourself. The tenants, the staff, and the townspeople are impressed with their new marchioness, as am I. It means a great deal to me." His eyes softened as he brought her hand to his lips. Without letting go, he rubbed her hand against his cheek. The faint hint of bristles tickled her skin. "What you said to Camden about us wanting to make Pemhill and its residents a priority was extraordinary. You made me feel as if I could conquer the world."

The look of gratitude in his eyes was something she'd never seen from him before. She drew near. "Thank you."

"I'm the one who should say thank you. I couldn't ask for a more committed partner or a more perfect wife. Together, we'll place our mark on Pemhill and leave it with pride for our son and the same for our daughter at Wrenwood." Alex took a deep breath and looked out the window. He played with her hand until whatever internal battle he fought was over. He gave a gentle squeeze and returned his gaze to hers. "I also wanted to apologize . . . for ever having any doubts about you or, more importantly, causing you any doubts about our marriage." He exhaled and his gaze captured hers. "I consider you the greatest gift I've ever received."

In that sweet moment, their marriage changed. Alex believed her. She suspected his apologies were rare. Without much reflection, Claire accepted it. It was enough to build their future. They needed to move forward.

She reached up and brushed her lips against the warm skin of his cheek. He turned and caught her lips with his. Each time she kissed him, the pull to be near him became stronger.

"My lord, my lady, I beg your pardon." Simms hesitantly cleared his throat. "The steward has returned with one of the tenants. There's a fire in one of the small granaries."

Alex nodded with a grim smile. "Sweetheart, I have to go. I'll be back soon. Don't wait up if it's late."

A fire in a granary was a danger to everyone. If it spread to the surrounding buildings, the last harvest would be lost. Depending on the cause, the fire and its fury could kill or maim dozens.

She'd worry until he came home. "Be safe."

He squeezed her hands one last time and left the room.

Claire asked Simms to keep her informed. Two hours later, she made her way outside. Toward the north, black smoke billowed upward, meeting the dark sky. The winds still came from the west, which did not bode well for a quick end to the fire or for a restful night. If the storm hit with enough rain, it might extinguish the flames. There was some comfort in the thought as she feared what the night promised to bring.

She walked the perimeter of the house, and Alex was never far from her thoughts. He'd be in the thick of things, trying to help those dependent upon him and Pemhill for their welfare.

Claire turned back inside for the long night ahead. She decided to retire early and have Aileen stay in her suites until Alex returned.

When she arrived at her chambers, she discovered Aileen flushed with a nasty fever. The poor woman looked as if she'd drop to the floor. Claire made the only decision she could before she sent her maid to bed. She would weather the night on her own.

The crack of thunder overhead jarred Claire awake. She sat straight up in bed and looked for Aileen. Immediately, she remembered she was at Pemhill and alone in her bedroom. Within seconds, another explosion hit. Then silence descended and surrounded her. Sweat beaded on her forehead, and her body began the uncontrollable but familiar trembling.

Another boom crashed in the distance. As she scrambled to leave the bed, her legs caught and tangled in the bed linens. Giant tendrils seemed to clench her body, fighting to make her stay. The more she struggled against the fabric, the tighter the grip became. The sick sense of drowning flooded her mind like that night at the river, but her father wasn't here to save her. Finally, Claire hurled herself out of the vise and stumbled to the window.

Lightning flew across the sky, and the flash rendered a clear outline of the trees swaying in the wind. Another bolt came straight down before splitting into four legs. Then the darkness returned.

Claire counted to forty before a low roll of thunder rumbled. She rushed to the armoire and flung open the double doors. The violent shaking of her hands made it difficult to grab the new pair of boots. Desperate to count again, she needed to know how much time she had before disaster struck. She'd slept in a linen shirt and buckskin britches, prepared for whatever the night might bring.

And it brought her worst nightmare. She rushed back to the window, closed her eyes, and willed herself to look again.

At first glance, the grounds were pitch-black. Then, out of the west, a bolt of lightning streaked in a faint line. Thirty seconds after the flash, the air crackled with a resounding boom.

Her stomach cramped with nausea. She'd vowed never again to be in the same deadly situation as her parents.

Long ago, her uncle's grief had caused him to confide the horrific details of her parents' accident to Aunt Ginny. He'd never meant for Claire to overhear, but she'd hidden from sight. Claire's father couldn't free her mother from the carriage. Her mother's heavy dress had caused their deaths when the skirt caught in the carriage wreck. Her father had fought to free her from the capsized vehicle, but the floodwaters had overwhelmed them both.

She balanced on one foot as she struggled with her boots. As illogical as it was, she needed the boots. With her two hands, she forced her right foot down the shaft with little success. With a hard fall, she landed on her backside as she tried to pull the damn thing off. She realized her error—there were no boot stockings. Aileen hadn't told her where she put them. Claire raced to the window, her heart pounding in her chest. She forced herself to watch the sky a third time. She needed boots to keep her feet warm and dry. She always wore her boots.

Claire took a deep breath, then exhaled. She repeated the pattern several times but stopped when she realized the night had stilled. Nothing stirred. The air hung heavy, without a breeze. She glanced to the left in time to see a single bolt of lightning hit the earth. She counted again. One, two, three. This time she made it to twenty before the thunder roared.

With little time left and little hope of finding her stockings, her only chance to survive was to take a pair from Alex.

She ran with boots in hand through the hallway connecting their apartments until she reached his dressing room. Every drawer within reach, she threw open. The first contained his folded cravats, and the second held personal items, including his razor. Another drawer across the room held a neat line of cravat pins and cuff links. Finally, the next drawer contained the boot stockings.

Claire gathered what she needed and turned to leave. A strong clap of thunder caused the windows to rattle in their sashes as the walls shook. The vibrations invaded her body, making her teeth chatter.

Unable to control the rising panic, she pushed her way through the unlocked door and entered Alex's chamber.

Claire clutched the boots and stockings in her left hand as she stopped to gather her bearings. Floor-to-ceiling windows covered the outside wall. She listened for Alex's breathing.

With her emotions in turmoil, she lost the ability to concentrate. Someone had left the windows opened, and the window coverings pulled. The force of the wind caused the bunched curtains to billow until they resembled an old-fashioned hooped petticoat for a court dress. She fought the panic that threatened to consume her and walked toward Alex's bed. She'd sit on the edge and wait for the storm to pass. Even asleep, his presence would provide comfort.

Deceptively, nothing except for the low rumble of thunder disturbed the night. She took a deep breath and smelled the moisture again. The rain would start any minute.

A blinding fire bolt lit the sky, its numerous streaks flashing to the ground. From the brief reprieve of darkness, she saw the storm clouds roll through the sky. Five seconds later the clap of thunder reverberated around the room, causing the floor to vibrate.

The thin thread holding Claire to her sanity stretched to the breaking point. Her thoughts confused and clouded, she stood frozen, unable to reach Alex as another bolt ripped through the sky and veined outward.

The only sound in the room was her own scream before she went flying through the air.

Chapter Ten

The boom of thunder woke Alex from his sleep. Lightning illuminated the room for a split second, accompanied by another rapid crescendo of thunder. That's when he saw him. In two steps, he reached the intruder and threw him to the ground as a scream sliced the air.

The interloper landed on his face. Alex locked the man's arms behind him. The feminine softness of the slight limbs offered no resistance.

"Don't." The small, childlike voice trembled in protest.

Lightning continued to blast the room in a shattering show of light. Stunned, Alex released his hold. Stark terror radiated from her eyes. A long braid of hair twisted around the front of her shirt—a man's shirt, tucked into a pair of buckskins.

Alex reared back. "Claire? Sweetheart, I'm sorry."

He heard her deep intake of air as she struggled to breathe. Then her words tumbled free. "Help me."

Alex caught her in his arms and hauled her to his chest. "What is it? Are you hurt?"

In the full blaze of the lightning, she shivered and

begged him for something he didn't understand. Her eyes were wild with terror.

"Darling? What are you doing?" Without waiting for an answer, Alex kissed her cheek and said, "Tell me."

Claire's drawn face was haunted with fear.

"Listen to me," Alex commanded. "It's all right. I'll help you." As she struggled in his arms, he bent down and picked her up. In one stride, he reached the bed. When he went to toss her in the middle, she clung to his shoulders for dear life, bringing him down with her. "What can I do?"

"Make it stop."

He caressed her neck as she buried her nails in his bare shoulders. "Make what stop?"

Thunder rumbled again, and she whimpered.

"Is it the storm?" That night in Lady Anthony's alcove, she had been scared of the storm but managed to contain her fear—until the thunder. Now, it all made sense why she'd reacted to him and rushed into his embrace. In an effort to calm her, he whispered in a soothing voice, "Let's close the drapes on the bed. That will help."

"Don't leave!" She was terrified, more frightened than the night of Lady Anthony's ball. Claire turned her focus from the window. She opened her mouth to respond but couldn't. Her eyes reflected a depth of torment he'd never seen in his entire life. She reminded him of a blackbird once trapped inside his room. The bird had careened from one place to another, desperate to find escape.

"Watch, Claire. I'm closing the drapes. Then, there's only us, nothing else. All right?" He kept his voice confident, but he was at a loss as to how to calm her.

Her chest puffed in and out like a small fireplace hand-bellows. His gaze held hers until he had closed all four curtains that framed the bed. Total darkness surrounded them. He kept his movements slow, in a careful, relaxed manner. She tried to roll away, but he found her by touch. In one swoop, he gathered her into his arms and placed her on his lap.

Alex mulled what to do next. He rested his chin on top of her head. She burrowed her face deep against his chest. He had to get her attention away from the storm. "Claire, the men and I put out the fire by midnight. Thank God, no one was hurt. I came to your room to say good night, but you were sound asleep."

When she didn't reply, he tried to engage her again. "What did you do this evening?"

"I took a walk, then went to bed." His chest muffled her voice.

Alex bent and kissed her cheek. "When did you wake?" His hands stroked the same path up and down her back. He repeated the pattern over and over, the rhythm designed to comfort.

"I don't know. Maybe hours ago." Claire trembled as another burst of thunder cracked. The storm's intensity had died down over the last couple of minutes. "Don't leave me."

"I won't," he whispered into her hair. Her plea sounded as fragile as it had the first night he'd seen her terror. He brought her tight against his chest. "Why are you dressed in men's clothing?" Not wanting to provoke a fight, he subdued the desire to know if these were the items she had ordered from the London shops. The information could wait until tomorrow. He coaxed her answer by kissing the sensitive area below her ear.

If he kept her interest, he could calm her. He rubbed his hands down her back and brought her nearer. Definitely, his wife was a sensuous piece dressed in breeches. To increase his torment, her breasts pressed against his chest. Her nipples were hard. He might not be able to survive the night himself if he had to hold her without having more.

Claire exhaled a breath, tickling his chest. "You'll throw me in an asylum if I tell you."

Alex chided, "Come now, I'll do no such thing. I commend your choice of tailor. You're well turned out." He gentled his voice. "You're scared. I need to know what this is about."

"I have a tailor in London who makes my clothing for nights like this." Resignation filled her voice.

He nipped her earlobe, then soothed it with a kiss. God, he couldn't get enough of her. He forced those thoughts out of his mind. She needed him.

Alex recalled Macalester's last conversation about the mysterious purchases of apparel. "Do your boots fit as well as the rest of your clothing?" He kept his tone light, trying to hint at his jesting.

"I have them made by Hoby." There was a slight tinge of huskiness and challenge in her words. She had no idea how seductive her voice sounded.

Nuzzling her ear, Alex replied, "I would expect no less from my marchioness." His tone turned serious. "Why for nights like this?"

"When it storms, I never allow my legs to become entangled in ball gowns or dresses or nightgowns."

None of this made sense. "Why?"

"I can't free myself. You won't understand."

Wrenwood was the cause of her fear. "This is about your parents?"

"I can't talk about this. Why are you naked?" she asked.

He exhaled a sigh of relief. If she noticed his lack of clothing, she had calmed somewhat. "I sleep this way. Do you like it?" Alex was determined to get a "yes" from her if he had to work all night. He rubbed his hand up and down her neck, much like petting a cat. Lightly, he placed another kiss on her ear.

"Yes. You're so warm."

Sweet victory flowed through his blood. Her panting had settled, and she moved her face toward his neck for her own nuzzle. "Are you more comfortable?" he whispered.

"Yes, but hold me for a minute or two."

He brought her tighter against him. As the storm departed, the thunder's boom was barely audible in the distance. The pounding tempo of her heartbeat had slowed. He'd push for answers later.

Alex traced a path under her shirt. Her skin shimmied as if startled by the touch. He gentled his movement and slowed his caress of the silky skin under her breast. He'd die a slow death if he couldn't have her.

She pulled away and rose to a sitting position facing him. With the slightest touch as soft as a down feather, she placed her lips to his.

Alex found her face in the dark. With a tender stroke, he slid his hand down the side of her face. He took his time and freed her hair from its braid. It was thick and curled from the moisture in the air. He carefully brushed it out with his fingers. With her head in his hands, he angled his lips and gently touched his mouth to hers. He heard her quick breath as she curved her lips to match his.

His kiss was calm. Slow. She needed to know there was no need to hurry. But Claire opened her mouth like a siren and lured him into her spell. Groaning, Alex took her mouth in a deep kiss, his tongue mating with hers. Her movements matched his in depth and intensity.

Alex drew back and kissed a trail underneath her jaw as she arched her neck. He explored the soft, fragrant skin until he found the hollow at the base of her throat. He kissed his way back to her ear. Nuzzling her earlobe, he murmured, "Claire, I've thought of you in my bed ever since the night at Lady Anthony's ball."

Claire placed her hand in his and brought it to her heart as her lips found his in the darkness.

Within a soft sigh—the sweetest sound he'd ever heard—she kissed his mouth, her lips exploring his.

From this moment forward, they would be committed to each other. All doubts and insecurities fell away. Tenderly, Alex sat Claire against the headboard. He fumbled with the buttons on the fall of her buckskins. With a tug, the breeches caught at her hips. His fingers traced the buttonholes until he found two he had missed. To distract her, he caressed her exposed skin, soft as butterflies' wings. Finally, gently, he pulled them off. She wore nothing underneath, and the sweet scent of her arousal made him stop and close his eyes. Overwhelmed by her fragrance mixed with musk, he was drunk with desire. Slowly, he caressed her calves, kneading and massaging, before making his way to the upper part of her legs. He would take his time with her tonight—show her she was safe. Show her all the pleasure she'd find with him.

Claire took his hand and kissed his palm. "Alex."

Tonight, her simple touch and gentle words left a permanent imprint on his memory. He would never forget the sound of her voice, the whisper of his lover. He leaned in and found her lips. Holding her in his arms, he moved his mouth to devour hers and everything she'd give him. He'd even devour her soul if she'd allow it.

The muscles of her stomach tightened when he slid his hands under her shirt. He touched and kneaded her breasts, breaking their kiss only when he raised the shirt over her head. In response, she moaned his name and arched against him.

His body hummed as blood raced through his veins. Eager to comply, he gathered her in his arms and moved to a position where he could lay her on the bed. He angled his body over hers, skin to skin. Possessively, he took one of her nipples in his mouth, laving it, sucking it, over and over until she whimpered. His finger outlined the other nipple, committing it to memory. The softness of her breasts compared with the hardness of her nipples fascinated him. With every touch, Claire's breath quickened. Her moans drove him to give her more—coax more from her.

"Please . . ." Claire moved her lower body against his.

His erection throbbed for its own attention. "Touch me, Claire." Alex found her hand on his shoulder and moved it across his chest. Her touch set his body on fire as if he had stepped in an inferno, and he groaned.

"Yes, that's it. Claire, hold me. We have all night together."

With short pants, she explored his stomach and hips. Alex's attention went to her thighs, where he moved her legs apart and touched her center. He parted her soft folds and discovered her wet heat. He struggled against the animal instinct to take her at that moment.

Claire pushed against his hand, whimpering. She wanted him.

Alex slipped two fingers into her slick center. She bucked into his hand, begging for relief.

With steady, controlled thrusts, Alex took his thumb and rubbed the taut bud of her sex. He caressed and fondled, each stroke of his fingers designed to take her closer and closer to her release. He brought his lips to Claire's ear, whispering, "So lovely."

Claire trembled and her sex began to contract. A long moan of ecstasy escaped from deep within her.

"Yes, that's it. I've got you," Alex soothed and coaxed as he sensed she was near a complete surrender.

Claire writhed against him as if she couldn't withstand the pleasure. Suddenly, she pulled him tight against her as her body clenched. Her cry escaped, and Alex moved his mouth to hers in a kiss, hungry to possess her.

As her shudders of release began to wane, Alex could

wait no longer. "Sweetheart, I've got to be inside you. I need you now."

Claire guided his cock to her center. Alex gathered her to him in an embrace and brought her leg to rest against his hip. He entered her slowly, inch by inch. Her hot pulsating core clasped his cock, drawing him deeper and deeper until his hips pressed against hers. It was divine, better than heaven. The feel of her soft skin and silken hair was exquisite. Nothing in his life had prepared him for this moment.

At her sharp intake of breath and immediate stillness, Alex forced himself not to move, though the pain of restraint proved excruciating. "Claire?" It was agony to stay still, but he needed her reassurance before he continued.

Her body relaxed slightly, and her fingertips smoothed his check. "I need a minute. I'm unaccustomed to this."

Breathing hard, Alex rested his forehead on the pillow next to hers. If he was stuck in this position for the rest of his life, it would be the sweetest torture to endure. He waited another moment. "Darling?" He found her lips. Her kiss, sweet and demanding, matched the desire he felt in his body.

"Don't stop." She exhaled and both her legs encircled his hips.

Thrusting again and again, Alex felt his own bliss cresting, the blind rush of desire coursing through his body as they settled into a rhythm. Her heat pulled him in and her muscles tightened as if she'd never let him go. Claire lifted her hips to meet each thrust. With a final surge, he threw back his head and came long and hard for what seemed like forever. Pleasure overtook every nerve ending in his body.

When his body returned to his control, he rested his head next to Claire's. Both of them were breathing raggedly as they tried to calm the storm they'd created. Alex caught her mouth in a primal possession, not letting up until he felt her respond. Slowly, breaking the kiss, he lifted his head and gave a solemn vow. "You're mine."

Stillness permeated the chamber. With his hands braced on either side of Claire's shoulders, he leaned down and softly kissed her twice. Then, after parting the curtains, he left the bed and dampened a cloth in the water on the vanity. He brought it back to the bed and gently patted her face. She shied away from him.

"Sweetheart."

Claire reluctantly turned toward him. Alex caressed her face with his hands before washing the rest of her. After he discarded the cloth, he climbed into bed. Gently, he gathered her in his arms with her back resting against his chest and brought the coverlet over them.

He rubbed his chin over her head and repeated in a soft cadence, "Sleep. I'll watch the night for you."

Claire answered in a soft whisper, "You're mine, too."

It took only a few moments before her soft, even breathing signaled her surrender to sleep.

Alex couldn't join Claire in her sweet slumber. He didn't want to analyze what had occurred or how it had changed their relationship, but he still harbored questions that only Claire could answer.

He was unaccustomed to having a woman in his bed. Always before, he had gone to their bed and left when he desired. Tonight was different. The thought of Claire sharing his bed was surprisingly peaceful.

Several times that night, he awoke to her caresses. She rubbed her hand lightly across his chest and allowed it to tarry by his heart. He found the need to return the touch without hurry until desire overwhelmed them. Alex made love to Claire again and again in a sleepy haze.

As he held her in the early morning hours, it was difficult to forget the image of her terrified, unable to deal with the storm. She had been lost in her fear. His presence had calmed her, but what would she have done if he hadn't been there?

It would be social suicide if she was in the presence of others and had one of her attacks. Even cocooned at Pemhill, Claire was susceptible to the curse rumors. If tales spread through the estate and village that her curse caused the granary fire and details emerged about her fear of storms, the stories would make it to London within days. He had little doubt it would fuel the *ton*'s favorite pastime. How could he protect her from those who would like nothing better than to ridicule his wife?

Were tonight's revelations the reason she had never been highly desirable in the marriage market? He couldn't reconcile the woman asleep in his bed with the cowering girl dressed in men's clothing.

A nag kept him from falling asleep. When Langham had told him Claire was fragile, he must have meant her fear of storms. It would explain the duke's words before their marriage. Did her uncle realize the extent of her terror? Had he decided not to share the information in fear Alex would walk away?

Alex wanted to believe the knowledge would have had little impact on his decision. But he wasn't that naïve. He needed to consider the matter again in the light of day. No question Claire performed laudably with the tenants and the locals, charming every single one. He believed, then and now, that she had become an admirable partner in his work. The question he had to face was whether the night changed him more than it had Claire.

The nag finally quieted, and sleep flooded his consciousness.

When dawn broke, Claire woke to the birds' cheerful chorus in a volume guaranteed to carry into the next village.

Spring was in full bloom, as attested to by last night's storm. When she stretched, muscles protested in places she didn't even know existed. At the sight of a sleeping husband draped over her body and a possessive hand over her waist, a sigh of contentment escaped her. Alex had been an attentive lover. Her passion had met his at every level, resulting in something she would never have comprehended without experiencing it.

Last night symbolized their commitment to each other. The intensity of their lovemaking could not have resulted from her fear of the storm. Alex's tender attention and the ensuing emotions were the reasons for her response.

Her happiness dimmed when she thought of how to explain last night's behavior. In the sunlight, such fears appeared without cause. At night, with the wind howling and the thunder roaring, it was a nightmare. Would he think her a freak, so fearful of a spring thunderstorm he should lock her up at the first sign of a drizzle? Or her behavior too extreme for normal society because of her panic?

Whether conceivable or not, her fears demanded she dress in men's clothing during storms. In her mind, the explanation was purely logical, a comfort that kept her sane if her fears turned unyielding. Last night reminded her of the night her parents had died. The storm's severity had blazed with power.

Involuntarily, she shook, and Alex's hand tightened around her in a hold to keep her steady. Claire felt his breath feather the back of her neck.

She turned, careful not to wake him. She gazed upon his face and looked to her heart's content. Year after year, she had dreamed of this moment, a quiet morning nestled in her husband's arms in a safe home of her own. Glorious was too feeble a description. It was everything and more than she had imagined. Alex was magnificent and the most handsome man she'd ever had the good fortune to see. Was it any wonder she reacted so passionately to him? With his mouth parted slightly in sleep and the dark overnight stubble on his chin, Claire's pulse quickened.

Her heart almost thumped through her chest when Alex drawled, "Are you getting your fill, or is something so amiss on my person you can't tear your eyes away?"

Claire instinctively moved toward him as her body commanded. He gathered her into his arms, and she was conscious of every part of him that touched her. Burying her head into his chest, she smelled their lovemaking and tried to get closer. His hands captured her lower back, bringing her flush with his rampant erection.

"Feel what you do to me. How will I get any work done if you throw a come-hither look when you pass me by? I'll be reduced to an adolescent, unable to control myself."

Claire kissed his chest. When she looked up, his face held a sleepy smile.

He took her mouth in a promising morning kiss. "Good morning, darling."

"Good morning." Claire returned the embrace. She loved his terms of endearment. It was hard to believe she was married to this man.

"Did you sleep?"

"Yes, somewhat." She stopped and raised an eyebrow. "If you'd left me alone, I probably would've gotten more."

He asked in a gentle whisper, "Are you all right?"

Warmth spread over her cheeks. "I'm fine . . . more than fine."

She waited for him to tease her again. He looked at the overhead canopy instead, and disappointment crept through her body like a thief.

"What happened last night? Were you remembering your parents' accident?"

Claire's shame intruded upon the perfect morning. She didn't move her head from his chest, as it was her only defense. His warmth and their time alone should have brought them closer. Instead, all she felt was a mortifying embarrassment.

His voice rumbled deep as he continued, "I've never—"

A brisk knock pounded on the connecting door.

"My lord?" Jean-Claude's voice boomed through the door. "I apologize, but Aileen is beside herself. She can't find the marchioness and wants to know if you've seen her."

"Don't enter," Alex commanded. "She's with me."

He became the seducer again and pulled her closer to his hard body. His low whisper met her ears, "And I intend not to let this beauty out of my sight for a while." He quickly kissed her neck below her ear and nibbled her earlobe while pressing against her. "I could take you now."

"Very good, my lord. I will let Aileen know," the valet called. "I want to remind you of your meeting with the steward. He has workers ready to start the granary rebuild."

With a groan, Alex kissed Claire on her cheek, then answered, "I'll be ready in a moment."

Alex turned Claire's face to his and looked deep in her eyes. "Last night—" He stopped. "I don't want to leave, but they're depending on me." He leaned over and encaged her in his arms. "I indeed will have you again soon. We are not through with this conversation, lady wife."

He delivered a quick kiss to her forehead, then rose from the bed. The loss of his heat was immediate.

Unperturbed by his nudity, he held out his banyan for her use. "Put this on. I'll be back before evening. We'll have dinner together."

Without a look back, Alex went to his dressing room, leaving the connecting door open. Claire slipped into the black silk robe. Mortified, she didn't think she could face Jean-Claude without turning maroon. When she hurried

past to make her way to Aileen, Jean-Claude delivered a
slight grin, then attended his naked master.

After Aileen made quick work of dressing her in a moss-
green riding habit, Claire headed downstairs for her morning ride.

The day gave no hint that a violent storm had hit last
night. Charles escorted her across the fields through a
shortcut to the granary. The damage, though a real setback,
was not devastating. However, the sight of Alex working
alongside his tenants with his shirtsleeves rolled up sans
jacket and waistcoat caused her to stop and study the scene
before her. All of these people, including Alex, were now
part of her life. With her new identity, she was no longer
the Lady Claire of the curse, but the wife of a marquess
who cared deeply for his estate and its people.

Earlier, Claire had taken her responsibility to Alex and
Pemhill to heart. She'd ordered a luncheon prepared and
enlisted some of Pemhill's under-maids to serve. Claire
took her turn and served food while Alex watched her
every move. As she served him, a secretive smile came to
his lips. A familiar shiver of awareness washed over her
when he stood near.

Mr. Landers, a longtime tenant at Wrenwood, diverted
Alex's attention with a set of drawings for the new granary.
Both men bent over a makeshift table as they examined
the paper. The tenant quickly nodded as Alex pointed at
the sketch.

Adam Stoddard walked to her side and nodded in Alex's
direction. "Without his quick thinking last night, we
might have had a real disaster on our hands. His Lordship
kept track of the storm's wind direction and instructed the
men where to put the fire out first. Otherwise, if the flames
had fueled an explosion, we'd have lost everything, includ-

ing lives. Lord Pembrooke has the respect of every man here."

"That's very kind. I'm not surprised he's well regarded."

"Aye, Lady Pembrooke. So are you. My missus told me what you and Lord Pembrooke did for my little Mary. Dr. Camden was out to visit that evening, and she's back to her sweet self. Once we go to market, I'll repay you."

Claire took a deep breath as his words wrapped around her thoughts. She was finally home. "Mr. Stoddard, will you accept Dr. Camden's visit as my gift for Mary's birth? She's quite special to me. She was the first baby I held after arriving at Pemhill."

The man's face brightened as he grinned. "Thank you, my lady. That's very generous." He tipped his hat. "I'd best get back to work."

She made her way back to the tables to help pack up after lunch.

"Lady Pembrooke, may I have a word?" Alex stood some distance from the others. Whatever he wanted to say, he expected privacy.

She tilted her head in question as she drew near. "Yes, my lord?"

"You are a wonder for sending this luncheon. The men needed the break." He captured her gaze and drew near. "Thank you for helping me."

"There's no need to thank me. I wanted to be here."

"I thought perhaps after last night's storm you might not feel up to . . ." He glanced at Mr. Landers and nodded. He brushed a fallen curl back behind her ear with a gentle touch that made her heart pound a little harder on the inside. "I must get back to work. I'll be home soon."

Later, Claire waited for Alex in a wispy silk negligee and matching dressing gown, both trimmed in rich, soft lace and pearls made for her wedding night. The pearls made it impossible to sleep in, but that was the point. Alex needed to see the adornment and then immediately relieve her of it. She'd never had the opportunity to wear it before, and tonight would be perfect for the seduction she had planned. She would have her wedding night, better late than never.

The connecting door opened and Alex entered. He held a bottle of Scotch and glasses from his chamber. When he saw her, he stopped midstride, and his eyes roved from the top of her head to her toes, then leisurely came back to her face. A wolfish smile graced his lips.

"Welcome, my lord." Claire laughed. "I'm happy you're here."

"Is that for me?" He prowled around her, ready to pounce. "You must not want any sleep tonight."

Chapter Eleven

Claire carefully dusted Alice Aubrey Hallworth's bronze nameplate. The cool darkness within the Elizabethan mausoleum was in direct contrast with the single sunbeam that slid through the leaded glass window. The light fell on Lady Alice's name as if favored by the heavens.

Claire had discovered the building within her first couple of days at Pemhill. She often came here when out of sorts and always left with a sense of peace. After she tidied a couple of stray leaves left over from the fall and winter, she placed several lilies on the old marquess's coffin. The larger bouquet was for Lady Alice. Claire liked to think that the young woman would have appreciated the gesture immensely.

She bowed her head. So far, the curse and all its ugliness had pretty much left her alone. Aileen hadn't heard a word of such talk among the staff since the brawl between Charles and the under-footman. Claire could continue to act in her own fashion without worrying about any rumors hovering over her.

With a deep breath, she tried to concentrate on the rest of her tasks today. Last night, Alex had informed her that

Lord Somerton would arrive tomorrow, and Alex had invited Dr. Camden to join them for dinner tomorrow, too. However, when her mental list of responsibilities drifted to the household and tomorrow's guests, she got lost in thoughts of Alex. The countless times they had made love over the last several days brought her closer and closer to giving him her heart. For all her caution, her heart was its own master and gave itself freely whether she protested or not.

The brightness of the sun briefly blinded her as she made the return trip to Pemhill. To escape its effects, she glanced at the few white petals that peeked over the edge of the basket she carried. She had kept just enough lilies for a perfect bouquet to set on her dressing table.

"My lady!"

Claire faced the mausoleum once again, where a young man slowed his horse from a canter to a gentle stop.

"Pardon me, my lady, but I was wondering if the Marquess of Pembrooke is in residence?" The young man slid off the horse and sketched a bow, his hat in hand.

His wavy brown hair was long and desperately out of fashion with the London crowd of dandies. His clothes were the exact opposite. The cut of his coat and waistcoat accented the expensive fabrics, and his boots were almost exactly like hers, the style obviously one of Mr. Hoby's.

Flustered, the man shook his head. "Please, let me begin again. I seem to have forgotten how to introduce myself properly. I'm Jason Mills. I mean Mr. Jason Mills." Another bow was freely given, but he made it brief. "The marquess?"

Claire smiled at the young man, who was obviously nervous and excited at the same time. "The marquess is touring the estate with his steward. He should return shortly. Come with me, and we'll see about getting you some refreshments."

She proceeded down the path, and the young man slowed his step to keep pace with her.

"Thank you for the hospitality. Do you live here, my lady?"

"I do indeed. I'm the Marchioness of Pembrooke."

Mr. Mills jerked his gaze to hers. "You're the marchioness? The marquess married?"

"Yes. You sound surprised." Hopefully, wherever Mr. Mills resided, the rumors of her curse hadn't made an appearance.

"I shouldn't be, Lady Pembrooke, but I've been away so long, and so much time has passed." Mr. Mills shook his bowed head. "Is Lady Daphne or . . . Lady Alice married?"

As she stopped to ask him his business, Alex crested the hill on Ares in full gallop. The two moved in concert as if made for each other. The sight never ceased to capture her breath.

He drew the horse to a halt from the path and away from the other horse to dismount. "Lady Pembrooke, you have company? Introduce us."

Mr. Mills didn't wait for her introduction. He stepped close to Alex in an awkward manner and then, as if remembering the correct etiquette, made a polite bow. "Lord Pembrooke, it's y-you I've come to see." He twirled his hat in earnest. His nervousness had increased to the point that he scuffed his boot against the grass as he stood before Alex.

Her husband's expression was blank as he examined the young man before him. "Do I know you?" His words contained a hint of haughtiness.

She closed the distance between them and placed her hand upon Alex's arm. The touch drew his attention to her. "My lord, this is Mr. Jason Mills. He was escorting me back from—"

"I wanted to join you, but the time got away from me." Alex's voice turned tender when he addressed her. Quickly, he returned his glare to the young man. "Weren't you a stable hand at the inn before you disappeared?" He lifted one eyebrow. "Your fortunes seemed to have turned."

"Yes, my lord. That's why I'm here. After I left Pemhill, I traveled to Lower Canada and made a small fortune in the fur trade. With that opportunity, I turned it into an export business. I arrived back in England two days ago and traveled here forthwith."

Alex narrowed his eyes but relaxed his shoulders. He placed his hand over Claire's and squeezed. She reciprocated the gesture with her hand on his arm.

Mr. Mills cleared his throat. The twirling of the hat had stopped, but he gripped the brim so tightly that his knuckles were white. "My lord, I'm worth over ten thousand pounds and expect that amount to double by next year if business continues to grow as it has."

Alex kept his hand over hers as she stood beside him. Whether it was intuition or a need to provide comfort, she closed the distance between them as a show of support for Alex.

"Congratulations." Alex relaxed his stance. "That's quite an accomplishment. If you're looking for investors, the only thing I can offer is a letter of introduction to Lord Somerton. He's fond of finding new opportunities. His business acumen is celebrated throughout London. He handles our investments."

The young man smiled but shook his head. "I've never been this nervous before. Please forgive me if I'm sounding dense. My lord"—his expression grew serious—"I've come to ask for Lady Alice's hand."

Alex took a sudden step back as if the words were a direct blow to his body, but he never let go of Claire's hand. She squeezed harder.

"Pardon me?" Alex's voice was barely above a whisper.

"I know it's a shock. Alice, I mean Lady Alice, and I had planned to marry when I returned from making my fortune. If she'll still have me, I promise she'll want for nothing. I come from humble beginnings, but I'm a hard worker and will continue to succeed. I can assure you, she'll be treated like a queen." Mr. Mills' gaze was fierce in determination. "Whether you approve or not, I'm going to marry her. Your blessing would mean a great deal to us both. Alice always spoke of you with the highest praise and genuine affection."

Alex didn't answer. Instead, he turned and walked to Ares. Claire had no choice but to give her attention to Mr. Mills. "Sir, I don't know how to say—"

"I do," Alex drawled. Pure rage twisted his face as he stood twenty feet from the young man with a flintlock pistol, the hammer fully cocked. His grip was steady and he aimed straight at Mr. Mills' heart. "To answer your question, you will not marry her."

The color drained from the young man's face. "What?"

"Before I kill you, tell me why you left her alone?"

The young man's eyes grew wide with fear. "I knew you would never allow a match between a stable boy and your sister. I had to prove my worth. It was difficult to post a letter, but I sent a few." His voice softened to a whisper. "Please don't tell me a falsehood so I'll leave. I love her."

"You love her?" Alex stood deadly still and spoke with a crisp enunciation. "Well, so did I when she moved to her permanent residence over a year ago. Befitting her status as a lady, her apartment is exquisite—outfitted with the finest velvets, white satins, and lace of the highest quality. The mahogany box is safely tucked away from the elements on a cold slab of gray marble in the family crypt."

"She's gone?" The anguish on Mr. Mills' face appeared

to turn into a physical pain as he grabbed his chest. "May I go see her?"

"No." Alex drew in a gulp of air. "When I kill you, it will give me great pleasure to know you'll be in hell while she rests in heaven." He took one step closer.

Claire had never seen this side of him, resolute and possessed at the same time. If she didn't stop him, he would ruin the young man's life and his, too, with one shot.

His forefinger bent to pull the trigger.

Without thinking, she stepped directly in the path of his aim. "Alex, no!" She stood far enough between both men that neither could push her out of the way.

"Stand aside. You don't know what he's done." Alex took a step closer, and she matched his movement. Only eight feet separated them.

"If you shoot him, you'll not only hurt him, but me. If you're tried for murder, I'll be left alone. You promised me at Lady Anthony's you'd never leave me." The tension between them made her weak. Her legs were about to give out, but she locked her knees and continued to face him. "Alex, he's grieving, too," she whispered.

He never lost eye contact but kept the gun aimed at Mr. Mills. "Get off my land."

In seconds, the young man had mounted his horse and was retreating the way he had come at a full gallop.

Claire stepped closer, but Alex turned on his heel with his back to her.

"Go to the house." The low rumble of his voice sounded like the first hints of thunder ready to burst through the night. He threw the pistol to the ground. Without a look back, he took Ares's reins and walked into the nearby woodland.

Claire dined alone. The exquisite meal sat before her untouched. Alex had been gone for hours. Earlier, she had checked the stables, but Ares's stall was empty. After the third course, she waved off the footman and waited for her husband in his study.

Newly built, the fire glowed with a warmth that should have brought comfort. Instead, she shivered as the cold surrounded her. Without knowing where Alex was or what he was doing, she would suffer through it.

"My lady?" Simms entered with an expression of worry that matched her own. "Is there anything else I can get for you?"

"No, thank you. Why don't you retire? I'll wait for Lord Pembrooke." Claire hesitated but decided to ask anyway. It made little difference at this point. "Has he ever done this before?"

"No, my lady." The butler shook his head.

"Thank you. If you hear anything, I'll be here." She rested her head against the back of the sofa.

The sound of clinking glasses woke her. She blinked several times to help her eyes adjust to the darkness. The fire was out, with only a few embers glowing. A fur wrap covered her body.

"You're awake, sleeping beauty." Alex caught his hip on the desk and cursed. He gently placed two glasses and a decanter in front of him. "Will you join me?"

"Are you well?" His lack of emotion tempered her relief.

He didn't answer, but the gurgle of whisky broke the silence. The potent smell filled the room. With a sip, he rounded the desk and handed a glass to her. He retrieved the decanter and sat at the opposite end of the sofa.

"Where were you?" she whispered.

He ran his hand over his face and exhaled. "Facing my demons and my failures." He took another drink. "I thought I understood Alice's action. Today was proof I failed in that also."

In the faint light, his neck muscles tensed and then bobbed as the liquid slid down his throat. She mimicked his sip.

With a spread of his arm against the wooden frame, he appeared relaxed and poised, but the energy between them told a different story. "You shouldn't have stepped in front of Mills." He took another swallow and emptied the glass. "You could have been hurt or worse."

She exhaled a deep sigh. Wherever this conversation led, she had to learn what haunted him. "I couldn't let you hurt Mr. Mills and be saddled with that pain."

"You see yourself as my salvation?" His impassive tone gave no hint as to his thoughts.

"Why did you want to shoot him?" His mood was frightening, but she pressed forward. "Tell me."

"He deserved it and, more importantly, I deserved to deliver his punishment." He leaned back, the movement slow as if he were in pain. "I will never forget the day I buried her. In the cold air of the crypt, I actually considered bringing her back to the house. Foolishly, I didn't want to leave her alone—in the dark." He took a deep breath and poured another glass. "That was the depth of my despair."

"I felt the same way about my parents." Her voice quivered, exposing her unease. She hadn't left her parents' side for five days after they were prepared for mourning. She prayed as hard as she could that it had been some dreadful mistake and they'd wake up any moment. She'd always wondered what she'd done to deserve such a fate. Perhaps that's when the curse had started. It would certainly explain her life.

She took a calming breath. This was about her husband's grief, not hers.

Alex inched his way toward her but retreated. "A hint of sanity returned when I glanced at my father's final resting place. He lies just to the right of Alice. I know he watches over her in death, as he always looked after all of us in life." He took another swig of whisky.

"A comforting thought for those of us left behind." She reached and grasped his hand.

He brought her hand to his lips. She was thankful for the gesture. It stopped his retreat.

Instead of a kiss, he rubbed his lips over and over her skin as if it brought him relief from pain. When he tired of the play, he brought their hands to his lap. "Under my father's watch, this never would have happened."

She waited for him to continue, but he appeared lost in his thoughts. She moved closer. "What would have never happened?"

The silence stood between them like a wall. Finally, he broke the quiet. "Alice left a note in my desk. She was"— he took a deep breath—"enceinte. She told me that the humiliation was too grave for her to face, so she took her own life." His voice was low, but his pain permeated every word.

Claire felt his anguish as he released his burden. She brought his hand to her mouth. "Oh, Alex."

He squeezed her hand in return. "She told me not to blame someone, a man she named. Immediately, I thought him the father. But tonight, I learned the truth from a young man who thought he was doing the right thing."

Her stomach clenched into a knot, but she forced herself to take a deep breath. Alex needed her. She leaned to embrace him, but suddenly he stood out of reach.

"You should retire. We've both had a long day, and there are several matters that still need my attention." He lit a candle and light filled the room. "I'll be up shortly."

"Shall I wait up for you?"

"I'm not good company tonight." His gaze caught hers. "Mother and Daphne haven't heard this story, and I'd prefer they not."

"Of course I'll be discreet." She stood beside him, unwilling to leave his side. If he grieved alone, she feared he would disappear again. "May I stay with you here?"

He shook his head, then walked back to his desk. "I've become that person I most despise. Someone who didn't protect their family. I failed to save her when I had the chance." The devastation in his eyes was hard to miss. He looked as if he were physically in pain.

Unable to control her response, she stepped closer. His words, his actions, and even his demeanor seemed desperate. Whatever comfort she could provide as his wife, she'd gladly give. It wasn't from a sense of duty, but from a desire to provide a safe haven where he wouldn't have to grieve alone. She had appreciated such efforts after her parents died. It was the least she could do for her husband.

"Claire, you're cold and it's late. Aileen is waiting for you to retire." He turned his attention to the papers on his desk. "I don't want to ask again. I want my privacy."

She really was cursed.

Aileen announced the marquess and her guests were waiting downstairs. When Claire descended the steps, Alex stood at the bottom like a guard dog while Somerton and Dr. Camden were deep in conversation.

Alex's eyes pierced the distance between them. They hadn't been in each other's company since she'd left him in the study. She concealed the inner turmoil that burned from his revelation last night and focused on their guests. Dr. Camden saved her from an awkward moment with a warm smile and a polite bow.

"Lady Pembrooke, as a bachelor, my evenings are devoted to either patients or reading materials. May I say this evening will be just what the doctor ordered?"

Claire laughed at his ill attempt at humor. As she'd learned from Aunt Ginny, a good hostess needed to make her guests feel welcome. After greeting Somerton, she turned her attention to Dr. Camden.

The party entered the ornate dining room and took their seats. After the footmen served the first course, she surveyed the length of the table. Alex met her gaze with fire in his eyes. He was dark and remote, like a gargoyle perched on a medieval castle. The man she had come to know over the past days was a million miles away tonight, and the turbulence of his emotions swirled around her. He needed time to erase his pain. That's why he was so distant tonight.

Somerton sat across from her and did his best to keep the conversation lively, asking for her impression of a new Egyptian exhibit in the British Museum. Soon, she and her guests had become engrossed in a discussion of the definition of art. Alex sat silent at his end of the table. Alone.

His behavior was unbearable, as evidenced by the awkward silence when Dr. Camden asked him a question, which he ignored. Before Claire could introduce another topic, Simms entered. "Doctor, the Briggs boy is at the door. There's been an accident. His mother—"

Dr. Camden rose to his feet. "Lady Pembrooke, I apologize and thank you for the hospitality."

Claire followed the doctor to the entry hall. Alex and Somerton stayed in the dining room. When she returned, both men were absent. She took advantage of the time alone and retreated to her sitting room. Within a short time, she had finished the daily bookkeeping for the household accounts. Satisfied there was nothing else that needed her attention, she made her way to the family quarters. The path took her directly past Alex's study.

Outside the door, the different sounds of masculine laughter blended together. Somerton had found a way to lure Alex out of his foul mood. With some luck, his newfound merriment might extend to her. A quick good night to both seemed appropriate under the circumstances.

Claire straightened her shoulders for courage, then raised her hand to knock on the study door. When her fist made contact with the heavy wood, it opened slightly. Crystal clear, the conversation floated in the air.

"Pembrooke, you're besotted. I'd even go so far as to say you're in love with her." Somerton's laughter rang out with a deep rumble. "All you did tonight was scowl at Camden or me anytime we said a word, let alone when we tried to engage her in a conversation. I'm afraid the good doctor will have nothing but trouble if he ever has to attend your wife."

Elation calmed the sting of their earlier discord. Everything she could have hoped, everything she had wanted—a husband in love with her—was right before her. It was wrong to eavesdrop, but nothing could pry her away.

"Don't torture me. That's enough." Alex's distinctive, arrogant drawl had turned into a snarl that resonated through the hallway.

"All right. I thought to get your mind off the matter. Obviously, I failed." Somerton's tone turned somber. "You can't challenge him. It'll leave Alice and the rest of your family exposed to gossip."

"What other option is there? The boy stood in front of me and asked to marry Alice. I could tell by the look on his face, he was the father." Alex's voice had deepened to a low rumble. "He'd been a stable boy at the village inn, but he was constantly here at Pemhill. I'd see them together, but it was all so innocent. They would play with the barn kittens, or he'd work in the stables. I thought he was trying to find employment here. By all that's holy, how could I have made such a mistake?"

Somerton's voice grew gruff. "Have you told her the truth?"

Alex sighed loudly enough that Claire could hear it through the opening in the door. "I'm not certain I would recognize the truth, let alone confess it. After the confrontation with that boy yesterday, I haven't been able to see a clear way out of this mess I've created."

Somerton continued in a milder tone. "Clear the air and tell her everything. That's the only way to ensure your marriage has a chance. The rest will come later."

A faint thread of dread started to unravel deep inside as she struggled to understand.

Alex continued in a tone of misery, one she'd never heard before. "How do I tell Claire I married her to avenge Alice? How do I tell her that everything I once valued in myself is a lie? Or that she was an innocent victim as I laid the trap, made the bet, and won? I won't divorce her, even if he spreads rumors they were lovers. Legal separation is an avenue I don't want to consider. Once I go to London and confess my sins to Lord Paul, I may never return." Alex paused, then his voice rumbled, "Why did Alice write not to blame him?"

Claire couldn't catch her breath for an eternity. Her body felt hollow, as if someone had carved out the pieces, leaving an empty shell. It took every ounce of strength not to fall or stumble to the floor. She had to see Alex's face. With a deep breath, she wiped her face, then entered the room.

It took a moment, but Somerton was the first to notice her presence. "My lady."

When Alex turned, his face held a look of disbelief. A tumble of confused thoughts assailed her, but she pushed them away. Her earlier dread had woven tentacles through every part of her body.

"Tell me." The silence between them grew tight with tension. Icy fear flowed into her gut.

"Claire . . ." Alex closed his eyes as if in prayer.

Somerton began to walk toward the door. "I'll retire for the evening."

Claire raised her hand to halt the earl's exit. Somerton stopped abruptly and avoided her eyes. Guilt washed across his face—he knew every ghastly detail. "No. If he won't tell me, you shall." She turned her attention to Alex. "You married me to avenge Alice? Now you're considering divorce or legal separation?"

He came toward her and reached to take her by the arm, but she stepped away. The pieces fell into the puzzle as if an invisible hand guided them.

"Claire, let's discuss this when it's just you and me." His tone was terse, as if the simple demand would make her stop.

"No. I want to hear it now." A soft gasp of despair escaped her lips. "You must have loved Alice greatly if you married me."

Alex's gray eyes showed a tormented dullness. He took a deep breath and finally answered, "Claire, don't do this."

Her heart stopped and skipped beats as if playing a game of Scotch-hopper. She fought against the pain until she trusted her voice not to break. "Lady Anthony's ball makes sense. How did I not realize this was about Lord Paul? He was the one you spoke of the other night." A bitter laugh emerged to hide the sting piercing every inch of her body. "You wanted whoever he promised to marry. It didn't make any difference to you. I could have been a 'duke's daughter, niece, or laundry maid.'" She threw his words the night of the Lady Anthony's ball back in accusation.

She walked around the two men and went to the side table that held the decanter of her family's whisky. She poured two fingers of the amber liquid into the crystal glass and downed it in one gulp. The fiery spirit slid down her throat and gave her the fortitude to continue. Claire waited for what seemed like hours for Alex's answer. She would force his hand. "Lord Somerton, what did my husband share with *you*?"

The earl shook his head. "Lady Pembrooke, I apologize for intruding on a private matter between the two of you."

Their tandem silence transformed her earlier hurt into a fury that would have rivaled the rage of the goddess Lyssa. "Obviously, it's not private if you know the details." Claire twisted to face Alex. "Who else knows?" Her clipped words were brusque. "You used that *damned* curse to trick me into marrying you. Were Honeycutt and his sister part of your plan?"

"No." Alex's voice grew in volume. "We both were caught in circumstances beyond our control." He crossed the space between them in three strides. "I would never have allowed you to face that scandal alone." He whispered, "Claire, you must know that about me by now. I was trying to protect you."

When she stepped out of his reach, Alex dropped his hands to his sides. His face clouded with an unease she'd only ever seen last night. She swallowed, and her mouth tasted vile, as if she'd eaten his confession. Everything she'd come to love and cherish at Pemhill had been stripped from her.

"You didn't protect me." Her breath caught as if she'd had the wind knocked out of her. She struggled to control the panic. It didn't stop the truth from assaulting her. "You were the one that placed that ugly bet at White's. The initials *L.P.* stood for Lord Pembrooke, didn't it?"

Alex stared at her and offered no answer.

Could the truth be that rancid? Claire's mind traced the sequence of events leading to their marriage. The night of Lady Hampton's party, Alex knew she wanted to wait to marry him. The bet at White's had forced her into a corner. She was desperate to protect her family, and Alex took full advantage.

"My lord, you are more contemptible than the *ton* members that used the curse against me for their own pleasure." She was surprised at the even tones of her voice as her body trembled over the indignity she faced tonight. "They used me as a ridiculous caricature of misbegotten luck. A joke, someone to laugh at." She curled her lips in a sneer worthy of a lioness. "You put McCalpin's and William's lives at risk. For what? Me? You used me as a weapon of hate and didn't have the honor or the courage to tell me so." She drew herself to her full height and walked out of the room.

Only when she shut the door behind her did her heart unravel with pain. What a fool to listen to the silly lies she had told herself. How had she not seen this? Alex immediately had stepped into her life to stop her from marrying Lord Paul. It had been a clear warning to proceed with caution, but she had allowed herself to believe in him and the promised fairy tale.

If love was not the basis for marriage, esteem and interest in one's spouse could hold a couple together. At least she had his interest. She was his first choice for retribution.

Claire stopped abruptly in the upstairs hallway and forced herself to remain calm. She would not allow his manipulations anymore. It would be hell, but she would face the *ton* and hear the latest rumors. Only then could she determine the extent of the damage to her reputation if Lord Paul spread the tale that she was his lover.

She'd go to her family in London—they'd protect her. She was a Cavensham. She would survive this. After tonight, she was finished with the curse, the lies, and the revenge. She would live her life the way she had always wanted. If it meant she'd forgo a husband and her own family, then so be it. She'd find happiness and an avenue to fulfill her dreams another way.

Upon reaching her chamber, she called for Aileen. The wheels turned in her mind as she decided when they would leave. She'd take Charles, since the lad had shown great loyalty. At all costs, she'd avoid Alex and Somerton. She wouldn't waste her time with either of them. Without hesitation, Claire locked the connecting door between their chambers.

If he came to her tonight, she could not withstand the pain. Alex had disclosed enough in the study that she understood his wounds were deep, too deep for her to accept. She choked on a sob, and her heart broke from the weight of the truth. She could have been anyone. Alex only married her because she had been engaged to Lord Paul.

When Aileen entered, Claire gave detailed directions for the tasks to accomplish before the morning. She would be in London by tomorrow night.

Somerton cleared his throat. "Pembrooke, I apologize."

"It's my fault. You tried to warn me, but I didn't listen." Dejected, Alex stood frozen in his study. Should he go to Claire and try to explain? Why would she listen? The devastation followed by disgust on her face haunted him.

"I'll need a second if he challenges me. Will you—" He cleared his throat in an attempt to hide the heaviness in his chest.

"Of course. Do you think it'll come to that? I can't see Lord Paul wanting to proceed with a duel. He'll soon be his father's heir."

"If I were him and I'd lost Claire to another man? There would be no question. Excuse me. I should talk to my wife."

"Tell her everything," Somerton called out as Alex left.

Somerton's words grated on his nerves, as every last one was the truth. He should have told her everything before they married. She had a right to know what he was up to and why. For the life of him, he had no idea why he hadn't been able to answer any of her questions.

The doubt in her eyes had struck him speechless. He'd failed her just as he'd failed Alice. She didn't want anything to do with him, which was the exact opposite of how he felt.

Besides reeling from the truth of Alice's death, he had suffered wretched jealousy this evening. His feelings for Claire were powerful and bewildering at the same time. When she left his study after last night, it took every ounce of will not to go after her and give comfort. At dinner, it took every bit of restraint not to punch Camden and tackle Somerton. They made her smile, and her eyes glowed with good humor. He wanted that power alone, not other men. He wanted those enchanting green eyes focused on him and only him.

In that singular moment when he'd looked down the table, all of his invidious envy had been honed to a sharp point against his best friend and a young country doctor. He personally had invited the men into his home and had then treated them abominably. He was worse off than he thought.

How could such an honorable goal result in such a horrid result? His wife was hurt and wounded because of his actions. His efforts to shield her from any harm had failed miserably. At every turn, he made mistakes when it came to caring for her. He didn't even recognize who he was at this point anymore.

He needed to take Claire into his arms. He needed her to understand and forgive him. He needed this guilt to be gone. All thoughts tangled, and his mind throbbed with pain.

He raced to her chambers two steps at a time. He knocked four times without an answer. "Claire?" Only silence welcomed him. When he twisted the handle, nothing budged. For a moment, he debated whether to knock the door down. No. It would be a selfish, barbaric act that would simply frighten her. He'd find her in the morning and talk through everything. Maybe with a good night's rest, they could both face this conversation with calmer heads.

The thought of sleeping alone held little appeal anymore.

The next day, Alex entered the breakfast room. Claire was nowhere in the house. Somerton was unusually quiet.

"Have you seen her?" Desperation leaked from his voice.

Somerton shook his head, but the look in his eyes was clear. He pitied him.

After he filled his plate, Alex sat down and commenced eating. He needed sustenance before he continued his search. Next, he'd visit the stable and look for Hermes. If the horse was gone, then she'd taken an early morning ride. He'd comb every square foot of Pemhill until he found her.

Simms entered and slowly walked toward him. "My lord, this was left on the entry hall table."

As if handed a death sentence, Alex hesitated, then accepted a wooden box and an envelope with his name written in Claire's distinctive hand. It was her stationery with the thistle pattern. She'd used the thistle seal for the wax, even after he'd given her the Marchioness of Pembrooke's seal.

With great care not to destroy the wax, Alex opened the letter.

My lord Marquess,

I have decided it is best for all if I go to London. I will stay with my family before making long-term plans. I have given instructions to Mrs. Malone as to how to address my leave.

> *If you have need of me, please communicate*
> *directly with the Duke of Langham's secretary.*
> *I truly hope you find peace and comfort in your*
> *actions.*
>
> *Claire Pembrooke*

Alex reread the letter three times to understand what had transpired in six short hours. He opened the box and discovered the witching ball smashed to pieces.

"What does it say?" Somerset was brave enough to ask. Simms bowed his head and left the two men to their privacy.

"She's gone to London," Alex replied with barely contained restraint. All he wanted to do was howl his rage at the havoc he had caused.

Somerton stared at the box. "What is that?"

"It represents a gift she once gave me." The pieces symbolized her trust that he stupidly had taken for granted.

"Pembrooke, I am sorry." Somerton added in a lower, huskier tone, "You should follow her."

"I wanted to get my affairs in order before I made that trip. I thought I'd have time to make amends to her."

"I'll accompany you." Somerton's voice carried a hint of sympathy coated with guilt.

The words died in the room, and the only sound was the scrape of Somerton's chair on the floor as he stood to leave.

Alex could not move for at least five minutes as he contemplated the impact of the letter. His inability to confess his actions and tell Claire his true feelings had caused her to leave him.

What had he done?

By late afternoon, Claire's naïve dreams of a meaningful marriage had been scattered like flotsam from a wrecked ship. On the road to London, she cursed out loud for believing she had a place in Alex's life and a home at Pemhill. Alex's silence about his actions still caused her breath to hitch in protest. Indeed, his acting abilities were extraordinary, as she'd personally evidenced at Lady Hampton's party and in his bed. Every masterful performance had been designed and executed perfectly.

At Langham Hall, Claire fell into the sofa in the blue salon. The familiar comfort was absent. The memory of Alex's proposal in the chair next to her shaded her every thought.

Aunt Ginny and Uncle Sebastian rushed in together. Her aunt drew her close and kissed both cheeks. "I couldn't believe it when Pitts said you were here. Let me look at you, darling."

Less demonstrative but as heartfelt as his wife's greeting, her uncle kissed her on one cheek. "Sweetheart, what's amiss?"

When it came to family, they could ferret out trouble a mile away. Claire took a deep breath in hopes she would not crumble until she revealed everything. Running back to London was too humbling an experience in and of itself, let alone having to offer a reasonable explanation as to why she'd left her husband of two weeks.

"Please sit down, both of you. I've left him. I've left Alex." She repeated herself more for her own benefit than anyone else's. "Please, do not stop me, or I will never get through this." Her throat clenched, but she continued, "Last night Lord Somerton arrived for a short visit. Alex and I had an argument the day before that we hadn't resolved." She paused to stop the threat of tears. "As I went to say good night, I heard him confess that the reason he married me was to avenge a wrong done to his family."

Aunt Ginny's eyes widened before she patted Claire's hand. "Oh, sweetheart, go on."

"I asked him to explain his actions. He refused to tell me anything. I got my answer by putting two and two together. The whole marriage was designed as revenge against Lord Paul."

Uncle Sebastian set his jaw while his eyes flashed. Her aunt pressed her hand to her heart.

In a stoic fashion, Claire forced herself to continue. "I'd like to stay for the time being with you. I've brought Aileen and a groomsman." Somehow she managed to get through her recitation without her voice breaking.

Her uncle's blue eyes softened. "Don't ever ask to stay here. Both your aunt and I consider you our daughter. You are always welcome. This is your home." With a gentle hand, he took her chin and lifted her face. The warmth of his fingers invited her to relax into his touch. A slight turn to the left and right allowed him a proper examination. "Claire, I will see that everything is well. Did he harm you? Hit you? Make you do anything you didn't want—"

Aunt Ginny stood and put her hand over her mouth.

"No, no. You misunderstand. He never harmed me. In fact, when we first arrived at Pemhill, he went out of his way to be considerate. I went to Wrenwood by myself, and Alex brought me home." She closed her eyes at the memories of Alex holding her tenderly in the portrait gallery. "He was kind and attentive when I was distraught."

"Let's go back to Pembrooke." Aunt Ginny spoke in a measured cadence. "Help me understand. What about this revenge?"

"I don't know much more." Claire stumbled on the next words, as she didn't want to reveal Alice's secrets. "I thought he was falling in love with me. He was the one who placed the bet at White's."

Her aunt and uncle shared a look that Claire didn't understand. Aunt Ginny's left eyebrow shot up. "Are you sure?"

"He didn't deny it—" Claire's voice finally broke, and the tears slid down her face. "I'm at a loss. I was so foolish. I fell in love with him."

She crumpled into her aunt's outstretched arms.

As Aunt Ginny patted her back, she whispered, "You're home, sweetheart."

In a deceptively gentle voice, Uncle Sebastian said, "Claire, I'll personally tear the bastard apart, limb by limb."

Chapter Twelve

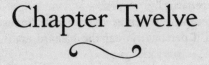

After forty-eight hours in London, Alex had reached his capacity to endure much more of the city or Somerton. The demands on his time, namely the frequent and plentiful tasting of his wife's family's excellent whisky, did not allow him to refine his skills as a gifted conversationalist with his uninvited guest, the earl. There were more exciting entertainments, such as staying upright, watching the room spin, and, in general, feeling disgusted with himself.

The study stopped revolving when Somerset blocked his view.

"Enough, Pembrooke." The earl scrunched his nose and turned away. "You smell like a sewer. Have you bathed since we returned?"

Alex jerked forward to grab Somerton's neckcloth but missed it by inches. Or was that feet? The distance was hard to judge. "Get out."

The earl narrowed his eyes and stepped out of Alex's line of vision. When had the bastard turned so ugly? What women saw in him was beyond comprehension.

"I don't have time for this," Somerton groaned. "I'm too

old to play nursemaid, and you're long past childhood. More importantly, you're incapable in this condition to make amends with your wife or put your life in order."

The room grew silent. Alex closed his eyes to enjoy the peace, but the ache that had seeped into every inch of his body returned. Claire was gone, and the weight of the loss crushed his chest like a boulder.

Alex growled but downplayed his displeasure when Somerton returned and escorted him to the kitchen. He'd put the earl to use. His whisky supply was running low. Somerton could fetch another bottle from Simms. Once they'd crossed the doorway, an oaken tub filled with water came into view.

"Is it laundry day?" Alex's confusion increased when his most trusted servant Simms stood at attention beside the tub.

Somerton bent down and threw him over his shoulder. Before Alex could protest, the earl tossed him in the tub.

The shock of the cold water was enough that he sobered—somewhat. "What the bloody hell, you sniveling sloth!" Water sloshed on the kitchen's slate floor, running as fast as his mouth. "You son of a one-legged whore, what do you think you're doing?"

Somerton checked the time on his precious pocket watch. "You cannot delay the inevitable. The longer you wait, the harder it will be. Go see her!" Somerton's roar caused Alex to lose his hearing for a moment.

By the time his ears had started functioning again, Somerton was long gone. A subdued Simms stood at the door. "My lord, I took it upon myself and asked the earl if he had any objection to keeping the remaining supply of the marchioness's family spirits at Somer House." Concern added to the deep crevices etched across the loyal fellow's face.

Alex shook the water out of his hair and heaved a sigh.

The insufferable Somerton was correct—again. He needed to get his house in order today. "You have my gratitude. But I'll let you go without a reference if you allow that foulmouthed bastard in my home again."

Simms wrinkled his brow. "I beg your pardon, my lord, but I believe you were the foulmouthed bastard." The butler straightened his jacket. "Will there be anything else, sir?"

It didn't take long for the news to sweep through London that the Marquess and Marchioness of Pembrooke were apart, which made Claire's decision for her first official outing with Aunt Ginny and Emma relatively easy. She chose a ball hosted by Lady Downing. It was a medium-sized affair with three hundred in attendance. An event that size allowed her the freedom to mingle if she chose without the constant fear of facing questions about Alex or the curse. Tonight, she'd determine the damage caused by his actions.

In the carriage, her aunt leaned over and gave a light pat to Claire's knee. "Promise you'll find me if you're uncomfortable or want to go back to Langham Hall? McCalpin and William are attending and will keep an eye on you and Emma."

Claire felt the corners of her mouth turn up. "I'll be fine. I shall follow Emma's lead this evening. The only ones who might pester me are the young ladies asking if I could introduce them to my male cousins. I'll be nothing more than a chaperone tonight."

"You deserve some entertainment. I'll see Sebastian dances with you," Aunt Ginny declared.

After greeting their hostess, Claire followed Emma to her circle of friends. She knew most of them and would venture to the chaperone's corner only if she wanted a reprieve from the crowd.

Claire waited while Uncle Sebastian was deep in conversation with a political crony. From nowhere, Somerton appeared. "Lady Pembrooke, may I have this dance?"

Claire hesitated a moment. "That would be lovely."

To refuse her husband's best friend in front of the others would set off a firestorm of rumors. She allowed the handsome earl to lead her onto the floor. Inwardly, she groaned when the first notes from the orchestra flooded the room. How unfair that her first waltz as a married woman was with a man not her husband. Her small sense of contentment for the evening fled. Her mood turned as fickle as a dandy's taste in fashion. She didn't want or need Somerton to take tales of her woe and loneliness to Alex.

"You look lovely tonight. I regret I didn't have an opportunity to tell you good-bye at Pemhill." His smile was charming, but she felt none of the flutters and skips she'd experienced in Alex's arms.

With an impartial eye, Claire scrutinized the earl. With his golden hair and straight Nordic nose, he was by far the most handsome man in attendance. The color of his eyes matched the aquamarine of her dress. As they made their way across the ballroom, the ladies of the *ton* seemed to sigh in unison. They rolled their fans in an attempt to capture his attention while longing painted their faces.

His seraphic looks had no effect on her. Over the last couple of days, her heart had told her everything. She was in love with Alex. She could never stop those feelings no matter how hard she tried.

"You could enchant any man here tonight." Somerton's voice was sinfully deep and rich, designed to make a woman's heart melt. "Have you been well?"

Claire looked deep into his warm eyes to decipher what trickery he played. "Of course."

"Pembrooke is in town," he said.

"Is that the reason for this dance? Did he send you as his emissary or his mole?" Claire kept a slight smile pasted on her face for the benefit of the crowd, but she prepared herself for any cajoling he threw her way.

"Are you always this direct?" A true smile broke across his face that made him even more handsome. "I have a new appreciation for what has made Pembrooke so befuddled."

"You must practice that drawl on a daily basis to attract women." Unfortunately for him, she was immune. "You didn't answer my question. Did Alex send you?"

A barely perceivable flash of pain dulled his beautiful eyes. "No. I'm here on my own accord. May I be frank?"

Claire nodded.

"Alex has been drunk . . . since you left Pemhill. His anguish over you is inconsolable."

His words caught her full attention. At the same time, she allowed herself a small dash of hope. She didn't offer a response for fear she would reveal her true feelings for Alex. She would not allow him to manipulate her again.

Somerton took a breath and continued, "I've never seen him like this, not even when his sister passed. What you overheard in our conversation—"

"My lord, I appreciate your efforts, and the dance has been quite lovely." She'd not listen to another word, certain her newly covered wounds would reopen and bleed onto the ballroom floor. Claire took her hand from his shoulder and attempted to withdraw her other from his, even though the waltz still played and dancing couples surrounded them.

Somerton tightened his grip almost to the point of pain. "Shall we continue outside?" Without waiting for her agreement, he whisked her out a set of open doors onto the balcony.

The evening's breeze was a welcome reprieve from the heat of the ballroom and the myriad eyes watching her with Pembrooke's friend. Claire leaned over the balcony. In the distance, a long rectangular wading pool was ablaze with floating candles. Below, several couples strolled the grounds, taking advantage of the beautiful night and the romantic view. Their destination must be the secluded pathways that led to Lord Downing's renowned topiary gardens. Concentrating on the view and the darkness would help hide the riot of emotions parading through her. She'd allow Somerton to finish and then find her uncle.

"He's too drunk to act. He stumbles through the day and keeps to himself. His feelings for you run deep," he whispered. The earl stood beside her and rested his arms on the stone balustrade.

Claire shook her head in disbelief. If only the earl's words were true. "He had the opportunity to tell me everything, yet he couldn't summon one word at Pemhill. I think you see things that aren't there. How would you feel if your spouse married you under false pretenses, just to use you for revenge? Trust me, it's not the strongest foundation to build a marriage upon. Why isn't he here?" She swallowed the pain that rose in her throat.

"My lady," he protested. "I've known your husband since we were both fifteen. His quest was to become a man that his father would respect. The previous marquess was a notorious taskmaster who would not accept anything except perfection from his heir."

Claire's chest tightened, but she tried to focus on one bubbling fountain in the distance to relieve her new unease at the earl's explanation for Alex's behavior.

Somerton took a deep breath, as if unsure whether to continue. "May I share something with you?" He looked back to the garden and waited.

"Please, continue." When he turned toward her, the desolation in his eyes was unmistakable.

"When I was fifteen, I foolishly followed Lord Paul into

a local pub one evening. We were all at Eton together."
Somerton looked to the ground.

After a moment of silence, Claire wasn't certain he'd
continue his story.

"The fool found a card game, and . . . well, he quickly
ended up owing over two hundred pounds."

"What happened?" Claire wondered what this story had
to do with her and Alex.

His gaze reflected tragedy. "The man who had won the
fortune was furious and threatened to kill Lord Paul for
not having the money to pay for his losses. Lord Paul
begged me to cover the debt with promises he'd pay me
within the week." He shook his head as if he didn't believe
the tale he was telling.

Somerton looked into Claire's eyes and drew a deep
breath. "I signed the note and stupidly thought I could
believe his promise. The next week there was no money
from Lord Paul. I asked repeatedly when he would have
the funds. His answer was always, 'Tomorrow.' Finally, I
was forced to ask my father for the money." He chuckled,
but the misery in his confession was visible. "My father
personally appeared and paid the debt. He called me a
wastrel and cut me off."

"Did you explain the circumstances to your father?"

"I tried, but he was livid." He laughed out loud, the
sound bitter. "Within the month, I became ill. Alex found
me in the stairwell of the dormitory. I was out of my mind
with fever. He paid for a doctor and took me home to Pemhill for the holidays, where I recuperated. I would have
died without your husband's help."

Claire brought her hand to her heart. "I'm so glad you
survived."

"As am I, my lady. I've never seen my father since."
Somerton turned and took her hand in his. "Your husband
loaned me the money to start my investment work. He's a

good man. I ask as a friend. Give him another chance. You both deserve happiness." He gave her a brisk nod. "He'll come for you." Instead of walking back into the ballroom, he took the balcony steps down to the lawn, walked past the wading pool, and disappeared into the night.

Claire stood alone. Somerton obviously owed his allegiance to Alex. She straightened her back and lifted her chin. The tale didn't excuse Alex's manipulations of her life and her dreams, even if it was for Alice.

She had learned early in life that you should appreciate what you have. Everything could disappear in a moment. She had left her own dream of a family at Pemhill along with her heart.

If only she could have left the pain there, too.

Claire straightened her dress, pinched her cheeks, and smiled. She had to survive another despicable evening alone, even if surrounded on all sides by the carrion-eating members of society.

At last night's ball, Claire had enjoyed a rather full dance card. The attention had kept her numb. Afterward, alone in her bed, the hours had lasted forever. Thoughts of Alex had invaded her dreams and kept her awake. Was he well? Had he quit drinking? It would be so much easier if she ceased to care for him. The awful truth squeezed her heart. No matter how hard she tried, she couldn't forget his rich scent, his expressive eyes, or the half-tilted smiles. She'd never be free of him. If Alex cared at all, he would try to see her.

The next day, Claire accompanied Emma to Lady Barrington's garden party. As she made her way to the refreshment tent, Claire passed Lady Amelia Goodhope and Lady Georgette Dinford. They had been introduced into society the same year as Emma and had enough savoir faire to navigate the slippery path through the *ton*'s inner workings. The young women were completely entrenched in conversation and didn't see Claire approach.

Lady Amelia fluttered her fan before her face and leaned toward Lady Georgette. "Did you see her? Why would she leave Lord Pembrooke after only weeks? That man is a walking dream. The curse must be true."

"Nonsense. As soon as she said 'I do,' the curse was over. Now, where's the fun?" Lady Georgette's lips curled into the slightest hint of a cat's tail. "My brother told me he made a small fortune with his bet at White's. He wants to thank her personally for marrying Lord Pembrooke."

Claire took a step in their direction, but reason pulled her back by her dress sleeves. She needed to find Emma and not waste precious time with the two girls. At least they weren't laughing about how she'd been a pawn in Alex's game.

Claire entered the refreshment tent and meandered around the structure as she searched for Emma. Just as she began to walk back to the party, her stomach turned inside out. Emma stood conversing with a gentleman to the side beneath a tree. She was with Lord Paul.

She flew to Emma's side without a greeting. "Emma, Lady Lena is in need of you."

"I'll see to her in a moment." Emma turned back to Lord Paul. "Perhaps one of these days I could examine your collection of logic and philosophy books?"

"Lady Pembrooke could act as chaperone," Lord Paul declared, his attention only on Emma. "I might have that first edition you're looking for."

"Oh, Claire, please say yes." Emma's eyes sparkled. Indeed, William was correct. Once her cousin had a book in mind, nothing would stop her from acquiring it. Even if it meant stirring up the rumor that Lord Paul had turned his attention to Emma.

"Let's discuss it later," Claire said.

"Good evening, my lord. I hope we'll be able to visit again soon. It's always delightful to find someone who shares the same interest in books."

He delivered an elegant bow. "I enjoyed your company, Lady Emma. Thank you for the recommendation of Mr. Bentham's works. Until the next time."

Somehow within the last several weeks, Lord Paul had recovered his sense of style. His clothes were impeccable and immaculate.

Claire watched Emma return to the party before she narrowed her piercing gaze on him. Whatever had she seen in him to think he was suitable as a husband? "I understand you're shopping for an heiress. I hope Lady Emma isn't on your list."

"Good evening, Lady Pembrooke," he mocked with a chuckle and a slight bow. "I thought you'd be overjoyed to see me."

"You must take some sort of perverted satisfaction in trying to rile me with your actions." She didn't need rumors that she was with Lord Paul or, God forbid, rumors circulating of Emma with him. If he thought Emma was a ticket to an heiress, he was mistaken. She would do everything in her power to keep them apart. She turned to leave.

"Claire, wait." His voice softened. "You and I have a lot in common. More than you realize. We're both victims of Pembrooke's manipulations."

Claire twisted to face him. "Manipulations? You, sir, are a master of such things."

He stepped close and lowered his voice. "Don't tell me Pembrooke shared that absurd story about his sister. You're more worldly than to believe such tripe."

She didn't retreat. "I know you're capable of anything."

"I will not deny I knew her. Bloody hell! Pembrooke and I were friends. I never intended to betray him. I woke up, and she was in my bed. Completely distraught, she confided in me. I tried to counsel her, but to no avail."

"What are you saying?" After Somerton's revelations and the hints of what had occurred between Lord Paul and Alex, her curiosity demanded she know more.

Lord Paul threw back his head with a sharp bark of laughter. "Your husband is a madman. One night at Pemhill, I went to bed quite foxed. When I woke, Alice was by my side. She was carrying. She tried to palm the child off on me. It was Pembrooke's unfortunate lot to believe her lies."

The words had the power to bring her to her knees, as if someone had kicked her. "Don't say such things."

"I'm quite certain I didn't sleep with her, if that's what you're thinking." His expression stilled, and he let out a breath as if defeated. "He didn't believe me when I said I wasn't the father."

She stumbled at his words. He reached out and steadied her. God, this was a nightmare.

"What you really should ask is how Pembrooke knew how much money I lost at the tables, and how he came to your rescue the same night."

Claire halted like a hare caught in a poacher's trap. "What do you mean?"

"He set me up to take you away from me for pure retribution of Alice's misfortune. Before the ink was dry on our marriage settlements, Pembrooke instructed lenders to give me unlimited credit to finance my gambling endeavors. All Alex wanted in exchange was information of my upcoming marriage to you. Your husband backed me with the intent to crush me like a beetle under a boot."

Claire leaned against a tree to stay upright. She had discovered the revenge plan by none other than the victim, Lord Paul.

"His first demand to *save* me? I immediately had to

break our engagement. He came to you at Lady Anthony's ball as a knight in shining armor." His furtive gaze haunted her. "Do you want the truth?"

The words were ugly, uglier than she could ever have imagined. She stared at him, not trusting to answer.

"He believed his motivation was pure. He didn't care whom he used, not even you. My dear, you're a victim as much as I am."

"*Stop*. You and I know Pembrooke didn't hold a gun to your head. You threw away everything, including me. I should thank him for my rescue after you told him I was your lover."

"I'm sorry. I should have never said those words." Lord Paul closed his eyes and shook his head slowly. "No one knows what I've lost, the least of which is money. I meant what I said at Langham Hall. I wanted to marry you. I saw what you were long before society acknowledged you." His voice became wickedly soft, like a caress. "Claire, I would have been wonderful to you and our children."

Her fingers touched her wedding ring as if it would protect her from his accusations. "Please, don't."

With a deep sigh, he continued, "I would have loved you like no other. Pembrooke can't give you that. He doesn't have room in that withered heart of his for you."

Claire stood frozen, uncertain she could answer without crumbling. "Neither you nor I can change the past. It's done." She drew away, but he grasped her arm, preventing her escape.

"Claire, walk away from him. Declare to the world you're finished with his lies. Let me give you the life you deserve." His voice had turned low and husky.

"Another revenge plan, my lord?" She moved out of his reach, hoping his ruinous words wouldn't wound any more than they already had. "I don't trust any of you. No, thank you."

"Think hard before saying 'no.' One more thing before bidding adieu—I was on my way to Leith for business the day that horrid bet was placed at White's."

She chanced a glance at the guests milling around the garden. Their laughter and conversation cascaded into a buzz that mimicked the ringing in her ears.

"Bring Lady Emma by someday. It would be lovely to see you." He bowed. "My actions have had the unintended impact of hurting you. I'm truly sorry, Claire."

His words floated in the air, and she couldn't force herself to watch his exit. No one at Lady Barrington's party knew her broken heart shattered into a thousand pieces in that instant. She bit down on her lower lip until she tasted blood.

She stared at the bright moon. Her whole life had turned upside down because of Alex's need for revenge. A red-hot poker being plunged into her chest would have hurt less than the pain she suffered now.

She had always held out a small hope that she and Alex would find their way together, but not now. She was insignificant to him. She heard the truth when he was talking with Somerton. He had actually considered a legal separation. A war of emotions raged through her as she walked back to the group. Ultimately, her pain grew into a huge knot that she pressed into a self-contained compartment deep within her soul. She'd not acknowledge this was part of the curse. To even consider the thought gave it and Alex too much power over her.

All those years of being at the mercy of the *ton*'s awful rumors had some benefit. It taught her the necessary skill to hide her emotions. It was easy to pretend to have a lovely evening when it was the only way to survive.

Partially hidden by the sculptured greenery of boxwoods, Alex waited at the edge of the property. For an agonizing eternity, Lord Paul enthralled his wife with whatever poison he spewed.

The evening grew into night, with a familiar London dampness chilling the air. It didn't bother Alex, since Claire held his attention completely. She mingled with the other guests, never staying long in any conversation except Lord Paul's rant. She moved through the crowd, always with an eye on Emma.

Undoubtedly, Lord Paul had told her everything. Alex closed his eyes and held his breath, a feeble attempt to master his guilt. He should have been the one to tell her.

He had received an invitation to Lady Barrington's gathering even though he wasn't particularly wanted. His rank and title within the aristocracy ensured he'd receive the request of his attendance. If he had made an appearance, Lord Paul would have kept his distance from Claire—another mistake on his part. The event was a perfect opportunity to mend the break between them.

Over the past couple of days, he'd read the society pages, examining the gossips for any mention of Claire. She made the columns daily. London craved to know what events she attended, what she wore, even who her partners were for the waltz. He smiled ruefully. The Marchioness of Pembrooke was an unqualified success in her own right. It certainly wasn't because of him or their current marital status. Even though society knew they weren't living together, the reasons remained secret. Thankfully, no mention hit the scandal rags. Nor was there any mention of the curse.

He had to thank Somerton for getting him back to a functional state after the two-day drunken soiree he'd thrown for himself. When he had come out of his stupor, it didn't take long to decide on the necessary course to get his wife home. He planned to visit Langham Hall. He would meet Claire, apologize for the conversation she'd overheard, explain everything, and ask her to return home. He wouldn't rest until he held her in his arms again.

He should have seen her as soon as he had arrived in London. He'd wasted precious time feeling sorry for himself and trying to find a way to explain his actions. Now, he had the added burden of dealing with Lord Paul's contamination. Plus, he had to figure out what to do with Mr. Mills.

Thoughts of Claire caused his throat to tighten. She understood his grief for Alice. She had provided comfort when he'd realized Alice wasn't the person he'd thought he knew. Claire valued what was important to him—his family, Pemhill, and its tenants. Her personality and work ethic fit perfectly with his. She had made love to him unconditionally, and he'd let her go without a fight.

There was only one solution.

He'd win her back or die trying.

"Mr. Mills, the Marquess of Pembrooke to see you." A young maid had escorted Alex into the neat but modest study. She nearly collided with Alex in her haste to exit.

He waited for the inevitable effect his title would have on Jason Mills, who sat at a large oak desk surrounded by invoices and bookkeeping records. The maid's response was minuscule when compared with his reaction.

"My lord?" The sudden movement to stand toppled the desk chair Mills had occupied. His wary glance shot to Alex's hands.

There was so much he wanted to hear from the young man standing before him. Alex lifted his arms in peace and to prove he hadn't come with a weapon. Mills continued to stare at him, as if weighing whether he could be trusted. If only he did possess the truth, it would make the upcoming task easier. Jason Mills had been important to

Alice, and by the end of their visit, Alex hoped to have a better understanding of Alice through Mills.

"Won't you sit down?" The young man swallowed hard and set his chair to rights. The tentative nod of his head at the chair across from him was confirmation Alex had a monumental task ahead of him.

"Thank you." How could he get the young man to accept his condolences? How could both of them find some peace in Alice's passing after the way he had ordered Mills from his sight? "Please, I've come to talk, just talk."

Mills exhaled the breath he'd been holding.

"I'd like to make amends for the horrid way I treated you at Pemhill." He ran his hand through his hair, desperate to find a way to talk about Alice. "If it hadn't been for my wife, I don't know if either of us would be here today."

Mills' brows set in a straight line.

"I truly apologize for my behavior. Alice's death is still . . ."

"I'm certain you were as devastated as me over her death." A flicker of sadness crossed Mills' face. "Would you care for a brandy?"

That was the last thing Alex wanted or needed after the last several days. "No, thank you."

Mills nodded again. The pain in his eyes and the tightness in his lips were evidence his grief was still fresh. Alex exhaled as the pain slashed through his chest. If he lost Claire and could never see her again, he'd be destroyed. If Mills suffered such an ache of the heart, Alex vowed to do anything he could to help the young man. He bowed his head and studied his clasped hands in a feeble effort to hide the rawness of the moment.

"I'm here because of Alice," Alex said.

"I just can't believe she's gone." Mills leaned back in his chair. "Will you share with me her last days?" He focused on Alex as if he could find some type of relief through conversation. "Did she suffer?"

Alex blinked. Whether he should divulge the circumstances of Alice's suicide wasn't a question he'd considered. It would be akin to flaying the man alive, pure torture. "Not physically. She went to bed one evening and never woke."

"I should've never left her. Never gone abroad to make my fortune. At least I'd have been able to have more time with her."

"Tell me how you . . . came to know Alice?" Alex's eyes clouded with visions of the past—his sister strolling into the barn without a care in the world. Hours later, she'd emerge with her face glowing.

"I heard you paid double what the village blacksmith paid for a stable hand. After work, I'd come and do odd jobs for your stable master, hoping for an offer of employment. I met your sister my first week. She was determined to rescue a kitten from the upstairs hayloft." Mills' eyes misted. "I offered to help. I fell in love with her at first sight. She might still be alive if I hadn't—"

"Mills, I don't think either of us can second-guess our actions." God, he wished Claire had accompanied him. She would have known what to say to offer comfort. "Probably neither of us could have stopped Alice from making the same choice."

"What choice?" Mills' gaze pierced the distance between them.

He was at a loss as to how to proceed.

"My lord?"

Alex's breath shuddered through his body. The man deserved the truth. "Alice . . . Alice was pregnant and killed herself. She left me a note."

The creak of Mills' chair broke the silence, replaced

with a low, soulful rumble. "A child?" He buried his face in his hands. "What have I done? I killed her."

"No, you didn't," Alex whispered.

"You had every right to shoot me. God, I wish you had—"

"Jason, listen to me. I've had the same thoughts and blamed myself every conceivable way. There are no answers or explanations. It was Alice's choice."

The young man swallowed. "I wrote to her several times to share my travels. Each time I made a game of it and underlined the letters in the words 'I love you.' I couldn't risk you reading my letters for fear you'd see her married before I arrived home to her."

"Very clever of you." The corners of Alex's mouth tugged upward. "You had nothing to worry about. I was in no rush to see her married."

"I'd gladly exchange places with the devil if it would bring her back. I'd give up everything to see her safe and out of harm's way." A fragile trail of moisture drifted into a slow descent down Mills' face. "I loved her more than life itself."

Each word sliced another part of Alex's heart. Jason's heartfelt devotion to Alice was an epiphany. He'd do the same for Claire. He'd give up everything, too. However, would he have had the intelligence and grace to recognize such a truth without this conversation?

Determined to avenge Alice's death, he hadn't seen what was under his nose the entire time. Somerton's lectures and repudiations turned into revelations he had failed to heed. He was a damned arrogant fool. Somehow, the universe had aligned in such a way that he'd received the greatest boon and found relief from the daily pain. He'd found redemption. He'd found Claire.

He'd wasted so much time on his revenge. Time better

spent on trying to find a way to heal from the impact of Alice's death. Time better spent helping Daphne and his mother grieve. Time better spent on Claire and their marriage. Instead of destruction, he should have focused on nurturing and building their life together. He saw things clearer than he had for over a year.

There was only one reason for his change of heart.

He loved her. Every breath he tendered was dedicated to Claire. Without her in his life, everything surrounding him would be a barren wasteland. Losing her would make life meaningless.

That was what Mills had lost with Alice's death—a haunting devastation from which a man might never recover.

Mills stared at the ceiling, but the redness and the agony reflected in his eyes were seared in Alex's memory. "Alice made me become a better person by giving me her love. She had so much faith in me."

"You're lucky to have experienced such a gift." Alex's chest tightened, as if a rope were squeezing the very life from his body. Claire provided the same comfort to him. If he ever won her love, he'd never again lose sight of what they had together.

Mills exhaled as if defeated.

Alex crossed the distance between them and held out his hand. "But Alice was fortunate to have had you in her life. I know that now."

"Thank you, my lord."

"Let me help you. My friend Lord Somerton is a financial and investment wizard. He can introduce you to his colleagues and business partners. It'll make your path so much easier now that you're home. Please. Alice would have wanted me to lend whatever assistance I can."

In answer, Mills stood and stared at Alex's hand again, his weariness replaced by sorrow. "On one condition."

"Name it."

"May I go to Pemhill and pay my respects to my beloved?" Mills asked.

Alex's breath hitched and his eyes grew moist at the tenderness in Mills' voice. "I'll send word of your visit. Stay at Pemhill as long as you like."

"That's very kind."

"I have a condition also," Alex added.

Mills tilted his head and regarded him.

"I hope you see past my mistakes and consider me your friend."

It wasn't quite a smile, but Mills' expression lightened a bit as he nodded his head.

"Somerton will be expecting to hear from you." Alex shook Mills' hand. "One more thing before I take my leave. Thank you. You've taught me a great deal today."

His sister had loved this man. She'd been too young to face the situation of a child out of wedlock, and she'd not come to Alex for help. He'd not make the same mistake with Daphne. He'd devote more time to his sister and her interests.

The most important lesson was how much he loved Claire, his wife. She'd given him hope and the ability to love again. He would not waste another second on his pursuit of revenge. There were more important things to accomplish—namely, convincing her how much he cared for her and her happiness.

Later that day, Alex dressed with meticulous care before heading to Langham Hall. He would never circumvent Claire's interests again. She was his wife, and he'd beg her to come home.

Within minutes of his arrival, Pitts personally answered the door. The icy greeting should have foretold the reception he'd receive.

After Alex entered the yellow drawing room, he paced, waiting for Claire's entrance. He would not leave without convincing her how much he loved her.

After a short wait, the Duke of Langham entered, followed by Lord McCalpin and Lord William. Their expressions were as dark as their hair, while their blue eyes flashed with fury. The proceedings looked somewhat like a military parade—or, more accurately, a walk to the gallows.

He wasn't surprised at the welcome. "Good morning, Your Grace. I've come for Claire."

The first volley didn't take long. The Duke of Langham was a formidable man when riled. Alex had seen enough of his oratory skills within the House of Lords to expect anything from him—except a single right cut to the chin.

The blow leveled him.

Momentarily stunned, Alex got up on all fours and shook his head to clear his peripheral vision. When he found his legs, he acknowledged his due by not defending himself. Langham took another swing, a straight hit to his abdomen. The punch knocked the wind from his lungs.

As Alex gasped for breath, Langham finally addressed him. "Did you think to use my niece, a Cavensham, without repercussions? Pembrooke, even you can surmise you've worn out your welcome. Pitts will see you out."

In a harsh, throaty whisper, Alex wheezed, "Your Grace, I've come to see my wife and take her home." He'd be damned if he'd leave without Claire.

Without hesitation, the duke grabbed him by the cravat and punched again, landing the hit square on the left side of his face.

Alex's head snapped backward. When he got his bearings, his face was numb. The metallic taste of iron seeped into his mouth.

"*Sebastian, stop,*" the duchess cried as she ran into the drawing room and grabbed her husband's arm.

"Ginny, he'll not speak to her." The duke's voice exploded across the room.

With the celestial dance center stage in his vision, Alex looked up and a vision of Claire floated in front of his eyes. For an instant, he forgot to breathe. She was more beautiful than he remembered. If he could touch her face with his hand for a moment, he'd die without regret. He took his handkerchief and wiped the blood from his mouth. He shook his head in an attempt to clear the jumble from his brain.

His eyes held hers as he addressed her while ignoring the others. "Claire. I'm sorry . . ." He stopped to swallow the blood in his mouth. "May we talk in private?"

The duke roared, "Ginny, get her away. Now!"

Claire stepped forward. "Alex?" Her voice softened and worry outlined her eyes. It was a sign from heaven.

"Now!" the duke demanded.

All hope drained as the duchess escorted Claire out of the room. When Alex flinched, the entire left side of his face felt as if it had fallen off. This was a harder challenge than he had anticipated.

The duke put a decisive end to Alex's misery. "Pembrooke, I take this personally. I encouraged Claire to marry you."

Alex cleared the blood from his throat once more. He ached to whisper, let alone speak at a volume the duke could hear. "With all due respect, she's my wife."

The duke's fury was still high as he shouted, "You'll not see her after you managed to make a bloody blunder of the whole affair. I have my solicitors looking at every section, every sentence, and every word of the settlements for legal action against you. If she doesn't want to have anything to do with you, I'll support her wherever she lives. She's no longer your responsibility." And without another word, the duke stormed from the room.

The day didn't improve once he focused on McCalpin and Lord William. He waited for whatever sentence they planned to execute. When the silence lasted too long for his taste, Alex asked, "I assume you want to have a go at me, too?"

"Pembrooke, we let our father have the first swing." McCalpin's voice was low. "Even though I won a tidy sum off that bet at White's, you tried to sully my cousin and family. I should tear you limb from limb, then feed you to my dogs. I won't kill you. But I guarantee you'll wish I had."

Lord William was much more vicious in thought and deed than his brother. "When he's done, I'll take great pleasure in what I have in store for you. I'll drag your sorry arse to McCalpin's estate for the night. I'm sure it will be described as self-defense."

Both took their leave without a look back. His treatment from the Cavensham family was not surprising, but he hadn't thought Langham would refuse to allow him to see Claire. If he could have had her in a room without their interference, he'd have convinced her to come home.

In order to win his wife's favor once again, he had to see her. Perhaps he needed to study the daily papers in greater detail. He'd have to start attending balls and other events. It was fortuitous he lived in proximity to Langham Hall. It would make it easier to keep watch.

Leaving Alex lying on the floor was one of the hardest things she'd done in her life. The urge to rush to his side and tend his wounds almost overpowered her. But if she had, Uncle Sebastian's anger would have erupted into even more violence. It was doubtful that Alex could have withstood much more of her uncle's wrath.

There had been a large amount of blood on his face and waistcoat. His breath had been short and labored. What if his ribs were broken? Claire choked with worry as she tried to catch a glimpse out the window. Alex exited the house and looked toward the second floor. Claire didn't move an inch, though he didn't know where her room was. Alex looked straight at her and sent her a swollen, lopsided grin.

An arm slipped around her waist. Emma pulled her tight against her and squeezed. "Your husband is still handsome, even if some of his face looks scrambled. At least his nose wasn't broken."

"Do you think he's all right?"

"Hmm, I think so. He walked out of the house without assistance." Emma led her into the attached sitting room. "Shall we go shopping? For books," she quickly added.

"Another time, perhaps." Claire would never admit it to another, but she was thrilled he had come for her. Alex's gesture in coming to Langham Hall must mean he felt at least something. However, the sole person she fooled was herself. She was the only one who had considered theirs a true marriage.

McCalpin and William stood when they entered. McCalpin took Claire's hand in his. "He'll be fine."

She broke away and walked to the window for a last look. William joined her and followed her gaze. He tipped her chin up and forced her to look into his deep blue eyes. "Tell me what you want, and I'll see it done. He'll not hurt you again."

"That's just it. I'm not certain what I want, but I'll not have him physically harmed." She studied all three of her cousins' faces.

"Claire," William chided. "You're such a spoilsport."

"Let's go to Hailey's Hope. I purchased a copy of Captain Cook's journal about his first voyage around the world." Emma tugged at Claire's arm. "Mr. Napier asked that I bring it and *you* the next time I visited. You could use a little fresh air, don't you think?"

McCalpin took Claire's other arm. "We'll join you."

Within a quarter hour, the quartet walked through the charity's large wooden doors. The incessant tension left Claire briefly as she enjoyed her time with the residents. She concentrated on their news and pushed aside all thoughts of Alex and the meaning of his visit to Langham Hall.

William never left her side. Determined she would enjoy her time, he told stories of their childhood exploits to the residents. The laughter grew in volume until McCalpin and Emma appeared to see what the commotion was all about. They quickly joined the group and tried to upstage Will.

Claire managed to slip away and worked on the letters asking for donations for the children's home. A knock at the door broke her concentration. Will leaned against the doorway with a smile of approval. A quick glance at the clock left her speechless. For two hours, she had been lost in her work.

"Thank you, William," she said. "I needed the time here today."

"Always a pleasure to have your company." He tilted his head. "My stories didn't drive you away, did they?"

She exhaled a long sigh of contentment. "On the contrary. They reminded me of all the great memories I've acquired since coming to live with you and your family."

"You love him?" William was never one to be tentative.

Her answer was a nod. It was all she could manage.

"There must be something redeeming about him, then."

When she returned home, Claire sent Aileen to Aunt Ginny with the message that she would not attend this evening's social entertainment. What little respite she had claimed at the charity, she didn't want to waste on another London ball.

She'd wanted to savor the time with her family. Any peacefulness she'd experienced from her visit to Hailey's Hope would flee once she prepared for sleep. Alex would no doubt consume her thoughts again.

Chapter Thirteen

The next morning Alex followed Claire to Rotten Row, but he took the long way around the park. The extra time allowed him to organize his apology. The opportunity was precious since there would be little chance her family would interfere.

He took a deep breath in readiness, then urged Ares forward toward the bridle path. But when the park came into full view, he was brought to a standstill by the unexpected sight before him. On horseback, Claire was animated as she talked to Lord Paul.

With wariness, Alex emerged from the mist. With a sharp turn of the reins, Claire took flight, with Charles beside her. Alex's leg twitched in readiness to spur Ares to gallop after her, but his priorities instantly changed. Why was she with him?

Alex felt the flinch of his jaw and delivered a hard, cold glare as he approached Lord Paul. His bruised face, a souvenir from his visit at Langham Hall, should lend a hint of menace to the confrontation.

Lord Paul took his time and looked Alex over from head to toe. "Nine shades of blue. Souvenir from your lady wife? Those colors are altogether dashing and a vast improvement over your normal visage."

"Stay away from my wife."

Lord Paul laughed, but the ragged sound held little humor. "Your wife prefers my company to yours. Some things never change." He tilted his head, then sidled his skittish horse closer. "Pembrooke, you should have never manipulated my life, or Claire's. You're the one who'll pay with a lifetime of misery."

If Lord Paul knew the full extent of Alex's wretchedness, he'd be satisfied with the result. "What's happened in the past can't be changed. Let's move forward—" The words fused together in Alex's throat. He clenched a fist and forced himself to continue. "I've received news that made me realize that I misjudged what happened with Alice. I misconstrued what happened between the two of you."

"Is that why my vowels were returned to me?" The smirk on his face didn't hide the flash of anguish in his eyes. "You think that gesture puts everything to rights?"

"No." He owed Lord Paul more than a curt reply, but it was damned difficult. "The deed to Willow House will be returned to you by the end of the day."

"My, my, someone's getting their house in order. Unfortunately, you always did come to parties late." The morning sun lent a malevolent expression to Lord Paul's face. "I asked your wife to come and live with me the other night at Lady Barrington's. We were discussing the details this morning."

"I don't believe you." To even consider such a revolting outcome made every nerve in his body stand at attention. He'd fight to the bitter end and still not give her up.

"Do everyone a favor and petition Parliament for a divorce. I'll marry her and give her the life she's always wanted. I'll even help by telling everyone she's my lover.

With both our fathers' ducal lineage, we'll withstand any scandal." His eyes bored into Alex's with a gravity seldom seen. "Within two years, we'll be on top of the social world, any disgrace long forgotten."

The solemn sincerity in his face caused an anger to explode inside Alex. "We'll meet in hell first before I'll allow that to happen. Perhaps we should just settle this on a field somewhere."

"As you taught me earlier, I'd much rather see you suffer long and hard." Lord Paul pulled his gloves tight.

"If you think I'll allow you close to my wife, you have a bed in Bedlam waiting for you."

"Watch me." Lord Paul allowed his white gelding to canter down the path. With a quick pull on the reins, he reeled the horse around and returned to face Alex. "When you started down this path, you dug my grave. I hope you dug another. You'll need it more than me." With a tip of his hat, Lord Paul was gone from Alex's sight.

The filth of Lord Paul's words washed over him. He let out the breath he was holding. God, what if there was a kernel of truth in his statement? He didn't want to think of the consequences if Claire wanted a life with Lord Paul.

Claire brought Hermes to an abrupt stop, took a deep breath, and hid in a small grove of trees. Her life had fallen into a well of emptiness. One man wanted her for a lover. Another had wanted her as a wife, as long as she served her purpose in avenging a wrong done to his family. For her own preservation, she had to escape Lord Paul and not yield to the tears that demanded release.

The sound of the chirping birds brought a moment's diversion before she accepted the inevitable truth. There was no denying it: She loved Alex and would never be free from wanting him. The loneliness threatened to swallow her whole.

Her chest tightened, and a small sob escaped. She had a difficult time catching her breath. One sob turned into another. The perfidious things turned into hiccups, and her whole world fell into the absurd. One last desperate sob dared to escape from inside before turning into an anguished, pitiful laugh. The sorrowful sound garnered more laughs until she found herself in a fit of hysterical laughter. She bent over Hermes in an attempt to lessen the pain in her chest. Unable to control her emotions, she slid off the horse and collapsed in a heap on the short grass.

When she moved to stand, the sound of Alex's voice startled her. "Claire, what in bloody hell are you doing?"

"Alex?" Where had he come from? She wiped the tears from her face with her gloves. The soft leather provided little comfort. In her haste to stand, her boot caught on the edge of her riding habit, and she stumbled. Falling face first, Claire waited for the hard impact of the ground that never came. Instead, she found herself in his arms. Her world righted itself as she felt the safety of his embrace. It was heaven until she looked at his face.

His gaze raked up and down her body before it shifted to her eyes. His face turned red, darkening the bruises on his left cheek. Claire automatically stepped away.

"Are you considering his offer?" His eyes flashed like the fury of an unleashed storm.

"Who?"

"Lord Paul." His nostrils flared, and his body stiffened. "I will not give you a divorce."

"No. I would never dishonor you or our families in that way." All of her emotions swirled in an anger that made their confrontation at Pemhill look tame. "It's inexcusable to accuse me of behavior that is indicative of you."

Momentarily stunned, Alex locked eyes with hers. "What are you referring to, madam?"

Claire bristled with indignation. "Lying, cheating,

conniving . . . Need I go on? Our marriage is based upon nothing but your deception and need for retribution."

A shadow of alarm crossed his face, and his demeanor calmed. Slowly, he approached her.

"Is that what you think? Everything at Pemhill was dishonest?" His voice was eerily quiet.

Her vexation scattered like a covey of partridges when set upon by a huntsman. Words and thoughts tumbled from her lips. "Those few weeks at Pemhill were my dream come true. I so wanted that life." She gave a stilted laugh to keep her tears from betraying her anguish.

He shook his head, denying her words. "Claire, listen to me. You misunderstood."

"I trusted you with so much. Pieces of my soul and heart I gave to you and no one else." She swallowed. The birds sang as if encouraging her to continue. "Secrets I told no one but you because . . ." *I love you.* She couldn't say it. Wary, she let her voice trail to nothing. "It mattered little. All you wanted was to ruin Lord Paul."

At Pemhill, she had never wanted to share so much of herself with anyone before, and look what she had received for her efforts. She was married to a man who had orchestrated their entire betrothal and marriage without her knowing the truth. At least she'd kept some of her secrets, the ones too shameful to share.

"I don't know what this is between us anymore." She took a deep breath so she could finish. "I thought I knew, but now with the revelations . . ."

He recoiled slightly, as if her words had truly hurt him. "Claire, stop."

With every ounce of strength she possessed, she looked into his eyes. "I was only important to you as a weapon to use against your enemy. If you desired our marriage to build your landholdings and fortune, I could have accepted your reasons." She sniffled even though it was unladylike.

"People of our class marry for those arrangements all the time." She grimaced and blinked so the tears would subside. "I was such a ninny. I thought our life was more than financial considerations. It's even worse. Our marriage is based upon hate and revenge."

"My actions were never meant to hurt you." His hand cupped her cheek. "At Pemhill, we were building our life. We were working on our future and the future of our family. Weren't you happy?" The low cadence of his voice coaxed her nearer.

"Yes, but for how long?" Her blood pounded while her face heated. "How many times have I trusted other men and lost?" She closed her eyes and shook her head in an effort to shed her confusion and humiliation. "Always before, I managed to make myself whole when I was torn apart. I don't know if I can endure it this time."

He brought his face closer to hers, blocking everything from sight except the intensity of his eyes. "Please, I'm going mad. I can't sleep or think anymore. Why were you with him?" His voice faded, losing its edge.

"I turned around and Lord Paul was there. Ask Charles if you don't believe me." As a fresh wave of courage bolstered her resolve, Claire stepped aside. "He's playing you, and you're allowing it."

"You're wrong. If I believed him, I wouldn't be here." He ran his hand over his face and grimaced when he touched the bruises.

Involuntarily she lifted her hand to offer comfort, then drew back. "Does it hurt?"

He gave a laugh, the humor never reaching his eyes. "That's not what causes me pain." After a long pause, during which he seemed to wrestle with his self-control, he spoke in an odd but gentle tone, as if he were coaxing a child. "Let's go back to Langham Hall and pack. I want to take you home."

His simple request unleashed the frustration that had lodged itself within her feelings of helplessness. "Do you hear yourself? Never once have you tried to explain your actions or apologize for what you have done. You cannot see the error of your ways. Are you so arrogant to think I'll return to Pemhill because of what you want?" She tried to swallow her annoyance, to stay civil, but it refused to desert her. "I don't know what I want anymore. But I'm going to try and find it here in London."

He lifted her chin, and for one moment her heart cried out in elation. He was going to kiss her. "Let me make this right between us. Give me a chance."

Caught off guard by the vibrancy in his words, Claire waited for his lips to meet hers; then reason came to the rescue and she turned her head. The jangle of a bridle broke the spell between them. Charles sat on his horse, holding Hermes's reins. The young man must have had ample time to witness the exchange. With a bright red face, he dismounted without looking at either of them.

Alex found his voice first. "Have a care. Do not leave the marchioness's side while she's in town. Help her mount."

Then he leaned toward her and whispered in her ear, "This will not stand, my lady wife."

With assistance from Charles, Claire took her seat. Her double-crossing heart faltered in admiration as Alex swung into the saddle with a refined skill that few men possessed.

With a single nudge, she fled the park as if Cerberus, the hound from the netherworld, was nipping at her heels. She never looked back.

Claire caught the sweet scent of roses that hung heavy in the air. Pitts guarded the entry with a large arrangement of at least fifty roses with blooms a riot of pink and red.

Aunt Ginny didn't hide her admiration. "My word,

Pitts, I've never seen so many different hues. Is that for Lady Emma?"

"No, Your Grace. This arrangement is Lady Pembrooke's, along with this parcel." Pitts handed the box and card directly into Claire's hands. "Delivered with the arrangement, my lady."

The card bore her title, written in Alex's masculine signature. She took a deep breath of the roses' sweet fragrance and tucked the memory away for later. "Pitts, would you have a footman deliver them to my room? Thank you."

He nodded and headed below stairs to see the task carried out.

Claire looked at the roses for several moments. They were spectacular, potent with fragrance and deep in color. The bouquet's colors spoke of passion, desire, and admiration. At least, she hoped it was not her imagination galloping away.

Her aunt whispered, "Take the box upstairs to open it. There's no need to upset Sebastian again. Later, you mustn't forget to tell me what's in it. I won't ask about the card." An understanding grin tugged at the corners of her mouth.

Claire ran to her bedroom. After the roses arrived, she locked the door. Taking one more smell of the fragrant bouquet, she sat at the window ledge. She opened the card, and her heart skipped a beat. His scent surrounded her when she pulled the note out of the envelope.

Forgive me. A

Instead of opening the small box immediately, she felt the weight of it in her hands. Slowly, she untied the ribbon that held it closed and opened the top. Inside was a dark blue velvet bag. She tipped the contents and gasped when a beautiful thistle brooch made of pink sapphires and diamonds set in gold fell into her hands. The fire from the gems made the entire room sparkle.

With reverence, she replaced the pin in its velvet case. Claire turned the events over in her mind and kept coming back to the same question. Why was he doing this? His actions toward Lord Paul and his insistence she return to Pemhill were not what she had expected. If he thought a bouquet and a piece of jewelry would erase the pain he'd caused her, he was more arrogant than she thought.

Her treacherous heart kept its steady beat, coaxing her to examine his actions more closely. Could she dare hope he might truly want her? Perhaps he realized the truth of her words that he needed to make amends. She fought the argument pounding for attention.

If their marriage had any chance of success, she'd be the one to take all the risk.

Claire grew tired of living in a permanent fog of misery. She needed a day trip, a short jaunt to see the countryside and smell the fresh air. It held the possibility of alleviating her mood, or at least putting some distance from her troubles.

She squinted at the bright sun in the sky as Charles assisted her into the curricle. A gentle, cooling breeze caught the bonnet ribbons tied under her chin and made them dance.

"Are you ready, my lady?" Charles played with the reins and sat on the edge of the seat.

The excitement of seeing an old friend made her anxious to start. "Yes. I'm ready." A sharp tug from the horses, and the vehicle lurched forward.

After an hour, she arrived at a small but well-kept cottage close to the outskirts of Leyton. Claire studied the pastoral setting with its beautiful gardens and green fields. She breathed the fresh scent of the country and immediately missed the tranquility of Pemhill.

"Charles, why don't you go to the inn for lunch? You may come back at three to collect me."

"Very good, my lady." He waited for Claire to receive an answer to her knock.

Before the cottage door fully opened, Lucy Porter's face beamed with joy. "Oh, my goodness, Lady Claire! You're a sight for sore eyes, you are. Come in." The petite woman called into the small house, "Uncle Roger, you'll never guess who's here to pay a visit!" When she realized she'd left Claire standing, Lucy exclaimed, "Come in this instant. Oh, my lady, if I'd known you were coming, I'd have made tea."

Claire gave the woman a big hug. "Lucy, I'm not intruding, am I? I wanted to escape from the city for a day."

Lucy's eyes glowed with laughter. "Uncle Roger will be delighted to keep you to himself."

After a quick nod to Charles that signaled he was free to go, Claire entered and took off her bonnet. She carried a basket she'd brought from Langham Hall and placed it on the table. "Here are some things Cook gathered for Mr. Jordon. His favorites, including those cheese scones he'd sneak to me if I turned up my nose at dinner."

A voice called from another room, "Lucy, is that Lady Claire come to visit? Bring her in!"

Claire hurried into the study, not waiting for Lucy. Her old friend stood before her. He tilted his head in an attempt to locate her approach. Claire extended her hand and squeezed his.

"Mr. Jordon, here I am." Claire finally felt some peace as she greeted her family's retired butler. Roger Jordon had held the position for three of the Dukes of Langham. He had served for forty-eight years before his failing eyesight forced him to retire. He received a solid retirement from the Cavensham family for loyal service, but Claire supplemented his income.

"My lady, please sit. I got a letter from Pitts that announced you'd married. I want to hear the news." Jordon's deep baritone still brought a smile to Claire's face.

Lucy came in with a small tray with tea and the fresh cheese scones. "My lady, will you pour? I'm late for an appointment at the village. I'm tempted to stay with you, but I hate to cancel on the dressmaker. I may never get another frock if she takes offense."

"Go ahead, and take your time. We'll be right here when you return."

"Uncle Roger, be on your best behavior. I'll return soon." Lucy's voice stayed in the air as she rushed out the door.

Claire turned to her friend, and the warm feelings of nostalgia rushed forward. "How are you?"

His eyes were bright, and he still held a butler's posture. However, his movements were stiff when he sat. He'd aged quite a bit over the last year. It took a few minutes for him to settle. "I'm well and happy. I enjoy my life and especially enjoy the visits from you." His warm smile brightened the room and her mood. He'd always been a true friend when she needed one the most.

Claire spent the next four hours telling him about her family and the details of their lives. She spoke of her marriage to Alex but left out their estrangement. There was no use upsetting the gentle man. She shared everything that had occurred during her visit to Wrenwood. He clasped both of her hands when she told the tale, giving her strength to share the experience.

A slow catharsis built from their conversation. She owed him everything. The visits did more for her than she imagined they did for him. Before she realized how much time had passed, Charles knocked at the door. Claire said her good-byes and promised to return soon.

On their way out of town, Claire stopped at the solicitor's office. The firm of Fitzsimmons and Walters handled her affairs for Mr. Jordon. She asked Mr. Fitzsimmons to keep a watchful eye on Mr. Jordon and Lucy. If their needs exceeded the yearly allowance, Claire wanted to know immediately. She could never repay the man for staying by her side after the accident. If Claire had it within her power, she would make certain he never wanted for a thing.

Chapter Fourteen

❧

At the crack of dawn, Alex received a missive from Macalester. Brief, it contained the address and name of the man Claire had visited in Leyton. A former housekeeper named Lucy Porter owned the cottage. Retired from a position in the Duke of Southart's household, she would have been well acquainted with Southart's second son, Lord Paul. The housekeeper's elderly uncle, Roger Jordon, lived with her. He was the connection to his wife, as Jordon had served as butler for the previous Duke of Langham, Claire's father.

The news that there was a connection to Lord Paul burned more than if he'd been run through with a saber, but he refused to let the torment paralyze him. Too much was at stake to wallow in self-pity and doubts again. On his own in London, he'd had many occasions to think of Claire and Alice. He'd idealized his sister and thought her completely innocent, but he'd done the exact opposite with Claire. He'd allowed his doubts to dictate his actions.

Posthaste, Alex ordered Ares, mounted, and departed for Leyton.

His jaw set, he stood in front of the small, well-kept cottage and made a vow he'd not rest until he'd uncovered every secret hidden inside. More important, he'd not let Claire go without a fight. Mills had made him realize how much he loved her. He had to convince her and bring her home.

With a brisk knock, Alex waited until a maid answered. She made him wait outside while she ducked behind the door to confer with her employer. Alex couldn't hear the conversation, but he heard a deep baritone voice rumble. The maid returned and escorted Alex to a closed door.

"My lord, Mr. Jordon is waiting in the study. If you need anything, please ring."

A tall, elderly gentleman grasped the desk with his hands and cocked his head. His eyes were clear but didn't rest on Alex. He looked out the window.

Alex crossed the room and stood in front of the desk. "I'm Lord Pembrooke. If you'd be so kind, I'd like a few minutes of your time."

The man continued to look out the only window in the room without facing Alex. With a slight bow of his head, Mr. Jordon extended his hand. "My lord, please sit down. If I may be so bold, it took you long enough to find me. I believe you and I have a lot in common."

When the old man continued to tilt his head without a direct look, Alex realized Jordon was blind. "You received a visit from my wife yesterday. I beg your pardon if I appear disrespectful, but I'm curious about your relationship and the reason for her visit."

Mr. Jordon laughed with glee. "My lord, it would be my pleasure. I don't get to extol the virtues of Lady Claire, I mean Lady Pembrooke, often enough. You have a remarkable and generous wife, a true Cavensham both in looks and, more importantly, in spirit and charity. If her father were alive today, I'm certain he'd be the proudest papa in all of England. No doubt he's one of the proudest in heaven." Reflecting for a moment, Jordon continued, "He loved that child, as did her mother. I was blessed to have been able to serve their family."

Before Alex could comment, Jordon continued, "You'll have to ask Lady Pembrooke why she came yesterday."

The man's arrogance was unexpected. Alex caught himself and refrained from answering with a cutting retort. Since Claire had come into his life, it seemed easier to get what he wanted if he stayed calm, though it was damned difficult sometimes. "Sir, help me understand. Who exactly are you?"

"I was the butler for the family when the fourth duke, Lady Pembrooke's grandfather, was alive. After his passing, the fifth duke, Lady Pembrooke's father, kept me on. I traveled with the family from estate to estate. Wrenwood became a favorite because of Lady Pembrooke's mother. It's where the duke and duchess met and fell in love."

Alex relaxed. He'd share a little information with the old man and see what he got in return. "After Lady Pembrooke and I married, we arrived at Pemhill for a short visit. Wrenwood holds a lot of memories for her." Alex believed there was no reason to tell the man how Claire fell apart.

Mr. Jordon looked directly into Alex's face as if able to divine the truth.

Alex held firm without a word. He waited to see if the old man would share his secrets. He wouldn't leave without answers.

The butler raised his nose in the air to take Alex's measure, then nodded his head. "You'll have to ask *Lady Pembrooke* your questions. I'll not betray a friend's confidences."

"Is my wife in trouble? Why does she give you money?" Alex ran a hand through his hair, and the questions tumbled from his mouth. "Did the Langham family not settle enough funds at the end of your service?"

Jordon practically growled at Alex. "My lord, I was with your wife when her parents died. That is the connection. She comes to visit on occasion."

Alex changed the tenor of the visit, as he was getting nothing from the conversation. "Mr. Jordon, please. I'm trying to help my wife."

The old butler raised an eyebrow.

Alex scrubbed a hand over his face and exhaled loudly. "The truth is I need help."

"I understand Lady Pembrooke visited Wrenwood alone. I hope you won't allow that to happen again." Jordon relaxed his posture and continued, "My lord, I assume she's never told you what she went through when her parents died?"

The old man held Claire in high esteem. There was something dignified and chivalrous in his tone when he talked about her.

"No, not yet. She's addressed the tragedy in general but not in detail."

"I don't know what troubles lie between you and Lady Claire, but the hesitation in your voices when you speak of the other tells me neither of you is comfortable in your marriage."

Alex had no choice but to confide in the impertinent old man. Otherwise he would get nowhere. "Claire and I have not had what one would call a smooth start because of my actions and attitude. I want to make amends but need help to know how . . ." Alex exhaled. "I need to bring her home."

"She's a rare gift." The butler waited, then laced his hands and placed them on the desk.

The old man surprised him. Jordon bowed his head and shook it before looking straight into Alex's eyes. "What that child went through would cause a grown man to lose his mind. But it's best if it comes from her."

Alex stood. It was time to leave and gather his thoughts. "I won't take up any more of your time, sir."

"Wait, my lord. There's a final issue to discuss. You're correct about the money. Even though the Langham family was generous to me, your wife provides me with one hundred and fifty pounds a year. I'm not certain why she does it, but it's appreciated."

Alex raised his eyebrows. This was an unexpected confession. The man obviously suffered guilt from taking the money.

"I keep the money in an account. After I die, I've given instructions all moneys are to pass to Lady Claire's children. I've never spent a shilling. If she believes she owes me something, she's wrong. I'm the one that owes the debt to her." The old man chuckled to himself. "She continues to provide me with her company and acts as if she enjoys visiting with an old man."

Alex took Mr. Jordon's hand in his own. "I'm pleased you feel that way. She is a gift. One I do not deserve. But one I'll attempt to earn every day by my actions toward her."

Mr. Jordon struggled as he stood, his bones creaking. "I want to see her happy."

Emotion tightened around Alex's throat like a garrote, but he continued. "As do I. Thank you. I want you to have the annuity Claire started on your behalf. Only, I want to provide it. Think of it as one man's payment of a debt to another. You kept my wife safe and sound until she went to live with her uncle, the Duke of Langham, and the duke, in turn, did the same for me. I can never repay either of you what I owe. Please keep the money."

"I'm glad you understand." Mr. Jordon bowed his head.

Something horrid had happened to his wife, and he was desperate to find out. Even though he was indignant with the elderly butler, he recognized loyalty. Jordon loved

Claire and would protect her at all costs. Witnessing the hurt and devastation on Jordon's face, he realized that the tragedy still haunted this man. If it haunted an elderly man, it would not be hard to imagine the magnitude of its impact on Claire.

Alex took his leave and made it back to his town house in record time. Nothing would stop him from seeing her tonight. He'd examined the paper and his invitations for any society events that might draw her interest. The only one was a mind-numbing musicale presentation at the Martins' home. Alex was fairly confident Claire was at Langham Hall. The unknown was how he would reach her.

He instructed Jean-Claude to prepare a bath. He dressed in dark, comfortable clothes and a long black cloak perfect for a night when he wanted to stay hidden.

After a short walk to Langham Hall through the back alleys, Alex waited outside the mews until the house grew dark and its occupants settled for the evening. His need to see Claire overpowered any normal sense of propriety. As the night stilled, he studied the structure. At all costs, he had to avoid Pitts raising the alarm. One go-around with the Duke of Langham was enough for any man.

Claire's room was on the second floor, close to the family wing. He noted the individual balconies that framed the windows. At the far end of the building, closest to the alley, a single window stood open. The ivy growing on the brick was thick and deep but wouldn't hold his weight. Another solution was directly above him. An easily climbable oak tree stood guard over Claire's quarters.

He made quick work of the bottom branch. The climb up presented little challenge, as he angled his way to Claire's window using the lower branches as stairs. His final step rested on the balustrade outside her window. With one jump, he swung his legs over and landed on the balcony.

With silent movements, he entered through the window and found his reward, Claire asleep and safely nestled in a giant bed in a small alcove to his left. Quietly, Alex brought a chair next to the bed and closed the drapes that framed the arched opening of the recess. He shrugged out of his cloak and coat, then removed his boots.

Careful not to wake her, Alex leaned over and placed a gentle kiss on the top of her forehead. He'd not leave until he discovered all her secrets. With care, he relaxed into a comfortable position in the chair next to her and felt the heaviness of the past several weeks start to lift from his shoulders.

Through the haze of sleep, Claire opened her eyes to discover a person sleeping in a chair next to her bed. The distinctive tilt of his head resting against the back of the chair proved it was Alex.

He moaned a protest and settled deeper into the chair. It was unlikely Aileen had let him in. Since they'd arrived in London, she'd only said his name with a curse under her breath. Claire scooted closer for a better look at his sleeping form.

Alex's breathing broke the stillness of the night. Sound asleep, he sat in the chair, his long legs stretched out. Shadows played along his face, making him appear younger and vulnerable.

When she had overheard his conversation with Somerton and he'd acknowledged his past actions, Claire didn't know if she'd ever be able to put his deception aside and forgive him. Her breathing grew shallow at the thought of giving up Alex and a family. In the short time they'd been married, he'd become so interwoven in her life, it would be difficult to ever forget him. He'd given her a glimpse of what she could become. She was a whole person when she was with him—not some empty soul because of grief.

He'd been kind and playful when he could have ignored her. He had protected her and given her refuge when she'd needed a retreat from the world. He'd told her over and over that he didn't believe in the curse. When they were together in bed, he'd made her feel emotions she'd never imagined. She became attractive, wanted, and desirable—all because of him.

Sometimes she daydreamed that she and Alex would have had a better chance for love if her parents were still alive and active at Wrenwood, but nothing productive ever came from would-haves. She'd wasted enough time through the years thinking of scenarios that might have occurred if she'd received a different hand from fate.

She sighed gently and left the bed to gaze at the quiet street below. Alex's sense of honor for his family drove every decision he made. By his actions, it was clear she was not a part of his decision making, nor was she a part of his family.

A gentle breeze stirred the air, and she sensed him move behind her. His arms were warm as he encircled her from behind and looked out the window. Much like the night at Lady Anthony's ball, he brought his mouth to her ear. He surrounded her, and she shivered at the touch.

"Claire, come to bed. I didn't mean to wake you. I had to see you." He kissed the side of her cheek, then slowly trailed his lips down. "I've missed this." The whisper of his lips against her skin caused her to swallow. "I've missed you."

"Did someone let you in?" She cleared her throat and tried to step away, but he held her close. "How did you get here?"

"No one let me in. I climbed the tree outside. Stay in my arms for a moment. You're cold."

For an instant she was at a loss when he loosened his embrace, but she realized he'd made the effort so she wouldn't feel trapped. "Why are you here?"

"The sky looked dark earlier, and I thought you might need me."

That nonsense caused her to step away and examine his face. The past day had brandished a rare blue sky with lots of sunshine. "The sky is filled with stars."

"The weather can be so fickle." He bent his head and rubbed his neck as he twisted it from side to side. "That chair isn't a fit bed for a dog, let alone a man my size."

His grin, sweet and endearing, made her catch her breath. For a moment, she was back at Pemhill—back to the life she wanted and the husband she'd always desired. She shook her head to clear the image. Her life had taken a different path.

"You're still shivering. Let's get you to bed."

"You're changing the subject." She crossed her arms.

He tugged one of her hands free and led her to bed. "I'll gladly converse on any subject you choose for as long as you'd like, but first things first." He rearranged the bed linens and efficiently got her settled. With a couple of tucks, he was apparently satisfied with his handiwork and sat on the edge of the bed with one long leg bent at the knee, resting on top of the duvet and the other propped on the floor. He took both of her hands in his. The darkness didn't conceal the penetrating brightness of his eyes. He searched her face as if he could reach inside and gather her every thought.

"I should go, but for the first time since you left Pemhill I feel content." His gentle gaze didn't hide his vulnerability. "I love you."

Her breath caught at his words. Wasn't this what she had wanted all along? Alex to come and proclaim his love? "Are you saying that so I'll let you in my bed?"

He tilted his head and regarded her. "No, of course not. We should talk first."

She pressed her eyes closed. At Pemhill, she had waited

to ask him to come to her bed and lost precious time with her husband. She'd been afraid of the risk. What about now? If there was a chance they could heal the chasm between them, she needed to meet him halfway. She needed to allow him in her bed and her heart. The hardness of his thigh brushing against hers through the bed linens didn't hide his heat or the shivers of want that rippled through her. "We can talk in the morning."

She threw back the layers he'd so carefully tucked around her and held out her hand. A ravenous need spiraled through her and spread a fire straight to her heart. He belonged in her bed.

With ease, he slid next to her and pulled her into his arms. The strength and beauty of him never ceased to amaze her. She leaned into his touch. The intangible bond between them may have taken a pounding, but it was still a force that could not be ignored. Chest to chest, legs to legs, his touch encircled her. It had been so long since he'd held her. His familiar scent reminded her of home.

When he'd said he loved her, everything else had diminished in importance—their unease with each other, even the curse. Tomorrow could wait. Tonight she wanted her husband.

Alex gently gripped her hip and pulled her body flush with his. She offered no resistance and even helped his efforts.

"I'm happy you're here." Her voice had grown soft.

"As am I." He pulled back slightly and kissed her cheek. He caressed her neck with his mouth once again, taking time to gently nip the tender skin beneath her jaw, then soothe it with a kiss. "You need comfort, and I need to give it to you, Claire."

She cupped his head in her hands and made love to his mouth—tasting and teasing his tongue with hers until they both moaned. Never before had she felt so open or vulnerable to another human being.

He broke the kiss and captured her gaze with his. "You're breathtaking in the moonlight. Your skin shines with a luster only the finest South Sea pearls could dare mimic."

With a reverent kiss to her forehead, he clasped one of her hands with his. He pressed a kiss to her palm, then placed her hand over his heart.

Burning for another taste, she took his mouth again. He seemed as desperate for her as she was for him. His hands pushed into her hair and cradled her head as he pulled her harder against him. His tongue explored her mouth, but she conquered his if the moans and grunts were any indication. Their kiss never stopped, as if both of them were famished for each other. He broke away, his breath coming hard. Never taking her eyes off his, she pulled at his shirt, signaling she wanted him rid of it. He stood, and with one tug his shirt flew over his head, exposing his bare skin. He stripped out of his trousers, then climbed back to her, offering himself for her pleasure. He was hers to caress.

Unhurried, she slid her hands down his chest, and his muscles contracted in response to her sure touch. She pressed her mouth to one of his nipples, then nipped it. He hissed and his jaw tightened. She trailed her fingers through the fine curls on his chest, and just before she reached his groin, she repeated the pattern. The growl that escaped him caused her to nip again.

"Let me," he said. "Let me see you—let me make love to you." With ease, Alex slid the fine lawn gown from her body and dropped it to the floor. Moonlight stretched across the room, bathing them both in its silvery glow. He pulled close and possessed her mouth. She answered in a promise of pleasures to come and pressed her chest to his.

She kissed the base of his throat, and it pounded. There

was no mistaking how much he wanted her, and he made a move to cup her breasts.

She turned over onto her stomach. "Alex," she warned in a whisper. Tonight, she wanted complete control.

"Hmm . . . ?" Moving on top of her, he brushed her hair to the side and kissed and nibbled the back of her neck. "My name on your lips is the sweetest sound."

He continued the assault of kisses as he braced his hands on either side of her. He rubbed his cheek against her backside. His whiskers skated across her skin in a tingling caress. All of it made her want to lose herself in this moment forever.

His fingers traced every inch of her, as if memorizing her body. He stopped and whispered against her skin, "You have the most darling dimples here. Would you like me to take you this way?" He dipped his tongue in one of the hollows. "I think you'd like it."

A shudder ran through her body. She forced herself to shut out the delicious image of him entering her from behind and pulled away. With a turn, she rested on her knees, facing him. He cradled her breasts in his hands and took a nipple in his mouth. His tongue pressed and circled. The pleasure lit a fire that roared through her blood, and she cried out. Her body hungered for more, but she forced herself to push him away. "I make the decisions tonight. Lie down."

He did as she commanded but took the opportunity to rub his body against hers as he moved to the center of the bed. Every inch of his skin burned hot, almost as if his body begged for her touch. The desire she had for him would never be satiated. She straddled him with her legs and took a position below his cock. "I want to be on top of you."

"Claire," he murmured. "You want to kill me."

She spread her legs and adjusted her hips to mount him.

She took his cock in hand. The velvet skin over his hardness never ceased to amaze her. She bent and licked the
moisture from the tip. Her gaze captured his, and his gray
eyes flashed with an incendiary desire that threatened to
consume them both.

"Hmm," she moaned. "Spice, salt, and the taste of the
forbidden." She flicked her thumb over the crown of his
cock, and it jumped in her hand. He fisted the bed linens
and clenched his eyes. Slowly, she straightened and brought
him to her folds. She was drenched and knew that excited him. She closed her eyes as she rubbed her wet flesh
against his. It was heaven, but she wanted more.

"Claire, enough," he whispered. "Take me inside you."

She brought him to her opening and slowly lowered
over him. When she was seated against his body, she
couldn't tell where he ended and where she began. Desire
and need pumped in her blood. She wanted to ride him to
completion and move until they were both exhausted. She
had missed everything about Alex in the days they'd been
apart.

He moaned in pleasure. Claire sighed in answer and
moved in a slow, controlled circle, up and down. She
lowered her body to his and ground against him—over
and over until the pleasure spread from her center and
thrummed throughout her body. Inch by inch she'd pull
away but never release his cock. Then she'd start her descent to repeat the pattern.

He held her hips in his hands to keep her steady. "Touch
your breasts."

She stopped moving, and her eyes widened. His gaze
flashed with unmistakable longing. Her movement became
more frenzied as the crescendo of her pleasure built toward
her release. Her breathing grew labored and her skin
burned. She was close. She moved faster as she traced her

nipples with her fingers, then pinched them. She threw her head back and splayed her hands on both breasts.

Her husband was coming undone as he watched her. He thrust his hips to meet her downward movements. Her center started to contract, and she leaned forward.

Alex reached between them and rubbed her clitoris, bringing her to the brink of climax. "Let go," he coaxed.

She closed her eyes and succumbed to the pleasure. She shuddered as the intense rapture roared through her again and again. When it ended, she slumped against his chest. Never had she experienced such intensity with another soul. She forced her mind to quiet and allowed her body to float on the last remnants of her release.

His arms surrounded her, and his heat warmed her cooling flesh. He reverently turned her so she lay on the bed. With her knees raised, he slowly entered her, then withdrew from her heat inch by inch as if relishing her. Again, he'd push inside, filling her completely. His gaze never left hers. "You've bewitched me. I can't have enough of you."

He was loving her so honestly, she felt exposed. He brought one of her legs over his shoulders. The change of position let him go deeper. Too overwrought with emotion to respond, she surrendered to the exhilarating sensation, her breathing ragged. He pumped his hips faster, more urgent. Claire clenched her muscles around his cock as he was on the verge. The feeling was exquisite. She closed her eyes and focused on the force of his release. Hot and hard, every muscle in his body tightened as he cried out her name and pumped his seed into her center.

Alex collapsed on top of her, and she pressed her lips against his shoulder. His labored breathing matched hers. She'd never experienced an orgasm like this. Its power had overtaken every one of her senses.

When he had recovered, he propped himself on his forearms and placed light, gentle kisses on her neck, jaw, and ear. He moved to her mouth. She drank in the sweetness of his kiss, savoring the feeling of satisfaction he gave her.

"My wife, my lovely wife." Alex gathered her in his arms as he lay on his side. "I love you." He caressed her, moving his hand slowly from her rib cage to the top of her hip and back again. He feathered kisses on her face, slowly moving to her neck, her shoulder, her chest, and her breast. "I don't want this night to end."

Claire sighed softly. Fascinated by the contour of the muscles and the feel of the soft downy hair splayed across his chest, she ran her hand lightly over his abdomen and traced patterns across the expanse of skin, his warmth intoxicating.

"Tell me about the night of the carriage accident," he whispered into her hair.

Her hands stilled. "Why?"

"I want to find a way to help and protect you." He tightened his grip on her hip and touched her lips with his for a brief caress. "If I had the power, I'd take every burden of those memories for my own."

Her pulse fluttered at the tenderness of his words. She forced herself to relax somewhat in his arms. Perhaps if she shared some of her past, it would help them open up more to each other. It might even allow them to discuss the night she had confronted him at Pemhill. If she could share her body, surely she could talk a little about that night. It was a risk, but she'd regret it for the rest of her life if she didn't try to mend this breach between them.

He cared for her tonight, and she wanted to trust him. She relaxed and allowed the memories to flood her mind. "My parents and I drove through a torrential thunderstorm to reach Wrenwood late one afternoon."

He leaned on his elbow, and his gaze locked with hers.

He wanted everything, but some parts she would not share with anyone. Ever. Otherwise, the millstone she carried would break the slim thread of control she had mastered over the years. It was her only link to sanity. "When we crossed the main bridge to Wrenwood, it collapsed. All I could hear were shouts and the wooden beams splitting. It was an eerie sound, how I imagined a ghost would wail."

He slid his hand around her neck, and his fingers cradled the back of her head. His gaze never left hers, but he didn't utter a sound. The touch kept her from floating away in the memories.

"My mother grabbed me to her side as my father stole a glance outside. Whatever he saw, he realized we were going in the river. He flung his body against us and wrapped both my mother and me tightly in his embrace."

He kissed her temple. "That must have been terrifying for you."

She nodded. "It happened so fast. We started to tumble and immediately slammed into something hard. Ice-cold water flooded the coach and we started to move swiftly. In seconds, we were submerged. The force of the water ripped the carriage apart, and I became separated from my parents." Her words knotted in a confused mass, and she swallowed. "I couldn't breathe and everywhere I turned it was black. I don't know how long I was down there. Somehow, my father found me and took me to the riverbank."

Alex shifted and lifted her chin. "What happened?"

She swept her fingers across his lips and ignored the question.

"Claire?"

"No more." To reveal anything else would rip her heart out. She lay on her back and stared at the ceiling. What little she'd admitted tonight left her numb, with nothing else to give.

"You make it sound as if you were a bystander and not actually in the accident," he whispered.

"I can't . . . don't ask me to share anymore."

"I want it all." He closed the distance between them and pulled her close. His arms bracketed her face, and his chest angled over hers as if to shield her from the horror. "Whenever you're ready, I want it all."

With no other words exchanged, he shifted and brought her back resting against his chest. He wrapped his arm around her waist, and they drifted to sleep.

Alex woke with his mind full from last night. As the first light of dawn broke, he felt the same contentment he had experienced at Pemhill. Careful not to wake Claire, he kissed her cheek and dressed. They were destined to be together. She'd welcomed him back into her bed and actually tried to share the horrors of losing her parents. She was starting to trust him again. She'd come home, and he swore he'd make her happy. He'd give her the strength to deal with the grief, and she'd do the same for him.

"Where are you going?" Claire struggled to sit up in bed.

"Good morning," Alex answered with a kiss to her lips. He shrugged his coat over his shoulders but decided to forgo the cloak. No need scaring the household staff this early. "I'm going home to change, then I'll return. I'll go through the servants' entrance. I've had enough climbing for one day."

"Don't leave—" Claire's voice caught as she whispered, "Stay a little longer, please. For me?"

Her plea was like a string tethered to his focus, and it pulled him back. "What is it?"

"I don't want you to leave. I don't want to say good-bye. Please, I want . . ."

"I'll be back. I promise." Alex sat on the bed and pulled her into his arms.

He could tarry a moment or two, anything to keep her mind off his leaving. "I've got a few things on my agenda this afternoon. Estate business, and I'm to meet with my solicitors about Mr. Jordon. What are your plans?"

As soon as the words escaped, Claire's body stiffened. Her face changed from longing to an expression that reminded him of a cold brick wall.

"Mr. Jordon?" Claire backed away to face him from the other side of the bed. The expression of disbelief chiseled on her face said everything. She knew the truth before he could confess it.

He cursed softly. He should have told her last night. Somerton's warning to tell Claire everything came back once again to haunt him. "We need to talk. Give me a chance to explain."

"How do you know him?"

Her pointed words stabbed like a stiletto knife straight through his chest. Alex rubbed his neck as the dread detonated. "Before you pass judgment"—he took a deep breath and released it on a sigh—"I had you followed to see who lived in Leyton. I thought . . . never mind what I thought."

"Did you think I was having an affair with someone in Leyton?" Claire spit the accusation out as her eyes burned with the truth. "*Oh my God*. You thought I met Lord Paul."

"No." Alex reached for her hand and squeezed. "Please, Leyton is important to you. I had to discover why you went there. I met Mr. Jordon. He and I had a wonderful conversation. He told me you send him money in gratitude." He stumbled with the explanation.

Her green eyes turned into a murky bog, a black pit he could not navigate.

"I'm grateful he was by your side all those years ago, and like you, I want to take care of him. I want to take over his annuity . . . for you." His explanation sounded thin and hollow even to his own ears. Bloody hell, she had the ability to twist his thoughts into a knot of anarchy. The aloofness and disapproving gleam in her eyes made it apparent his explanation wasn't passing muster.

Her long lashes brushed the tops of her cheeks as she smoothed the sheets. "I want to hear it from your own lips. Why were you having me followed to Leyton?" She stood and put on her robe. When she looked at him, her green eyes flashed. He couldn't tell whether it was from tears, anger, or both.

He felt like a thief after the tenderness they had shared last night. If he didn't answer, they'd never move past his mistakes. "Before I met you at Lady Anthony's ball, I hired a private investigator to discover everything about you."

"Before Lady Anthony's?" Her glare burned through him, then her eyes widened. "You're the one responsible for Mr. Thornley at Hailey's Hope?"

"His name is actually Macalester."

"No wonder Uncle Sebastian couldn't find him. All this time I held my breath, ready for the *Midnight Cryer* to publish the Lady Claire exposé." She laughed, but the brittle sound held no humor. "Your investigator asked practically everyone about my curse. *You* wanted to know about *my curse*." Her tone of voice carried an unmistakable accusation: he had betrayed her.

He took a deep breath and shook his head. He'd not lose her again. "I don't believe in that *bloody* curse, and I never have. I wanted every piece of information I could gather before we married. I discovered you had a solicitor in Leyton that received semiannual payments, then I found out you visited Leyton a few days ago to see an old butler. I thought he might provide some answers."

"Here's your answer." Claire walked to the door. Before she opened it, she addressed him in a low whisper, the unmistakable agony resonant in her alto voice, "You stole the last refuge I had from the curse. Hailey's Hope never suffered the taint of that ugliness until you . . ." She cleared her throat. "Until you sent your private investigator. Can you imagine how I felt when I discovered someone was snooping around and asking about the curse at my *mother's* charity?" Her voice grew stronger, and she spoke faster the angrier she got. "First, it was the manipulations to make me marry you, then the bet at White's, now an investigator that taints everything in my life. I won't live under suspicion, and I won't live with the lies. I proved how I felt last night. It's not enough for you. It's never enough."

He tried to grab her hands. "Claire, listen."

She stepped out of his reach, and that's when he saw her tears. "I've given as much of myself as I could. My trust, my support, my soul. I don't know how to make you happy. I don't think I ever can."

His panic started to rise. Alex rushed forward to hold her and make her listen. She opened the door to leave the room before he could stop her.

"I need—" She closed her eyes as she struggled for control, and her voice echoed her weariness. "I'm tired, Alex. I'm so tired of not being enough. I'm not enough for anyone at this point."

"Claire, don't leave."

"It's best if I visit Lockhart for a while. I need some distance. We'll have papers drawn up on how to proceed. After the children's home is established, I'll arrange to live in Scotland and manage my affairs from there. I'd planned on opening up another facility in Edinburgh anyway." Claire turned and walked out of her bedroom. She headed toward the stairs.

Without thought of who might be in the hallway, he rushed after her. The light from the hall lamps made her appear like a sprite about to disappear into thin air. "Claire, don't do this."

She stopped in flight and returned to him. Her eyes searched his face as if to impress every feature, muscle, and line to memory. "Could you not tell how much it all meant to me?"

Her simple question ripped his insides apart. "I'm your husband. I love you."

"It's not love if you doubt me." She grimaced and clenched her eyes shut. "God, I was such a fool to share something as private as the night I lost my parents. I allowed you to slip past my defenses. I can't bear to live under your cloud of constant doubt."

He overpowered the rising need to cry out for the pain he'd inflicted upon her and their marriage. He had to convince her to see reason. "Claire, I want to help you."

She leaned close and raised her hand to caress his face. "There are things I'm ashamed of, as they define me as a person. But I told you as much as I could. You keep pushing for more, and I can't give it." She closed her eyes for a moment.

He leaned his face into her hand. He was desperate for her touch but feared he would scare her away if he pulled her into his arms. "Whatever it is, I don't care. I'll still love you."

"My secrets . . ." Claire's soft voice continued, "Perhaps this is for the best. If we're apart, the curse can't touch you."

Alex risked raising his hand to return the caress. "There's no curse. Tell me everything, and I'll help you. I promise." The desire—no, the *need* to touch her soft skin was overpowering.

She stepped back as if frightened and shook her head. "All I ever wanted in my life was you," she said. "You were always my dream. I just never got a complete glimpse, never saw your face, until the night at Lady Anthony's. After last night, I wondered if I could return to Pemhill with you . . ." She cleared her throat. "Not now."

He never remembered begging in his life. Now, he'd sell his soul to the devil if he thought he'd have a chance in hell of keeping her. "I love you."

The words died in the hallway after the soft whisper left his mouth.

She'd disappeared down the steps.

Alex stood rooted to the spot. The only sound he could hear were her words over and over in his head: *All I ever wanted was you.* When Langham put his arm around his shoulder, Alex became aware of his grief.

"Pembrooke, go home. You've done enough damage here to last a lifetime." The duke led him down the stairs.

Chapter Fifteen

Claire tried to ignore her maid's shocked expression, but the blasted woman looked like a baby blackbird trying to catch the last bit of worm from a morning meal. Aileen's mouth gaped open as Claire fired off instructions on what to have moved from Wrenwood to her Lockhart estate outside of Edinburgh.

Her mind furiously ran through the plans for the next day, next week, and next month. She had to escape Alex and her own agony, the sooner the better.

"I want to hire however many people necessary to make this move in the most expeditious manner possible. I'll ask my uncle for help in transporting the portraits from Wrenwood to Lockhart. When do you think my clothes will be packed? We should ask Mrs. Malone to send my books from Pemhill." Claire looked over her shoulder. "Aileen, are you listening to me?" She hardly ever felt exasperated with Aileen's actions. But it was best not to challenge her fortitude today.

"Yes, my lady. It's just we haven't been to Lockhart in five years. Forgive me, I'm trying to understand everything."

Aunt Ginny swept into Claire's room like a ray of sunshine. An appropriate comparison, since both entered at will without knocking. "Darling, I heard you're leaving."

"Good morning. You've heard correctly. I thought to stay for Emma, but my circumstances have changed. I'm meeting with Uncle Sebastian this afternoon to determine how best to proceed with the marriage."

"Aileen, would you see about some tea or coffee for Lady Pembrooke?"

"Yes, Your Grace," Aileen answered.

A hint of remorse clouded Claire's thoughts, but nothing would persuade her to stay. She could speed up her plans if she left Aileen in London. In the morning, she'd start her trip and leave the arrangements and packing to Aileen—a brilliant solution. She'd even hire her own outriders. Any argument against her traveling by herself would be moot.

"Aunt Ginny, I'm going to open a children's home close to Lockhart. Perhaps I'll call it Hailey's Gift. You and Uncle Sebastian must come for the grand opening." She flung open a wooden chest and scowled. How had she collected so many stockings? "Is there anyone on your staff that could travel as my maid? Aileen will stay here. Once she arrives in Edinburgh, I'll send the Langham servant back."

"Tell me you don't love him, and I'll leave right now," her aunt said flatly.

She stopped packing and squeezed a pair of pink clocked stockings in her hand.

"I saw your face the last time he was at Langham Hall." Her aunt softened her voice. "Sweetheart, you love him."

Claire would not let her aunt ruin her newfound peace. She laced her voice with an emotion that closely resembled a discussion of the weekly cleaning schedule. "Yes, well, sometimes that doesn't matter. I have no future with him."

"That sums it up prettily." Her aunt's lips tilted with the shadow of a smile. "Have you told Alex how you feel?"

"I've tried. He's his own law."

"You can't expect a successful marriage if you don't work through your problems." Aunt Ginny exhaled rather loudly for such a small woman. "It defies logic. Neither of you can mend this break if you're in Scotland."

Claire threw the stockings onto the middle of the bed. "There's nothing to discuss. He used me and had me investigated because he thought I had a lover. I'm moving forward with my life. End of story." She sorted through her gloves. Anything to keep her occupied and distracted from her aunt's pointed questions.

"You belong to one another now."

"Please, I must finish this." She picked up a pair of ivory silk stockings and threw those next to the pink ones. She reached for another and then stopped; her hands fluttered to her sides. "He wants things from me . . . things I can't give him."

"What things?" her aunt whispered.

Her thoughts coiled, ready to burst in admission, but she bit her cheek. "He wants personal things, my parents, the accident . . ."

"Perhaps he's the right one you can finally share this with?" Aunt Ginny squeezed her shoulders. "Sweetheart, learn to give one another what you both want and need. You can do this. Pembrooke sounds sincere—"

Claire pulled away. "Not now."

"I'll find out what's happened between the two of you. I'd rather hear it from your lips, but I'm not above going to him for answers."

"Enjoy your visit," Claire called out. The pile of stockings resembled the shape of a small mountain on her bed.

"My lord, the Duchess of Langham is in your study." Simms handed Alex the calling card.

"Thank you." Alex walked down the hall with the faint

hope that this was the final confrontation over Claire. First it was Somerton, then Langham, and now the duchess. It would make a perfect ending to a perfectly lousy morning.

When Alex saw her, he suspected the visit was more than a set down. She looked worried. Taking her hand, Alex greeted her without emotion. "Your Grace, welcome."

The duchess launched into the purpose of her visit without a by-your-leave for arriving at a time when most of London was still abed. "You must know why I'm here, my lord." Her blue eyes bored into his. "Why is Claire moving to Lockhart? Why is she acting as if this move is nothing more than a ride in the park?"

It would be more comfortable to face a trampling by a team of wild horses than a confrontation with another Cavensham. He'd already had his heart tattered to shreds by Claire. "Your Grace, I am at a loss."

With the full force of an Atlantic gale wind, the duchess blew apart, her apparent hold on patience exhausted. "If you want to save this marriage, you had better tell me everything. I'll handle the duke and the settlement and annulment nonsense, but I need ammunition to stop Claire. If you can't or won't tell me, then this is what you both deserve for your respective stubbornness."

Alex froze in stunned silence. She looked like a goddess of war, ready for battle. She never moved as she waited for his response.

"Won't you please sit down?" He had never expected Claire's aunt would be an ally of his. Shocked was putting it mildly. Yet he still possessed the wherewithal not to look a gift horse in the mouth.

After the duchess settled in the chair in front of his desk, Alex followed suit and sat at his desk. "This will not be brief. May I offer you tea?"

The duchess's expression softened. As if this were an ordinary social call, she offered him a sweet smile and

said, "No, thank you. However, I'm quite certain something stronger than tea would be more refreshing when
we're finished."

After he concluded telling her the whole sordid tale, the
duchess looked at the floor for a moment. "Do you know
about Claire's experience with her parents' death and
Wrenwood?"

"What do you mean?"

"Her inability to tolerate thunderstorms, her reaction to
Wrenwood?"

"Not enough." Alex leaned back. "She won't share
everything that happened that night."

"Sebastian and I don't understand the extent of her
trauma either." She took a deep breath before her face became shadowed with grief. The duchess rose from her
chair, then started to pace back and forth. It seemed the
only way she could tell the story.

"The drivers, outriders, and groomsmen made it safely
to land and tried for hours to find the family and the carriage, even sending for others to help. The day ended without any sign they survived. The next morning, with little
hope left, they saw Claire struggle through the deep mud
to reach them. The carriage had capsized and the rushing
water swept it down the river. The duke brought her to
shore about a half a mile downstream, then went back to
free his wife." Her speech faltered, then she turned to
him. "She had waited for them both through torrential
storms all night. Sebastian speculated that a wheel caught
Margaret's heavy dress, and she was unable to free herself.
Michael must have stayed down in the water to free her,
but . . ."

Alex shifted in his seat to hide his discomfort over the
horror. My God, his Claire alone on the riverbank as she
waited for her parents.

"The search resumed and the next day, their bodies

were found." The duchess's voice barely rose above a whisper. "The storms that lashed Wrenwood during the week were relentless. No one could leave or enter the estate as the creeks and rivers flooded their banks."

"I remember that season." Alex waited for the duchess to continue.

The grief on her face turned into pain. The story could only become worse. Tears came to her eyes. "My darling girl never cried and stayed in the drawing room where her parents lay in repose. They didn't resemble . . ." She cleared her throat. "Claire screamed and was inconsolable when the staff tried to cover the bodies. Mr. Jordon was by her side day and night. He couldn't get her to move. Meanwhile, the thunder and lightning never stopped."

Alex thought about his wife as a little girl, all alone. An emotion seized his chest much like a punch in the stomach. No wonder she was adamant about home and family. She had witnessed her parents' death and was alone for hours before she found shelter with her rescuers. The sorrow of those moments pummeled Alex. He felt something wet on his face and realized it was his own tears.

"Finally, after five days, Sebastian found a way to cross the river. He raced into the house and picked Claire up in his arms." Tears glistened on her smooth cheeks. "She never shed a tear." She bowed her head.

"Your Grace, she was a little girl in shock. I've seen her grieve. She cares—she cares deeply." Alex faltered in his silence before he could continue. "It's a scar, one that many of us carry when we lose a parent. It doesn't define Claire."

The duchess dried her tears and gave him a slight smile.

"My actions may indicate otherwise, but I truly care for your niece."

Her gaze held his captive. "You can't let her go to Scotland."

"I won't." It wasn't a promise he took lightly. He would bring Claire home.

"Thank you, Pembrooke." The duchess reached over and patted his arm. "Shall we have those refreshments we discussed earlier? By chance, might you have any of Claire's mother's whisky?"

Later in the afternoon, Sebastian escorted Claire into his study and closed the door. He took a deep breath and sat on the edge of his desk, facing her. "I know you're in the middle of preparations for travel, but we need to have this conversation before the rumors get worse." He wiped his hand over his face. Her situation had taken a toll on him, too.

"Thank you. I want to know my options. Have you heard from your solicitors?" Claire controlled the quiver in her voice that threatened to expose her weakness. That she was actually contemplating annulment or a permanent separation from Alex caused her stomach to cramp.

The curse was real.

"It's not easy, sweetheart. It never has been. There are few reasons to support a petition for annulment. If Pembrooke lacked the ability to consummate the marriage . . . I trust that's not the case, since I found him in the family quarters early this morning."

Claire bowed her head to hide the heat from her cheeks. "No."

The duke cleared his throat. "Yes, well . . . He's not a close relative, so that avenue is closed. He's not legally insane, but in my mind it's debatable." His gaze was tender as he shook his head. "The solicitors have examined every corner of the marriage settlement. There are no grounds."

"Can't they find something he lied about in those pages and pages of documents?"

"Claire, you won't win. The solicitors examined the

document from every angle—dissected every fact. You'd be a laughingstock if you tried to proceed. The House of Lords, everyone, would side with Pembrooke if you challenged him."

Her uncle had employed the best legal minds in London. If anyone could produce a rational reason for annulment, her uncle's solicitors could.

"Most intelligent people would say Pembrooke kept you from becoming a victim of Lord Paul's ruin. Others would say he saved you from the curse." Her uncle rolled his eyes in disgust. "Can you imagine your life if you were married to that wastrel and his gambling? Pembrooke saved you from a certain type of hell I wouldn't want for anyone." His voice softened. "Especially you."

"What about divorce?" The words escaped before Claire could rein in her thoughts.

"No! Not under any circumstance. Pembrooke would have to petition Parliament and stake a claim you are an adulteress for a divorce. I won't allow it. What if you're pregnant? He could declare your child a bastard. Even if you stayed in Edinburgh for the rest of your life, every person you'd meet would turn their back on you."

"There must be something." One hot tear plunged to her dress. She refused to allow any others to follow.

Her uncle pulled her into his arms. "I'd be doing a disservice to you and dishonoring my brother if I allowed you to get out of this marriage. My anger was raging when I told Pembrooke I'd keep you away from him. Sweetheart, you're his wife." He released her from his embrace and stared into her eyes. "Take my advice. Try to find a way to work this out with Pembrooke. I'm not saying live together in harmony, but find a way to exist with one another."

"You don't understand." Claire took a deep breath. "It hurts too much to love him and pretend I don't. How can

I escape this torment?" Her anguish had steadily increased as every option disappeared.

"I agree. He's made a mess of things. Try to find your way in this marriage. It's work. All marriages are. It might not be too farfetched to consider living with him. If it's too big a sacrifice, then live apart. I've seen it hundreds of times. You're one of the lucky ones. At least you have the means to do what you want when you want."

"I'll consider it." Claire dried her eyes and turned to leave.

"Have dinner with your aunt and me. We'll make an appearance at Lady Dalton's ball."

"Thank you. I'll see what Emma's plans are for the evening."

"Before you go . . . earlier when I said you are my daughter, I meant it. When I picked you up at Wrenwood that godforsaken day and held you in my arms, you became a part of Ginny and me."

Claire smiled through tears that threatened to fall again. "I'll never forget. You and Aunt Ginny provided a home and a family when I had none. I love you both."

"I'm going to hang your parents' portrait at Falmont if that's agreeable with you."

"That would be lovely, Uncle Sebastian."

His cheeks turned a deep crimson, and he nodded his dismissal without looking at her. "Well then, that's settled."

When Claire left the study, part of her burden had lifted. Every time she visited Falmont, she'd see her parents. No matter what her future held, she was fortunate. She belonged to two loving families.

"Claire, hurry, please. I've already promised the next dance to someone, and I don't want to be late." Emma had taken special care with her appearance tonight, an obvious attempt to capture someone's attention. They were in the receiving line to greet their hosts, the Earl and Countess of Dalton.

"Lady Pembrooke." The earl took Claire's hand and gave a slight bow. "Lord Pembrooke has already arrived. He asked that I tell you to save your first dance for him." He leaned forward to whisper, as if sharing a grand conspiracy, "But not if I may have the honor."

"Thank you, my lord." Claire smiled, but her stomach dropped at the news that Alex waited for her. The last time she and Alex attended the same ball, the curse took center stage. What would happen tonight?

The countess batted his arm with her fan. "You old rogue." She clucked her tongue. "You better save it for me." The countess turned to Claire and gave a wink. "We're delighted you could attend."

"Thank you." Claire left the couple and walked to Emma's side. "Perhaps we should leave."

"Nonsense." Emma didn't appear the least concerned with the news. "You can't hide. Take the opportunity to show him he has no effect on you. Besides, this is your last ball before you leave for Scotland." Her cousin squeezed her hand. "Wish me luck. I'm trying to secure two books this evening. One is that first edition of Mr. Bentham's essays. But my first dance partner has a new memoir he wants to discuss. It would be perfect for my collection. Angela Tarte's diary."

"Who is Angela Tarte?"

"An eighteenth-century capitalist." Emma flashed a brilliant smile as if it were Christmas morning. "In a manner of speaking."

"As in business?" Claire might as well have been talking to one of the potted palms. Emma skated down the steps and found a group of friends. Claire followed but kept to the perimeter of the ballroom in an attempt to hide, weaving around the rows of flower arrangements and liveried footmen with trays of champagne. If she watched Alex, she could keep out of his sight. It was difficult since she always tried to keep an eye on where Emma was and whether she was greeting friends or dancing. She'd allow Emma her dance with Lord LaTourell or whoever her mystery man was, then demand they return to Langham Hall. If she was lucky, they'd leave before Alex could find her.

After a short break, the orchestra performed a new set, and Emma found a dance partner who was an old family friend. It was one less thing to worry about this evening. The ballroom had grown crowded and the heat insufferable. Claire took advantage of the opportunity and escaped outside. The urge to check the sky never left her. Earlier, a light easterly breeze had changed directions and now came from the west.

She walked to a deserted part of the balcony and inhaled the fresh air. Out of the corner of her eye, she saw someone approaching.

She turned to offer a greeting and found Alex by her side.

A rakehell grin turned up the corners of his mouth. With a lazy look, he placed his hand on her lower back and gave it a slow caress. "You received my card." With his eyes flashing like a summer storm, Alex glanced at the brooch, then directed his full attention to her.

Claire placed her hand on the brooch. Her fickle heart melted a little at his smile.

"Will you?" With a tilt of his head, he leaned forward.

She took a step back to keep some distance between them. He was too close and far too tempting. "Will I what?"

"Forgive me?" His gaze searched the depths of hers.

She took a deep breath. "Alex—"

He brought his finger to her lips to stop the words. "Don't answer." His face softened with his endearing lopsided grin. "Dance with me instead?" He took her hands in his and waited for her decision.

Every muscle in her body relaxed. The beastly cad knew the effect it would have on her ability to say no. She nodded but regretted it immediately. The evening would end with her picking up the pieces of her broken heart again.

Alex escorted her to the center of the floor, ensuring every guest could see their interaction. He placed his left hand on the small of her back and pulled her close. Her cheeks heated. The proximity of their bodies provided the kindling to start a firestorm of murmurs and titters. The fans of the matrons and chaperones snapped and flapped vigorously, hiding the comments about the couple's behavior.

Claire tried to keep her face calm as the guests watched the performance. His arm became a steel band clasped about her waist. "Alex—"

"My darling wife, if this is the only way I have of getting your attention or spending time with you, then so be it. You've caused me to take such drastic action." He smiled for the benefit of the crowd.

"Please let me go," she whispered. The orchestra launched into the waltz, and they began dancing.

Alex brought his head close to her ear. He inhaled her scent and let it out. "Not while I have a breath in me." He brushed his lips over her ear and then swept her around the floor, never taking his eyes off hers. When he spoke again, his voice was tender, almost a caress. "Never."

A strange sense of relief welled into a deep pool inside her chest. Claire chose to ignore everything except the dance. After the waltz, she would let her mind and heart battle for the claim on her spirit. For now, she concentrated on her steps.

However, her disloyal body wouldn't let her concentrate on anything but Alex. It was heaven in his arms. With little effort, she could stay here all night long. When she looked over her shoulder at the other dancers, she remembered Emma. A quick search of the dance floor revealed her cousin dancing with Mr. Jackson.

Alex's brows came together. "What is it?"

"Emma's not been herself lately, and I promised Aunt Ginny I'd watch her. Lord Paul sought her out the other evening at Lady Barrington's party. I broke up their conversation, and she's been acting strangely ever since." Claire waited for Alex to tense his arms, but there was nothing.

His held her gaze without anger. "Yes, I saw you with him that night."

Butterflies fluttered low in her stomach. "How did you know? You weren't there."

"Darling, I was invited but attended from afar."

Claire waited three steps for control over the tumult created by his confirmation that he had followed her. "He had quite a bit to say, as you might imagine. I warned him off Emma, but he told me what you refused to admit." This time his arms did tighten around her.

"While painting himself the hero." Alex looked away, as if something else more important had caught his attention, then turned to study her.

He held her close until the dance came to an end. When they stopped, he fastened her to his side. "Come with me." He led her into a small draped anteroom away from prying eyes.

"My lord, I regret bringing the subject up in such an inappropriate place. I must find Emma." Claire tried to escape from his grasp.

"We're not done." Alex pulled her into the corner under the anteroom's wide staircase leading to the third floor. It lent an immediate privacy, since no one would look for them there. He leaned his hand against the wall over her head and closed the distance between them.

His familiar citrus scent surrounded her, and immediately her mind wandered to the sensual memories of Alex covering her when they'd made love in her bed. If she didn't get her disloyal thoughts under control, her heart would never survive the night.

"Claire." He brushed his lips across her temple before he continued. "Come home. I will make amends, I promise. Right now, I can't think straight. There's so much to say, but all I can think of is how much I've missed you." He pressed his lips to the sensitive spot on her neck and trailed kisses to her earlobe. "I've never begged in my life as I am now."

She had to stay strong. "Why? Will it be another victory over Lord Paul?"

Alex's eyes widened. Then some undefined emotion broke through the depths of his gray eyes.

She didn't flinch, nor did she back down.

With a sudden movement, Alex pressed her against the wall. His mouth possessed hers with a kiss of passion, a passion primed to explode. When he stopped, Claire felt a keen loss of balance. She leaned and placed her head against his chest. With the rapid pounding of her heart, she didn't trust herself to stand on her own.

He rested his head against the wall. His fingers twined around the loose tendrils of hair on the back of her neck. "I plan to take a walk. At this moment, I want you so much I think I'll frighten you." He took a deep breath and slowly released it, as if trying to calm the rage of emotions he held tight inside. "I know I frighten myself."

He stepped away from her, and she almost cried out at the loss of his touch.

"Afterward, I'm going to find you, and we'll finish this one way or another. Agreed?"

If she spoke now, she'd beg him not to leave. All she could manage was a single nod.

He returned to the ballroom without a glance back. She wanted him to look at her so she could see his brilliant eyes once more. She brought her hand to her mouth and felt the remnants of their kiss, bruised lips, and the heat of his touch. She should have listened to her head and not her renegade heart.

When she had regained her composure, she entered the ballroom. Scanning the dancers for Emma's pale yellow dress, she allowed her gaze to drift from one side of the floor to the other. There were few takers for the reel, a physically demanding dance and not a favorite for most of the attendees. Another waltz would follow.

Claire found Lady Lena Eaton with Emma's friends, enjoying a break from the dancing. "Have you seen Lady Emma?"

"I believe she danced with Mr. Jackson until he twisted his ankle, then said she had to return home for an emergency."

"How long ago?"

Lena furrowed her forehead and tapped a gloved finger against her check. "It was after the quadrille but before the reel. Perhaps a quarter of an hour? I'm not certain, Lady Pembrooke."

A fresh-faced young lady named Miss Jane Hosmer stood alongside Lady Lena. "Lady Pembrooke, Emma didn't leave the dance floor with Mr. Jackson."

"Oh really? Did you see her?"

The corners of the girl's mouth dipped into a frown, and she nodded. "She returned to our group. I overheard her tell Lady Daphne that Lord Paul had located a book for her."

"Thank you." It took supreme effort, but she maintained an appearance of calm with a smile pasted to her face as she hurried away.

Emma was nowhere in sight. It wasn't her cousin's typical behavior to leave without informing someone of her plans. After Claire scoured the refreshment area, she entered the card room to find McCalpin or William. Neither was present. He aunt and uncle wouldn't arrive until after midnight.

Her search of the public areas including the outside balcony left her with a cinched throat, which was a blessing because it kept her from screaming. She needed Alex, but she regretted the way she had left his company and had no idea where to find him.

Claire moved around the room and attempted to appear as if she were on a stroll. As she made her way to the front entrance, Lord Somerton stood as a sentry to the ballroom exit.

"Lady Pembrooke, you aren't leaving, are you?" Somerton dipped his head and sketched the customary bow.

"Yes, I must go." She would wait as good manners required and make small talk. Otherwise the man would know something was amiss. She silently tapped her slipper underneath her skirts.

"Have you seen Pembrooke?" Somerton looked about the room as he asked the question.

The blasted man wanted her to attend to Alex. "I believe he's taking a stroll around the ballroom. You might want to check the card room. If you'll excuse me, my lord." Without waiting for his reply, she continued to the entry.

She asked the head footman to call for her carriage. Fortunately, it waited out front. As the Langham footman assisted her up the steps, Claire whispered in his ear, "Once we're off the grounds, I need to return to Langham Hall as quickly as physically possible." Soon the carriage rumbled out of Lord Dalton's drive. When the estate was out of sight, the driver gave the signal. The carriage whipped forward.

She prayed they'd be in time to stop whatever was

happening between Lord Paul and Emma. As soon as she
was able, Claire exited the carriage on her own and opened
the front door. "Pitts!"

"What may I do for you, Lady Pembrooke?" After years
of service, the butler had become a master at deciphering
emotions. He handed her coat to the under-footman and
gave her his full attention.

"Come with me." Claire led him to the blue drawing
room, where they would have privacy. "Have you seen
Lady Emma?"

"No, my lady. You are the only one home." He handed
her a sealed note. "This was just delivered for you."

Claire's heart beat in a wild dance that kept pace with
her erratic pulse. In the same elegant writing she'd become
familiar with at Lady Anthony's ball, the message was
from Lord Paul.

> *My dearest Claire,*
> *Your cousin has decided it's urgent she meet me
> at the Black Falstaff Inn tonight. She sent a note
> earlier for me to meet her here. In my humble
> opinion, it would be beneficial for all of our sakes
> if you came posthaste. I'll have a private room
> reserved.*
>
> *L.P.B.*

Inside, ice-cold dread wrapped around her chest and
made it difficult to breathe, let alone speak. Emma had
willingly gone to meet Lord Paul. She was ruined.

Charles entered the room and joined them. "My lady,
is there something I can help you with?"

"Lady Emma is missing." Her steady voice commanded
everyone to pay attention. At this juncture, Claire couldn't
wait for the rest of the family. "Charles, saddle Hermes for
me and prepare a carriage. Make certain it's one without

the ducal seal on the doors. You'll follow me in the carriage to the Black Falstaff. Keep our destination quiet to the rest of the staff."

"Yes, my lady." The groomsman nodded and left.

"I'll change. Pitts, send word to the duke and duchess and have someone search for McCalpin and Lord William."

"Of course, Lady Pembrooke." Pitts left to carry out the instructions, and she rushed to her room. With Aileen's help, she made quick work of changing into her riding habit. With the threat of a possible storm, she couldn't ride in a carriage.

Scenarios that only spelled disaster for Emma crowded her mind. If anyone saw Emma traveling by herself or on the road to the Black Falstaff, she'd face ridicule of a magnitude that would rival Claire's curse. Without further thought, Claire returned to the blue drawing room, where Pitts and Charles waited.

Claire's riot of emotions quieted, but she twisted her fingers together to quell the shaking of her hands. "It's time to leave."

Why did Emma go to Lord Paul? What did he want with her?

Chapter Sixteen

Claire rode next to Charles as he drove the carriage on the dark road. The coaching inn was located no more than three miles outside London. After riding for almost a half hour, they were close to their destination.

Overhead the stars had disappeared, replaced by nothing but blackness. The moon held its grip on the night sky in the east. Brief flashes of lightning lit the west. The wind increased its velocity, as if trying to outrun the incoming storm. She called forth every bit of courage she could scrape together to face what they'd find at the inn. Deep down, that all-too-familiar terror tried to push her determination out of its way as it swelled in waves. She tightened her hold on Hermes's reins. She had to find Emma.

They approached a small bridge over a creek, the water's swift flow violent. Claire slowed the horse and gasped at the sight before her. A narrow suspension bridge swung in a choppy motion as the wind intensified. It was barely wide enough to accommodate two horses, let alone a full-sized carriage.

She had no control over her body's trembling. She bent low over Hermes to escape the assault of leaves and debris that swirled through the air. It took all her willpower not to turn and ride away. The fear on her face must have been visible. Charles stood by her side and grabbed the reins.

He raised his voice over the wind's shrieks. "My lady, shall I take the horse over and come back for you?"

"No. Go back to the last bridge and cross over. It'll accommodate the coach. I'll make my way across this bridge." The wind threw the hood of her cloak over her head.

"Take this." Charles gave her one of the carriage lanterns. He climbed into the driver's seat. With one command to the horses, he circled the coach to face the opposite direction, then stopped. "Are you certain, my lady?"

"Yes, go. I'll meet you at the inn." She didn't watch him drive away. Otherwise she might never find the fortitude to face the bridge. A shiver rolled down her back and caused her leg muscles to tighten. The horse must have taken her reaction as a command. In seconds she was in front of the bridge.

With a deep breath, she dismounted while holding the lantern in her left hand. With her other hand, she brought the reins over Hermes's head. There was little doubt she would not be able to ride across. It would be an impossible feat for her to stay seated in the saddle.

The distance to the other side was probably no more than a hundred feet. Whether it was ten feet or ten miles, she'd rather face the fires of hell. That wasn't an option, as Emma was on the other side.

The winds had died down, giving her a reprieve to cross. With a silent prayer, she took the first step and pulled the reins behind her. The wooden planks beneath her feet were solid. That one step gave her enough confidence to coax the horse to follow.

The rushing water below roared with an intensity that swallowed all other sounds of the night. Her breath grew shallow, and her heart pounded for her to retreat. She held the light in front of her and concentrated on each step without looking into the water. Her horse showed no sign of fear and followed at her pace. Flashes of the night she and her parents crossed the river at Wrenwood tried to break her concentration. She refused to succumb to the nightmare and continued her trek across.

With only twenty feet to go, she walked faster. With no warning, vicious winds assaulted her, and her hood blew over her face, momentarily blinding her. The bridge creaked as the wind propelled it into a bobbing motion. With her right hand, she grasped the rope that served as a handrail. The reins followed her movement. Her grasp tightened until her hand throbbed from the pain. She stilled and drew great gasps of air. A trickle of sweat found its way down her chest.

The horse nudged her back, and she took a tentative step. She swallowed some of the fear and forced her way across while she kept a firm hold on the rail. Once on land, she leaned into Hermes and stroked his neck. The sign of affection and words of praise helped her find her own succor—they had made it.

After a few minutes, her hands had stopped shaking and her heartbeat had calmed. Without help or a mounting block, she searched for a way to climb into the saddle.

"Claire!"

The shout came from behind. She held the lantern to her side and looked back at the bridge. Alex held his own lantern and stood in the middle, pulling Ares's reins behind him.

"Claire, wait for me." The short cape of his greatcoat whipped against his shoulders as the force of the wind surged. The next instant his horse reared as the bridge swung wide. Alex fell and rolled off the edge. A frightened Ares shot forward and galloped past her.

Tremors rolled through her body as Alex labored to haul himself back onto the bridge. He held on to the rope with one hand and grasped a wooden plank with the other. She tried to scream his name, but the sound lodged in her throat. The bridge swung, then snapped back into place as if trying to throw him into the creek. Alex pulled half of his body onto the bridge.

Claire fell to her knees and curled into the littlest space possible. Nearby, a tree limb broke free in a booming crack. She forced herself into a sitting position and pushed aside the numbness. This time, she'd not lose her loved one. Whatever the sacrifices, she had to save Alex.

The onslaught of the wind continued. Without thought to the consequences, she ran toward him, then stopped on the edge of the bridge as if held by a force against her will. Every inch of her trembled, but she couldn't let her fear overpower her. She thought of nothing else but taking slow, even steps until she reached his side. She didn't let loose her hold on the bridge railing. After what seemed like hours, she came within two feet of Alex. Claire broke free of the invisible hold on her body and set the lantern down. The flame flickered as it clashed with the savage winds.

Pure instinct took over. She got to her knees and grabbed him by the arms. With every muscle in her body, she pulled while he held on to the rope and the plank. What little strength she provided was enough. He levered the rest of his body up.

They both rested for a moment, then Alex helped her to stand. "I owe you my thanks." He inhaled with a deep breath, then released it. "That's not something I want to try again in the near future."

"I—I thought I was going to lose you." She wrapped her

arms around his neck. His greatcoat whipped around them both.

"I'll not go that easy." The deep rumble of his laughter vibrated within his chest.

His ease made her relax somewhat, but she didn't loosen her hold around his neck.

"My lady, you give me cause to hope." He cupped her face with his hands and brushed his thumbs over her cheeks. "I'm a lucky man if you're worried about me."

"I would have done anything to . . ." Claire didn't finish but turned toward the darkness ahead. With Alex behind her, the lantern's light made it difficult to see much of anything. "How far is it?"

Alex placed his hand around her waist and pulled her close. "Not more than fifty or so feet. You hold the lantern, and I'll keep us steady by holding the rope."

Her heart pounded, and she closed her eyes. She willed her feet to go forward, but instead she turned in his arms. "He told me not to move."

The wind blew between them. He turned them in a direction that blocked the gusts from assaulting her. "Who?"

"My father."

Her throat tightened. She'd never imagined she'd confess what happened that night. Not now, not on this bridge. Her body jerked, but it made little difference. She'd almost lost Alex tonight. There were so many things she wanted to say. She'd become a master of keeping that night buried. Once she started, the whole story would tumble out.

"The river was black. Everything surrounding me was black. I couldn't see anything. My lungs burned with the putrid water I swallowed. I couldn't breathe, and I couldn't break free. Somehow, he found me and grasped my hand. He brought me to the surface and swam to the riverbank."

Alex pulled her tight against him as if he'd never let her

go. His hand cradled her head close to his. This near to him, the wind gusts were incapable of stealing her voice.

"The last words he said to me were, 'Claire, stay here. Promise me you won't move.' He shook my arms gently and forced me to look into his eyes. All I could see was his worry and raw fear. 'Promise me,' he demanded."

Alex smoothed her hair, and each stroke of his hands encouraged her to continue.

"I nodded once . . . twice . . . I can't remember how many times. Then he dove in the black water. I waited all night." She shook until her teeth chattered. "I didn't move from the spot as I watched the river. Nightfall came, but the rain wouldn't let up. Everything was black except when lightning ripped across the sky."

Alex kissed her cheek. He squeezed her as if giving reassurance she'd be all right.

Claire swallowed, determined to finish. She wouldn't keep secrets any longer. "I waited while the rushing water crept closer. I'd lost my shoes, and the water covered my bare feet." She pulled back so she could watch the expression on his face. "My feet were so cold I couldn't feel my toes. I didn't think he'd mind if I scooted back a few feet—" Her voice cracked. "I never saw either of them again." She buried her head into his chest to escape the pain. "It's asinine, but I always thought if I hadn't disobeyed him, they'd have come back for me."

She stepped away from the comfort of his arms. The wind gusts had died down. His eyes never left her face.

She turned to the bridge and summoned what little courage she had left before she faced Alex. "Deep inside, I think I caused their deaths. When the curse first made its appearance, everything made sense. The truth is . . . I'll . . . I'll never overcome this fear. Ever. Now, you know everything."

"You didn't cause their deaths, and you're not cursed.

Our grief and guilt for being left behind makes us try to find some reason, some cause for such senseless tragedy." He stood close but didn't touch her. "Your pain makes my heart sick for what you went through. None of it makes a difference to me." He clasped her shoulders and stared into her eyes—seeing every piece of her shame. "Do you understand? It doesn't make any difference. I still want you as my wife." His voice thickened. "Thank you for telling me. I'm honored." He touched her face and brushed the wild loose hairs away from her face. "Let me help you get across. I'll not leave your side."

She bowed her head and fought the tears that stung her eyes.

"It's all right. I'm right here." Alex brought her close until her cheek rested against his chest. Hoping to escape the pain, she buried her head.

She froze, finding it difficult to form a response, then turned to the end of the bridge. "I—I can't do this. Leave me here." Her whisper was lost with the gust of wind.

It was inconceivable that Alex heard the words, but he coaxed her forward. "Claire, you *can* do this. I'll not let go, I promise." He took a step. She wrapped her arm around his waist and fisted his greatcoat in her hand. She tried to stop him, but he moved forward. If she was going to stay by his side, she had to take a step.

She mimicked his movements, never letting go. Step after step, she walked beside him as they made their way across. The rush of water below was louder than the wind, and she could feel the rising cold mist hit her face. She couldn't see the water, but she could hear the frantic pace of its flow. As if the night couldn't get any worse, the wind kicked into a high dance with the bridge that caused it to sway back and forth. The wood groaned under the strain. Her cloak wrapped around her legs. She tried to keep her footing but lost her balance and fell into a heap.

Her fall caused the light to extinguish. Alex knelt by her side and attempted to pick her up in his arms. "Are you all right?"

Blackness surrounded them. Her panic took control. She grasped a wooden slat and wrestled away from him. She didn't have any idea where she would go, but she had to find solid ground. She couldn't catch her breath, and the water rushing below grew in volume.

Alex stopped her retreat by grabbing her arms. "Listen to me, sweetheart. We have no choice but to go forward. Right now Emma's no more than half a mile away at the inn. We're so close. No doubt she's frightened, Claire. She needs you." He took her face in his hands. She couldn't see anything, but his lips found the corner of her mouth as he spoke. "You have my promise. I will not let go."

She clenched his coat in her fists and held on. Her sanity depended on it. She forced herself to stand with his help. Somehow, she gathered strength from him and the words he had whispered. With a single nod of her head, she pulled him forward, and he gathered her in his arms.

"We're almost there, love." Alex kissed her softly on the lips. "Let's find Emma."

The wind lost some of its furor but managed to give a mighty gust as she clung to his side. Another flash of lightning lit the sky, illuminating the horses at the end of the bridge. A more subdued Ares had joined Hermes at the end of the bridge. Claire had ten feet to go, so she concentrated on Emma.

Relief flooded her as she reached solid ground, and for the first time she could take a deep breath. The air rushing through her lungs was as sweet as the smell of honeysuckle. She had made it across with Alex's help. She turned as he came up behind her. "It's trite, but thank—"

"No, Claire." His voice turned gentle. "I should be the

one thanking you over and over for saving me. I have no place in this world if you're not beside me."

They arrived without fanfare to find the inn's courtyard quiet. The wind had picked up again. Claire's cloak whipped around as if trying to take flight.

Her color had returned after the ordeal at the bridge. Watching her, Alex realized that she had more strength than any other person he knew, including himself. She was here because of the love she felt for her cousin. If only he had earned such a gift from her. He closed his eyes. After everything he'd done, he could only hope she'd allow him to make amends somehow, some way.

The stable hands rushed forward to give a welcome. Alex helped Claire dismount and threw a coin to each man. "Attend to our horses if you'll be so kind. I'm not certain how long we'll be." He turned to Claire. "Shall we, my dear?"

"As ready as I'll be, my lord." Claire took a deep breath and took his arm. "How did you find me?"

"Somerton found me outside on Lady Dalton's terrace after you left. I went to Langham Hall, and Pitts disclosed what was happening. I followed immediately."

His wife's green eyes widened with worry. "Do you think Somerton knows about Emma?"

He nodded. "I asked him to keep an eye out for her. He wouldn't say a word against her. Claire, we'll find her. My carriage should arrive shortly, then we'll all leave together." To himself, he promised he'd see his wife and Emma safe, then discover what Lord Paul's endgame was in tonight's affairs.

When they entered the inn, the main dining hall appeared filled to half capacity, with no sign of either Emma or Lord Paul. The other patrons didn't bother to look up at their entrance or give any sign of curiosity. The inn's

owner, a man about sixty years old with a full head of
white hair and a round midsection, approached with a big
smile. With a bow of his head, he gave a hearty greeting.
"Good evening, my lord. How may I help you?"

"We're here to meet Lord Paul Barstowe." Alex kept his
voice low.

A low rumble of thunder rolled overhead. Claire moved
in front of him as he addressed the fellow. A gust of wind
blew through an open window, and she shivered visibly.
He stepped forward to close the distance between them to
provide a sliver of comfort.

"You must be Lady Pembrooke." The innkeeper smiled
at Claire. "I'm Thorpe Webster, the owner. Welcome to the
Black Falstaff. The gentleman is waiting in the private dining room. Please allow me to escort you."

The innkeeper walked briskly through the small, cramped public room that led into a small hallway. The inn's
smarmy-eyed patrons watched their every move. Webster
didn't stop until he'd reached the last door on the right.

"How many are in his party?"

Webster didn't look at Alex. "Just Lord Paul Barstowe."

Claire didn't blink. She glanced at Alex and gave a
slight nod to indicate she was ready.

Webster used his knuckles to make a short staccato rap
on the thick wooden door. "If there's anything you need,
please let me know? Lord Paul has already ordered food
and drink."

Alex put himself between Claire and the innkeeper.
"No, thank you. We'll announce ourselves."

Alex raised his eyebrows. Claire nodded once and
stepped behind him and to the side, out of the doorway.

Alex slowly turned the handle. He threw the door open
and stepped inside. Several candles jumped a jig in protest
against his quick entry. A nicely built warm fire lit the
room.

Lord Paul stood at their entrance, then snorted in disgust. "For all that's holy, Claire, why bring him? I'm trying to keep this exchange rational and hopefully discreet."

"I'm delighted to see you, also." Alex forced the urge to throttle Lord Paul back into some semblance of control. He needed answers before he unleashed his fury over Emma. "Where is she?"

"I don't know. I thought you were her." Lord Paul addressed Alex, but his gaze darted repeatedly to Claire.

She stood in the doorway, frozen. "Where could Emma be?" Her pale face and wide-open stare hinted at the depth of her panic.

Alex gently took her arm, then closed the door. "What did you do to convince Emma to meet you here?"

"Claire, he proves my point by jumping to conclusions." Lord Paul shook his head. "Two hours ago, I received a note from Lady Emma asking me to meet her here. She wants a first-edition anthology of essays I have in my collection." His gaze settled on Claire. "If she arrived here alone, no telling what type of welcome she would have received. Likely, someone would recognize her." He slipped a note from his coat pocket and handed it to Claire.

"Why here?" Alex asked.

Lord Paul lifted his chin and trained his cold gaze on him. "She said she'd never visited a public tavern or taproom and thought it would be a grand adventure."

She scanned the letter and handed it to Alex. "He's telling the truth. Why would she do this?"

Lord Paul closed the distance between them. "I don't know, Claire. I thought a private dining room and your presence as a chaperone would be the best way to keep her reputation."

"I don't know what to say. That was very thoughtful and considerate of you. Emma's behavior lately is becoming increasingly odd." Claire folded her arms around her waist. "Where is she?"

"I wish I knew." Lord Paul's tone mellowed into a low hum.

"You and I should try to find her," Alex said. "Once my carriage arrives to take my wife home, we'll leave."

Lord Paul stared at Alex as if he were a stranger, then nodded begrudgingly. "I agree."

Alex exhaled and returned the gesture. The rancor they had shared over the past year wouldn't come into play this evening. Lord Paul was doing his best to help Emma. Tonight, they worked for a common cause—protect a young woman who needed their assistance.

Lord Paul gathered his coat and hat. "I'll take the Old Post Road heading north and stop at every inn and tavern on the way." He hesitated and narrowed his gaze on Claire. "Lady Pembrooke." Without saying another word, he left the room.

Alex followed. "One thing before you leave."

Lord Paul leaned against the wall as if bored with the world. "What is it?"

"Why lead me astray about Alice?" Alex asked. "Tonight you're a chivalrous knight for a damsel in distress. Why?"

One eyebrow slowly rose. "It's plebeian, I know"—he exhaled a deep breath—"but I once considered our friendship one of the most important things in my life. In my youth, wherever I went, chaos followed in my wake. You had the ability to calm the waters, so to speak." He looked down and shook his head with a deadened laugh. "I was prepared to lose your friendship if it meant you'd be spared the pain of knowing Alice was pregnant by a stable boy. I always thought one day you'd figure out the truth and seek me out."

Alex stared, not believing what he was hearing. The revelation was disturbing but comforting at the same time.

"However, you exceeded my expectations. Now, you're the one causing chaos." Lord Paul placed his hat on his head. "To answer your last question, I'm quite fond of Claire and Lady Emma."

"What about Somerton?"

"Please, spare me," Lord Paul drawled. "He's wound up tighter than that insufferable timepiece he carries every minute of the day." With a resigned breath, he continued, "I'll consider it."

With a pivot, Lord Paul strolled to the end of the hall and abruptly turned around. He regarded Alex with a slight hesitation in his hawklike eyes. "I apologize for disparaging your wife. It was the only way I could lash out at you."

He didn't wait for a reply and turned the corner.

Alex exhaled. After they found Emma, he'd consider Lord Paul's answers. Right now, his wife needed him.

When he entered the room, the look on Claire's face told him everything. She was at her breaking point. "We need to look for her separately. You should probably head south on Chase Road. As soon as Charles returns, I can search with him—"

"No. We search together. However, we'll wait for whichever carriage arrives first, yours or mine. We'll need it for your cousin."

A quarter of an hour later, Claire paced back and forth before the fireplace. As Alex reached to gather her in his embrace, the door slammed against the wall.

The Duke of Langham stood before them. Anger distorted his face. He looked like a warrior prepared for battle.

As if it were second nature, Alex's hand caressed the small of her back before he grasped her waist and pulled her into his protective embrace. Whatever rebukes the duke delivered tonight wouldn't deter him from Claire. "Your Grace."

"Where is she? Where's Emma?"

"We don't know. She's not here," Claire answered. "Lord Paul explained Emma told him to meet her here. He's headed north to look for her. We'll head south."

"Bloody hell!" the duke bellowed. Worry flashed from his eyes. "Are you certain Lord Paul's story is the truth?"

"Yes." A small river of relief flowed through Alex's veins. The duke's wrath was for his daughter and not him. "I have my horse resting downstairs. Tell me where you'd like me to look, and I'll leave immediately after I've seen Claire safe."

"Emma is a horrible rider and can't go long distances." Langham pulled a map from his greatcoat. "Pembrooke—"

Charles burst into the room. The young man became tongue-tied when he saw who stood before him. The duke appeared at wits' end, stressed and tired. "Spit it out, son. We've got to move quickly."

With a catch in his voice, Charles finally conversed without stammering. "Your Grace, Lady Emma is in her bed at Langham Hall."

"How do you know?" Claire's voice betrayed her shock.

"My lady, the carriage broke a wheel because of the mud. I took one of the horses and rode back for another. When I got there, Pitts was waiting with the news."

"Thank God." Claire closed her eyes. Her body softened in Alex's arms.

The duke turned, his full attention directed at Charles.

Charles swallowed hard. "Aileen woke Lady Emma. She asked Lady Emma where she was this evening. Lady Emma said she was at Lady Dalton's ball."

With an unmistakable sigh of relief, Sebastian turned to Alex. "Pembrooke, thank you." The duke extended his hand to Claire. "You need to come with me. Your aunt is distraught over you both."

When Claire left Alex's embrace to take her uncle's hand, the lack of her warmth caused a roar of emotions to rush forward. He couldn't let her leave this room, not before he made her understand. Alex's fingers grasped her arm through the thick riding habit. "Claire, wait."

She paused but wouldn't face him. Instead, she studied his hand. "My lord, we'll continue later when both of our heads are clear."

Langham tugged her hand to signal it was time to go.

Uncle Sebastian took Claire's hand in his to assist her into the carriage.

Claire stepped away, and her lips tickled as she felt the first hint of a smile. "I'm going to take your advice."

"Finally, someone listens to me." Her uncle had his own grin tugging at his lips. "Which advice are we talking about? Or would you like for me to guess?"

"I'm staying with Alex and going home." She laughed, and the sound soothed every piece of her. There was no use holding it inside. Saying the words caused the stress and pain of the evening to lift from her shoulders. For once in her life, she didn't feel the suffocating weight that had been her constant companion. "I love him. I'm going home."

"I always knew you were wise beyond your years." He leaned down and kissed her cheek. "You'll be happy. Will you both come over tomorrow? Ginny needs to see you and hear it directly from you."

"I promise." Claire watched as he fitted his large frame through the carriage door and sat on the forward-facing bench.

He leaned down and caught her gaze. "For what it's worth, I believe your father and mother would be very pleased with your choice and your husband, too."

"I like to think so, too. But I thought you didn't care for him, particularly after your altercation," she said.

"I was rather angry that day. My hand is still bruised." He scrunched his face as if tasting something sour, then reached across and caressed her cheek. "I saw him climb our oak tree the other night. He's a determined devil and wouldn't leave you alone. That's when I knew he loved you, if he'd risk confronting me again."

Alex rushed down the hall and outside to stop Claire from leaving with her uncle. The quiet of the inn's entry confirmed his worst fear. He was too late. They were gone.

His earlier experiences had taught him to recognize failure. This was it. His mind flooded with the sinking revelation that he'd lost Claire forever.

The innkeeper stood by his side and gazed about. "Did His Grace leave?"

"He just left." *With my wife.*

"Not often we get such a distinguished guest. I didn't even have the chance to offer him some of our fine ale." Webster sighed in disappointment. "Good night, sir."

With legs made of granite, Alex found his way to the courtyard.

The black ducal carriage, well-oiled wheels still creaking in protest, had turned onto the road back to London, with Langham and Alex's marchioness inside. How much longer would he be able to say she was his wife? He closed his eyes and bowed his head. How could he have failed in winning her back?

He started for the stables, then halted midstep. Claire stood alone in the middle of the courtyard and faced him.

He made quick work of the distance. "Are you waiting for someone?" Had he actually asked the question out loud?

His carriage arrived and stopped before them for the return trip.

"I am." She dipped her head in a nod.

His chest tightened as he waited for her to continue.

"My husband."

There was something hidden beneath her calm and determined visage, something he couldn't identify, but it was something that cast him in a sea of unease.

"Charles is riding Hermes." She glanced at the moon breaking through the clouds. "Alex, it's time to finish whatever this is between us."

Chapter Seventeen

A lex waited for as long as he could to prolong the inevitable. His carriage rumbled down the same path the Duke of Langham had taken. Claire sat silently across from him.

"When you first left me, I thought to fight to keep you to the bitter end. Now, I only want what will make you happy. I can offer you peace. You can go anywhere or do anything without my interference."

The worst of his statement—or, good God, call it a confession—had escaped his lips. Nothing else mattered now. It was out. He chanced a glance at her face to see her reaction. She bent her head until it appeared to rest on her chest. Only those glorious mahogany tresses were visible. She sat so still. Time to make his final plea.

"I pray you don't want this, but I'll abide by your decision." He dared to clasp her chin and raise her face to his. "You need never fear that my future actions are motivated by revenge. I'm finished with that life. My solicitors returned Lord Paul's vowels and the deed to his estate."

Her eyes glistened as they sought his.

"I found Mr. Mills in London. I've spent time with him.

Enough to know you were correct. He's a fine young man who loved Alice very much. He's heartbroken. I've introduced him to Somerton, who promises to find him some investors. I've also invited him to Pemhill. I think Alice would have appreciated that." He exhaled, and the exhaustion threatened to swallow him whole. He leaned forward to escape the lead weight on his chest. "Logically, I'm not responsible for her death. However, it may take my heart a little longer to believe it."

"You're making the right decisions, Alex. I'm so proud of you." She took his hand in hers and squeezed.

"I want you to have something from me." She started to protest, but he silenced her with a raised hand. "Shh, let me. I've donated twenty thousand to your campaign for a new children's home. I even got Somerton to match the amount. In exchange, I negotiated the right to name the facility from your solicitor. I thought you could name it in honor of your father and mother." He closed his eyes and exhaled. "Perhaps Wrenwood might still be needed for a daughter . . . our daughter." He didn't dare look at her for fear of rejection.

Tears streaked her cheeks. This was a hundred times harder than he'd thought. He'd cut off his right arm rather than see her suffer. If he could just hold her, maybe he could lessen her pain as well as his. However, he had to finish this.

"One more thing." He took a deep breath to garner the strength to confess the last. "I realized you wouldn't marry me after Lady Hampton's party. It didn't matter you weren't a virgin. Neither was I, so how could I judge you? Alice had suffered because of her choice, and I would never let you go through that alone. You see, I already cared deeply for you. So much so, that if you had been carrying Lord Paul's child, I would have accepted it as my own." He tilted his head back and drew a deep breath, hoping it would provide some extra time with her before she discovered his duplicitous behavior. "That explains why I secretly placed the bet at White's under my initials. Everyone assumed it stood for Lord Paul. It was the only way I knew how to keep you. It was wrong. Whatever you decide, I promise never to harm you or yours again. You have my word on it."

He cleared his throat and swallowed as moisture gathered in his eyes.

"You're the most important person in my life. Now and always. Even if you aren't with me, you'll always be cherished and at the forefront of my thoughts and all my decisions. I love you with all my heart." With a deep breath, he continued, "I never knew I could feel this way until you came into my life. No matter where you are or who you're with, my heart will always be true to you."

His chest constricted with pain as he kissed her. His lips tightened not with passion, but with love and respect. He waited to see if she'd respond. She didn't move or make a sound. It was much like her kiss when they'd married. The pain increased to a point he didn't think he'd survive. He pulled back slowly, not certain how to go forward.

"I'm not going to Scotland. I don't want a life without you either."

He heard the words but didn't comprehend what she was saying.

"I love you. I gave you my heart at Pemhill. When I did, I meant it forever. I take my fidelity seriously and would never hurt you." The look on Claire's face became tender. "You've seen the scars and faults I carry, and you still love me. You've made me believe I'm not cursed. If I was, I'd have lost you tonight on the bridge. But, I didn't." She reached for his hand. "You've given me more than I thought I'd have in this world."

Alex pinched his brows, unsure if he could trust what

he was hearing. He understood when the warmth of her smile embraced him.

"I came to you thinking I wasn't worthy of being loved and thought I would never experience it. What became the most painful was thinking you'd never love me."

His eyes burned, and he blinked hard. "Love, you had my heart the entire time in your possession."

"I love you," she whispered. Her voice was as sweet as an angel's breath. "With everything I am, with everything I have, I love you."

Claire's words caused any response to lodge in his throat. The pulse in her neck beat in a wild rhythm. He reached out to feel the power of it with his fingers.

Claire tilted her head to look into his eyes. "All I ever wanted was for you to share my life and build a family. When you came to find me tonight, it was as if my eyes finally opened. I saw a man willing to risk his life for my cousin because he puts family first. You were willing to protect what I value, my family. You showed me the depth of your love."

"Claire, I promise I'll never make you regret marrying me. I know I said the same words that first night, but my only path is to make you happy."

"Pembrooke, you're in for a delightful treat this morning." William's deep whisper cut through the quiet in the salon. "When these two get going, it's quite a sight to behold."

Claire stood next to her husband and her two cousins McCalpin and William. They were a safe distance from the center of the salon, where a somber Emma sat like Joan of Arc and waited for her lecture.

"Pardon?" Alex's hand rested on Claire's lower back, and the weight grounded her and kept her from flying to Emma's side. "What are you referring to?"

"Emma and Uncle Sebastian. It's rare he ever reprimands her. With Aunt Ginny beside him, this will not be pleasant for any of us," Claire said.

Emma stiffened visibly as Uncle Sebastian repeatedly paced the entire length of the room. "Father, I have no notion why anyone would believe I was to meet with Lord Paul in a private dining room at the Falstaff."

Her uncle stopped midstride and delivered a glare at his daughter. "Oh? You don't understand the circumstances we're concerned about? Why do you suppose I had your maid wake you up at the crack of dawn?"

"Father only uses sarcasm when he's furious. It's time to stir things up a little bit," William whispered. His face instantly transformed from humor into solemn concern. "Emma, I would have gladly escorted you home." His deep voice echoed around the room. "I arrived only an hour after the ball started. I couldn't find you. I was worried sick."

"William, stop," Claire whispered. Emma and her uncle didn't need any outside interference in this discussion, and Claire wanted to hear every word spoken between the two. How could Emma have left the ball without telling her?

Alex leaned close to her ear. "I'm impressed with the little scamp. She'd make a fine barrister. She said private dining room. That's not the language written in her note to Lord Paul. She wanted to meet in the tavern or public taproom."

"Care to place a bet on how long it will be before he spirals out of control?" This time William addressed the comment to his brother.

"No." McCalpin narrowed his eyes and closed the distance between them. "If you'd done as I'd asked and escorted Emma and Claire last night, neither Father nor our sister would be in the middle of a tangle."

"There was a time you loved to wager on these matters," William muttered. "You've become an abysmal bore."

Claire laid her hand on McCalpin's arm. This upset him as much as it did her. "She could have easily disappeared under William's nose too."

"Are you suggesting I can't keep track of my own sister?" William raised both eyebrows. "Claire, you should be thanking me. If I'd attended the ball with Emma, you and Pembrooke would still be apart. I take full credit for your reconciliation."

Alex's lips turned up. "Seriously? It was only several days ago you wanted to kill me."

Aunt Ginny gracefully sat down next to Emma. "A young woman named Jane Hosmer overheard you say Lord Paul had a book to give you. Is that true?" Her voice was even, but her face indicated she was barely holding on to her ire. Uncle Sebastian had stopped pacing and now stood behind his wife with his hand on her shoulder in a show of solidarity.

"No." Emma fidgeted. "If I'm interested in a book, I'm always willing to pay a fair price."

"That's not an answer," said the duchess.

The room quieted as everyone waited for Emma's response.

Eventually, Aunt Ginny let out a long sigh. "Your father and I have always encouraged your interest in books. Last night gives me pause."

Uncle Sebastian continued his relentless questioning. "Why did Claire receive a summons from Lord Paul Barstowe to come to the Falstaff?"

Emma delivered her own heavy sigh. "I have no idea. The last time I saw him, he approached me at Lady Barrington's. He asked if I was enjoying my Season, and we talked about books, specifically Mr. Bentham's essays. It was quite innocent. Then Claire pounced like a protective lioness and ordered me away."

The duke narrowed his eyes to slits and glared at Emma. "Would you care to comment about the missive?"

"What missive are you referring to, specifically?" Emma lifted a brow. "If I'm to be condemned, I'd like to see the evidence."

Uncle Sebastian shot a glance to Claire, as if asking if she had the note. She gently shook her head.

"Shall I say that's not quite what happened?" Alex whispered in her ear. "You really didn't pounce. You'd been looking for her for quite a while if memory serves me. Plus, I saw the note last night."

Claire smiled and shook her head. "If we interrupt, it'll go on forever. I'll talk privately with her later."

Understandably, the protective side of Alex had emerged. Since losing Alice, he was always aware of Daphne's itinerary and plans. Because Emma was Claire's cousin and his sister's best friend, Alex's concern naturally extended to Emma as well. She may not like it, but Emma had a new man in her life who watched over her.

"Let me explain the situation, young lady," Uncle Sebastian bellowed, like a bull in full rage. "You are to stay away from the likes of him or any other man without my approval." The duke's gaze settled on the expansive view of Langham Park through the salon's windows. The room grew deathly quiet, until finally he turned to Emma and exhaled. "Your mother and I have made a decision. You'll leave for Falmont tomorrow. An extended stay at the family seat will put an end to this nonsense. Your Season is over."

Emma stood and gracefully straightened in a movement that caused the silk of her dress to whisper. "If you have further need of me, I'll be in my room." With her chin tilted several inches higher, she left without a glance acknowledging her brothers or Claire and Alex.

"I'm glad we didn't wager." William scowled. "That wasn't nearly enough of a show. Emma has learned some strategy. She left them hanging."

"She's been *bloody* sent to Falmont, Will," McCalpin muttered. "God save me from ripping your head off."

William's veiled expression didn't hide his sympathy for his sister. "I'll go with her. There's not much entertainment here anyway."

Emma's banishment to the family's ancestral seat caused Claire a moment of regret for her part in her cousin's punishment. A year ago, Emma would have never considered such an outing, let alone try it. When Claire and Alex had discussed last evening's events with her aunt and uncle this morning, Somerton had joined them. He was the one who had found Emma and returned her home without anyone being the wiser.

"How will your family explain Emma's absence for the rest of the Season?" Alex asked.

The penetrating gray of his eyes had the power to make her forget everything else except for him. "My aunt and uncle will travel with her and stay for a week. When they return, they'll say it was her preference to stay at Falmont."

"I'll go find Somerton, then let's take our leave," Alex whispered. His breath felt like a kiss against her neck. "It's time to go home."

"I'd like that very much." It was the start of their new life together. "Perhaps we could go see Emma in a couple of weeks?"

"I've always wanted to visit Falmont." Alex's astute gaze softened. "We can find your parents' portrait."

Claire nodded but didn't answer. Was it any wonder why she loved this man?

The next week, Claire woke to find herself cocooned within Alex's arms. For the last week, he had kept her close by his side. The sense of peace caused her to smile. A slight hint of thunder sounded in the distance. She chose to focus on her dreams.

She found his hand close to her waist and wove their fingers together. Warm thoughts of Mr. Jordon, her cousins, Sebastian and Ginny, her parents, and, most important, Alex greeted her this morning. Her confidence and belief in herself would grow stronger because of those relationships. They defined her.

Her heart continued to pound even and strong as her future came into clear focus. She loved Alex now more than ever.

Moreover, he loved her. She would never tire of the sentiment.

When he had said those words, her old life had stopped and a new one had started. She said a prayer of thanks for her marriage and for her husband. They were committed to helping each other forget the scars and live the life they were destined to share.

Claire let out the breath she held in relief.

Alex drew her close and nuzzled the back of her neck. "I love you." He gently kissed her neck. "Wherever you are is where my home is. When you said you belonged at Wrenwood, you were wrong. You belong with me and I belong to you."

The curse was finally and irretrievably broken.

Epilogue

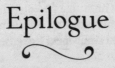

Eleven months later at Pemhill

Claire allowed a soft sigh to escape. Alex and she had chosen well. Emma and Somerton stood before them, each holding one of the children.

Emma held Michael Alexander Sebastian Hallworth, the Earl of Truesdale and the heir to the Marquess of Pembrooke, during the christening ceremony. A perfect gentleman, he held his cousin's gaze with a cool, calm demeanor. Emma kissed the little fist he waved at her. She was rewarded for her kind attention with a gurgling smile and a soft "ooh." Emma returned the flirtation with a kiss to his forehead.

Her son was a natural-born tease, the paragon of the ideal male. Claire pursed her lips to keep from laughing. Truesdale was much like his father.

A bloodcurdling scream erupted in the room. Beside her, Alex started forward to rescue his daughter, but Claire kept him from interrupting the ceremony with her hand on his. With her ears ringing, she assessed the Earl of Truesdale's older sister, Lady Margaret Virginia Alice Hallworth. Lady Margaret bucked and twisted in her godfather's arms, then stiffened like a wooden plank. The

Earl of Somerton tried to calm the baby with a pleading *shhh*. He managed only to enrage her more. Resolute, the baby would have none of his heavy-handedness and managed to throttle him in the nose with her little hand.

Though a mere five minutes older, Lady Margaret let everyone know she was in charge and found the whole proceeding, particularly the cold christening water, disastrous. Her personality matched that of her cousin Emma perfectly.

Before the ceremony continued, Emma exchanged Lord Truesdale for Lady Margaret. The baby immediately ceased her protests and closed her eyes.

After the presentation to the family, Emma reluctantly released Lady Margaret to Alex, and Somerton presented Truesdale to her. The earl's loud sigh of relief garnered hard stares from the babies' grandmother, the Dowager Marchioness of Pembrooke, and the twins' great-aunt, the Duchess of Langham, her sweet Aunt Ginny.

Uncle Sebastian pounded Somerton on the back. "You need to practice how to charm the ladies. Lady Margaret made a cake out of you."

"Excuse us, Father. Lord Somerton and I need to discuss the remaining events." Emma casually led Somerton to the other end of the room.

Claire contemplated the two godparents as Alex brushed a kiss across Margaret's temple. "Darling, let's take them upstairs for a nap. Our daughter looks miserable."

"Do you think Emma and Somerton will attend their weddings, birthdays, and other celebrations?" she whispered. By then, Uncle Sebastian had strolled over to attend Aunt Ginny.

"Don't rush things, love." Alex laughed. "I can't even think about next week. Besides, the role of a godparent is mostly for appearances' sake."

Claire glanced at Emma and Somerton at the far end

of the room. Both were standing far too close, with their heads together. Somerton laughed at something her cousin had said and raised his hand as if to push one of Emma's stray curls behind her ears. His hand froze in the air as if he suddenly remembered the impropriety of touching her cousin.

Claire shook her head, then placed a kiss on her son's hand. "Not with these precious two. I expect both Emma and Somerton will be heavily involved in their lives."

Claire gently rubbed her son's back after putting him down for a nap. The poor dear had a horrible case of the hiccups after his last feeding and didn't care for them at all. Every time he closed his eyes for a well-deserved nap, another popped up and surprised him. After his busy day with the christening and the endless cuddles and hugs from the family, he was exhausted.

Alex strolled into her bedroom with Lady Margaret. The baby focused her attention on his face and tried to grasp his nose. Alex deftly avoided her maneuver and caught her tiny hand between his lips. Her eyes widened as she grinned. With a stealth grace inherent in a Hall-worth, she lifted her other hand and accomplished her goal. Apparently satisfied with her effort, but unimpressed with her father's startled chuckle, she let out a yawn. Alex placed her next to her brother in the custom-built cradle shaped like a swan.

Claire's heart skipped a beat as Alex first caressed their daughter's cheek, then turned his attention to their son. "They're perfect, aren't they, sweetheart?" He placed his arm around her waist and drew her near.

She leaned back and rested her head against his shoulder. "Perfect and beautiful."

"Just like their mother." Alex kissed the top of her head. "Remember when I told you I wanted a boy and a girl?"

"How could I forget? You wanted to eat them." She tilted her head and caught the brilliant light in his eyes. "They've certainly changed our lives, haven't they?"

"Indeed, love." With a gentle kiss, Alex paid particular attention to his favorite spot directly below her ear. "You've made me the happiest man in the world."

"Sometimes I can't believe my good fortune." She closed her eyes and savored the moment until her curiosity got the better of her. "Did you see how Somerton and Emma kept eyeing one another throughout the christening? They failed to come upstairs after the ceremony."

He tightened his embrace. "You're not suggesting—"

"They're developing a regard for one another." She turned in his arms to gauge his reaction to her theory.

"No, you're seeing things that aren't there. It would require Somerton get close to a woman. He's never let that happen in all the years I've known him. You saw how awkward he was with Emma when she took Margaret from him. He could barely touch her."

"I'm afraid you're wrong. There is definitely something between the two of them."

"Leave it, wife. I have better things for you to occupy your attention." He stole one more glance at the sleeping babes, then took her hand and pulled her into their dressing room that led straight to the adjoining bedroom. "Let's take advantage of the peace and spend some time alone." A glorious smile spread across his face.

She was only too happy to leave it.

Coming soon . . .
Don't miss the next novel in this sparkling new series!

The
BRIDE WHO
GOT LUCKY

Available in November 2017 from St. Martin's Paperbacks